*For my beautiful Eve, Mum and Dad.*

# SONS OF BRUTALITY

## DANIEL JEUDY

danieljeudy.com.au

Copyright © 2021 Daniel Jeudy

ISBN: 978-1-922565-09-9
Published by Vivid Publishing
A division of Fontaine Publishing Group
P.O. Box 948, Fremantle
Western Australia 6959
www.vividpublishing.com.au

A catalogue record for this book is available from the National Library of Australia

All rights reserved. No part of this publication may be reproduced, stored in a retrieval system or transmitted in any form or by any means, electronic, mechanical, photocopying, recording or otherwise, without the prior written permission of the copyright holder.

# FOREWORD

Let's get something straight right at the start: I am intimately familiar with every word of Daniel Jeudy's debut novel. In fact, I have read it twice now. I enjoyed it more the second time. In fact, the second reading was purely for pleasure. And this foreword represents my futile attempt to convey the beauty of Daniel's work.

I read a lot. But I confess that quite often I will stop reading a novel before the halfway point. I become bored, perhaps. Or the language is less than it should be. Maybe the characters do not excite me.

Daniel, though, has excited me with *Sons of Brutality*.

The first time an author excited me—the first time I literally could not put a book down—was in the summer of 1981. I checked out Stephen King's *Firestarter* from the Buder Branch Library. For three days, I carried the hardcover book with me. I loved every page. I secretly wished the story would never end. After I returned it to Buder, I bought a copy from Target (I think). I've reread it several times.

I didn't carry Daniel's book around with me in my backpack. But I've carried it in my head. And parts of it have followed me into my dreams.

Meet Addison Mowbray, the jaded, hard-boiled veteran detective investigating the homicide of two young women whose mutilated bodies are found in the Hollywood hills. While Addison is a damaged soul, wrestling with unresolved childhood trauma and a fondness for liquor, his cynical philosophy and regrets have never affected his abilities as a detective. As a criminal profiler and hunter of serial killers, Addison has a unique ability to identify and understand the killers he tracks. He knows that he's not looking for a glamorous artist-genius like Hannibal Lecter. He is on the trail of an ugly evil.

*Sons of Brutality* takes the reader into a world of drug-fueled Satanists, snuff clubs, and killers who engage in every lust the world has ever known. We meet characters driven by madness, uncontainable urges, men and women who seem to exude an almost godlike invulnerability. Daniel introduces us to the rich capitalist who spent thirty years assembling a posse of affluent lunatics. We get to know a misogynistic wife beater who kills people for the Armenian Mafia.

Addison and his allies explore the city's underbelly to find their prey. What they didn't expect was the ability of these killers to make police investigations disappear.

What I did not expect was Daniel's ability to make me turn the page, to read past the halfway point, to suppress my desire to sleep to finish just one more chapter. Then, finally, coming to the final page, and simply wanting more.

Michael McConnell<br>June 18, 2021

# PART ONE

"Shadow deepens shadow, deception gives fire to flame.
I tell you, you cannot beat the grave at its own game."

From the song *Shadows*
—*written by Leigh Marks and Daniel Beltran.*

# ONE

Detective Addison Mowbray looked up at the crescent shaped moon, conscious of a dull ache working its way to his shoulders. He thought about the last time he'd been here at Griffith Park, hiking in the hills with his son. The sky had been a cloudless blue, with oak trees soaking up the Californian sunshine; the dead female with two missing hands who lay sprawled on the carousel was in stark contrast to that perfect day.

Homicide made its first incursion into Addison's life when he was seven years old. That experience had hurled him toward a police badge and determined his view of the world. There was a time when he had trusted in the providence of God and the inherent goodness of people. Then his father was shot, and the darkness that pierced his heart began corrupting his soul. The grief was suffocating, but it had shaped his perception and prepared him for a career in homicide in a way no textbook ever could. He'd been working in the LAPD for almost three decades and occasionally got the inkling to try his hand at something new, though the idea always evaporated. Policing was all he truly comprehended in a life marred by solitude and dissonance.

Addison stared down at the body and scowled. The old carousel made him uncomfortable. There was something about the intricately carved jumping horses and their jewel-encrusted bridles that distracted his thinking. It wasn't dissimilar to how the fortune-tellers' tents at traveling carnivals had made him feel when he was a boy.

A memory came of watching his son ride the carousel a few years earlier, how the atmosphere had shifted when the military organ began its marching tunes. It was as if the music box released unseen darkness, a yesteryear evil that attached to the children while they went up and down and round and round. The young woman lying dead at the edge of the wheel intensified his aversion, and he half expected to hear the sound of a coyote howling at the moon.

Addison took a deep breath to readjust his focus before moving away from the body until he arrived at the periphery of the crime scene. He shone his flashlight in a ten-foot arc while he advanced in tiny circles, sweeping the area. Finally, he stood over the corpse again, looking at the body from every available angle, giving the victim one final opportunity to speak in a way that didn't require words.

Criminal ineptitude often played a starring role in resolving a case, and a perpetrator's sloppiness could come in various forms. Occasionally, he struck it lucky; however, most cops didn't expect to find a perfect fiber or presume the first piece of evidence would land them at the killer's door. To achieve success in the Homicide Division, a detective needed good instincts and a whole lot of flexibility. Addison usually got a sense of whether an offender was careless, and he sure as shit wasn't getting those feelings here. Whoever was responsible for murdering the girl on the ride didn't appear to be the blundering type. He'd figured as much when the first body landed at the Hollywood Bowl four days earlier.

Headquarters had called while he was making his way home from a destined-to-go-nowhere dinner date. An old buddy who worked in the Commercial Crimes Division organized the night in Newport Beach with a recently divorced neighbor. Things had started off well enough, but their discussion soon became forced, punctuated by the kind of silences that suggested the outing would be a one-time thing. Perhaps he needed to connect with a prettier version of himself, a middle-aged, whiskey-guzzling woman with sleep concerns and good natural inheritances. It wasn't as if he were completely past it. Standing at a little over six feet tall with thick brown hair and a lean build, he was in reasonable condition, all things considered.

His mother named him after the town of his birth, and that

town represented a past he could never escape. Addison, Texas, north of Dallas, was a humble city of simple-living folk, renowned for its generational continuity. Addison boarded the first train to California a week after his twenty-first birthday but still planned on moving back once he retired. He believed the stillness there might teach him to sleep again without the assistance of booze and pills.

Checking the time on his watch, Addison wondered what might be behind his partner's delayed arrival. The sound of shuffling footsteps ended his reflection, and he turned around to see Detective Stan Glover from the Special Assaults Section make his way down the small hill above the clearing.

"Evening, Mowbray," Glover called.

"Hey, Stan," Addison replied wearily.

"No rest for the wicked, hey?"

Addison sensed his colleague's reluctance when he got an impression of the corpse, watching as the out-of-shape detective sucked in a few deep breaths. Stan Glover was a heart attack in waiting, all wheezy, plum-faced, and oozing with sweat. His sloping chest ran into a potbelly that hung over his belt, and his crooked teeth were stained yellow by nicotine.

Glover was wearing a cheap gray suit with a faded red tie twisted beneath his jacket. In his fifties with receding ginger hair, he was counting down the days until retirement. Addison didn't think he'd last long drinking cheap cocktails by the pool.

"I thought you were headed to San Francisco for a wedding."

Glover shrugged his shoulders. "What can I say, Mowbray. My wife's dumb-as-dog-shit cousin got himself caught in bed with the wrong woman. Three days before the ceremony, no less. We got a call yesterday: the whole thing's been canceled. I can't say I'm bothered, though; I'm not keen on San Francisco and its blatant leftist dogma. If it were Vegas, then I might be feeling a little pissed."

"Good for you," Addison replied with no genuine interest.

"So, what are we looking at here? Is this going to be falling back on HSS?"

"What's the body saying to you, Stan? We have a clothed female on a carousel with no apparent signs of sexual assault, and she happens to be missing both her hands."

Glover's face remained blank.

"This victim here, she's not the first," Addison continued. "There was another body with missing feet up at the Bowl three days ago. The unsub branded the shape of an inverted Christian cross onto her breast. I'm guessing the examiner will eventually discover the same symbol on this girl here. Both the scenes present like a copybook."

Glover stayed silent.

"Surely you've heard about this," Addison said.

"Yeah, of course. But I'm not about to sweat over a case I'm not involved in."

Addison didn't imagine he sweated much over anything these days.

"So, HSS has got two serial killers working the city at the same time, then," Glover remarked while struggling back into an upright stance.

He was referring to the vigilante who'd started blowing holes into hardened felons over the past twelve months. It would be hard to find a detective anywhere who felt sympathy for the scumbags being targeted; however, the shootings impacted the department for obvious reasons. Mainly because the perpetrator dropped a toy police badge beside his victims, and almost everyone in the city believed the killer was a cop. The body count stood at four, all of them grade-A assholes.

Addison didn't bother with a response as the two detectives continued standing by the amusement ride, lost in their thoughts before Glover ended the silence.

"I have to say: everyone was astonished when Collins handed the vigilante file to Miles and Ramirez, considering their tender age and general lack of experience."

"I'm sure Peter and Carlos will do fine. It's not as if they're incapable."

"Just saying, man. Those two are still wearing diapers, and that investigation has gathered serious steam. Put it this way: if it were my ass on the line, I'd be slapping it down in front of a cop who's closed a few more cases than they have."

"The times they are a-changing."

"You're certain this will be falling on you guys?"

"Pretty much guaranteed."

"I can go home, then?"

"It ain't my job to facilitate your responsibilities, Stan. But I don't think there's going to be anything of a sexual nature discovered here tonight."

Glover looked at the dead girl again.

"You got anything yet, or you flying blind?"

"Nobody has even come forward to identify the first victim. All we have are two attractive young blondes with missing body parts. As for motive, your guess is as good as mine, but I wouldn't be discounting an attraction to the occult."

"Well, for everyone's sakes, I sure hope you find something soon. Pretty white girls chopped up in the Hollywood Hills? It'll become a major pain in the ass if it drags on much longer."

Addison bent in toward the victim, blowing his fringe off his forehead. "Good things come to those who wait . . . Bad things too, I suppose."

"Has the examiner taken a look yet?" Glover asked.

"She's up there with the photographer. My assumption is she's having a cup of tea."

"Who is it?"

"The fact that I just said 'she' with a 'tea' should tell you who it is."

"Coniglio."

"Bingo."

"Well, here's to hoping she clears me off this thing nice and fast."

Addison remained crouched beside the body; his palms were clammy inside latex gloves as rivulets of sweat trickled down his forehead. He reached for the hip flask of whiskey in his coat pocket, running a finger around the ribbed metal cap as Glover sidled in again, trying hard to give the impression he was working.

"It's like I've said, Stan, this is going to land on us; that much I know."

Glover stared out into the darkness.

"There are probably all kinds of nasty prowling those hills."

Addison stood and rubbed at the pain behind his knees.

"That's just the world we inhabit," he replied, inhaling the pleasant fragrance of mixed chaparral that could be detected floating through the air.

Glover kept his eye on the night. "What do you mean?" he asked.

"I'm referring to the incursion of wickedness in modern times. Evil can be found in one form or another almost anywhere nowadays. Even right here on a children's ride."

"You ever consider cashing in early?"

Addison was about to reply but refrained when he noticed the examiner closing in.

"Evening, gents." Coniglio greeted them with a dazzling smile. "You fellas will need to let me squeeze in here. Otherwise, we might end up working past sunrise, and I don't want to be playing outdoors in the heat that's coming."

A deluge of brilliant light suddenly penetrated the darkness as artificial illumination bore down on the carousel to make the corpse appear like a figure made of wax. Addison spotted a young man he didn't recognize moving hesitantly toward the crime scene. It didn't take Coniglio long to pick up on his blank expression. "Gentlemen, this is my assistant, Dominic Beltran; he's brand new, right out of the box."

"Well, he ain't gonna stay that way long," Addison said.

"No, Mowbray, I don't imagine he will."

Coniglio tried passing her flashlight to Dominic by extending an arm behind her back, but he just continued standing around like a goofball. Certain examiners would have been quick to point out the kid's unawareness; however, Coniglio just waited for him to wake up, without speaking a word.

Addison analyzed Coniglio while she carried on with her work, taking in her long dark hair, soft complexion, and bow-shaped lips. Her deep-brown eyes radiated intelligence, and her compact figure always looked appealing no matter what she wore. Coniglio was a year older than him but appeared younger than her age. She was easy to get along with, exhaustive in her work, and never obstructed the detectives.

"What do you think?" Addison asked her.

"Looks like a slam dunk match to the body at the Bowl."

Coniglio lifted the dead woman's shirt to unveil a brand in the shape of an inverted Christian cross on her left breast as Addison wiped the sweat from his eyes.

"I'm sure we'll find ketamine in her system as well," Coniglio said.

Addison sensed Glover withdrawing—he had two feet out the door. "Well, if HSS is going to be catching this one, I'm going to head back to the car for some shuteye, unless you want to call it now and send me off to my desk?"

Coniglio slowly shook her head. "The car will have to suffice for the time being."

Glover didn't hide his disappointment. "Give me a holler if anything pops up."

"Uh-huh, I don't imagine you'll have to stick around for too long."

Glover began moping his way back up the rise. "Later, Mowbray."

"Yeah, see you, Stan."

Addison kept his gaze fixed on the victim's face. If it weren't for the streaks of mascara, it would almost seem like she was asleep. The wounds on her wrists were identical to those found on the first victim's ankles. Neat, but in no way surgical. Her skin appeared as if it had recently been sprayed with a tan, and Addison assessed her age to be mid-twenties.

"The serial killer part looks to be in the bag," Coniglio asserted.

"Yeah, sure seems so."

"That didn't take very long."

"Not long at all."

"Did the perp call it in again?"

Addison wiped away a thin film of perspiration from his brow, the sweet aroma of chaparral replaced by the harsh tones of stale piss and human shit. "No one's said anything to me at this stage."

"You gonna stick around?"

"Like I got a choice."

"I'll get her moved once the photographer is finished, then I'll take a closer look at the body and see what it tells us. In the meantime, if you've got anything else you want to ask me, you know the drill." Coniglio looked up, smiling, her eyes sparkling in the light.

"I need to locate my partner."

"The young ones, huh?"

Addison looked across at two cops standing on the other side of the tape who flashed in blue and amber with the lights on their cruiser. "He's thirty-one, so the justification of youth doesn't stand. I guess he can still act like one, though," he replied.

"Oh, come on, Mowbray. What were you getting up to at thirty-one?"

Addison considered the question but decided to disregard it. He watched Coniglio's assistant again and saw how the kid's ambiguity remained; it seemed his approach was to just stay out of everyone's way. Addison took a knee and pointed toward the end of the victim's arm. "Do I have to ask what you think he cut them off with?"

"Almost certainly a butcher's bone saw. The wound is fairly straight, and the skin around the surface of the arm indicates a sawing motion."

The rumble of a V8 engine rolled over the crest of the hill behind them. Addison watched as his partner's Chevrolet Silverado pulled in beside his F100.

"Mister thirtysomething has finally decided to grace us with his misunderstood presence," he griped while straightening to shake the dust from his trousers.

"Play nice, Mowbray."

Addison raised a thumb in the air as he made his way back to the parking lot, where the two uniforms stood by, disinterested, passing the time in conversation and cigarettes. He ducked beneath the tape and ambled up the moderate slope on tired legs, moving in behind the coroner's van to remove the hip flask from the pocket of his blue linen coat.

He unscrewed the cap like a hooch hound before taking a healthy swig of whiskey. Addison quickly returned the flask to its place of concealment and rounded the corner, where he saw Jed climbing out of his truck.

"Hey, kid," Addison said irritably. "Nice of you to show up."

A sheepish grin came over his partner's face while he watched Addison trudge over to his Ford in search of a cigarette.

## TWO

The sound of Katherine's screeching reverberated inside Edward's mind like a withering echo as he placed her hands inside a snaplock sandwich bag. He'd been trying to recall the touch of Linda's lips, but his memories diffused like smoke in the breeze, so instead he thought back to the way she looked when they first encountered one another.

Her dress had been patterned with miniature lavender roses, while her sandals had displayed her perfect toenails sparkling in green. He had loved the way her blond hair underscored the color in her eyes and how her breath smelled like an infusion of sandalwood and raspberry. It was difficult to comprehend that six years had passed by since he'd run a blade across her throat at the Adelanto Compound. "We'll be together again before long," he whispered, looking down at the bloodied goat's head pentagram on the floor.

Dark purple veins had begun to branch along the back of Katherine's hands, which caused Edward to smile as blinking candles continued burning around the room. The cold blood inside the brass canister shimmered like liquid rubies; its fragrance resembled freshly poured iron, and Edward chuckled while he considered its taste.

Katherine's eyes were filled with horror when she released a final breath, her face frozen into a soundless scream as her tongue dangled out of the side of her mouth. When he carved away her wrists with a bone saw, his passion burned like a fever. For now, the flames had subsided. Edward's throat felt dry and abrasive as though he'd spent the evening feasting on sandpaper. He raised the canister to his lips and supped the blood, grinning red as it soothed his gullet on the way down into his stomach.

The smell of Katherine's fatality saturated the ether. He could sense the gray entity he'd unintentionally conjured up during the final stages of his ritual. *Did the demon represent Linda's consciousness?* Edward kept his gaze directed away from the baleful figure smeared in congealed plasma, not wanting to meet the awful contest he felt coming from its existence. To do so might result in his brain melting like jelly on a pile of hot embers, so he concentrated on what he intended to do with the girl still caged in the dark.

Griffith Park was situated on the eastern point of the Santa Monica Mountains and consisted of four thousand acres of parkland. The ideal site to unveil his corpses without the likelihood of having to encounter waves of people. He provided the LAPD with the location of the body once he was back on the freeway to ensure Katherine was put on ice, just as he'd done with Emma Paul four days earlier.

After all, these women were his offering to Baal to gain assistance in luring Linda's spirit home. It didn't feel right to leave them inside a dumpster or conceal them out in the desert like most of the trash he'd butchered over the years. Nevertheless, his charity toward their remains was entwined with a crooked purpose. Everything he staged was soaked in conceit, but hey, that was just the Californian posture.

Edward wasn't impeded by conventionality. His actions were always determined by what layer of himself he chose to feed. Modern society was hinged on the middle classes remaining enslaved within its system of deception. Most citizens existed like fish in a bowl, content with acquiring their ridiculous values from adulterated sermons on morality. Even the revolutionaries had become insignificant as they recited existentialist philosophies without having any understanding of what it was they needed to resist.

America's youth were duped into spending money they didn't have by corporate dictators who peddled their wares into the subconscious. Then there were the colleges that absorbed updated versions of yesterday's knowledge and labeled it an education. It was all such sheer fucking mindlessness. Edward pursued his immoral practices whereby he answered to no one, and as such, he was free to do anything his black heart desired.

He raised himself from the vintage leather couch and walked across the living room, where he studied his reflection in one of the many mirrors mounted inside. His smoothly shaved skin appeared incandescent as his eyes gleamed like two black pebbles. Every muscle on his naked body was sinewy and lean, and the razor-sharp features of his elongated face gave an impression they had been etched from granite. Katherine's blood had colored his teeth a soft shade of cherry, and his impeccably curved scalp was akin to polished glass.

Edward's house remained under a constant shadow. The boarded windows encouraged flickering candlelight to sway among the photographs of mutilated corpses on the walls, performing a funeral waltz with the dead and rotting. His occultist literature collection was stacked on the floor like a twisted little shrine—providing another doorway to Satan.

He wanted the bodies to spawn intrigue as each new corpse produced more energy than the one before. Exposing them in the hills added to their mystique and engendered the kind of extravagance he required. Every component needed prudent consideration if he were going to resurrect the only person who'd ever come close to fulfilling him.

Linda represented a promise of always from the moment they first met. In the end, they would get to spend an eternity among the flames, but for now, the infernos could wait. After all, forever was a long time in which to be burning. Her face was a sun in the corridors of his memory as the demon began to slowly fade away, and he was determined to bring as much of her back as was possible.

# THREE

Addison gazed aimlessly at the panoramic picture of Dallas hanging on his bedroom wall. He felt exhausted, yet sleep remained out of reach—as if its location were hidden somewhere on a map he didn't know how to read. His insomnia began soon after his father's homicide, and the condition had only worsened over time.

Every detail from that tragic night continued to haunt him. The final words his father spoke when walking out the front door, not to mention the Godawful sounds he heard coming from his devastated mother as she shrieked her soul away the next morning. Addison recognized the permanence riding upon the crest of her cries the moment they'd awoken him. Carter Mowbray was shot twice by a drunk he'd pulled over for a busted taillight, and he died alone in a ditch by the side of the road.

The sudden heartbreak shepherded a quietness into his life he'd been entirely unprepared for. A manifestation of silence so deafening and final there was no way to escape its vacuum. Losing his father at such a young age caused a chasm of disparity to develop within Addison's mind as time leached the memories he tried holding onto. Nowadays, he would often find himself questioning whether any of it was real because the only thing he had to depend on were the faded photos inside his mother's albums.

Addison checked his clock radio while he straightened the tightness behind his knees, thinking how it sucked to be aging. He snatched a bottle of Irish whiskey off the floor, unscrewed the top, and drank, appreciating the trail of warmth as the liquor flowed down inside his belly.

It was after five am by the time he finished writing up the report for Griffith Park. The first fingers of dawn had started peeling away the darkness when he pulled into his driveway. Addison had gone straight to bed after walking through the front door. He'd considered whether there might be a secret meaning to life while he lay there on his back and how a man's days could start to feel a lot like treading water.

When he took away all the hours spent at work, what was left? If a person was lucky, they might get to view their world through a pair of rose-colored glasses for a period, pretending everything was dandy. Then something unanticipated crept in a back window to burst their bubble of contentment, shoving them toward a place of irrelevance alongside everybody else, entirely demoralized while imploring God for an outpouring of purpose to justify the point of their existence.

Addison had long given up on self-actualization ever landing on his doorstep, and he sure as hell didn't have many expectations of finding some deeper sense of fulfillment. He believed the world was broken all right, and destiny would eventually take most people down a path of disappointment and straight into the bitter embrace of sorrow.

He'd also reflected on the occultist symbol the perpetrator was branding onto the victims and considered how the burns might influence the investigation. At first glance, the inverted cross might appear to be nothing more than a swipe at Christian morality, but Addison understood the unprincipled darkness behind the satanic doctrine. He'd seen more than enough wickedness in his time and could usually anticipate when something horrible was closing in. Imagining what each girl went through roiled his stomach, yet the concept behind the symbology unnerved him even more.

Addison returned the bottle to the floor and cast his eye around the bedroom. *So, this is what the good guys look like.* Two mounds of dirty clothing were piled in the corner, and he couldn't recollect the last occasion when the place was orderly. Addison purchased the Valley Glen bungalow one year after his ex-wife moved to Phoenix with their son. The suburb predominantly consisted of low-income households and racial minorities, a noticeable step down from the three-bedroom home they'd owned in Eagle Rock.

Still, it scarcely concerned him whatsoever because, apart from missing Nate, his life felt no different here. Certain things within the neighborhood were kind of cool, such as parking next to The Great Wall of Los Angeles, where he would numb his mind with liquor, striving to make sense of all the colors and various shapes with a belly full of booze. The artwork was over half a mile in length and portrayed the history of California as seen through the eyes of women and subgroups. A night spent at the Tujunga Wash provided a momentary reprieve from the tendrils of hostility inside his head. Some days Addison would sit at home questioning everything he thought he'd already known about himself, applying the blowtorch to his character as a way of passing the time until his shift began.

He'd encountered every kind of human filth while sifting through the abattoirs of the city's most depraved killers. Examined the fruits of wickedness from a personal distance and seen things ordinary people only hope to experience from within the pages of a book. Justice had a face, and it didn't come muscled up with a purity of heart. Regular was just a portion size for any detective who worked homicide in a big town like LA. Normal gets snatched away, and there isn't much chance of getting it back.

Addison lit a cigarette as he stretched for an ashtray on the floor with his foot, cussing when some old butts spilled onto the carpet. He inhaled deeply and looked at the photograph of his son by the window. It seemed like an age since he'd last seen the boy, and it would likely be a good while until he saw him again.

He blew a thick plume of smoke up at the ceiling as he began making his way toward the bedroom door, where an onset of lightheadedness nearly floored him. When Addison stepped out into the hallway, he leaned against the wall as a way of maintaining his balance. He waited until everything stopped spinning, then continued into the bathroom, where he raised the toilet seat and closed his eyes, thinking of the dead woman on the carousel with the two missing hands.

Even though Addison hoped the scumbag responsible might one day get what they deserved, he also understood they likely never would. He took one final drag on his cigarette and dropped it into the bowl, doing his utmost to disregard the bottle of Valium on the ledge of the window. Three or four of those blue babes with a big glass of whiskey, and everything went quiet for a few hours.

He often considered the prospect of whether he might be a little crazy but never arrived at a conclusion either way. If he was losing his mind and then somehow located it again, it would never be the equivalent of the one that went missing. Just like if a busted truck door were banged out and resprayed—scratch away the exterior, and all the original damage could be found patched underneath.

Addison hitched up his track pants and walked over to the sink, conscious of the morning sun transforming his house into an oven. He turned on the faucet and splashed cold water onto his face, dropping his head to restore his balance. The sound of his phone filtered down from the bedroom, and he began making his way up the hallway on unsteady legs.

Addison stumbled across the room and dropped onto the bed, snatching the Samsung with his left hand. "Mowbray," he croaked.

"Hey, Mowbray." It was Lieutenant Jevonte Collins.

Addison didn't react right away, as he waited for his head to stop twirling.

"You there, Mowbray?"

"Yeah, Lieutenant, I'm here."

"We've managed to hook ourselves a break on the body."

"Oh yeah . . . which body and what break might that be?"

"The one from last night. We got a name and an address. The victim's partner just walked into the Hollywood station house two hours ago. Apparently, her girlfriend hadn't been home since Monday morning, so she decided to come in after hearing about the murder on the news. The detectives took her over to the coroner, where she gave a positive ID."

Addison plucked a pen from the jacket he'd worn the previous night, automatically reaching for the notepad he kept inside his bedside drawer.

"Girlfriend, you say?"

"That's right, Mowbray, she's gay."

"I see."

"The victim's name is Katherine Schneider. She comes from a wealthy Jewish family; her daddy owns a big fancy law firm on the East Coast."

"Swell," Addison replied, thinking how that fact could become a pain in his ass.

"So, the address is one-eight Elmer Avenue, North Hollywood, and the girlfriend's name is Angela Brown."

"Okay, Lieutenant. I'll get right on it. Has anyone called Jed?"

"Nope, I thought you might do that."

Addison was well accustomed to the department's penchant for cutting corners.

"I want you and Perkins to swing by and see if you can extract anything more than what she's provided already. She was extremely distraught when the detectives spoke with her earlier, and they may have missed something. Have you had an opportunity to listen over the call yet?"

Collins was referring to the killer's MO of directing them to the victims' bodies.

"Yeah, I played it through a few times when I got back in this morning."

"What can I say? You were right on the money about the first victim being the work of a potential serial murderer, which means we've got ourselves another one. As of this moment, you and Boy Wonder can clock as much time as you need to get this done. Did you finish writing the crime report when you got back here last night?"

Addison stifled a yawn. "Yeah, I did."

"Great, I'll have a look at it shortly. The toxicology results will be back sometime in the afternoon. If her blood shows traces of ketamine, then we're gonna need to start digging around to see if we can find where the cocksucker is getting it from. Maybe he works at a healthcare facility, or he's tight with somebody who does.

"I've already informed the sergeant that you and Perkins will be reporting directly to me, so there's no need to check in with the big prick unless you require something. I'm anticipating the mayor will soon start shouting about how these homicides are impacting the city's trade, and the captain wants to set up a hotline for anybody who might have relevant information. Which means you'd best be preparing yourselves for all the whack jobs. Keep me in the loop with everything as it unfolds, Mowbray, and make sure you shave, 'cause we're going live to press at five-thirty."

"Okay, then."

"Thanks, Ad," the lieutenant replied before the line went dead.

Collins was a decent boss and very hands-on with his management style. Most of the men Addison previously worked under operated in more of an overseeing role. They left the groundwork to their detectives and swooped on anybody who tried punching out extra hours.

Lieutenant Collins wasn't known to implement strict policies and rarely scrutinized his detectives' practices with a magnifying glass. The captain, on the other hand, was an entirely separate story. He was the most penny-pinching individual found anywhere within the department and not just in matters concerning the job. It was hard to know what was more important to him: closing a red ball case or ending the year under budget.

The policing landscape was a vastly different beast from the one Addison cut his teeth on during the nineties. To be accepted back then meant being somebody who wasn't prepared to concede ground, but detectives these days were much less inclined to break rank. Temperament was quickly being supplanted by diplomacy as officers became increasingly cautious of taking the kind of gamble that might see them step outside procedural guidelines, even when it meant breaking a case open. There were too many hazards involved, and no one wanted to find themselves stuck at their desk all day going bat-shit crazy while internal affairs set a fire beneath their ass.

Addison slid across to the edge of the bed again, debating whether he should heat the iron and press a shirt before quickly discarding the idea. There was something off about going to the effort to look sharp while the brass discussed a homicide victim. It felt too much like sticking a knife through someone's heart with a smile on his face and a bandage in his hand. Addison dialed his partner's number and was surprised when Jed answered so quickly.

"Hey." The kid's voice sounded hoarse.

"What are you doing?"

"Nothing, I was still in bed."

"Well, get yourself up; we've got an address for the victim from last night."

"Seriously? Fuck, that was quick."

"Yeah."

"When do you want to head over?"

"I was hoping you could swing by to pick me up in about an hour; the address is over in North Hollywood. Her girlfriend ID'd the body."

"This morning?"

"Yeah," Addison replied, mildly irritated at having to elaborate.

"Okay, Ad, I'll be there soon."

"And make sure you look respectable, whatever the hell that means. Collins made a point of saying we're going to press at five-thirty."

"And that affects me how, exactly?" Jed asked.

"If you're lucky, you'll get to stand on camera with the boss and appear Californian."

"Sounds like a real blast. I'll jump under the shower and then head over. You want me to grab you anything on the way?"

"Nah, I'm all good, kid. I'll see you when you get here," Addison replied, ending the call and reaching for the bottle again.

Most people presumed he and Jed were as distinct from each other as any two persons might possibly be, but that was incorrect. They shared several common traits, most of which boosted their chances of getting into trouble. Even so, the kid was reliable, and as far as Addison was concerned, loyalty and liquor were the two best friends a detective could have.

# FOUR

Narek Avakian wiped a piece of lavash around his bowl and scooped up the remaining sauce from the porridge, appreciating the different spices before washing it down with a mouthful of sweet red wine. There wasn't anywhere in the city he'd rather have dinner than his cousin's Armenian restaurant. Erik was an absolute maestro in the kitchen, and Narek made sure he dined there at least three times a week.

The temperature outside continued to rise. Everybody on the West Coast was bracing themselves for another hot fucking day. Narek was five years old when his family migrated to the USA during the summer of 1979, and he'd adapted to the dry heat without a problem. Like many other Armenians who flooded into Los Angeles at that time, the Avakians found a home in the suburb of Glendale. The neighborhood was located eight short miles from Downtown and provided its residents with an unhindered view of the Verdugo Mountains.

In the year before the Avakians landed, ten local broads were murdered and raped in the surrounding area in what became known as "The Case of the Hillside Strangler." Two black-hearted Guinea cousins were responsible for the carnage. Just a couple of sick fuckin' Wops who awoke one morning and started killing women as a way of getting some kicks.

Narek remembered how the local kids exaggerated their crimes to frighten each other while they roamed about the streets after dark. The embellished stories created an urban legend that continued to evolve long after the greaseballs were caged.

There would have been an entirely different ending to the situation if the Armenian Mafia were around when everything unfolded. The boss was adept at smoking out a target, and he used a dull blade on any perverts stupid enough to prowl in his territory. Davit would have enjoyed opening them up before dropping their carcasses on the street for everyone to see.

 A detective on the payroll had provided information about the new nutjob dumping bodies up in the hills. Narek didn't have any problem understanding how somebody might find pleasure in killing but drew the line at murdering innocent women. He was well known for losing his head with bitches on occasion, mainly when some mouthy fuck checked his patience by getting lippy. But a good slap put them straight real fast, so ten minutes later, he might be found shoving their cunt face into a pillow while he fucked them in the ass. Still, each of them had what was coming, and they all walked away from the experience breathing.

 He never understood why certain predators ended up sobbing when they got themselves caught, neither. Nor the way they attempted to excuse their behavior by telling the world about all the horrible shit they endured as kids, fabricating a sob story as the primary reason for why they turned into a monster. And it was generally everybody else's mistake, like maybe their mommy didn't love them enough, or their daddy was a hooch hound, or some other piss-weak reasoning. Like there was a justification for why they implemented their illness and became the twisted monsters they were always destined to be.

 Narek had just turned fourteen when the Armenian Mafia was established in an East Hollywood parking lot during the summer of 1988. He'd been working on the fringes at the time, selling dime bags of weed for one of the older boys. Four years later, he shot a man dead, a crime that elevated him to the next level within the organization. The Armenian Power quickly transformed into a structured syndicate, no longer resembling the loosely organized street gang they were in the beginning.

 The people at the top got to make all the rules, and blind allegiance was essential for anybody hoping to clamber their way up the chain. A kid must be prepared to stick around and prove themselves by doing whatever the bosses instructed. Eventually, they might be afforded an opportunity to commit a crime there was no coming back from.

Narek made his bones by whacking a neighborhood rat in 1992. Sammy Bedrosian was just a bottom-feeding junkie with loose lips. They sprung a trap to lure the bastard down to Pelanconi Park with a promise to provide him some low-priced crack. Narek had been faithful from the get-go and jumped at his chance to be a triggerman.

He recalled waiting in the darkness while his heart pounded against his chest like a kick drum and how the anticipation became so intense, he almost pissed his trousers. When he finally spotted Bedrosian coming toward him in the distance, his stomach twisted and roiled because popping someone for the first time was so much harder than people could imagine.

Any aspiring hitman must engage in a confrontation with their own mind, regardless of how tough a kid might be or how desperate he was to be a part of something. Nothing had been more challenging than pulling the trigger on that rat fuck all those years ago. He'd pumped five bullets into Bedrosian's upper body, thinking the job was complete. After all, five slugs from a high-caliber revolver should kill a man dead, right? What the asshole taught him was that people rarely go easy when it comes to dying.

It sure as hell was nothing like what he'd see in the movies. Bedrosian's lungs kept squealing in protest each time he attempted to draw breath, pushing crimson bubbles out the holes in his chest. Narek stood over him for a while, captivated by the confusion inside his eyes and the way they failed to comprehend what was happening. Then, when he'd seen enough, he placed the barrel on his brow and blew a big fat hole out the back of his head.

Shooting someone up close was freakin' messy, too; his jacket got covered in blood, brains, and bone fragments from all the spray back. Narek struggled inside his mind afterward, thinking about all kinds of weird shit as he attempted to deal with the reality of what he'd done. There'd even been a brief period where he endeavored to balance the morality ledger by doing good things for random people, like helping an old lady with her bags at Walmart or throwing a few extra dollars on top of the bill at the diner. One time his guilt even saw him buy a sandwich for a homeless bum.

It was liberating when he realized there was no need to do any of that shit. Nowadays, he didn't even blink when it came time to put a slug into someone or stick a blade through their guts. Hell, he could even dismember a body with half a smile on his face, and when he put his head down at night, he slept like a fuckin' baby.

Murder became his bread and butter, but he also trafficked drugs, extorted local businesses, and promoted illegal gambling. Narek had been involved in organized crime for more than two decades without doing serious jail time. Although his blessed luck almost ran dry the previous year when the LAPD connected him to a gat he'd used in a murder.

The close call didn't take place due to any carelessness on his behalf, and there was no forensic breakthrough from DNA left behind at the scene. He always applied meticulous planning to his work, irrespective of the payout. But when the weakness came from the confines of his own organization, it created the perfect catalyst for a fall.

Narek returned the piece to the guy he'd purchased it from; the cocksucker had provided him with multiple firearms over the years and could be relied upon to make them disappear. Yet, for some bizarre reason, he got careless by throwing the gat into a dumpster in East Hollywood. Making matters worse was his associate sourced the Smith and Wesson from a local kid who'd lifted it from his father's underwear drawer.

A group of youths eventually stumbled upon the weapon when a union strike prevented the trash from being collected, and they were spotted fooling around by a passing patrol car. Ballistics paired the piece with the slugs the examiner pulled from the body, and then the LAPD traced it back to its owner.

He didn't imagine the detectives encountered many obstacles in getting the kid to fess up, and when his associate faced a murder one rap, the snitch made a deal by naming Narek as the shooter. If it weren't for the boss having a contact in evidence to compromise the gun, he'd likely be caged up like a dog right now.

Instead, he spent a few weeks inside LA County Jail while the piece was made inadmissible before being released back onto the streets without charge. The rat disappeared into witness protection, which meant he remained temporarily out of reach. They would eventually track him down and send him to hell, squealing like a pig. Then they'd take turns at tossing a quarter in the air to figure out who got lumped with the task of putting the asshole through a meat grinder. It might seem a little extreme to most, but that was the way things got handled in Narek's world.

His cousin's restaurant was located on North Pacific Avenue, and they sometimes used the kitchen to make their plans. Davit insisted on having the building swept for listening devices each month even though he never really went there much. The boss was about as paranoid as any person could be, and his mood swings were legendary. He had even managed to work himself up about the vigilante who was popping bad guys around the city.

Narek didn't understand why he wasted a thought on the dick and would accept an encounter with the son-of-a-bitch at any time. After all, most of Narek's fortune had been acquired by putting souls underground, so his attitude to any threat was—*take your best shot.* Crime had provided him with abundant riches, but he understood what it felt like to be poor.

There was an endless flow of discrimination imposed on the citizens who resided in many neighborhoods around the city. Watching rich white cocksuckers live the dream on cash they never earned was rough. Being broke in LA was like getting sucker-punched each time he went to sit down for a meal. It's why people were prepared to risk their lives pushing dope on street corners, dodging bullets, and doing whatever it took to make bank.

Narek was momentarily startled by the kitchen door swinging open and looked over as Bedros Darbinyan came lumbering inside. The old-school bruiser was one mean bastard who'd come to America four years earlier. Bedros had an enormous raw-boned frame and a huge belly. He was the complete opposite to Narek, who was muscular and lean with a smooth tanned complexion. Narek also had a full head of hair and great looks while Bedros was receding and ugly as fuck.

The big gangster strode across the kitchen and embraced Narek, kissing him on both cheeks before his deep-set eyes scanned the room for food. When his thick fingers found the leftover bread, Narek shook his head, watching as Bedros stuffed lavash into his gob.

"I've never met a person who eats like you," he confided. There were times he'd seen the asshole grab a meal in a house where they'd just shot someone in the face.

"It keeps me strong," Bedros countered in accented English.

"Did Davit explain what he expects?"

"Ayo."

"Good, so you understand he wants us to make him suffer."

"Of course, of course," Bedros assured him.

Narek pointed toward an industrial refrigerator on the other side of the kitchen. "Erik has put something in the cooler for you."

Bedros's smile was broad in appreciation. "You are good, my brother, always thinking of me."

"That's because I need you to be focused."

Bedros looked down at the leftover porridge in Narek's bowl. "When the time comes for action, I am always ready. Where is the harissa?"

Narek jerked his head at a pot warming on the grill. "Make sure you leave some for the paying customers, you greedy fuck."

# FIVE

Angela Brown's 1920s bungalow was obscured by an oak that loomed across the front yard like some old, enchanted tree. A bay laurel privacy hedge ran adjacent to the sidewalk, concealing a garden that presented like an ocean of living color. There was a red BMW parked in the driveway, and the property was positioned at the end of a cul-de-sac. A redevelopment program had transformed North Hollywood in recent times to satisfy the demands of its changing demographic. The revamped NoHo Arts District was drawing a fresh crowd of artists to the neighborhood, and the infusion of cafes, craft beer bars, and vintage clothing stores only added to the hipster feel.

"Does this lady know we're coming?" Jed inquired through glazed eyes.

Evidently, his partner had smoked a blunt that morning.

"I don't think so," Addison responded casually, making his way along a winding stone path to the front door, where he checked the time on his watch and stole a sideways look at his partner's face. Almost every cop stepped outside stipulated protocol on occasion. They all experienced mental trauma on the job and dressed their scars accordingly. So long as no corruption was involved, then it was all fair play as far as Addison was concerned. At the end of it, Jed's reasons for smoking weed wouldn't be much different from the ones that sucked him down a whiskey bottle each night.

Most cops were optimistic at the start of their career; however, their liveliness was usually supplanted by disillusionment in no time. When a uniform was required to respond to the same domestic settings each week, it started to feel kind of pointless. And watching repeat offenders get released early eventually created strong impressions of loathing. But it's not until something wanton suddenly got thrust upon them that a copper's opinion became forever skewed. Like feeling bullets whiz past their face during a license check or the time Addison stepped on the decomposing body of an infant inside a Compton crack house.

If an officer made it into homicide, they wouldn't be tending to any aspirations of leading a typical life. It required grit to graft out a career as a murder cop, working from inside a labyrinth of despair while chasing monsters on behalf of ghosts.

Addison had discovered that hell was often situated next door to heaven and how a couple of steps could provide the variance between a person living or dying. All the detectives in HSS toiled hard to provide resolution to the victims' families, and they occasionally experienced the victory of taking crumbs of justice to those left behind. But their principal motivation was always about limiting the tally of the dead.

Addison rapped on the doorframe and took a small backward step. He listened to the echo of padded footsteps approaching from within before a hesitant voice inquired, "Who is it?" from behind the frosted glass.

"It's the LAPD. We'd like to speak with Angela Brown, if she's home."

Addison began to consider whether he might need to repeat himself when the door creaked open to reveal a diminutive woman in her early thirties. She looked up at him through hurting eyes and rumpled brown hair. A sprinkling of light freckles dusted her cheeks, and the expression on her face highlighted her strain.

It felt invasive to impose themselves on someone who was in such an early stage of grief. There would always be many questions she'd never have answers to, certainly none which made a lasting difference. Angela was attempting to find her way through the most isolated condition a person might ever know. Addison stopped trying to alleviate people's anguish after coming to the realization there was no respite to be had in a situation that found him standing at the door. The best she could hope for was to witness her girlfriend's killer get apprehended, then find some way to move forward with her days.

"Are you Angela Brown?" Addison asked in a sympathetic tone.

She nodded slowly. "Yes . . . Yes, I am."

"I'm Detective Addison Mowbray, and this is my partner, Detective Jed Perkins. Would it be all right if we came inside to speak with you, Angela?"

"I guess so," she replied. "Come on in."

The detectives followed her down a narrow hallway and into a spacious living area where they watched her slump down into a mahogany chair.

Addison took a seat on a sofa opposite and pondered whether he should make arrangements to come back another time. The woman's heartache was inescapable. Her only available options were to ride with the pain or ingest something to circumvent her mind.

Angela appeared waifish and unkempt as if she'd spent the past few months couch surfing. Her purple nail polish, nose piercing, and handcrafted silver jewelry displayed the neighborhood's alternative sway. Dressed in a pair of faded track pants and a black T-shirt, she seemed indifferent to how she presented herself.

The living room was decorated with an Asian flair. A Japanese wall mirror was encircled by Shinto dancing masks and charcoaled sketches of geisha girls. Photographs of flooded rice fields were displayed on a bookshelf, and a red rug covered a large portion of the white tiled floor. A coffee table that divided the space between them was littered with magazines and papers, diverging from the neatness so prevalent throughout the house.

Addison studied the various artworks, wall hangings, and ornamentation on display, thinking of the good times shared here. He waited while Angela gained a small portion of composure, prepared to give her as much time as she required.

"I can't believe any of this," she finally managed. "Like, maybe it's just a bad dream, and I'm going to wake up to find Kath walking through the front door." Her voice wobbled with instability as she combed slender fingers through her hair.

Addison glanced at his partner. The kid had been distant on the drive over. "Is it all right if I start with some questions?" he asked, watching while Angela dabbed at her eyes and nodded her head.

"When did you see Katherine last?"

"Monday morning, before I left for the office. It was around eight o'clock."

"Was she going to work, as well?"

"Unh-unh. Kath didn't work," Angela replied, dabbing her eyes once more. "Her daddy deposited an allowance into her account at the end of each month."

Addison offered a compassionate nod of his head. "He's a lawyer over in New York, is that correct?"

"Not just a lawyer; he owns a big firm right in the heart of Manhattan."

"Do you happen to know where Katherine may have been going?"

Angela's eyes filled with tears, and she dropped her head into her hands. "She was headed up to the hills to do some modeling for an art class."

Jed stirred on the couch, but Addison maintained his focus. "Do you have an address for the place?"

"Give me a second; it's written down on a card in the kitchen."

Angela appeared stiff as she got to her feet and shuffled out of the room.

"A rich nonconformist with a German surname," Jed said evenly.

Addison was surprised by his partner's ignorance about Katherine's Jewish roots. "German?" he asked.

"Yeah. Schneider sure sounds like a German name to me."

Addison regarded Jed with a quizzical smile. "Schneider is also a common Jewish surname, and Jewish she certainly was."

Jed started to reply but checked himself when Angela reentered the room.

"The address for the art class is two-twenty-four Mount Hollywood Drive," she said, falling back into the mahogany chair. "It's up by Cathy's Corner. I drove to the house yesterday when she didn't return my calls. There's just an old guy living there who we've both known for quite some time. Jerry told me the class ended at noon, then Kath had a coffee with him before riding off on her Vespa."

Addison jotted everything down in his pad.

"Did you provide the detectives with the registration and licensing details for Katherine's Vespa this morning?" he asked, not wanting to waste time going over particulars they already had on record.

"Yeah," she replied, "I did."

"Do you have reason to believe Katherine may have gotten herself mixed up with bad people? Could she have become involved with anything unsafe?"

"No," she replied, shaking her head. "Kath grew up on the Upper East Side of New York; she went to the best schools and never had to do a single thing her whole life. Experiences are what mattered to her, and she was always chasing something new. Her daddy pestered her about finishing her degree, but Kath loved the freedom here in Los Angeles. California was worlds away from the influences she contended with back east. It wasn't unusual for her to fly off for a few days, but I knew something was amiss when my calls were still going unanswered by the following afternoon."

"Have either yourself or Katherine socialized with people who practice any pagan forms of spirituality in recent times?" Addison asked.

"Well, we're gay, so there's that."

It was easy to hear the defensiveness in her voice.

"Sorry, Angela, that's not what I meant at all. I'll be more precise. Did Katherine associate with anyone who adhered to the principles of satanism or Black Magick?"

Angela wrinkled her nose. "Not that I know of, and if Kath had any dark spiritual leaning, she would have definitely spoken to me about it."

Addison smiled kindly. "What about brothers, sisters?"

"She had a younger brother, Anthony, but they weren't very close."

"Were there troubles between Katherine and Anthony?"

"No, there was nothing like that. They weren't tight, but it wasn't as if they disliked one another. Anthony works in the family business and takes his career seriously, while Kath was very much the opposite."

"Do you know where Katherine may have gone after the class?"

"No, I don't." Angela was blubbering now, leaning forward to cradle her head in her hands. "That's why I drove up to speak with Jerry at Cathy's Corner—"

Angela glanced over her shoulder when an incoming call filtered into the room.

"I'm sorry, is it okay if I answer that?"

Addison nodded. "Of course, it is."

Angela smiled languidly before exiting the room again.

Jed stretched his arms over his head. "An art class, hey."

"Yeah," Addison replied. "We'll need to get someone to head up there."

His partner focused on something across the room. "My first time was three years ago, man," he said.

"Three years ago? What do you mean by that?"

"Nothing. Just thinking out loud is all."

"Care to elaborate?"

"It was three years ago when I walked into my first homicide case. Old Jason Connolly was the lead detective, and I remember being excited," he said sarcastically. "Can you believe it? I was fucking thrilled to be in the room with the Scottish prick."

"What are you saying, kid? You don't want to be here?"

Jed laughed with disdain. "No, what I'm saying is I'd prefer to be just about anywhere than where I am, man. I mean, how many inquiries end up being stuffed inside some cardboard box and deposited away as evidence? It's not like we get the satisfaction of giving the sons of bitches a good tune-up at the station like they did in the old days."

"You want a day of reckoning?" Addison countered.

Jed exhaled with frustration. "Sure. I mean, why the hell not? Maybe the vigilante has got it all right, brother, and we don't even fucking realize it."

Addison had been involved in similar conversations over the years because, at some point, every cop got to feeling this way. The arm of justice could be excruciatingly slow in its execution. Whenever they apprehended a suspect, it marked the beginning of a drawn-out judicial process while waiting for the case to go to trial. Then there was the task of gathering witnesses and conferring with the attorney general, not to mention the time they spent doing nothing as the prosecution and defense went back and forth with their plea deals.

"I hear what you're saying," Addison agreed. "But doing our best to ensure there's not another Katherine Schneider will have to be retribution enough."

"Yeah, man, I know the freakin' score, but it would be kinda sweet if we could send some of 'em to County all busted up instead of smelling like fuckin' roses."

The sound of shuffling footsteps ended the discussion, and they waited for Angela to reenter the room. She looked fatigued as she padded back to her chair.

"Sorry," she said. "My phone's been running hot all morning. I made a couple of calls when I found out about Katherine, and word spread really fast."

Addison offered another understanding smile. "So, is there anything else that comes to mind about Katherine? Changes in her patterns, or new people she started seeing in the last few weeks?"

Angela appeared to give the question serious consideration while reaching for a fresh tissue. "No, it's like I've said already; Kath had a very cruisy lifestyle and the freedom to do just about anything she damn well pleased. The modeling started a few weeks back as a favor to Jerry, but apart from that, there was nothing out of the ordinary."

Addison scribbled something down before looking over at Jed. "You all good?" he asked.

"Yeah."

Angela's eyes remained down in her lap, and Addison waited until she raised them again before speaking. "Thank you for meeting with us at such a difficult time. I hope you manage to find a way to get some rest. We'll be in touch when there is any information to pass on. In the interim, if anything fresh comes to mind, then please give me a call." He extended an arm across the table and handed her his card.

"Thanks," she replied as her focus returned to her lap.

Addison got to his feet. "We'll see ourselves out."

Angela didn't respond, seemingly lost inside a memory that would never be built upon as the detectives left the room and walked back down the hallway.

"What the hell is going on with you, kid?" Addison asked once they were outside.

"Nothing, why?"

"I know you can be quiet at times, but you didn't speak a word to her in there."

"What did you want me to say, Ad?"

They continued back down the path in brooding silence. Addison waited as Jed unlocked the doors before climbing into the passenger seat and checking the time.

"You hungry?" Addison asked.

"Yeah, I guess I could eat," Jed grumbled.

"How about we order a couple of burgers and debrief. We'll be standing in front of the cameras with Collins later, so I guess we should at least try to be prepared."

"For what? It's not like they'll be asking me anything."

"Yeah, hopefully we'll both remain invisible. You feel like sharing a whiskey with this old hound?" Addison suggested, knowing his partner would never knock back an opportunity to have a couple of lunchtime shots.

"Sure thing, what about the burgers?"

"You okay with drive-through?"

Jed nodded. "But I'd prefer Taco Bell."

"Taco Bell it is, then."

Truth be told, he didn't even feel hungry and would have been happy enough to skip food altogether. Whiskey was their go-to play whenever things got tense, because a seedy bar and a few glasses of liquor rarely failed in raising the mood.

# SIX

Coniglio breezed into her kitchen on naked feet, where she poured her leftover tea down the sink before walking back toward the sunroom. She was dressed in a yellow vest with matching boxers to combat the heat; however, the temperature continued to rise as streams of perspiration trickled down from her hairline. Another day like this, and she would have to consider purchasing a second air conditioner for the bedroom.

Her apartment was situated on Sunset Boulevard in Echo Park, a scruffy East Side neighborhood known for its live music, great food, and quirky boutiques. It was completely different from the coastal town in Oregon where she'd been raised. Florence was a place where children played unattended after dark and chased fireflies along the Siuslaw River.

She remembered searching the trails near Heceta Lighthouse with her brothers and how the sound of laughter was as familiar as a cool ocean breeze. A blue sky always lured her to the water, where the Sea Lion Caves provided a glimpse into the marvel of nature. There were lasting experiences contained within each season. Those magical days had promised to last forever before quickly passing by. It sure was an amazing universe for an adventurous little girl to begin learning about life.

Coniglio's father was a first-generation Italian American and possibly the only migrant to be found within a hundred miles. Frank was a loving man with a kind heart and easygoing manner that made everybody feel entirely at ease. She couldn't think of a single person who didn't end up head over heels in love with him.

Her mom was a totally different story, though, always awkward in shared situations because of the impediments she chose to surround herself with. She could reveal many things about her dad, like how generous he was or the commitment he had to his family. But whenever she thought about him, what first came to mind was the steadfast way he held to the American flag, even in circumstances where patriots might consider his faithfulness less than deserving.

If she ever found a guy with half his devotion, her life would be a portrait of happiness. Her marriage came to an abrupt conclusion in 2010 after she discovered her husband in a motel room with a younger woman. She'd participated in the occasional fling after the divorce, but her experience of sex without love was underwhelming. It was the very reason why she felt so comfortable with being single until the right man came along.

Her philosophy in life was to absorb every piece of grandeur that came her way, although it wasn't about running toward anything obvious. Countless hidden surprises were waiting to be encountered in everyday living, like the sugary aroma of a freshly baked donut or the color of the evening clouds in July. Transient beauty was almost everywhere; it just floated by most people unnoticed.

Coniglio nestled into the cushions of her daybed and closed her eyes. The sunroom was her favorite spot inside the apartment, where she came to absorb the sounds of activity as they drifted up from the street below. She began reflecting on Detective Mowbray and his plaintive undertones.

There was something about the guy and his tangled presentation which appealed to her. Mowbray might be a little bowed and broken, but there was also completeness to his complication, a precision to the manner he carried out his duty and picked up on the stuff others missed. She certainly had never met anyone more underrated on the job.

She thought back to the previous night when he was stretched out inside his truck and how he appeared to be lost in the fizz of his own thinking. Johnny Cash was playing softly on the radio as he puffed absently on a cigarette. It was as if he'd been awaiting an echo of the victim's voice to start calling from the darkness or a spectral flashback that captured the moment of her murder. She recognized the presence of historical pain inside him and presumed his scar ran deeper than just policing. Coniglio was conscious of his marriage breakup, but whatever was responsible for his hurt seemed to have been with him for much longer. There was a softer side to him as well, an edgy warmth that draped his manliness, which was evident in the way he connected with his incredibly good-looking younger partner.

The sun illuminated motes of dust in the air, so Coniglio straightened her leg into the light. Her skin appeared youthful as if the secret to agelessness might be found within its ancient glow. She was in excellent condition for her age, something she never took for granted. Her work demands could quickly get in the way of a healthy lifestyle, and the odd hours sometimes affected her sleep patterns. It was difficult to discuss her profession with everyday folk; many of her friends questioned why she'd even decided to become a forensic pathologist at all. Dinner parties were the worst because she could rarely explain herself in a manner that satisfied people's curiosity.

Coniglio turned her head and scanned the living room with genuine appreciation. Her complex consisted of twenty-one apartments over three floors. The other tenants were mainly young professionals who kept to themselves. A caretaker attended to the pool area each week, and there were never many noise complaints. It provided a different vibe to the bungalow she'd rented in Venice Beach, and the change of scenery had proved to be refreshing.

She began thinking about the victims from the Hollywood Hills and felt a shiver working down her spine. Her angst didn't have anything to do with what the bodies looked like; she was no longer traumatized by the condition of a corpse. It was more the reality of them being conscious while their body parts got hacked away that tightened her belly. The homicides of the two young women had managed to subvert her core. She understood the ketamine would have alleviated a significant portion of their pain, although it likely just made things feel more misrepresented in the process. There had to be a fundamental reason why the perpetrator was administering the drug, but she remained clueless as to what it might be.

Forensic pathology evolved in leaps and bounds over the last few decades to provide the dead with an opportunity to speak from the grave. Alger Mortis disclosed how Katherine Schneider died roughly four hours prior to them arriving at the carousel, which enabled Coniglio to determine the location of the primary crime scene to be somewhere within a ninety-minute driving radius of the reserve. It was easy to identify the common denominators between each of the victims, and the LAPD made a quick decision to go public with the details. There was nothing to be gained by keeping a lid on the circumstances.

Coniglio examined the polish on her toes and decided a fresh color was long overdue. She'd been painting her nails, shaving her legs, and moisturizing her skin for what seemed like forever; pampering remained a part of her daily routine.

The bathtub was calling. Perhaps she would light a scented candle and fix herself another cup of tea while soaking to the voice of Carlotta Chadwick. She still intended to go for a stroll down by the lake and wanted to get back in time to watch the boys deliver their gruesome news to the citizens of Los Angeles.

# SEVEN

The Frolic Room was Addison's favorite place to go whenever he found himself caught up inside a shitty day. Filled with yesteryear charm, the small, no-frills venue maintained a well-stocked bar and the drink prices never fluctuated. There were portraits of movie stars on the walls and a collection of Al Hirschfeld sketches, while the jukebox was an archive of contemporary music. A diverse beer selection was available, and the cigarette machine proved handy on those occasions when he sat on a chair for longer than expected. The dive bar was situated next door to the Pantages Theatre, like a speakeasy on prime real estate. Addison had been frequenting the joint regularly for thirty years.

Collins was expecting them to be standing by his side when the cameras rolled out in the evening, which meant they couldn't go getting loaded on whiskey. A cop might have gotten away with such things in the past; however, the times had changed. Management could no longer ignore errant conduct due to the scrutiny that came with holding a public office.

City Hall was a ruthless beast, and a good community profile was tantamount to career longevity. Besides, most people carried a camera in their back pocket nowadays, increasing the likelihood of police misconduct making the evening news. But a few drinks wouldn't hurt, and a pause might help improve his partner's hangdog attitude.

Addison heard the familiar cry of squeaking hinges when Jed swung the door open, bringing a blast of cold air onto their faces. A lingering smell of sickness floated above the fumes of hard liquor; a hundred bottles fashioned a glittering glass wall beneath the space lighting. The joint was empty except for two Latino hoods hunched at the counter.

Jed led the way to the bar, where a young blonde with jade green eyes came gliding over to serve them. Addison ordered two double whiskeys, impressed by the speed in which she returned with their drinks. The girl offered an exaggerated smile when asking for his money before focusing on her fingernails.

The hoods nearby had started cussing under their breath after catching a glimpse of Addison's badge when he opened his wallet. Dressed in tank tops with baggy pants, they flaunted gang-related ink over their arms. Gold chains hung loosely around their necks, and white scars protruded through their buzz cuts. Addison considered whether they might become a problem as he leaned against the bar.

The blonde was making eyes at his partner, so he coughed to get her attention. She took his cash with a sigh before he left two dollars on the plate as a courtesy.

Addison glanced down the bar at the two men again. Ordinarily, he wouldn't give a damn, but he was mildly comforted by the fact they were beside him rather than Jed.

"How are ya doin', kid?"

"Don't sweat it, Ad; I'm all peachy."

"Well, you ain't been saying a whole lot today."

"I'm just thinking is all."

"Seems you been doin' a bit of that."

Jed's attention returned to his glass. "Yeah, I guess. It just feels like everything is stuck on repeat, you know what I mean? Same old bullshit over and again."

Addison studied him while he endeavored to form a picture of what he might look like after another ten years on the job. "Yeah, I know what you mean."

They both stood there for a bit.

"How'd your date go last night?" Jed asked.

"Like they always do, buddy."

"I wasn't aware you went on enough of them to complain about, hotshot."

Addison chuckled. "Well, I guess it depends on who you're comparing me with."

"Don't be so humble, man. I'm bettin' the ladies love that Texan cowboy shit you bring to the table. It'd be like stepping out with Elvis and Eastwood at the very same time."

Addison snickered again, only louder. "Elvis? I don't think so. How about you? You still seeing that little waitress, Rosie, who you told me about?"

"I am. Rosie's a cool chick who doesn't ask any stupid questions, and I don't get the impression she wants to hang out with me 'cause I'm a cop. She's good company, too."

"Good company, hey? Nothing beats good company. An easygoing woman can be a hard thing to find." Addison could feel the hatred coming off the two thugs beside him and turned around to pick out a position on the back wall. "How about we go and sit over there so we can speak in private," he suggested casually.

"Sure thing," Jed replied, already making his way toward the dark end of the room.

Addison ordered two more whiskeys, pointing to the back corner.

He'd taken just a few steps when something hit the back of his skull. Addison watched a quarter rattle across the floor, and he turned to face the assholes at the bar, but they continued pulling on their beers with ridiculous straight-ahead gazes.

His legs jammed when his father's face flashed in his mind, and he needed to push the image away. If he didn't, he'd likely march across the room, and once things kicked off, he probably wouldn't be able to stop. Addison never considered himself much of a fighter, but that didn't mean he shied away from a contest if the circumstances required it. Almost every scrap he'd been involved in was a consequence of something like what just transpired. He moved on with justifiable anger and sat down to focus on his partner.

"Who stole your drink?" Jed teased.

"What?"

"You look like someone stepped up to take a piss inside your glass. You should see your face, man. Are we drinking here or what?"

Addison squeezed out a smile. "I'm a different person, one moment to the next partner. You ought to know that by now." His tone lacked lightheartedness.

"You know what you need?" Jed asked in all seriousness.

"That's a tough one."

"What you need is to come to Santa Monica and catch a wave with me at dawn. When the swell crashes over your body, it makes you feel brand new. At least for a while, anyway."

Addison raised his eyebrows. "Take a look at me. I have a hard enough time putting one foot in front of the other. How do you think I'd go riding the water? I've got enough things I suck at already."

Jed was about to respond when the blonde appeared like mist to place their glasses on the table. Addison slipped her a ten and told her to keep the change.

"Hey," Jed objected. "It's my round."

"You can grab the next one. It'll save me having to walk across to the bar."

The girl tried her best smile on again, and Addison laughed silently within, thinking how his partner made him feel invisible at times.

"Can I get you guys anything else?" she asked.

"No, we're good," Addison assured her, watching as she gave Jed a final lingering glance before dragging herself back behind the bar.

The kid was California personified, and he came with a loose aura that could sometimes be mistaken for apathy. His youth had been spent on the beach, where school was an afterthought to the surf culture and party lifestyle. He was raised by his single mom, an airy-fairy take-everything-as-it-comes woman who invested her years chasing after men. She loved him dearly despite her flaws, and her cop brother had always been close at hand whenever her son needed to be pulled into line.

Jed's uncle persuaded him to apply for a place at Elysian Park Academy, where he graduated top of his class. The kid sometimes played possum with the other detectives in the division, but his brain was what got him noticed in the first place. He was encouraged to sit for the detective exam after impressing the sergeant with his street smarts and instinct.

Much of Jed's sparkle had dissolved over the past six months. It wasn't easy staying switched on in the killing game. There used to be an old sergeant at the Parker Center who had this one phrase he would repeat to the rookies who arrived ready to save the world— *You cocksuckers better get used to finishing second, and you best be doing it quick.*

As far as policing went, no truer words could be spoken, but it was the utter contempt that gnawed away at Addison more than anything. The disrespect at getting a quarter thrown at the back of his head while he was trying to have a quiet drink.

"Anything jumping out at you on this case yet?" He asked.

"Nothing besides the obvious."

"Which is?"

"We need to pray the sick bastard screws up soon. Either that or we catch ourselves a lucky break, and somebody calls the hotline with game-changing intel."

Addison inhaled the fumes of his whiskey. "We'll get him," he answered evenly.

"How the fuck does anybody's life get to a point where they start cutting young women into pieces for pleasure? Remember that piece-of-shit kid killer, Marshall Brooks, who'd come down from Fresno whenever he was in the mood?"

"I don't think I'll ever be able to forget that piece of filth."

"The Brooks investigation is hands down the worst case I've worked on. His commitment to killing those boys was almost unprecedented. Now, I don't know why, but this kinda has a similar stink about it. You feeling me?"

"Yeah. I know where you're coming from."

"Then there's the speed between the bodies and the way he's calling them in. It's almost as if he needs them to be discovered right away. Like the cocksucker's impatient for the world to see his work. Even the inverted Christian cross is muddying the waters. If something doesn't turn up soon, we're gonna end up with a lot of pretty corpses on our hands."

Addison considered his glass while he reflected. The kid was right. Aside from the occultic symbology, there wasn't much else for them to go off.

Jed swallowed his drink and raised his glass in the air. "You want another one?"'

"One more, then we should probably head back."

"One more it is, then," Jed answered, setting off toward the bar.

Addison believed a few more shots might result in them staying in the joint to commit career suicide. Everybody knew they'd missed out on the vigilante case due to his weakness for hard liquor, so he didn't want to screw things up here.

The explosive sound of splintering glass crashed in his ears, and he looked across to see Jed advancing toward the assholes at the end of the bar.

"What the fuck did you say, dickhead?" Jed raged, arms extended on either side of his body as he stared down the challenge.

It took a moment for instinct to kick in before Addison jumped out of his chair, moving fast for a middle-aged drunk with bad knees. He watched the first hood lunge at his partner with outstretched arms as Jed pulled him in hard, smashing his forehead down onto the prick's nose. The tough dropped like lumber, his face shattered, groaning incoherently and barely conscious. Blondie was hollering from behind the bar, and Addison realized how Jed would be brawling security if this had kicked off later in the evening.

Thug number two snatched a beer bottle and moved forward.

Jed ducked beneath the sideways arc of his intended blow, driving hard with his shoulder to spear him into the ground, where he unloaded a flurry of punches. When Addison arrived a moment later, he hooked an arm around the kid's neck and dragged him toward the door. His partner thrashed about in a fury.

"You hear what these fuckin' assholes said to me?" Jed roared.

Addison hadn't heard but could still feel the dull throb from where the quarter had connected with his melon. He continued dragging his partner away from the scene.

"We need to get the hell out of here," he reasoned as they scrambled for the exit.

Addison was pissed with himself; he knew about Jed's hot temper and should never have allowed him anywhere near those sons of bitches. They burst through the door into the sweltering afternoon heat, making tracks away from his favorite taproom. "Are you trying to get suspended or what?"

"Fucked if I know," Jed declared, storming up the sidewalk to his ride.

# EIGHT

Narek lowered his window to check the side mirror for anyone who might be using the street behind them. He'd been thinking of a dancer from the boss's titty bar in a bid to alleviate his boredom, but the memory of her cunt created an ache in his balls that only left him frustrated. Narek parked beneath the canopy of a eucalypt while they waited for Jamie Callahan to arrive home. The air inside the stolen Chrysler felt like a breath from hell as it coiled around his body like invisible fire.

Bedros appeared aggrieved by the conditions as if the humidity were a personal slur sent down on them by the hand of God. He sat slumped in the passenger seat, stuffing food down his gob while he fanned his face with a stick magazine. His rusted-on expression of hatred affirmed how he'd be ready for action when Callahan returned.

His partner was the cruelest individual Narek had ever encountered: his forthright approach embraced his stoneheartedness. The big bastard always inflicted more brutality than was needed, and when they whacked someone, his eyes smiled. Violence was an indispensable commodity in organized crime; being feared was the best security a criminal could have. Bedros had proven himself to be reliable, and he never needed much encouragement to make a person scream. He discussed murder and rape in terms of endearment, and it didn't bother him any if a target happened to be a woman.

"How much does this Agarka owe?" Bedros asked through a mouthful of grease.

"Seventy grand," Narek replied, disgusted.

"We'll have some fun, then?" Bedros roared, spraying harissa onto the windshield.

"Oh yeah, we'll have some fun, all right."

Killing for cash could be an absolute blast. The severity of the craft got the heart racing, and the variables meant things never became dull. Davit often wanted people killed in terrible ways; it just depended on what they'd done wrong and who they'd done it to.

The rim job they were waiting on had made an error in judgment, and even though everyone could make a poor choice on occasion, rarely would the consequences of their stupidity be so considerable. Jamie Callahan had managed to fuck shit up for himself after approaching them to coordinate his wife's abduction.

It was a hasty piece of Irish cocksuckery aimed at getting her wealthy folks to pay a fee for their daughter's safe return. The boss agreed to terms with the dipshit when he promised half the payment or fifty grand if things went belly-up.

The lady's family had come to the party with the dough, so they released the bitch as soon as the money changed hands. It should have been an easy earn for everyone involved, but the slippery cocksucker had been lying about the size of the payoff from the very start. Mrs. Callahan's abduction generated a lot of media attention upon her return, which meant the actual ransom amount eventually came out in the wash.

Davit used some Mexicans to snatch the woman and transport her to a safe house at Redondo Beach. The Chicanos were promised twenty large for their effort on the condition she was not interfered with in any way. Vato criminals were mostly scumbags in nature and similar to dogs when it came to fucking—renowned for putting their dicks into anything with a heartbeat. The reason Davit ventured outside of Armenian Power was to ensure there'd be a sheet of separation between himself and the authorities who came sniffing about afterward.

He often recruited hardened felons prepared to luck out for a smaller slice of the pie if a job contained a high element of risk. A citizen might question how he could do this, but it was all super fuckin' easy. The Armenian Mafia was notorious for their unchecked savagery, with hundreds of soldiers to call upon whenever a threat needed to be enforced. Their influence didn't end on the street either. Davit kept a chief judge who could arrange for corrupt officials to preside over a hearing, provide intel on the prosecution's evidence, or obtain a witness's address.

Everything came down to the dollar because even the most upstanding residents would usually look the other way for a price. America had been hoodwinked into believing their legal system was beyond reproach. Still, the OJ Simpson murder trial displayed the kind of exploitation that could be purchased in the good old US of A.

Bedros wriggled while he attempted to get his shirt unstuck from the front seat. "Has this Gyot paid Davit any money?" he asked.

"What do you think? Of course he paid. He just didn't pay enough. The boss even gave him extra time to come up with what's owed, but the douchebag never got the message."

"Not very smart, this Irishman."

"No, brother, not very smart at all."

The thing was, seventy grand's a fair chunk of change, and it's never good business to squeeze the trigger on someone without first trying to recoup what was owed. Callahan had gotten the chance to make things straight by handing over the fifty he'd shorted them, plus another twenty on the top as a gesture of goodwill. Narek believed he would have moved heaven itself if he'd understood what would happen if he didn't.

Instead, he fed the boss a bullshit story about the press getting the ransom wrong. How he ever imagined they'd accept such a lame excuse was anyone's guess. The stupid bastard would have been better off hiding behind a sheet of clear glass in the middle of the fucking day. Still, Davit gave him one final opportunity to square up, but the dumb cocksucker just threw it right back in his face.

Callahan claimed he'd used the money square his outstanding

gambling debts, then he pleaded for an extension, promising to come up with a more lucrative outcome. The situation confirmed there were no limits to the foolishness of some folk. Narek likened it to a person charging toward an incoming tornado with an umbrella in hand.

So, now the mick fuck needed to be dealt with. It wouldn't be clean with a slug to the back of the head, either—not after the way he'd insulted the boss. Besides, the asshole deserved what was coming after agreeing to hand his wife over to a bunch of Mexicans. If a man wanted fast money, then all he had to do was buy a shooter and steal it from someone else. Narek was going to enjoy spreading the pain load around his body.

The boss expected Callahan to be gutted like a hog and left on the driveway so his wife could observe his disgrace. Should Davit ever happen to toss a person his leftover bone, they best be grabbing it with both their hands, then burying it someplace where nobody would ever find it.

Narek watched grease dribbling down Bedros's chin and quickly turned away, unable to escape the harsh sound of his chewing.

"Can you try to eat a little quieter?"

Bedros grinned with meat-flecked teeth.

At least he wasn't talking Narek's ear off; there was nothing worse than being stuck in a car with someone who babbled on about everything they'd been doing for the past week.

Both men stiffened when a black SUV came up the street, watching as the vehicle slowed before turning into Callahan's driveway. Bedros wiped the grease from his hands on his trousers and quickly opened the door.

"Come on, let's go kill this chent," he said, pulling a ski mask over his face.

Narek gripped the handle of his blade as he entered the killing void, readying himself to unleash some Armenian justice.

"Make sure you take him from behind," he instructed as he stepped into the sunshine.

*I'm gonna carve him up real nice.*

Narek intended to extract every dime from Callahan's body, and he didn't have the responsibility of cutting the chent into pieces when they completed the job. They still needed to take a drive over to Watts and kick the color out of some African gang banger later tonight, so it was going to be an asshole of a day.

The sound of Jamie Callahan's car door set them into motion like a pair of hungry lions tracking prey. Narek smiled hatefully beneath his mask and fell in behind his partner as they made their way across the peaceful suburban street.

# NINE

Late afternoon shadows crept across Sean Brody's front porch as he looked out at the suburban street in Melrose Hill. The familiar smell of summer floated through the air— a fragrance he once found soothing. His colonial bungalow was positioned on a leafy, oak-lined street in the neighborhood's historical zone. The simple front garden featured a hedged lawn and wooden planter boxes that ran adjacent to the driveway. Sean was dressed in short pants and a white LAPD shirt while he reclined in a chair with wide armrests, feeling like two halves of the same person—one alive and spirited, the other dead and weighty.

There was nothing remarkable about his physical appearance to leave a lasting impression inside a stranger's mind, except perhaps his eyes. They were pale blue and contained a glassy coldness that contradicted the innocence of his face. Sean's sandy hair, sun-freckled skin, and average height just didn't stand out in a crowd. Though not handsome in a traditional way, women would often become attracted to him over time, drawn by his character's quiet intensity. His mother told him he'd come into the world composed, and maybe that's why he was so accomplished at killing dangerous people.

The details of his last shooting were becoming hazier by the day. Like a scene from a movie, he'd watched while intoxicated on the sofa. Sean frowned as he tried to recall Mario Bocelli's face after he fired the first bullet into him. He could remember laughing while the fat asshole pleaded for mercy and the way his hands groped at the air in search of something to catch onto, but everything else was clouded and fuzzy.

Each execution had numbed his inner torment for a brief

period, exchanging antipathy for a fragile stillness that enabled him to get through the next few months. However, the disgust never failed to return, as if committed to infecting the base of his soul. Sean embraced this inconvenience without much bother, and it simplified certain things that might otherwise be perplexing. He'd already chosen his next target—handpicked the piece of shit right off the LA court records before commencing his research.

Sean removed a fresh beer from the portable cooler beside him, watching as two kids raced each other up the sidewalk on pushbikes. He raised his can to the sky, thinking of no one in particular. "To serve and protect," he mumbled while undoing another button on his shirt. It seemed like a lifetime since he last enjoyed anything normal. Sports no longer made much sense, and reading a book only left him feeling irritable. Even sex was tedious, because he was often unable to get himself out of first gear. At least the rage kept half of him alive. His hatred was set in stone, hard-won inside the trenches of a city brimming with human filth.

The stench of reprobates and scumbags seeped from the cracks of just about every zone in Los Angeles. Worthless murderers resided in almost every neighborhood around the county—corrupting suburbs with the secrets they concealed in their hearts. Killing such people made Sean's universe smell sweet for a while. Hell, for a few days, it made the godforsaken city smell good enough to eat.

His parents raised him to understand it was always best to withhold judgment whenever possible, a tenet he'd attempted to follow until his partner was senselessly gunned down three years earlier. Nowadays, his attitude was stuff 'em all. Retribution was the best game in town, and he came packing a dirty big Ruger that knew nothing about grace.

When the sun moved behind some clouds, it sucked the color out of the world for a few seconds. The front garden appeared gray as if it were reflecting his current mood. Sean tried thinking of happier times devoid of tragedy and violence, but it was useless. Loathing was now part of his DNA, and it guided him through the gutters of the people he hunted.

When Sean first learned of the young women dumped in the Hollywood Hills, he began toying with the notion of abducting his victims. He'd imagined all kinds of ways to make a criminal suffer but didn't want to start deviating from his course. It was too risky, and cops don't usually cope well inside a prison. Besides, why would he begin chasing an abstraction when everything was ticking over like a Swiss clock? He was going to take a drive out to Glendale tomorrow night in the hope of getting up close to his next target. He wanted to look into Narek Avakian's face and feel the man's arrogance up close. Smell his aftershave and hear his voice.

Sean thought back to the day he graduated from Elysian Park Academy. He remembered the pride in his father's eyes, his mother's gentle smile, and how they snapped enthusiastically on their cameras to capture the moment for all Sean's relatives; however, it was like he had lifted the details from somebody else's life.

A desire to help people inspired him to become a cop. Sean had genuinely believed he could make this cancer of a city a safer place—*the irony of it all*. What a chump he'd been, holding onto such unattainable ideals. The closest he came to fulfilling those ambitions was blasting a handful of crooked assholes off the face of the earth. Now he stood at the center of a paradigm that divided law enforcement and criminality with an untraceable pistol in his hand.

A green Nissan pulled into the driveway next door, and he watched as the married Rachel Munroe waved at him with a flirtatious smile. She performed this bullshit whenever they happened to cross paths. Her blond hair was in a ponytail, and she was dressed in tight shorts and a little pink tank top to highlight the fake tits her husband had provided.

"How are you, handsome?" she called in an inviting, kittenish tone.

*Fuck off!* "Same as always, thanks, Rachel," he replied. It was a token attempt at congeniality on his behalf, but it still left him feeling dirty.

"You really must come for dinner soon, or I might start thinking you don't like me. Wait a minute . . . is that why you keep declining my cooking, Sean—because you don't like me? I don't think I could deal with such a scenario."

Sean looked away as Rachel leaned into the car by raising her butt in the air.

"How's Greg?" he asked, his tone dripping with sarcasm.

Rachel snickered.

"As boring and predictable as always. It's enough to cause a woman's mind to begin swirling with all kinds of naughty thoughts. You know what I mean?"

Greg was a pompous little prick, but that didn't make it right for a man to start fucking his wife. Rachel should just leave and find somebody else instead of bleeding him dry for new tits, plump lips, and liposuction. He ignored the question.

"Anyway, the offer is there, honey. All you need to do is take me up on it whenever you're feeling in the mood. You won't be disappointed, I promise."

Rachel winked seductively as she began making her way to the front door of her house with swaying hips and two bags of shopping. Sean took another pull on his beer, thinking how even the law-abiding citizens could be real fuckin' assholes in LA.

# TEN

The room was pitched in a blackness that ran deeper than night, and a flawless silence made Jennifer feel as though she was detained inside an anechoic chamber. Her breathing sounded rushed, and there was harried desperation to the way her lungs searched for air. The reek of stale urine occupied her nose while the scent of congealed blood remained lodged at the back of her throat. Jennifer's sobbing was persistent and heart-wrenching, as it spilled out from every fiber of her being. Her soul crushed beneath the conclusive nature of what was to come. As she lay in the darkness, Jennifer thought back to when she first awoke inside the cage after being abducted from the parking station on Sunset Boulevard.

"Shhhh, it's okay," Katherine assured in a half-hearted whisper.

"Where am I?" Jennifer shrieked, rattling her handcuff against the steel cage. "What the hell is going on? Who are you?" Her head pounded with unrelenting pain.

"My name is Katherine Schneider, and I'm not sure what this is all about. I'm caged here as well. I was set upon while hiking in Griffith Park on Monday afternoon."

Jennifer had been feeling untroubled and happy after completing her yoga class on Tuesday morning, emotions that suddenly seemed utterly foreign to her as if they belonged to someone she'd hardly known. Her mind swirled in frightened confusion, nothing about this situation made any sense.

"I think the asshole who kidnapped us is after a ransom," Katherine uttered.

Jennifer gradually calmed, though not much. "Why do you think that?" she asked.

"Well, he hasn't tried to rape me for a start. He's provided a comfy pillow, drinking water, and a bowl of spaghetti. Then there's the fact my father happens to be extremely wealthy. I'm guessing your folks aren't short on money, either."

"No, not really . . . they're upper middle class."

"Well, there you go. I'm sure everything will turn out okay. I just know it will—my intuition has never failed me in the past. What's your name?"

"I'm Jennifer . . . Jennifer Hill."

As the girls talked over the next few hours, they shared a lot about themselves, quickly establishing a bond that created a sense they had been friends their entire lives.

"When we eventually get out of this freaky shit show, you'll have to come over to my place for dinner and drinks," Katherine suggested. "We can discuss our ordeal and celebrate arriving home in one piece. Angie is a fantastic cook. It's another reason why I love her so much. She's also hilarious. I think she could make just about anyone smile."

There was a vitality to Katherine that resisted the hopelessness of their position. A liveliness Jennifer was never going to jump on board with.

"You should eat something," Katherine encouraged.

"The thought of food makes me queasy right now. Maybe later."

"I've had a few mouthfuls . . . it's not too bad. I think whatever drug he used to knock us out with must have suppressed our appetites. Hopefully, this nightmare gets resolved soon. It already feels like I've been stuck in the dark here for an age."

Jennifer understood precisely where she was coming from because time felt so subjective. Each second was like an eternity, yet an hour might pass in the twinkling of an eye. It was as if they were under the meter of an inter-dimensional clock, which compressed everything into a ball one moment, only to stretch out the edge of forever the next. There was little relief from the simmering psychological torment.

"How long have you and Angie been together?"

"We started dating in 2016 when I arrived from New York. I met her at a party in the Hollywood Hills. At the house where I modeled for the art class before being abducted from Griffith Park. Angie is like the opposite to me in almost every way. That's why we blend so well together. She rarely misses a day of work, hardly ever drinks, and wouldn't dream of taking drugs. Me, on the other hand . . ."

Jennifer forced a laugh.

"Why don't you have a boyfriend?" Katherine asked.

"The last two guys I dated turned out to be assholes. When I broke it off with Damien last year, I decided that I needed to have a season or two in my own company. It turns out single life is a whole lot more fun than I was expecting. I get to go wherever I want, dress however I feel, and there are never any arguments about what show to watch on Netflix."

Katherine giggled. "Men are assholes: full stop. Some of the gay guys I know give a whole new meaning to the term *bitchiness*. Angie calls it the curse of having a set of balls."

Jennifer smiled, momentarily forgetting that she was being held against her will.

"Damien was the most self-absorbed person I have ever come across. He was fine so long as everyone's attention revolved around him and what he liked talking about. I don't know what I saw in him, to be honest. He didn't even have a sense of humor."

"I'm guessing Damien was easy on the eyes."

"Oh yeah, but there was nothing below the surface of his skin."

The girls shielded their eyes as a burst of light came through an opening door; they were unable to make out anything beyond the sudden brightness. When her vision adjusted, Jennifer recognized the man who had "accidentally" smashed his case into the back of her car a few days earlier. The guy insisted on exchanging personal details so he could reimburse her for the damage. She watched in a state of panic as he walked across to Katherine's cage and grabbed a fistful of her hair, pressing a cloth down over her face while she flailed hopelessly in futile resistance.

When Katherine's body stilled, he smiled at Jennifer through crooked lips and shuffled his way toward her cage. She attempted to snatch the rag from his hand as it came through the hole beside her head, screaming and crying, pleading for him to stop. Jennifer felt a sting in her eyes and fire in her nostrils. Then her mind drifted away into a heavy black void of emptiness. If only she could have remained there.

When Jennifer regained consciousness, her brain drifted amid a sea of fuzz, and the room was stooped and twisted out of focus. Everything appeared to have been crafted with unnatural curves, seemingly rising out of a liquefied floor. The surrounding area had become spectral shadow with boarded windows and flickering light—photographs of disfigured corpses covered much of the walls, removing all hope of a happy homecoming. A sickening euphoric giddiness gripped Jennifer's mind, and she felt like a rubber doll, no longer the person she'd always understood. The monster had secured her limbs to a thick wooden chair as Katherine struggled at the center of a goat's-head pentagram on the floor, splayed like a suckling pig.

"Please stop this," Katherine pleaded, her words sounding slurred, barely decipherable through pale pink lips. "My father has lots of money; he'll pay whatever you want."

Candles burned on the five points of the circle, and Jennifer knew something unspeakable was about to occur. The psychopath represented evil in its purest form, applying himself in a manner to suggest he'd been imposing this kind of torment for many years. An oily sheen covered his pallid white skin, and the veins in his arms protruded like long purple worms. There was a foulness to the ether around his body as though his impression was tainting the air itself. The muscles on his arms rippled in a molten way, while his callous eyes resembled two black marbles with nothing human inside them. They peeled back her thoughts and piled her in horror like a layer cake of concealed nightmares.

Katherine's shrieks were unbearable as the psycho pressed a

burning iron onto her left breast, singing a nursery rhyme while stroking her face. He smiled at Jennifer, dancing around the room with a bone saw in his hand before taking up a position by the pentagram. Katherine bucked like a prairie horse as he began cutting through her wrist with slow, purposeful motions. The corroded metal stench in the air caused Jennifer to vomit. It was so hard to breathe . . . then her bladder failed, and the warmth in her tights increased her confusion. His drug gorged upon her senses to make everything distorted, producing powerful waves of synthetic bliss and an erratic form of peace, ramming a toxic mix of ecstasy down her throat while she sat front row as Katherine was hacked up alive.

Jennifer shook her head violently to throw the recollection from her mind, drawing her thoughts back into the here and now. Her mouth was cardboard, and she reached for the bottle of water inside the cage. Gooseflesh crept down the skin on her arms as rivulets of sweat stung her vision. Her body cooked in fever as the air tickled her nostrils, each breath making her want to sneeze. There was a bowl of spaghetti by her side, but she would never even consider eating it. She'd watched him lick Katherine's blood off his fingers like chocolate sauce. Jennifer wriggled over to where her wrist was cuffed and twisted her body to alleviate the sharp pain in her arm. She examined the restraint for a weakness, for a way to break free of its hold. It was funny, though not in a laughing manner, that despite her knowing escape was futile, she continued revisiting the possibility.

Jennifer believed everyone likely considered, at one time or another, the concept of dying under horrifying circumstances. When she was a girl, she would hold her breath until her lungs were about to burst, imagining drowning underwater. Jennifer also reflected on how it might feel to be shot and wondered what the pain was like for a person wasting away with terminal cancer. However, none of her conjecture had prepared her for the looming horror she'd witnessed in the outer room. Her body seemed to be undergoing a preternatural evolution as grisly images sparked a wildfire at the center of her consciousness.

Katherine had died screaming under the weight of their captor's malice, and soon, Jennifer would be departing similarly. The blare of Katherine's screeching was the harshest sound Jennifer had ever heard. She would have done anything to tear it from her memory; however, the quiet inside the room intensified her understanding. Her dread was spinning on an unbreakable loop and moving with perpetual motion. She thought of random things while lying there in the darkness, such as debating her cousin about why Donald Trump would make a lousy president and feasting on peanut butter sandwiches with her brother at the lake house when they were kids. Jennifer considered whether her father might eventually find a way past her murder to continue buying a season ticket at the Staples Center. She remembered all the people she'd taken for granted. If only she were able to see her parents one final time, draw them close and tell them how much she loved them.

Her body trembled in waves—her head throbbing with an ache that probed down the sides of her neck like poison ivy. Silence rested heavily within the room like a pool of water. The stillness was laced in anticipation to make her brain feel electrified and skittish. When a burst of light finally arrived to push back the darkness, she turned her head and saw the monster standing in the doorway—a rag dangling in his left hand.

"Hello, sweetheart," he said.

A groan rolled up her throat in search of an exit. Jennifer's stomach was a nest of vipers as he moved forward to slip an arm through the hole beside her head. She felt the cold dampness contained inside the cloth as it pressed against her face and struggled to turn away, but the force of his hand offered no course of action to her weakened body. Her brain glitched as streams of hot urine trickled down the inside of her thighs, and she recognized his disgusting, crooked smile before the chloroform kicked in to close her mind.

# ELEVEN

Addison made his way up the staircase to the county coroner building in Boyle Heights while his partner stood near the entrance above smoking a cigarette.

"Your joints playing up again?" Jed asked.

"Yeah, and I don't imagine they'll be improving anytime soon either."

His bad knees were the result of two injuries he'd suffered while playing football for the Lone Star Rangers in high school. The issue hadn't concerned him until he hit forty, and they'd been getting steadily worse every year since.

"Have you had them seen lately?"

"I went to a doctor last year, who wrote me up for some Vicodin, but it didn't help much. Besides, I don't want to go adding painkillers to the mounting list of vices in my life."

Jed took a drag on his Winston and wiped away the sweat from his forehead. "You ever thought of getting a cortisone injection?"

Addison grimaced as he ascended the final few steps. "I've been tossing around whether to have them cleaned out for a while now. But maybe I should get an injection first. A needle is more appealing than going under the knife."

He would already be feeling uncomfortable if it were anybody else making such a fuss over his health. Addison was familiar with the way Jed could sometimes niggle over things like a woman. However, his partner's heart was honorable, and his motives were genuine. The kid didn't nurture an exaggerated ego or concern himself with gaining external recognition, and they had figured a way past every hurdle. Jed's approach to life helped Addison gain a new perspective in areas outside the job. It's why he hadn't bothered revisiting the barroom situation from the previous day.

His former partner had been as challenging to work alongside as any person could be. Daniel Redmond maintained an itchy trigger finger which brought an underlying sense of volatility to every situation. Redmond employed a kick-the-door-down-and-force-a-confession approach to complicate even the most straightforward investigation. It wasn't at all surprising when internal affairs sent him into early retirement.

Addison waded through the accumulation of turds left in his wake before eventually emerging out the other side with his boozy reputation intact.

"The cortisone will make a massive difference," Jed continued. "And you won't think about chewing on that other crap when it's done."

A lingering silence produced a moment of awkwardness.

"You catch the news this morning?" Jed asked as he flicked his butt onto the road.

"Yeah, I did, unfortunately."

The brutal nature of the crimes and the short time frame between each victim ensured the investigation was the biggest news story for two days. Still, a particularly shameless murder in Monterey Hills had snatched the headlines this morning.

Addison waited for Jed to toss his cup into the trash before making his way inside. The corridors sparkled in perfect cleanliness, and he wasn't keen on the synthetic freshness soaking the air. For some reason, it made him feel as if he needed to take another shower.

There was a time when he would arrive here in eager anticipation. But like most other things in his life, the enthusiasm faded until it became just a part of the job. The detectives walked in silence, caught inside the myriad of thoughts running through their heads.

Addison remained a short distance behind Jed as they rounded the final corner to the coroner's office, watching while his partner knocked on Coniglio's door with the back of his hand. It seemed a matter of seconds before she appeared all bright-eyed and ready for action.

"Mowbray, Jed, how are you boys doing this morning?"

They both responded how they were doing fine.

"Well, don't just stand there looking all serious, fellas, come on in."

Addison followed his partner into the room as Coniglio took up a position behind the desk to begin shuffling paperwork. Jed took a chair by the door as Addison sat beside him.

The office was drenched in random color, and there wasn't anything medically related on display. Band posters decorated the walls, while a bookshelf next to the detectives overflowed with a sea of paperback novels. A stereo on the floor balanced a crooked stack of CDs, and three small cactus plants encircled a water feature in the corner.

Addison must have sat in this position on a hundred occasions and couldn't believe how many things he'd missed. The examiner's desk was perfectly ordered, which contradicted the abundant flow of creative clutter so prevalent throughout the room.

When Addison returned his focus, Coniglio's smile made him anxious.

"Thanks for coming in," she said. "And I have to say, you boys did some nice work in front of those cameras last night. You looked great up there, the both of you."

Neither of them reacted, though Addison took note of the fact she'd been watching.

"What have you got for us?" he asked.

"I have a few things, but don't go getting excited, because it's nothing that's going to blow the case open. I can certify the primary crime scene is within a ninety-minute driving radius of Griffith Park. I can also confirm a few matters we already suspected to be true. Some new information has come to light, as well."

When Coniglio finished speaking, she pushed a transparent plastic pouch across her desk.

Both detectives leaned in for a look.

"What is it?" Jed asked.

"A few strands of blond hair we lifted off the back of the victim's shirt. The lab called this morning to confirm the hair belongs to our Jane Doe from the Bowl. Which tells us the perp is holding the victims in a common area before he kills them."

"The lab isn't wasting any time, then," Addison mused.

The county and LAPD laboratories shared the same building and always had a lengthy backlog of bodies that needed to be worked through. Waiting on results could often take longer than desired, particularly when a case wasn't deemed to be a high priority. Addison had established a few decent connections inside both departments throughout his career and wasn't afraid to use them if he needed something back ASAP.

"This investigation is now the department's number one priority," Coniglio revealed. "So, you boys won't be sitting around waiting on results."

Addison nodded to convey his curiosity had been satisfied.

"Now, remember how we couldn't make sense of why there was spaghetti in the first victim's stomach?" Coniglio asked them.

Addison leaned forward, anticipating what she was about to say.

"The question has an answer of sorts, Mowbray, but it creates complications."

Addison raised his hand into the air to show he wasn't getting carried away.

"He must be offering the victims a meal while they are detained," Coniglio continued. "What his reasons are for doing this is anybody's guess. Perhaps it's a way of dragging things out, or maybe it's a ploy to hide his intentions. Anyhow, Jane Doe decided to consume a plateful, while Katherine Schneider ate a few mouthfuls. I'm presuming Jane was probably held captive longer, and hunger found a way through all the fear."

Addison reclined in his chair again.

"The techs confirmed the same guy called them in. Were you

aware of that?" he asked.

"I suspected as much, but nobody confirmed it with me till now."

"When I listened to the recordings again the other night, this one thing jumped out at me. Maybe it was the tone of his voice or the fact he's making the calls at all. But it comes across as he cares about them in some bizarre, contradictory way. What I know for sure is it doesn't feel like a blatant flouting of the law."

They all reflected over what Addison said before Jed cut in with a question.

"Did you find any trauma besides the brand and the removal of her hands?"

Coniglio shook her head.

"Nothing to indicate he willfully attempted to inflict a physical injury. There's bruising on her right arm from a handcuff. It was harder to identify because he'd cut away her hands from below the wrist, but I managed to find chafing farther up the arm. There was also bruising near her ankles and a tear in her groin. It appears she was splayed in the same manner as the first victim. There are nasty rope burns on her lower legs, too.

"Now, I understand how I'm not a detective, but the more time I get to spend on this, the more plausible it seems the perpetrator is attempting to perform a ritual killing. Whether or not he's serious or just trying to throw you off course, I can't say. Although he sure goes to a whole load of trouble in doing things the way he does.

"We know he secures their limbs when he works on them, and he shackles their arms to something as a way of keeping them captive. The lab also discovered several polyester fibers in Katherine's hair. They're the kind used in the manufacturing of pillows, which fits with your line of thinking, Mowbray, about him having a twisted affection for them. I believe you might be on to something there; it's certainly worth considering what his motivation could be for offering comfort."

Addison glanced at his partner, who was bouncing his legs with an expression of hatred on his face. "You okay?" he asked.

Jed appeared embarrassed by the question and sat back to become rigid in his chair. "Yeah, of course, I'm all good."

Addison wasn't buying it; however, he knew better than to press him.

Jed deflected by clearing his throat.

"What about the ketamine?" he asked.

Coniglio referred to the papers on her desk. "There's ketamine in her blood, but there's also something else that came back which we didn't pick up on in Jane's system. There are high levels of chloroform in Katherine's blood. It was administered only a matter of hours before we arrived at the reserve. I'd considered whether he might be using the ketamine to assist him in binding their arms and legs, but I now believe he uses the chloroform when he abducts them and then again when he secures their limbs. He must be injecting the ketamine before the killing starts. At least, that appears to be the situation with Katherine Schneider. Now, I have a theory on this, but I'd be interested to hear what your thoughts are."

The detectives remained deep in thought, and Coniglio began watching Mowbray.

Addison uncrossed his legs to commence speaking his mind. "He's knocking them out with the chloroform when he moves them, which makes a certain amount of sense if he's preparing his bone saw. But why the hell does he even bother using the ketamine if they're already out? Are you implying he's jabbing them with the drug and then going to work?"

Jed shook his head in disgust.

"What?" Addison asked.

"The sick asshole is putting them to sleep, and then he's getting them high on drugs before he starts the process of cutting away his pieces."

Coniglio's eyes expressed the revulsion she was feeling, and she unconsciously scrubbed her hand against her shirt as if she had encountered filth.

"Yes, that is precisely what I presume he's doing. Which means he has access to a supply of very decent ketamine. The drug in the victims' blood is hospital grade, so it would definitely mask the pain and maybe even stop them from passing out."

Jed's forehead compressed into a knot. "He might be getting the ketamine from a medical facility, but I don't believe chloroform is even used in hospitals anymore, is it?"

"No. Chloroform isn't used medically, but it can still be found in most colleges around the country. More specifically, in their science departments. The only other place I can think of where he might be getting it is through the dark web."

Addison's phone began vibrating in his coat pocket. "It's headquarters. I'm going to have to take this," he said, pressing CONNECT and putting the phone to his ear. "Mowbray."

"Hey, Ad, it's Thompson. How are you doing?"

"Well, I'm alive, Bill. I know that much."

There was a short pause before Thompson responded.

"It appears another girl has been taken. She's been missing since Tuesday after leaving for a yoga class on Sunset Boulevard. The girl's name is Jennifer Hill, and her roommate's been trying to reach her for a couple of days. She knew where her friend usually parks and decided to take a drive out there this morning. It turns out the car is still there. She got all hysterical and freaked out, so the attendant watched the security footage from the night in question. The abduction is all on tape, and physically, she's remarkably similar to the other two."

"Been missing since Tuesday, you say."

"Yeah."

"Has the area been secured?"

"No, the red flag came up just ten minutes ago. Everyone's heading over there now."

"What's the address?"

"The parking station is at 3246 Sunset Boulevard, Hollywood."

"Right-o, we're on it."

"Good luck, Mowbray."

"Yeah, thanks."

Coniglio and Jed stared at him in dreadful anticipation. When a homicide detective landed on a crime scene, it usually meant it was already too late for the victim. It's like installing security on a door after everything inside the house has been lifted. But for now, Jennifer Hill might still be breathing.

"Seems our perp has gone and grabbed himself another girl," Addison said.

Coniglio released a faint whistle as Jed cursed beneath his breath, both aware how every second was now a matter of life and death.

# TWELVE

It was just a matter of fortune that the house happened to be situated between an empty warehouse and a vacant lot at the end of the street. Watts could be a dangerous neighborhood and certainly not an area where Narek would choose to spend his night.

Bedros appeared as if he felt unhinged by the drawn-out proceedings, which might prove hazardous for the young slut and her hog-tied fuck buddy on the floor.

The girl gaped anxiously at Narek while he checked his gold Rolex and silently questioned why Davit had decided to go off-grid. He strode over to the window on heavy legs and peered outside through a small crack between two tattered curtains.

There wasn't a cloud in the sky as the morning sun beat down onto the property. Narek mopped the sweat on his neck with a soggy napkin and thought about how much he wanted to be home right now, relaxing with a beer while the air conditioner blasted cold onto his face. How anyone managed to get by without HVAC was a mystery, yet the toasty conditions were the least of his concerns.

The job was meant to be easy-fuckin'-peasy, like taking a dump in the morning after climbing out of bed. They were expecting to break a few of Dewayne Jordan's ribs to ensure he never went near the girl again, then drive back to the club. Hayk Sargsyan paid for Davit's help after hearing the stories of his daughter's sexcapades circulating the hood. Narek understood why Hayk wanted this done and brought Bedros along to ensure he received value from his investment. They'd been looking forward to putting a boot into the bastard, but sure as fuck weren't supposing on making him graveyard dead.

The last fifteen hours had been draining, and fatigue now made everything more complicated. When Narek finished twisting his knife inside Callahan's guts, the prick's innards were dangling around his ankles as he squealed through bloodied lips. The Irishman pissed himself before his peepers went cockeyed and clouded over in death. His execution was performed over one exceptionally long minute. Then they torched the Chrysler in the Los Angeles River culvert and hung out at the club until it was time to head over to Watts.

Narek sponged his neckline again, cussing in Armenian while he tried to cultivate a strategy that didn't involve hearing from the boss. He'd already exhausted every available option to get a message through and needed to be mindful of overstepping guidelines. Narek felt lost at sea, like trying to send a letter home by dropping a bottle into the ocean while sharks circled the raft.

What made matters worse was they wouldn't be in this squeeze if someone had monitored the joint beforehand. A little planning might have prevented them from strolling through the door with nothing but their dicks in their hands. Not that Narek would bother expressing his displeasure when they eventually found their way out of this jam.

After all, it was the boss who'd contended there was no need for any surveillance.

Hayk also had provided certain assurances, so Narek intended to hit him up for additional costs should his daughter get to leave here alive. His oversight contributed to them being trapped inside this dump, sweating their asses off like Christmas hams while Lado Fucking Jordan went stiff on the floor. Stinking the room up like a medieval sewer.

Narek observed the girl as she attempted to comfort her fuckboy by stroking the side of his face while he wriggled about like a maggot. It was nauseating. His patience for cocksuckery had long expired, and it required iron-cast resolve not to put a bullet into their heads. However, Davit fixated on them keeping the girl safe, and their future might come crashing down if they defied his instructions.

Bedros was wilted into the couch in such a way to convey he

didn't plan on moving, a wicked scowl pressed to his features as he grappled with the rising heat.

"Hey?" Narek called.

"Aya."

"Check your phone."

Bedros stared back at him like a stone. "It's in the kitchen."

Narek dropped his head to prevent his rage from spilling over. "Why the fuck did you leave it out there?" he demanded, incredulous. "Get up and go grab the damn thing. Do you want to get home or what?"

Bedros struggled to his feet as the hatred in his eyes became more pronounced than usual. Narek could empathize with his attitude. They should be unwinding in a state of calm serenity by now, not stranded in some shithole between Lynwood and South Gate.

Everything seemed to be on course when Hayk gave them a key to Dewayne's house and the time his daughter would be there. The old coot insisted on the girl being present when they kicked the stuffing out of her colored friend, thinking it might discourage her from making a similar error again.

Narek was surprised to find Lado slumped on the couch when he walked through the door, but that was nothing compared to what he felt when the prick went for a gat on the armrest. The scene could have quickly concluded with him, and Bedros sprawled out on the living room floor like two lumps of Swiss fuckin' cheese.

Fortunately, he reacted fast by firing three rounds into the cocksucker before they stood watching while blood exploded from the artery in his neck. The violent spray of dazzling red soon became a lazy surge, a final song from his rapidly dying heart, then Lado's hand dropped from his throat, and he slid from the couch like an oversized corn snake.

Narek's decision to fit his Glock with a sound suppressor proved to be astute. The familiar pop of gunfire would have enticed more punks to the scene, tooled up for war.

He cast his eye around the room and shook his head in disgust. It was the type of dive where other people's trash got to find itself a new home. The dilapidated old bungalow was typical of the low-income, urban lifestyle prevalent in many neglected neighborhoods around the city—undesirable suburbs where racial minorities were required to scratch an income from below the poverty line. Narek couldn't comprehend how anybody got accustomed to existing this way. It might seem a better alternative to death, but it sure as fuck wasn't living.

The walls inside were probably white at one time but had transformed into a greasy beige color from grime buildup. Two couches positioned in the center of the room appeared filthy enough to prevent Narek from taking a seat. He considered the PlayStation console and the interactive TV standing on top of a chest of drawers, the fancy stereo in the corner, and the plastic chairs scattered throughout. Another confrontation felt more plausible by the second, and they only had nine bullets and Lado's gat between them.

Hayk's girl was whispering into lover boy's ear, but the asshole received no comfort from her words. Dewayne's eyes were pleading white saucers, ready to explode from their sockets. Narek looked down at them with loathing while he covered his nose to mask the foul reek of shit drifting up from the corpse.

*Was it any wonder why Hayk wanted to drag her away from this pair of dirtbags?*

If she felt conflicted right now, what would she be like when he got around to finishing Dewayne? There was no way for this situation to conclude with the tar brother still breathing. The only reason he hadn't popped him already was that he couldn't risk sending the girl into a meltdown. Her wailing might attract unwanted attention, and he hadn't been authorized to "silence" her.

She failed to comprehend why they were waiting to hear from the boss, and there was only one reason for wanting a word with him: to determine whether she got to go home to daddy or put through the mincer with her two colored friends. When Davit apportioned her welfare to them, there hadn't been a pair of bodies in the equation.

Narek was typically prepared to put a wager on most things, and if he were offering odds on the conclusion, he'd say her chances were about fifty-fifty. It would all come down to the boss's presence of mind and where his paranoia levels happened to be.

Bedros trudged back into the room. His look communicated he was nearing the end of the line—as far as waiting around was concerned.

"And . . . ?" Narek asked.

Bedros shook his head in silence.

Narek wanted to smash his fist through something, but besides the chents on the floor, there was nothing for him to fucking hit. At a pinch, their problem might appear to be somewhat multifaceted, but the only thing keeping them here was Narek's fear of making the wrong decision. The bitch resided in Glendale, which meant the waiting game was their safest option for now. It would be a significant risk to instigate a play without hearing from the boss, and a poor call might result in dismemberment on the slaughter room floor.

When Narek felt a vibration coming from his back pocket, he pulled out his Blackberry in a burst of anticipation, quickly reading the message before flipping Bedros the phone and pointing toward the kitchen. Bedros appeared disgruntled, cussing in Armenian as he made a big exit.

Hayk's daughter began whimpering, and Narek considered the inviting curves of her body. She was easy on the eye with her long mane of dark-brown hair, smooth caramel skin, and perfectly rounded titties. It would be a shame if Davit ordered them to make her fish bait. Besides, they already had enough to get through with the task of hacking away the brothers.

Narek turned his head at the sound of Bedros's approach and saw his partner raise a thumb into the air. So, the girl was going to make it home after all. He still needed to inform her about what would happen if she ever decided to open her pretty cunt mouth.

Then after they disposed of the waste, he could finally head home, get a blowjob from Anna, and find some relief from this incessant fucking heat.

# THIRTEEN

A strong LAPD presence was assembled inside the parking lot on Sunset Boulevard as more detectives arrived to help the forensic team sweep the area. Addison observed a lab technician dust Jennifer Hill's car while waiting for Jed to make his way back from the office upstairs. Word of the kidnapping had found its way to the press and Jamie Callahan's murder was no longer their main priority. The girl's abduction would be the opening news slot on every network before day's end.

Major investigations chew into police reserves, and the homicide division usually found itself being split down the middle. It wasn't like they could pause the murder rate. Detectives were just expected to pick up the extra slack until things cooled off. A lot of heat was coming down the line right now, and Addison didn't imagine the pressure would be getting released any time soon.

The lieutenant was speaking with a forensic team leader about how he expected the scene to be processed. Collins carried himself with a noble impatience that came from spending a lifetime on the job. Standing at over six feet tall with a muscular frame, he radiated a physical presence that made him hard to overlook. Collins maintained a high level of fitness, and his terrific looks made a strong impression on the ladies. Addison often heard the women at the office calling him Denzel Washington, but they also understood he was utterly devoted to his wife. Most cops lost a portion of their intensity by the time they hit fifty, yet Collins was sharp as ever and expected everyone to uphold his standards.

He didn't need to holler to get his point across. Nevertheless, when the shit hit the fan, it was best to be doing more than what might ordinarily be expected if one didn't plan on seeing his other side. Collins had arrived at the scene in a pair of denim jeans and a white, long-sleeved shirt, a noticeable change from the dark suits he favored.

Addison began thinking about whether the first two victims were the only people the perpetrator had ever murdered. A season of carnage often occurred when a psychopath found a way past any lingering concerns they might have had about taking a life. The urge to reoffend became irresistible, like a contagion of bloodlust that defied all reason. It wasn't much different in the way a junkie craved the sting of a needle.

Killing distributed dopamine into the brain, and an offender's perversity usually increased as they pursued an elevated state of exhilaration. If Jennifer Hill were eventually killed by the perpetrator's hand, it would take his tally to three girls in a single week, a murder frenzy by any standard.

The lab team combed the ground around the girl's blue Honda, searching for fibers and trace evidence. They didn't extract noteworthy data at the first two scenes, and Addison didn't expect that to change here. His thoughts were interrupted when Jed came striding through the door behind him.

"How'd it go?" Addison asked.

"It's all done. Holbrook's bagging up everything now, and Rodgers just came back from the yoga joint to take down a statement from the attendant."

Addison recognized the presence of hostility in his partner's eyes. "You get a look at the tape?"

Jed nodded before spitting on the ground. "Yeah, and it sure as shit doesn't look good for the girl."

"What's your gut saying?"

"That it's our guy who snatched her. The piece of shit drives down here while she's getting out of her car and parks his van opposite. He just sits around until she comes back, then moves in on her from behind that wall over there. She's completely unaware of his approach and appears to be rummaging for keys inside her bag. The perp wraps his arm around her throat and covers her face with a rag. When she passes out, he drags her across to his van. The whole thing is done and dusted in under a minute. It seems Coniglio was right about the chloroform being used in the abductions."

Addison considered whether Jed had been adversely affected by the footage. "You doing all right today, partner?" he asked.

"Yeah, sure. Never been fuckin' better."

The disparity between his statement and mood was apparent.

"Well, at least we've got something we can report to the lieutenant."

Jed forced a laugh. "You think? I wish you the best of luck with that. My guess is he'll find a way to get uptight about the situation, and the chloroform will likely feed his obsession about finding where those drugs came from. I might be wrong, but the way he's marching around this morning, I'd rather just stay the fuck out of his path."

"I'd imagine you're probably right," Addison agreed.

Jed smiled. "What's the story with you and Coniglio?" he asked.

"Say again? What do you mean, me and Coniglio?"

"Come on, Ad, there's this thing that descends whenever the two of you are together."

Addison's face reflected his astonishment. "What the hell are you talking about? What thing?"

"A vibe like you're both doing everything you can to hide what you think of each other. It kinda reminds me of junior high when all the girls would stand around tapping their feet while they waited for the boys to make the first move."

Addison was about to disagree when he noticed the lieutenant closing in.

"I think you imagine things," he asserted.

Collins maintained a loose regulation on proceedings while he strode across the parking lot. It was easy to understand why he'd gained so much reverence from the cops he'd served with. Jed remained unconscious of the boss's approach as he examined something in the corner behind him, so Addison nudged him with his elbow.

"Mowbray, Perkins," Collins greeted.

They didn't get the chance to return his acknowledgment.

"Your investigation is fast becoming a clusterfuck. I've got everyone from the captain to the mayor lining up for a grab at my ass right now, and this latest turn of events is only going to increase their squeeze."

A brief silence passed between them before Collins continued his rant.

"It appears a matter of time until there's another body up in those hills. Does either of you care to hazard a guess on what parts of her will be missing?"

Addison couldn't recall the last occasion he'd seen the man behaving this animatedly and wasn't sure how to respond. He just nodded with a look of earnest contemplation.

"You're both on call around the clock until we catch this slippery fuck, so make damned sure that you keep your phones with you at all times."

It wasn't like they didn't know that already.

"And I expect you to remain clear-headed," Collins revealed. "I don't care how we get this cocksucker. Just get him off the streets and into a cage."

Collins looked from Addison to Jed, then back again.

"If either of you somehow finds a way to screw this up, you'll find yourselves working burglary out of Hollywood station faster than a speeding ticket. I'm sure they'd love to have a couple of homicide detectives on their team."

"We understand," Addison countered. "We won't let you down."

"That's good to hear. All available techs are trawling through the victims' social media accounts, and the calls have started coming in faster than we can answer them. You'll need to get somebody to follow up on every half-decent lead.

"I've also got people canvassing the hospitals in the local area because the ketamine he's using isn't coming off the streets. We're in the process of collecting as much CCTV footage as we can get our hands on. Gas stations, tolls, the whole shebang. With any luck, we'll be able to triangulate where this filthy fucking animal is operating from."

Addison suddenly found himself thinking about how the chloroform might affect the deployment of manpower, deciding now was the time to tell the lieutenant about it.

"Are you aware Jed and I were with Coniglio when we received the call about the missing girl?" he asked hesitantly.

Collins stared at him with unblinking eyes.

"The examiner uncovered traces of chloroform in the Schneider girl's blood. It appears he's using it when he abducts them. Jed had a quick look at the tape upstairs, and the video supports the hypothesis. We think he uses the chloroform again as a convenience when he gets them from wherever they're being detained. Then he injects the ketamine before he starts killing."

If Collins appreciated the new information, he wasn't making it known. "And why the fuck am I only hearing about this now?" he fumed.

"It's like I said already. We just learned of this."

"You got anything else you'd like to share while we're here?"

Addison nodded. "The lab found a pillow fiber in the victim's hair, which indicates there must be a common area where he's holding them."

"Did Coniglio have an opinion on where he might be obtaining the chloroform?"

"Yeah, she explained he could find it in most college science labs around the country. The only other place she thought he might be getting it from was the dark web. We received the call out soon afterward and didn't get to go any deeper with her on it."

Collins remained silent.

"There's another thing," Addison said, watching as Collins raised his eyebrows.

"Well, go on."

"Coniglio believes interest in the occult might be the inspiration behind these murders. She thinks the signs are too aligned for the concern not to be genuine."

Collins appeared unimpressed and perhaps even annoyed. "Listen, Mowbray, the last thing we need right now is to whip the nation into a fix about the prospect of some devil-worshipping nutjob prowling the streets. Nothing good ever came from all the satanic panic that engulfed America's suburbs during the nineties, certainly sweet fuck all to support the idea any such people existed beyond the realms of imagination. Do you remember the kind of shitstorm those three boys caused down in West Memphis?"

The lieutenant's reaction wasn't entirely unexpected.

"I'm not proposing we release details about any of this. But Jed, Coniglio, and I are of the mind that the ritual nature of these crimes may turn out to be the real deal."

Collins exhaled. "How, exactly?"

"Well, he's branding an inverted cross onto the victims, for a start," Addison countered, looking toward Jed, who remained silent by his side. "Then there's the manner he goes about his work, which suggests his connection to these women may not be completely random. The asshole splays the victims, keeps body parts, and doesn't sexually interfere with them. What I do know is we aren't dealing with a typical thrill kill degenerate, and he isn't taking the kind of risks that scream it's only a matter of time. My instincts are saying the ketamine is integrated into whatever it is he's striving to do. At a pinch, I'd say we're chasing a person of high intellect, and I don't know why exactly, but I just can't shake the feeling he's working his way toward something."

Collins shrugged. When the silence went on for longer than anticipated, he rolled his hands to encourage Addison on to the point.

"We need to be thinking about more than just finding chemicals, is all."

Collins smiled and clapped Addison on the shoulder. "All

right, then, Mowbray. You boys come and see me when you're both finished here and give me everything you've got."

"I just did," he replied.

Collins winked intuitively and began slowly shaking his head. "Just come and see me when you're done," he reiterated evenly before turning on his heel to begin making his way back to Jennifer Hill's blue Honda.

Addison faced his partner. "Thanks for the input."

"Trust me, Ad, I could sense him waiting for a chance to rip my ass."

His partner's intuition was superb; he usually read most situations like a book.

"Yeah, you're probably right," Addison agreed, reaching for his cigarettes.

He began wishing for a breakthrough development—for anything to make him feel like they'd found a way into the game.

# FOURTEEN

Paige Harding sat in a Bladen recliner chair inside her Huntington Beach villa, rubbing moisturizer onto her freshly shaved legs. She decided to skip her afternoon exercise class and was watching an update on the latest abduction by the Hollywood Hills serial killer. Her boyfriend had called from the office half an hour earlier to make sure she felt safe being at home alone. Greg was an on-the-rise business developer for a sports agent who specialized in promoting college football stars. He was concerned by the notion Paige fit the profile of the women being targeted. It was a charming gesture, a little unnecessary perhaps, but sweet just the same.

She met Greg at a Pomona College bar in the fall, and they moved in together six weeks later. Paige wouldn't necessarily say she was head over heels in love with him, although his good looks and incredible body were easy to embrace. Paige's parents couldn't deal with the reality that Greg was thirty-five years old and didn't belong to a church. They expected her to date someone with a college education who *loved* the Lord. Her mom had attempted to sabotage the relationship at every turn. Consequently, she hadn't spoken with her much of late.

Even though Paige was raised in a Christian home, her faith only existed as fleeting interludes in neglected corners of her mind. There were too many self-righteous hypocrites in the church—too many judgmental people like her folks who looked down their noses at someone just because they didn't have a tertiary qualification.

She placed the lotion down by the side of her chair and raised the volume on the TV. A correspondent was speaking grievously about the unfolding situation outside a parking station on Sunset

Boulevard. The missing person was a woman named Jennifer Hill, an attractive blonde who was abducted after her yoga class on Tuesday afternoon.

Maybe Greg was right in believing she needed to be more careful. Still, California provided an endless assembly line of beautiful blondes, and Paige didn't consider herself to be overly attractive anyway.

She watched a swarm of media descend upon a couple of detectives as they exited the parking station to begin making their way up the street. One of the cops was a middle-aged, rugged-looking man with a thick mop of brown hair and a weary face. The other was blond, sun-kissed, and sexier than Brad Pitt in *Legends of the Fall*.

"Talk about making a girl consider breaking the law," Paige uttered, observing while the detectives hurried away from the cameras, displaying an intense loathing for all to see.

A female reporter from Fox chased after them, firing multiple questions as her crew struggled behind. Paige wasn't disappointed when the younger detective turned to face her. "God damn it, lady, you need to back the hell up. People are grieving right now, and all you care about is making sure you get your cutesy face on the tube tonight. How many ways do you want to ask us the same freakin' thing anyway?"

The plastic-faced correspondent appeared stunned as the detectives crossed to the other side of the road without looking back, weighed down by the mounting pressure to apprehend the monster they were hunting.

Paige flicked the channel over to MTV, searching for something less intense, surprised to discover an old INXS concert at Wembley Stadium from the nineties.

Greg was taking her to Santa Monica for shrimp and steak later tonight, and then they were heading to the rooftop Standard Bar in the city for drinks with a few of their friends. The summer break had been tedious after her best friend abandoned her by taking a vacation to the French ski fields. Paige's ongoing problems with her folks had made the holidays forgettable, not to mention the fact they had stopped her allowance.

Greg was on a very decent salary, but he already paid the rent and supported them both, so she hated asking him for money. Nevertheless, she was due to have herself some fun, and for whatever reason, sensed good vibrations for this coming weekend.

The least she could do was see to it that her appearance might take his breath away. Paige slipped off the recliner and removed her panties while she padded her way toward the bathroom. She needed to finish preparing her body for their big night on the town.

# FIFTEEN

The activity inside the office had subsided as Addison tried to take advantage of the lull by realigning his focus. He'd been going over the video from the parking station all afternoon and was still no closer to any kind of a breakthrough. Documents formed a pile on his desk, and the time on his computer confirmed his shift had ended an hour ago. His brain felt murky as he attempted to push past another headache that branched down the sides of his neck.

Their meeting with Collins had mainly been a revision of the conversation from earlier in the morning. However, Jed still managed to annoy the man by suggesting that the chemicals search was a waste of everyone's time. The lieutenant had insisted they keep the inverted cross out of the media, and it wasn't hard to understand his reasons for doing so.

If the press indicated the murders contained a satanic undertone, it might generate spot fires of unnecessary paranoia to drag the investigation off course. Those kinds of details would fuel the madness by stirring people into panic as they became uneasy about anybody who happened to be even vaguely peculiar. Although, a red flag would arise if any information referenced satanism or the occult.

Jed had spent the afternoon reading through the statement provided by Jennifer Hill's roommate before starting a chronological chart from her last known location. They needed to establish whether the girls were being stalked in the days leading to their abductions or happened to be in the wrong place at the very worst moment.

Addison had told his partner to head home at the end of their shift after noticing how tired he appeared. Fatigued cops had the propensity to make bad choices. Besides, he wasn't a believer in driving people beyond their limit unless it was essential, and Jed was already displaying signs of being gassed by lunch.

The CCTV footage on his computer screen was a window into the working practices of an active psychopath, and he remained hopeful of seeing things with a fresh perspective. Addison leaned back in his chair and stretched his neck to ease the buildup of tension in his shoulders. He rubbed at the dryness in his eyes, thinking how essential it was that he found a way to get some rest later tonight.

There was an arrogance to the manner in which the perp offended, but his actions didn't come across as spontaneous. Addison took the video back to where the girl was fumbling for car keys in her bag while he swallowed a mouthful of soda. He must have already examined the footage forty times and still wanted to scream out "Turn around!" on each occasion.

The perpetrator moved in swiftly as Jennifer remained oblivious to the danger until he coiled his arm around her neck. She struggled hard in a spirited attempt to break loose, but his biceps were inflexible, and she soon lost consciousness after he smothered her face with a rag.

It took him twenty-seven seconds to incapacitate her and an additional thirty to drag her limp body across to his white GMC van. The perp appeared on the footage one final time when he gathered Jennifer's bag, then he climbed into the vehicle and drove up the exit ramp onto Sunset Boulevard. His features were concealed by a bandana on the lower half of his face and a trucker cap pulled down over his forehead. He wore workman's overalls with sleeves, and besides his average height, there was nothing that could help identify him.

Addison considered whether the woman might have detected something of what was waiting for her inside the parking lot. A thread of hesitation leading up to a moment where she found herself becoming afraid for no apparent reason.

There'd certainly been times when Addison had sensed an impending threat before it materialized. He was able to feel the danger among the cords of uneasiness that began weaving through his gut to form a blend of tension that stood out from his everyday anxieties.

His mom attempted to teach him how best to stand against badness soon after his father's murder. She believed there were only two ways a person could react when darkness came knocking on the door. They either chose to confront the wickedness and endured the inevitable pain that followed, holding firm while they waited for their wound to be transformed into a scar. Or they ran away to spend the rest of their life jumping in the shadows. Irrespective, the unrepentant nature of genuine evil always demanded more from its victims than they were comfortably able to give.

Addison's contemplation ended when he heard the lieutenant's influential voice coming from the other side of the office. He was communicating with a new detective, and his tone suggested he remained very much on edge.

When Collins finished talking, he began striding toward Addison, who turned in his chair, believing it best to preempt the man's interest right now. It sometimes felt as if he expected everybody to have a telepathic connection to his presence. Still, Addison wasn't in the mood for his impatience and hoped any discussion would be brief.

Collins pulled up uncomfortably close before launching into a monologue.

"I've just received confirmation that the plates on the van were stolen out of Bakersfield in October 2015. The tech team is in the process of viewing CCTV footage from every camera they can gain access to, but so far, there's been nothing from any of the main arteries out of the city. My guess is he's probably switched his van someplace nearby. The captain has insisted that we continue our efforts at finding where he's getting the ketamine from, so fingers crossed we get a bite soon."

Addison's work cube was hardly expansive at the best of times, and the lieutenant's enormous frame made him feel like he was stuck inside a matchbox.

"And as far as calling him out through the media is concerned, there's no way I'm prepared to sign off on that," Collins said before bending down to look at the image on Addison's computer screen. "If we go firing off an antagonistic remark before Jennifer Hill's body shows up, it's only going to encourage the press to ridicule us when it eventually does. Then I'll be the one left standing in front of the brass while they question me on whether our approach contributed to a young lady getting cut into pieces. The last thing I need is for them to start accusing us of inspiring a psychopath."

Lyn Holbrook was the one who had advocated the oblique tactic of calling out the killer on national television. Addison considered it a ridiculous suggestion that would only give the impression they'd run out of ideas, yet Collins was rambling as if he were responsible for the proposition. He flirted with the notion of correcting him but decided to let it slide. Collins's agitation would intensify with each new victim, and every detective in homicide had made peace with the reality that Jennifer Hill was already dead.

The lieutenant was staring at Addison as he awaited a reply.

"Well, I can't see how this will end with the girl breathing. Not unless the perp makes a mistake, and so far, everything points to him not being the screwing-up kind of lunatic."

Collins appeared nonplussed. "So you keep on saying."

"Jed and I want to dig around to see if we can locate any practitioners of satanism in the county who might be willing to give an opinion on matters. Surely there's gotta be someone who knows something about what's going down, and people who play around with voodoo often network in groups."

Collins's bland expression communicated a desire for Addison to be more expansive.

"Look, I don't want to keep going on with the same old stuff, but there are multiple aspects to suggest these murders have an occultic connection . . . I'm thinking Ramirez, but with more direction."

"You know I trust your instincts, Mowbray, and I'm not implying you're off the mark. So, do whatever you must but be sure you do it fast. I don't need people to start suggesting my lead detectives have gone running down some fucking rabbit hole in pursuit of imaginary monsters. Agreed?"

Addison nodded as Collins looked at his wristwatch and began rolling his shoulders.

"Where's boy wonder?" he asked.

"I sent him out to do something earlier and told him to head on home when he was done. I need him sharp," Addison emphasized.

He didn't feel like watching Collins work himself up over Jed, and he sure as hell didn't want the kid to start kicking stones, but it was easy enough to comprehend why the man might be looking for an ass to chew, and his partner always made for a ready target.

"How much longer you plan on being here, Mowbray?"

"I'm going to run through the footage of the abduction a couple more times, and then I'll call it a day. You had any success finding a college that's down on some chloroform?" he asked disingenuously to get Collins thinking of something other than how much longer he intended to stick around.

"Have you been listening to a word I've said? I just finished telling you I'll be persisting in our endeavor to locate where he's getting those chemicals. Besides, you got any idea how many college laboratories there are in the state of California?"

Addison hoped Collins would ease up. The day had dragged on, and he still needed to stop for some Buckeye on the way home. His hands had started shaking again an hour earlier, and his belly was protesting his decision to skip lunch. He wanted to heat lasagna and kick back on the sofa while he watched sports. Have a quiet moment where he got to think about something other than dead girls with missing body parts.

"You spoke to your kid lately?" Collins inquired.

"Nope, not since last week."

"Don't let it get you down. You know how kids can be; they sure are difficult to figure out at times. As you're aware, mine are all grown up and moved on, but the way they relate to me is always changing. I quit trying to figure it out years ago and just try to make them understand they can always come to me."

Addison nodded before allowing the comment to hang in the air. He didn't feel like discussing his kid or the concerns he had that the boy might stop taking his calls altogether.

Collins picked up on the feeling their conversation had reached its end and began to withdraw. His perception wasn't surprising; after all, the man was a detective, and cops are usually switched on to the things left unspoken.

"You have yourself a good evening, Mowbray, and try to get a little rest because you don't know when your phone is going to start ringing."

Addison smiled uneasily.

"I'll sure try, Jevonte."

Collins took a final glimpse at his computer screen then began moving away in his unmistakable stride, ostensibly fixated upon whoever happened to be his next port of call.

Addison leaned back into his chair to shake out the tremors from his hands. He planned on having enough whiskey to get himself a decent sleep but would have to remain vigilant about not going over the top. Collins was right in saying a call was coming. If not tonight, then perhaps tomorrow, or the day after. Which meant the option of drinking himself into a coma was very much off the table.

# SIXTEEN

Narek listened to the muffled sounds filtering in from the dining room as he sat inside the kitchen of his cousin's restaurant eating porridge. He was in a shitty mood by the time he'd finished scrubbing out the trunk of his Buick at the boss's warehouse. The task of making a couple of bodies disappear was no picnic lunch and not anything a sound-minded person would decide on doing in their spare time.

Davit's mincer made things easier, but the stench of mashed innards might be the worst smell a person could encounter. Like always, the two of them had grit their teeth until the job was complete. They occasionally got lucky whereby the stiff's bowels weren't clogged with shit, though that only occurred every blue moon.

It wasn't like he'd been expecting the Boogie brothers to smell like fuckin' roses, but their stink turned out to be exceptionally rotten, probably from all the fried chicken, hush puppies, and grease that they ate.

Bedros's incessant gorging had combined with the terrible odor to put Narek off his food, which resulted in him turning his nose up at Anna's breakfast when he arrived home. There must have been something about the way he slid his plate across the table that got her pissed. She'd started bitching at him like a whiny dog.

His wife had been fortunate he was feeling exhausted at the time and just decided to allow her complaints to pass by. Nevertheless, she knew when to quit being lippy and quickly moved out to the living room to mope silently in front of the TV.

Narek provided her with many beatings over the years. His brutal floggings left her curled into a fetal position on the floor. She somehow always managed to crawl back to their bedroom eventually, where she'd lay beneath the sheets, pissing blood and trembling in darkness with the curtains closed. Anna could be a stubborn little bitch whenever she got backed into a corner, and Narek had needed to whack the defiance out of her during the early period of their marriage. Most women came to realize which side of their bread gets buttered, and his wife was no different. She mainly was compliant these days, though he still surprised her with a good sucker punch every few weeks to maintain his authority.

By the time Narek arrived at the restaurant in the evening, his appetite had returned, and he dished out his porridge like a greedy bum. Erik always prepared his recipes from scratch and never included any premanufactured sauce or ingredients from a can. The eatery was named Yerevan in tribute to the Armenian capital and had gained a status for offering authentic cuisine with a point of difference.

Narek checked the time on his watch. The boys were due to arrive in ten minutes to drive over to the boss's titty bar in East Hollywood. They were going to be getting high with some premium snatch as a way of letting their hair down to celebrate a job well done. Davit kept a stash of Colombian powder locked in the office safe to complement the liquor flow and assemblage of sluts he supplied them. The night shift dancers were all in sublime condition with the kind of asses that might prove capable of turning a faggot.

A shameless smirk spread across Narek's face while he played with a thick gold chain around his neck. Few people experienced life in the manner he did, and even though he was required to do vile acts on occasion, it was still a small price to be crowned a king.

When Narek explained to Hayk's daughter how the morning's event was going to unfold, he'd gone into incredible detail to communicate what would happen to her family if she decided on making a fuss. He'd spoken loud enough for Dewayne Jordan to hear every word, smiling brazenly as the kid lashed about in futile resistance. The girl's initial denial was soon replaced by acceptance so that when he fired the slug into the back of her lover's melon, she'd appeared almost serene, finally comprehending the extent of her good fortune. This shift in attitude was relatively standard for anyone who faced a similar set of circumstances. She was barely even whimpering by the time they dropped her home to daddy. *So much for fuckin' love.*

They didn't leave a mess behind at the scene. Jamie Callahan's execution had already caused a public uproar, and their DNA was all over the house. The spacious trunk in the Le Sabre sure proved handy. After driving to the back of the property, it took them less than five minutes to load the bodies before Bedros doused the joint with gas, lit a match, and they were gone. If the LAPD investigated the Jordan brothers' disappearance, nothing connected them to the Armenian Power, and Hayk had paid for the job, so he wouldn't be talking, either.

Narek had observed the girl in the rearview mirror on the drive back to Glendale, wholly taken by her undeniable beauty. She appeared much more glamorous than he'd first realized as she brooded silently in the backseat, and he intended to check in on her at some point to see how she was holding up.

Maybe he'd ask her to come with him to the restaurant for a nice traditional meal. Afterward, their date would conclude inside a room at some cheap hotel on the edge of town where he'd spend the entire night fucking her brains out. Pounding away at her tight little cunt until she went all bent and bow-legged. One thing was for certain; he'd make sure she never contemplated sucking another boogie cock ever again.

He slid the leftover dumplings across the stainless-steel benchtop as he kicked back his stool, slowly making his way into the main dining area. Things appeared to be winding down in the restaurant. Most customers were now enjoying a coffee or eating their dessert as Erik waved a goodnight from behind the bar.

Narek responded by raising a casual hand before heading out onto the dark street. The night air was muggy, but much less so than it had been at any time this past week. He flipped open his pack of

Salems and removed a cigarette with his lips, drawing deeply as the blue flame ignited the tip. He held the smoke in his lungs, appreciating the relaxed sensation while the nicotine fed his craving.

He noticed a solitary figure moving steadily toward him along the footpath, partially obscured by shadow. Narek reached for the piece he always carried at the back of his belt. The stranger wore track pants with a black hoodie, and there was a stupid smile on his face as he pulled up a few yards from where Narek was standing. Just a loopy white boy with no street smarts, it seemed.

"Hey, man," the stranger greeted. "I'm sorry to come upon you in the dark like this, but can I grab a light, please?"

Narek observed closely while the outsider removed a hand from inside his pocket and placed a cigarette to his mouth, silently questioning himself on what sort of cocksucker chose to wear long sleeves during the middle of a fucking heatwave.

"You might want to be a little more careful about who you approach around here, cracker," Narek warned while passing his Zippo.

Coldness swirled through the stranger's pale-blue eyes while he lit his smoke.

Narek sensed something akin to fear.

The hooded male returned his lighter and said, "Thanks, pal, you have yourself a real good evening now, ya hear? And I'll be sure to take your advice the next time I'm in the neighborhood." Then he turned around to start walking back from where he'd come.

Narek watched the stranger through a squinted glare as he puffed intermittent plumes of smoke into the air. When the threat had passed, he released his grip and began slowly shaking his head, grateful for the fact no one had been around to witness the brief exchange.

He felt a bit red-faced by his apparent twitchiness, but he didn't trust the look in the bastard's eyes or the way he suppressed his smirk. The stupid asshole was probably just another whack job; after all, there were plenty of them to be found wandering the city.

Still, if they happened to cross paths again, he wouldn't want to be entertaining himself in the same fashion, or Narek might feel compelled to wipe the smugness off his face for good.

The sound of a horn blaring from up the street ended his reflection. He turned to see a freshly scrubbed Bedros leaning out the window from behind the wheel of a silver BMW.

"Come on, brother," he called out, grinning from ear to ear.

Narek strutted toward his friend on happy legs, greeting the other men inside the car while he climbed into the front seat. He quickly forgot about the stranger with the polar gaze as they pulled from the curb and drove off into the night.

# SEVENTEEN

The old fan by the window rattled like an angry snake, but the dusty blades didn't alleviate the stuffiness inside the bedroom.

Jed was thinking of the gangbanger assholes he'd confronted inside the Frolic Room and how Addison hadn't spoken a word of the situation since the event. He had a real mellow buzz going on from the blunt he'd just smoked with Rosie, and the heaviness of his eyelids suggested sleep wouldn't be hard to find. The investigation remained at an early juncture, yet he already felt somewhat jaded by the process.

Working homicide was nothing like they made it out to be on the television. Jed's days were becoming increasingly condensed, and they sure as hell weren't making many impressions on the murder rate. Every division was seriously understaffed, which affected the performance capability of the entire department. The sons of bitches at the city hall needed to fund a decent recruitment drive instead of sitting back in their comfortable chairs, complaining about the county's increased crime rates. Presuming to have an appreciation of what it's like for cops on the street.

Detectives were taking on impractical caseloads, while their uniformed buddies continued to be run ragged on each shift. And despite the additional responsibilities, there was seldom any conversation when it came to increasing their shitty salaries.

Policing was a terrible career choice for anybody with aspirations of attaining personal wealth. The only coppers Jed knew of who made decent cash were a handful of reprobates from the gang and narcotics division—a sprinkling of unethical scumbags who'd often get exposed to the kind of dirty money that enabled them to engage in underhanded transactions. The corrupt narcs in GND solicited the services of reliable crooks. Then they massaged the evidence into their crime reports to make everything fit.

Even so, most GND officers were honest and only came under suspicion because of the few shitheels who disgraced the badge. Jed had been informed of the corruption by a buddy named Clarence Gooding, who was part of the GND surveillance team. As far as he was concerned, justice couldn't find them soon enough.

Jed and Clarence were in the same graduation class at Elysian Park Academy. They caught up for a drink each month at the Gaslite Bar in Santa Monica with another police friend named Sean Brody.

Clarence could come across as a little abrasive at times, mainly because he wasn't shy about speaking his mind whenever something got him pissed. He was known for continuing his work off the clock and sometimes struggled with finding his place in a team-first environment. Some people considered his techniques to be borderline renegade, but everybody knew Clarence walked a straight line as far as bribery was concerned.

Jed's other pal worked in uniform over at UCLA and was doing his best to push through a tricky period while recovering from an incident in South Central LA. The tragedy unfolded when the patrol car Sean was driving got sprayed with bullets after he responded to a call regarding suspicious activity. His female partner died at the scene, and even though Sean's body had mended from the various wounds he'd received, his mind remained fragile, forever damaged by the experience. There was no apparent motive for the brazen attack, and every informant they dragged in claimed to know nothing about what occurred. The LAPD used all its resources to locate the culprit, but despite a substantial reward and a concentrated public appeal, the perpetrator remained at large.

Jed covered a yawn with the front of his hand before wrapping an arm around Rosie's lower back. He appreciated the company tonight and enjoyed the delicate touch of her fingers while she caressed the skin on his belly with soft, swirling strokes.

"I'm going to draw a picture on you," she said in an unvarnished way.

"Huh?"

"I'll draw a picture on your belly. You have to figure out what it's supposed to be." She remarked, her voice bridged somewhere between song and statement.

"Sure."

He certainly didn't have much enthusiasm for the game but did his best to follow the movement of her finger as the sensitive trace made the hair on his arms prickle.

"Well?" she said.

"I dunno."

"Oh, come on. That's not how you play the game. You've at least got to try to guess. What do you think I might have drawn?"

Spending time with Rosie was never tricky; she was like honey to a sore throat in the way she cleared his mind of any undesirable junk. It was the very reason he found himself participating in a kid's game while stoned out of his mind.

"Is it a flower?" he asked in a noncommittal tone.

"Nope, try again."

"Mmm . . . is it a person?"

"Yes, it is. But who could it be?" The sing-song element of her idiom connected her words into a swaying question mark.

"You?"

"Uh no. That would be a little narcissistic, don't you think?"

"Not really . . . maybe, okay. So, is it me?"

"Yay!" Rosie clapped her hands in soft applause. "Well done, my clever detective."

She raised her head from his chest and flashed a toothy grin. Her cheeks brightened as she wriggled up to his face and kissed him tenderly on the side of his mouth. She gazed into his eyes with a deep penetrative stare.

"What's up with you tonight?" she asked.

Jed recognized the strain of concern on her smooth features and how her breath smelled like red candy. When he remained quiet, it prompted Rosie to break the silence.

"It's almost as if you're jammed someplace where you don't want to be. I know you said you don't discuss your job, but if you ever feel like getting a load off your chest, then you oughtta know: I'm a good listener, and I never judge."

Jed didn't doubt what she said. He'd identified something different in her from the moment she came gliding over to take his order at Big Dean's Café. There was a clarity in her green eyes that reminded him of the ocean surface at daybreak.

"It's just the work," he said eventually. "The last couple of days have been a real pain in the ass, and I can't see how tomorrow is going to be any better."

Strands of blond hair fell either side of Rosie's face. She was measured and considerate in the way she approached life. He appreciated the intellect that resided beneath the exterior of her cruisy personality—how she looked for answers outside the circle of societal reasoning.

"Is it because of the psychopath on the TV?" she asked eventually. "The one who's killing those young women? Is that what's bothering you tonight?"

"Sure, it's playing a part, but it runs deeper."

"Deeper how?"

It was the first time they'd come close to broaching the subject of a case he'd been working on, and he was a little surprised to find it didn't bother him. Jed knew there wasn't much point in attempting to answer her question ambiguously.

"Have you ever been in a position where you're expected to do things in a very particular way, despite knowing that if you went about stuff differently, the benefits could be permanent, and the result would come a whole lot faster?"

Rosie's eyes sparkled, and he wanted to lose himself inside her contemplation.

"Well, if I found myself in the position you just described," she replied with rich sincerity, "I guess I'd figure out a way to do things how I wanted them done. Particularly if it meant righting a few of the wrongs you're always facing."

Jed stared up, hopeless, at the ceiling. "But what if it means breaking the law?" he whispered.

Rosie propped herself up on her elbows. "Some laws are begging to be broken, I guess," she replied before nuzzling into his neck to run fingers through his sun-bleached hair.

It seemed she had heard enough, so Jed released himself to the heaviness inside his body while they lay together in peaceful silence—thinking how Mowbray was probably right in saying that good company was hard to find.

# EIGHTEEN

A sense of disorder flooded Meagan Banks's mind as she drove her luxury E Class Mercedes along the Mojave Desert trail to arrive at the Filii Reprobi compound. The secret complex was situated down Highway 395 on the outskirts of Adelanto, about one hundred miles from Los Angeles. An eighteen-foot reinforced concrete perimeter ensured no outsiders could gain access to the premises. The local folk believed the center was a storage facility for hazardous materials.

The Old Man's motives for wanting this meeting were no mystery. Meagan was responsible for supplying Edward with the drugs he'd been using in his adventures, a decision which now put her in the firing line.

Meagan understood how Edward's project wasn't going to continue indefinitely, and she believed all the external aggravation would soon dissolve when it concluded. If it were anybody else exploiting her services in such a flagrant manner, then she'd possibly have genuine cause to be alarmed. But Edward was like a masculine reflection of herself in many ways—it was the very reason she'd chosen to participate in his dangerous game. Besides, the sacrifices had started having the desired effect in the spirit realm.

Linda's ghost had already made a fleeting appearance a few days earlier. It had been a thrill when the bitch slithered out of the Badlands to adjoin with Meagan's consciousness. Depositing images as Edward screwed her ravenously, like a man condemned to never reaching his fill. She had always found sex with him to be extraordinarily fulfilling, even when it was standard and the sanguine Magick got placed on the shelf. It was difficult to articulate how great it felt to be fucked by a guy while the essence of his dead girlfriend swirled restlessly inside her.

She parked her car beside an old Joshua Tree and killed the engine before scanning the adjacent area for anyone who might be hiding among the shadows. When the darkness presented like a scene etched in charcoal, she straightened a kink in her auburn hair and examined her makeup in the rearview mirror. Her almond-shaped eyes exuded sultriness, and there weren't any signs of tension on her elegant face.

The reflection about Edward's hard cock had made her sticky, so she slipped a hand between her thighs to readjust her panties into a more comfortable position. At least there was a gorgeous, young Mexican boy waiting for her back at the beach condo in Malibu.

Javier had smooth olive skin and was always prepared to satisfy her needs, never wearying with the task at hand. She acquired her slave from a Mexican drug cartel for fifteen thousand dollars ten months earlier, which turned out to be money well spent.

Meagan extended her legs as she withdrew from the Mercedes in a swish of gracefulness to begin making her way toward the entrance of the church. The tarnished exterior was all that remained of the congregation who once worshipped inside the building. She perceived the wickedness percolating within. An obscure presence raked beneath the cracks of the door in search of something vulnerable to infect. The dark essence was conjured into existence when the previous reverend smashed his wife's face apart with a bat while she slept inside. His random violence had left the victim unrecognizable as he pounded her bones to chalk. The preacher eventually swallowed a shotgun to put a moniker on his fury before the chapel was abandoned to the Mojave sun.

Many of the local folk remained wary of the building's tragic past. Even the agent who sold them the property had been tight-lipped during the process, as if declaring the event might somehow unleash a thirty-six-year-old demon upon their wretched little town. It was all so ironic.

The maniacal reverend was to blame for initially dethroning the site of holiness, but his actions still paled in comparison to what had taken place there since. The humblebrag church had become a Filii Reprobi sanctuary. A black altar of sacrifice for a people well-practiced in lawlessness, where horror was a certainty for those unfortunate enough to be detained inside. The Old Man stored an assortment of runaways underground for the occasions when they all gathered in bloody celebration each month. Their captives were mainly neglected persons confined inside cages beneath the main chapel, entombed without hope while they awaited some horrible end.

Meagan had partaken in countless death offerings over the years, slaughtering a range of citizens from across the country. When she considered the multitude of victims who could be attributed to Filii Reprobi, it provided her with a sense of invulnerability. Despite the sheer volume of killing, not one of them had ever been apprehended. The Old Man's sphere of influence extended to Capitol Hill, and his associations enabled them to remain hidden in plain sight. Every Filii Reprobi was instructed on the significance of regulating their passion to ensure they never attracted outside interest.

An associate must bring something exceptional to their society and have the means to present a sophisticated front. They never dressed in ridiculous costumes to rip a cutting edge across someone's throat, enjoyed the finest exotic drugs, and regularly fucked one another's brains out. Still, human butchery was what truly connected them. Murder was their art form.

Meagan felt a fresh wave of apprehension as she approached the church's doors before gliding inside on light feet. She caught sight of the Old Man lighting candles at precise intervals on the other side of the hall; it generated an outbreak of fluttering wings at the base of her belly. Meagan considered stepping back outside to recompose herself but presumed a withdrawal might be interpreted as a symptom of guilt. She'd become a participant with Edward from the moment she provided him the drugs, and her impetuosity had the potential to bite her on the ass.

The Old Man would be expecting to receive a truthful account of the facts, and she couldn't risk responding to his questions in an impromptu manner. Whatever misgivings he had wouldn't be because young women were getting abducted and killed. It was only due to the corpses being left on display that there was a need for this discussion at all.

It had been several years since Meagan felt jittery about meeting a man. She extinguished her anxiety after tracking down the two assholes who'd raped her at college. They were delivered to a Filii Reprobi property situated in the Los Padres National Forest, where she spent a couple of days rejoicing with a few close friends. They'd taken their time on the fucking creeps, pulling hot entrails through the small incisions she crafted into their abdomens. Her surgical skills came in handy whenever anyone set their sights on maintaining a pulse.

Meagan never allowed herself to be cowed by much nowadays; however, the Old Man could somehow breach her defenses without even trying. She tugged nervously at her peach-colored skirt while she gazed around the exquisite hall. Everything within contravened the simple presentation on the outside. The gallery was a triumph to Victorian ascendancy, combining the charm of nineteenth-century pomp with Southern flair. Traditional chaise couches provided comfort throughout, and a collection of Marcel Duchamp sculptures rested in the corner. Yet, it was Robert Campin's Netherlandish masterpieces that Meagan appreciated most of all.

Italian river stones were fitted into esoteric designs on the ceiling, while the floors displayed a black and white Masonic checkered pattern. A giant goat's-head pentagram hewn from the highest quality Mesoamerican jade was peerless as the centerpiece inside the room.

The Old Man didn't give any indication he'd noticed Meagan's presence as the candlelight created flickering shadows that danced along the wall. He appeared captivating in a blue cotton suit, a white V-neck shirt, and alligator-skin boots. His shock of thick gray hair was combed back carelessly, and his chiseled features were apparent in the sparkling light.

Most men presented fragile by the time they hit seventy-two, but the Old Man didn't exhibit frailty in his movement. He was of a moderate height with broad shoulders and strong hands, the flesh on his body remained firm to touch. His greenish eyes blazed experience, and there was something about his stare that made Meagan want to stay and flee at the same time.

"Are you going to come inside or just continue standing there like a mute?" he asked with his back turned, proving how he didn't need his vision to recognize an approach.

Meagan slinked her way across the room and released a faint breath of reprieve when he extended a hand, accepting his palm into her own, brushing over his skin with a stroke of her slender fingers. She couldn't resist running her tongue along her upper lip; there had always been a sizeable part of her that craved his touch.

"You must know why I've asked you to come."

"Yes, I believe I do," Meagan confirmed, watching while he clapped his hands in a deliberate move to return any dust particles to the floor.

"And?"

"There is absolutely no reason for you to be concerned about the ketamine or the chloroform. Supposing that is what's troubling you. No one can trace them to me."

The Old Man appeared rigid while he considered her response; the candles' reflection made his eyes smolder like two living caverns of eternal flame.

"We operate in perilous times," he declared dispassionately. "Edward's actions have generated far too much excitement among the public. I know that a couple of extremely hardy detectives are now leading the investigation into the bodies he's dumping in those hills. This pair of nosy bloodhounds have earned a reputation for being men who won't go away easily. I can't get my head around what it is he's trying to achieve. The manner he's going about his business is not how I expect my people to operate. So, will you please fucking enlighten me as to why he is behaving in such a way?"

The question caught Meagan off guard, and her doubts quickly returned, as if formulating a satisfactory reply was an act of folly. All the planning she'd done on the drive over seemed inadequate. She felt a flash of relief when the Old Man continued.

"There are so many other locations he could have used to dispose of those bodies: places in the desert where they would never have seen the light of day."

Meagan locked onto his gaze as he took her in, contemplating whether she should apologize for her part in supplying the chemicals and be done with it. Instead, she decided to be clear in the hope of appealing to his unbridled spirituality.

"He's attempting to resurrect a ghost from seasons past and believes he will achieve a more favorable result by creating a brief period of publicized chaos." She wiped away the dampness from her palms on the back of her skirt. The Old Man understood the science involved with building sacrificial energy, and even though he remained silent, she could tell her words had found their mark.

"He's just trying to increase the vitality within each offering," she continued.

The Old Man closed his eyes to reflect over the fundamentals of what she'd said as Meagan felt the edginess return to her belly. "How many?" he asked coolly.

"What?"

"The women, how many more are there going to be?"

"He intends to kill another four."

"Are you aware of what the penalty will be if this thing runs askew?"

"Yes, I am," she said, doing her utmost not to shuffle her feet.

"All right, then, so be it. Who is she?"

"Sorry?"

"The woman whose spirit he's attempting to bring back. That's the very reason you said he's bleeding out young blondes and exposing them in the hills, is it not?"

"Yes, that's right."

"Who is she?"

The urge to lie became irresistible.

"Linda. H-He's hoping to bring back Linda Jones," she said with a stutter.

The Old Man didn't register a reaction as his eyes turned into cold fire lights. For a while, it seemed as if he was going to keep on staring right through her.

"Now I see," he replied finally, turning around to leave her standing in the middle of the room while he continued with the task of placing candles.

# NINETEEN

Addison kept a lazy eye on his bacon while he placed his Samsung down onto the kitchen benchtop. He'd awoken an hour earlier in a bad headspace and decided to fix something for breakfast in the hope it might improve his disposition. His dreams had been a flickering reel of swollen faces, red lights, and spectral images of dead kids with clouded eyes who accused him through wintry lips. Then, when he'd awoken, his hair was soaking, and his brain felt like Jell-O, as if he'd been rugged up sleeping inside a steam room.

He'd spent ten minutes deciding whether he should be making more effort to reach his ex-wife before concluding it might be wise to hold off until he felt less irritable. He needed answers to why Nate wasn't returning any of his messages but didn't see much point in quarreling with the woman unless it was necessary.

Michelle was not a vindictive person, which raised the possibility she might be involved in a new relationship. It wasn't as if he'd have an issue with her moving on; however, he did want to know if a stranger was hanging out with his kid.

When he arrived home from work the night before, his mind had been full of static, and the muscles in his neck were compressed so tightly it made turning his head feel like a form of self-flagellation. He ended up taking three Valiums with a glass of whiskey after dinner and drifted off to sleep watching TV on the couch. It was the most extended rest he'd had in days, and despite the night terrors, his brain felt much more cohesive for the experience.

Addison released a yawn as he cracked a couple of eggs into the center of the frypan before casting his eye around the banged-up kitchen. It was a small space, even for just one person who didn't care much for food. The faux marble countertops were all faded down the center, and most of the flimsy cupboard doors needed replacement. Michelle would have been in his ear if they were still together, chattering on about impracticality as a means of pestering him for an upgrade. Addison's requirements were less complicated than his ex-wife's because his appetite had charted a downward trajectory these last few years. There were still occasions when he would climb out of bed craving something, but those days came around infrequently.

Whenever he wanted a dependable lunch, he'd get into his truck and take a drive to Bill's Cafe on Spring Street. The small, no-frills diner was popular with many detectives in homicide, and their omelets were something else. He used to take Nate to Bill's on a Saturday afternoon when they were living at Eagle Rock. Afterward, the two of them would stroll down to Chinatown while discussing basketball, the Dallas Cowboys, and what it meant to be a cop in LA.

The memory of those past weekends burned like hot embers within Addison's heart, so he redirected his thoughts to avoid any underlying bitterness from taking root. He'd come to appreciate how nothing good resulted from holding on to his anger during the fifteen years he'd waited for his father's murderer to face execution. The hatred he dragged around impaired his ability to be present in most relationships, while his mom preached forgiveness in a vain attempt to help him move forward with his life.

She'd been mindful of communicating her message in gentle terms without minimizing his grief. Perhaps if he'd taken some of her advice, his affairs wouldn't be in the mess they were today. His resentment tainted whatever he set his sights on, and it was only after witnessing the lethal injection doing its thing that he was able to release a portion of his anger. Nevertheless, he still needed to contact Michelle to determine what was going on and stipulate how the current setup wasn't working.

Jed was supposed to be arriving in an hour, and Addison was hoping his partner's presence of mind might be in a much better place. They would be taking another drive up into the Hollywood Hills to meet with a woman who moved within occult circles.

Elizabeth Plume had phoned through to HQ the previous day as Addison was heading for the door. He recalled speaking to her at the Parker Center in 2009 about a case he'd been working on. The detective who delivered the woman's message explained how she asked for Addison by name. He didn't hesitate to return the call after remembering her background before arranging to meet at her home the following morning.

Plume would probably describe herself as a spiritual consultant who specialized in connecting people with esoteric material and New Age mysticism. When she initially approached Addison eight years earlier, he was embroiled in a nationwide search for an outcast associate of an Alabama religious cult. The scumbag was wanted on two counts of first-degree murder, but his profile exploded when the body of a teenage girl was discovered in the Los Angeles River Basin with his DNA inside her. Plume's assistance didn't result in his apprehension; nevertheless, her info helped them secure a verdict.

Conferring with Plume might be considered as something of a long shot. They were becoming increasingly desperate, and Addison's core sense about the perpetrator being active in occult circles wasn't shifting. There'd been nothing to indicate the killer planned these crimes on impulse, and he suspected the inverted cross was more than just a calling card.

He'd worked several cases where the offender left an autograph and couldn't shake the feeling the symbol signified a more precise connotation. Regardless, the time had come for them to get inventive and broaden their search to ensure they knocked upon every door. For even if the offender's motives weren't as complex as Addison believed them to be, he wasn't coming across as a degenerate who would come unstuck because of an inability to control the perversion.

Addison chewed his overcooked bacon with disinterest before swallowing a mouthful of juice to help get the meat down his throat.

He still needed to jump under the shower and wanted to be sure he finished his morning whiskey by the time Jed arrived. Addison had managed to stay astride of the drinking to this point, but going cold turkey was never a bright idea. Complete abstinence would cause several other problems to arise, and he intended on consuming just enough liquor to keep his hands from trembling during work hours, and not a drop more.

The breakfast was abysmal, even by his standards, so he scraped the leftovers into the trash as a wave of vertigo came over him. Addison steadied himself by reaching out for the counter as he waited for the kitchen to stop spinning, thinking about the bottle of whiskey he'd opened during the night. When the dizziness subsided, he dropped his plate into the sink, stretched out a crick in his neck, and started toward the bedroom on rickety legs.

# PART TWO

"Air grows cold, I won't despair, I set my face like stone.
For the glory and the end of fear."

From the song *Stay Awake*
—*written by Leigh Marks.*

# TWENTY

The aroma of frankincense permeated throughout Elizabeth Plume's fancy living room as the two detectives waited for her to finish speaking on the phone. Addison had contemplated asking her if he could open a window, but he didn't want to offend and was already picking up on a feeling that she may have been having second thoughts about contacting him in the first place.

Plume was a striking woman in her fifties who wasn't afraid of expressing her opinions on life, politics, and everything in between. She was pretentious with an edge of entitlement attached to every gesture. Her finely arched eyebrows contrasted the straight-line symmetry of her nose, while her cheekbones balanced the surgically enhanced features on her face. Plume's lips were softly inviting, which complemented her sharply etched jawline and long raven hair. She didn't appear to be a day over forty, and her luminous aqua-colored eyes had a feline quality to them. An erotic ambiance seemed to fill the atmosphere around her, and Addison took another long glimpse at the curvaceous legs projecting from beneath her red summer dress.

The spacious room displayed contemporary artworks and expensive ornamentation, and hard-bound leather tomes filled the bookshelf behind the detectives. A ceiling to floor window provided an expansive view past the city to frame the rambling metropolis of Los Angeles into a moving picture. The sleek modular couch where Addison was seated could have easily accommodated another twenty people, while the sandstone walls and rustic timber flooring were crafted from the highest-quality materials.

When Addison spoke with Plume in 2009, their meeting

occurred within a smoke-stained interview room at the LAPD's previous headquarters downtown. The Glass House was considered an architectural masterpiece in 1955, though most of its mystique had faded by the eighties.

That outdated office complex was like a cesspit compared with these luxurious surroundings. Addison had been taken aback by the extent of the woman's fortune when they pulled into her gated drive that morning. He understood how real estate in this part of town never came cheap but had still been expecting her home to feel less upmarket.

Plume farewelled whoever she was speaking to and placed the phone onto the armrest beside her. She released a groan while maintaining a rigid back as she eyed the detectives suspiciously from across the room. Plume's legs were crossed as she tapped a foot in the air like she was searching for an opportunity to send them on their way.

"Sorry for the disruption, but I did need to take the call," Plume said through the thinnest veneer of restraint. "Now, where were we? Oh yes, that's right. Now I'm not sure if I've understood your previous question. Although, if I'm correct in presuming you're asking me whether I associate with people who approve of homicide, then my response would be an emphatic no, absolutely not. I'd consider that to be a very ignorant inquiry and more than a little offensive. There is far too much prejudice directed toward people who choose to go against the tide of general acceptance. I'm sure we can all agree nothing prodigious is ever accomplished by holding onto a partisan mindset."

Addison found himself growing frustrated by the uppity sounds of displeasure he could hear in the woman's speech, even more so when he considered how she'd been the one who instigated contact with him. Nevertheless, she might have vital information up her sleeve, which meant he needed to try to win her over.

"I can certainly agree with you when it comes to preconception, and I apologize if I've given you the impression that we've come here today because of a belief you may somehow be involved in a crime. I understand how insulting such a premise would be for you."

Plume regarded him with a kind of expressionless boredom like he was an uneducated shitheel from a backwater river shack. A ghost of a smile threatened to touch the edge of her mouth before she unveiled a row of perfect white teeth.

It required a concentrated effort for him not to say anything objectionable.

"You're not originally from these parts, are you?" Her decree was rich in arrogance.

"What betrays me?" he asked facetiously. California had transformed many things about him over the years; however, his dry Texan drawl remained as strong as ever.

Plume dismissed Addison with a wave of her hand and set her eyes on Jed.

"I intend to provide you with information. Why else would we be sitting here today? Whether it has relevance to your investigation, I can't say. However, before I begin, I'm going to require assurance that my identity will be withheld from everything you do moving forward. If you cannot guarantee my anonymity, then I'll bid you both farewell, and you can show yourselves out the front door. I have no interest whatsoever in being a known participant in this investigation. Are we clear?"

"You have our word. I will leave your name out of all of our records, irrespective of what you might end up telling us," Addison assured her.

Plume held his eyes for ten seconds before responding. "Very well. I can only hope you turn out to be a man of your word. Let me kick things off by saying this information comes with two key disclaimers. Firstly, and most importantly, it would seem, is that I'm in no way certain whether the people whom I'm about to speak of exist. Secondly, my learned experience is that most doomsday cults and spiritual crazies usually disband over time. They break apart from the inside long before anything significant emerges. Now, the only reason I contacted you is that I was informed the victims are being branded with an inverted Christian cross."

Addison and Jed stared back at her with perplexity.

"Where did you hear that?" Addison said. His tone wasn't quite accusatory, but it probably wasn't far from being so.

"From a friend whose husband works for the coroner. Anyway, if the people I'm thinking of are somehow involved in these crimes, then you will have your work cut out for you. It would suggest they have been doing this kind of thing for several years while remaining very much underground. They won't be recruiting people on Facebook; I can assure you of that."

Jed leaned forward with a pen in one hand and a notepad in the other.

"So, what you're saying is you might know people who could be implicated in these crimes, but they may also be nothing more than a fairy tale?"

Addison observed Plume while she drummed her red manicured nails on the armrest of her chair and pondered his partner's question.

"Nightmare," she replied eventually.

Jed appeared to be momentarily confused. "Excuse me?"

"Most of the fairy tales I've read concluded with a happy ending."

Jed leaned back into the sofa as Plume elaborated.

"When a person has been active within the occult universe for as long as I have, they are going to hear whispers on occasion. It may help if you consider that the people I associate with practice a blend of spiritism, which is considered strange to average folk, perhaps even a little frightening. We exist in confidence, and we're told of peculiar rumors from time to time. I have realized that most of the spooky stuff is nothing more than legend, no different to vampires or werewolves roaming the woods. Though, if a story like this did contain an ingredient of truth, then I'd imagine anyone found sharing it may find themselves dancing in flames."

"I can understand how you might have reservations about

passing on information, Ms. Plume, but we could use your help here," Jed reasoned.

Plume unfolded her legs and leaned into the armrest of the chair. "Please, Detective Perkins, you may call me Liz," she replied.

Jed flashed his winning smile. "Like I was saying, Liz, I can appreciate why you might be apprehensive about disclosing certain details to us, and we wouldn't expect you to place yourself in harm's way. But two girls have been brutally murdered, soon to be three, and we need to either intensify the direction we're now heading or change our focus altogether. So anything you can tell us would be greatly appreciated."

Plume returned to an upright posture, knitting her fingers before consigning her hands to her lap. Addison recognized a specter of darkness sweep inside her eyes, an expression to suggest she'd spent her lifetime gazing into things that were best left undiscovered.

"I really can't give you much at all," she replied candidly. "Certainly, nothing I can confirm as fact. But I was informed about a supposed group of dangerous individuals several years back, and a story may be all it is. Nevertheless, if the narrative I heard is genuine, then I wouldn't be the least surprised if they were involved. I remembered hearing how the inverted cross is meant to have great significance to their spiritual compass. So, when my acquaintance told me about the brand, I decided to give you a call."

The detectives reflected on the information for a moment.

"Does this story of yours have a name?" Jed asked expectantly.

"I don't know any name, but there is a person who might. He's extremely private, and I'm not certain he will even be prepared to speak with you. The man I'm thinking of is a revered demonologist named Harry Bath. Harry knows much more about these allegations than I do. I'll provide you with his details, but whether he decides on entertaining you will be entirely up to him."

"We'd very much appreciate that, Liz," Jed said.

Plume turned her attention to Addison.

"Please be sure to withhold the details about our meeting here today when you contact him. It might destroy my credibility if you don't. And if those stories are true, I don't even want to begin thinking about that."

"Is this Harry Bath located in the Los Angeles area?" Addison asked.

"Kind of. He lives down in Simi Valley, and he's a retired priest."

Plume appeared to appreciate their reaction, smirking.

"Oh, don't be so astonished, gentlemen. The world which exists behind the door you are now knocking on is composed of many shifting shadows. Think *Alice in Wonderland*, but a creepier version written for adults. The stubbornness of organized religion has been striving to eliminate occult practices since the beginning of time, yet witchcraft continues to flourish worldwide. Magick is extremely popular nowadays, even inside the LAPD, if my memory serves. Anyway, let me go find Harry's details for you before I change my mind."

When Plume finished speaking, she raised herself from the chair in a sleek, effortless motion and glided out to another section of the house. It left the detectives to sit in thoughtful silence and consider some of the things they'd just heard, quietly wondering what might be waiting for them on the other side of the door.

# TWENTY-ONE

Jennifer lay bound and trembling on the floor, whimpering while Edward stared down at her in silent consideration. He could feel a sophisticated terror scratching its way out through the pores of her skin, an omnipresent fear that got his heart racing as she squirmed about, hopeless, in the center of the goat's-head pentagram.

Her movement implied she was no longer inhibited by the ketamine he'd injected into her neck seven hours earlier. Edward had spent the night twining terror to her every thought, and it was now time to increase the misery. Adrenaline began its surge while he applied a blowtorch to the steel brand. Bloodlust blistered his core as visual descriptions flickered behind his eyes to create an expectancy that never found lasting satisfaction.

The girl's wailing intensified as she caught sight of the hissing blue flame, and Edward barely resisted the impulse to cave her face in with his boot. He had stopped dispensing the drug to ensure she comprehended the full sting of his blade. There wouldn't be any need to cut through bones today, and the pain might help extract the energy from inside her body.

Conventional sacrifice was about maintaining equilibrium. The controlled violence was entirely different from the pandemic-like ferocity he unleashed during regular killing frenzies. A symbiotic relationship connected physical suffering and psychedelic terror to produce a twisted association rooted in morbidity. Edward always submerged his subjects within the bowels of defilement until they became malignant beneath the intensity of their torment. The slightest adjustment in either direction could significantly impact the variant planes of Magick, so there was never much latitude for conjecture.

Edward would have spent longer preparing the offerings if it were feasible; however, he needed to get a wriggle on before the Old Man intervened. He understood the gamble he was taking by leaving their bodies in the hills. Still, if he had abided by the rules and disposed of the corpses, the raging furnace of community fascination could never be factored into the conclusion. Edward assumed somebody would alert him if the Old Man decided to entangle himself in matters. Meagan Banks, for instance. She was incredibly supportive of the initiative, although her loyalty likely hinged on how well he fucked her.

The first time he witnessed a human heart get ripped from inside a rib cage, it released endocrine shocks through every part of his body, creating a hardness in his chinos that lasted for hours. Edward thought he surrendered everything to Filii Reprobi that night, adopting his destiny with gratified giddiness while his senses indulged upon the woman's grave misfortune. Her horror remained despite the emergence of death, articulating the gravity of her affliction through filmy eyes as life began curdling inside her. An arcane spirit soaked the hall afterward, penetrating his bones while it slithered around the place to attach itself on the living. It was entirely impossible to rationalize such potency with anybody who hadn't experienced it.

Edward didn't consider his defiance to be an act of impertinence. It had taken six months of internal deliberation to arrive at a resolution, and he was no longer receiving satisfaction by protecting his stake in the game. His obsession with resurrecting Linda's ghost was the driving force behind him disregarding the Old Man's regulations. There were no guarantees he would emerge from this venture intact, but he'd grown indignant toward the people who had determined Linda's sacrifice as being categorical to his initiation. Perhaps he might have felt differently if time deleted her presence from the fabric of his memory; however, she continued haunting him from the shadows.

When the brand began to glow orange, Edward reefed Jennifer's shirt over her face and pressed the hot steel down onto her breast, smiling while she howled over the whistle of burning flesh. The sweet aroma of cooking skin filled his nostrils. He absorbed the jolt of her screeching as the Reaper's essence drenched the atmosphere in restless anticipation. Jennifer was gaping up at him with mortal dread. Her eyes sailed at half-mast as her words spewed out in garbled surges, still attempting to plead with a nemesis who would never relent.

Edward floated across to his bureau to fetch a barber's razor from the drawer, singing "Peter Pumpkin Eater" while making his way back. He crouched beside Jennifer's head, where he sampled her tears with a pasty cardboard tongue. She was searching for air in shallow gulps as Edward brought the blade down over her ear to trigger a penetrating rodent squeal that filled every crevice inside the room.

He applied rough strokes to break through the cartilage on the side of her head, appreciating the crunchy sound of tearing flesh as Jennifer's cries bounced around the walls. She began growling like an animal caught in a trap, and when the ear broke free, he dangled it between two fingers like a rabbit's tail.

"You really ought to change your perspective. Hold tight to every moment because you don't have many left," Edward declared with a humorous sincerity. "I'm going to slash the main artery in your neck as soon as I finish removing your other one."

He reached for an old brass canister on the floor. "That's why I have this."

\* \* \*

Wickedness engulfed the room as Jennifer pulled against the ropes with a futile resistance. Fear had coiled its hands around her throat from the very moment she'd awoken inside the cage; even so, this present horror was something else entirely. She no longer felt trapped within some twisted cartoon of malevolence. Those delusions had been extinguished; in their place came the judgment of eternal suffering.

Jennifer wailed as Edward began working on her other ear, yet the sound of his deranged cackling penetrated her brain. She sensed his perversity whenever he leaned in. The proximity of his presence generated an influx of bile at the back of her throat. A metallic stink infused her nasal passages as her lungs contended with the concentration of his cruelty; Jennifer's shrieks came out in raspy whispers. His hand was severe as it gripped her hair like a vice, and she didn't notice when the last strand of flesh surrendered its grip. A racking cough rattled her lungs, shook her bones, and fired nails through her chest. Obscene images tormented Jennifer's mind while a mystical perception resisted the fade of her body.

She heard him talking, but his voice was now gurgling liquid going down a plug hole. Jennifer's resistance had dissolved when he tilted her head to rip his razor across the side of her neck in a slashing arc. The dull thudding inside her brain became louder than anything she had ever heard. As if someone was standing at the center of her mind banging away on a steel bucket. Everything transformed into a kaleidoscope of angry color, then darkness spread across the room as a gray wraith descended to consume the light.

Jennifer saw herself making sandcastles with her brother on Venice Beach when they were kids before the soothing tone of her father's voice began calling her name. A lifetime of remembrance flashed perfectly behind her eyes, and she recognized her grandmother waiting in the distance with outstretched arms as blackness crashed over her like a wave.

# TWENTY-TWO

They were anxious to contact Harry Bath and needed to act super-fast if Jennifer Hill was to have any hope of being found alive. Addison had already made several attempts to reach the priest in the afternoon, but his calls went unanswered, and there was no way for him to leave a message.

Collins was back at his desk after a lengthy meeting with the captain, meaning they would soon be required to bring him up to speed with the latest information. The prospect of having to engage in an exhaustive discussion about a cleric who summoned demons didn't invoke much excitement, and things might prove less complicated if they managed to get a hold of Harry Bath beforehand.

Addison searched the internet for any demonologists located in the county while Jed continued creating the timeline, he'd started piecing together the previous day. The detectives working the phones generated a persistent hum as an atmosphere of heaviness settled inside the office. Everybody felt the mounting pressure, and no slapstick humor was bouncing back and forth.

Addison was in the process of calling the priest's number again when the lieutenant's voice came booming from across the room. "Mowbray, Perkins, my office. Now."

A morose expression spread across Jed's sun-bronzed features as if an audience with Collins might be the very last thing he wanted to be a part of right now.

"Relax, buddy," Addison assured him. "I'll take the lead on this one."

Jed shoved his hands into his pockets like a kid who expected a scolding as they began making their way through the cubicles. Their progress stalled when Detective Lyn Holbrook announced herself by leaning into the aisle and rolling her eyes.

"Like that, is it?" Addison asked.

Holbrook and her partner, Tom Rodgers, were seated on either side of her desk.

"Yeah," she replied. "It sure has been a whole load of fun in here today."

Holbrook was a frumpy woman in her early forties with strawberry blond hair, thin lips, and weird brown eyes. Most of the detectives in HSS referred to her and Rodgers as the odd couple, mainly because Tom was built like a truck and fancied himself a ladies' man. At the same time, Holbrook was quite unattractive and forever traversing a path of singledom.

"How are things going?" Addison asked casually. "You find anything useful?"

Rodgers appeared stuck somewhere between uninspired and bored shitless.

"Nah, we've found nothin'. Been tied to these phones all morning like a fuckin' house mouse while Sarge shits down our throats. Collins has been riding him like a bitch on heat, so it's probably best to avoid the man if you can."

Holbrook tossed a stress ball at her partner and smiled.

"The Sarge lost his head with Tommy boy twice this morning," she said playfully. "He's getting about the place with fire in his eyes while he searches for someone to feed on."

Addison nodded aimlessly.

"Are you guys still calling healthcare facilities?"

"Nope," Rodgers replied. "We're presently focused on animal hospitals and local colleges. The captain decided to appeal to the city hospitals through the press to save time. He thinks it might be easier to get hold of this stuff through a vet."

"Well, it's hard to question his reasoning there."

Holbrook swung around in her chair. "Shit, Perkins, don't you look thrilled to be here." Her flippant interjection came with a mock-toothed grin.

"Well, you wouldn't want us to start stepping out with a can-do attitude. If we did that, you might find yourself becoming irrelevant around here in no time."

"Oh, what a sharp little peanut you are. So full of wisecracks and spunk. Maybe there's a solitary brain cell somewhere inside that stoner head of yours. But, man, why you always got to be so freakin' serious?"

Jed gawped at her. "I guess it depends on how you feel about innocent women being tortured and killed. Is it something you think we need to be serious about, or not really?"

Holbrook dismissed him with a sigh, opening the door for her partner to cut in.

"You should've been here to see the lieutenant rip young Steer a brand-new asshole this morning," Rodgers said comically. "Poor little thing looked like she was going to melt into the fuckin' floor. I reckon if Mendez hadn't been standing by her side, she might have bolted out the front doors of the building, never to be sighted again."

Addison allowed the comment to hang. Whenever a female got reprimanded in the office, a handful of regular assholes would mill around to snicker at their embarrassment, a practice which he had no interest in being part of. Female coppers had more than enough rubbish to deal with without adding a public correction to their day.

Take Holbrook, for example. She was constantly fighting for validation within an environment dominated by testosterone. A wide-ranging consensus still existed among many men that their counterparts were little more than secretaries with guns. America's left may have declared war upon the residual chauvinism of years past, yet sexism prevailed inside most district houses. Holbrook probably worked harder than anybody in making her way to the HSS division. She had a well-rounded set of skills and never hesitated to get her hands dirty in an investigation. Nevertheless, she was often subjected to archaic jibes from her male contemporaries.

The detectives turned around when the lieutenant called out impatiently again, his big frame filling the passage which led to his office door. He didn't appear at all pleased by the prospect of having to twiddle his thumbs while they indulged in conversation. The man wasn't familiar with being put on hold.

Addison farewelled his colleagues as they began moving on.

"Adios, amigos," Holbrook quipped. "Here's to hoping you find a way to have some fun in there, Perkins. Best to keep that serious face on for a while longer, I imagine."

"Thanks for the sage advice, Lyn," Jed called over his shoulder. "Perhaps while I'm busying myself with this investigation, you could wander off someplace to go fuck yourself."

When they entered the lieutenant's office, he was already behind the desk with his arms folded. Collins looked at them both with a frosty scowl while they found a seat.

"What do you want to know?" Addison asked him.

"Everything, Mowbray. I want to know every fucking detail. So, did you learn anything useful from the witch?"

"She provided the name of a priest whom she believes may have relevant information."

"A priest, you say?"

"Yeah, that's right, a priest."

"Tell me, Mowbray, why the fuck would a priest know anything about this specific asshole we find ourselves pursuing? Has he recently undertaken a stunning confession, or are you hoping he might have received a word from God?"

Addison was about to reply when Jed interjected.

"Plume said there had been whispers about a group of people who are rumored to be into some extremely unpleasant shit. She thinks if this group's existence is more than just gossip, then it would contain the kind of shitheels capable of killing in a manner that befits the crimes. The witch also clarified how the inverted cross is supposed to have a certain significance to these people. So, there's that, and he's a retired priest."

Collins's observation went from Jed to Addison, then back to Jed again.

"Do I detect a tone of mockery in your words, Perkins?"

"No, sir, just letting you know what she said is all."

The lieutenant kept Jed under the scrutiny of a furrowed brow.

"You're beginning to sound more like Mowbray with each passing day, which is mighty fine in principle. It just so happens your partner has a bunch of redeeming qualities. However, I do hope you eventually close as many cases as he has. Heck, if you somehow manage to achieve his numbers, then I might even be receptive to the sarcasm I believe I just heard." When Collins finished, he turned back to Addison. "So, I take it you'll want to keep running with this whole satanist angle, then?"

"Not necessarily a satanist angle, but I would like to remain open to the possibility the perp might have more than a fleeting interest in the occult, at least."

Collins appeared lost inside his head. "Isn't Elizabeth Plume the same woman who came forward with information in the middle of the Randy Johnson investigation?" he accused.

"Yes, she is."

"And will you remind me how that turned out again?"

"Her info was solid."

Collins rolled his eyes. "Well, can you enlighten me as to how a retired priest supports this hunch of yours?"

"It appears Harry Bath may not have been your typical kind of priest. He was likely involved with certain practices a man of the cloth shouldn't be playing around with."

"Our resident witch has implied he's into the same hocus pocus bullshit as she is, then, I take it?" The lieutenant was smiling, but not in a happy way.

"She also informed us there might be witches and the like working right here in the department," Jed said with a straight face and wooden eyes.

A humorless laugh exited Collins's mouth while he gaped in amazement.

"Isn't that just fuckin' something. Maybe I can take this

information upstairs and explain how my lead detectives still haven't found anything more to link the homicides to satanism, but they have warned there might be witches working among us in the LAPD. The brass might suggest we head down to Santa Monica and jump off the pier as a way of seeing how many of us float... Are you both fucking with me right now?" he bellowed.

"Look, all I'm saying is we need to go talk with the guy," Addison reasoned. "If nothing solid comes from it, then we'll be straight back in here searching for fresh leads by morning. And when Jennifer Hill's corpse turns up, we will be more than happy to follow any other angle you might feel is relevant. But as of right now, there isn't much else to go on when it comes to a motive. And no matter which way I look at this, those two bodies, the manner they were killed and kept, it certainly appears to be very ritualistic."

Collins nodded with pursed lips.

"We're going to be issuing a computer-enriched photo of the Bowl victim to the press sometime in the next hour. Have you been made aware of this?"

"Nope," Addison replied. "Hopefully, someone comes forward because her identity would help construct a more detailed timeline between the victims."

The softening behind the lieutenant's eyes suggested he appreciated the response.

"Okay, Mowbray, you boys go and speak to your priest. But if you want to continue working on this approach, then you'll need to come back with something more substantial than a rumor about a group of people. From where I'm sitting, the only door this cocksucker may have left ajar is wherever it is he's getting those drugs. There's a ton of info coming in on those phones, and I don't have nearly enough people to work through it all."

Addison decided to change the course of their conversation.

"Did the lab guys lift anything from Jennifer Hill's car?"

"Nope, not a single darn thing. All the fingerprints inside the vehicle have now been accounted for as well. Flatmates and friends, that kind of thing."

Jed reclined casually in his chair, content to clam up again.

"All righty," Addison said. "We'll keep trying to get hold of Harry Bath. See if we can't schedule a meeting with him for tonight or in the morning."

"Anything else?" Collins asked.

"Nope."

"Perkins?"

"I'm all good."

"Goodbye, then," Collins said dismissively.

The detectives got to their feet before breezing out the door.

"That was fun," Addison observed.

Jed chuckled. "The thing about Collins is, he's just a good old barrel of fuckin' laughs. At least we managed to secure a reprieve from working those incoming phone leads."

Addison felt the beginnings of another headache forming inside his temples.

"Yeah, well, it sure as hell ain't gonna last long if Bath doesn't hit us up with something substantial," he remarked while moving toward his desk in the hope of finding a couple Advil.

# TWENTY-THREE

Edward lifted Jennifer's corpse into the back of his Ford Transit cargo van, where he wrapped her remains in a canvas sheet. He examined her clouded blue eyes, fixed wide and staring at nothing. Jennifer's lips were parted in a strange half-smile, and he documented how even in death, she presented as beautiful.

Part of him felt dissatisfied to be releasing her shell without first humiliating the body. It was like eating his favorite pizza without cheese. Nevertheless, he wanted Jennifer's splendor to remain apparent when the LAPD arrived on the scene.

He closed the sliding door on the van and looked out across his property to Munz Ranch Road in the distance. His modest acreage was situated on the periphery of Palmdale, a pleasant town on the opposite side of the San Gabriel Mountains to LA. Edward purchased the land two years earlier for a tidy sum, not that the inflated price bothered him. He inherited a fortune when his father passed away, so the cost was never a deterrent if he wished to acquire something. Edward took his financial standing for granted. He'd been born into privilege, and his Southern bloodline continued to provide him security from the grave.

Everything changed once he decided to try his hand at bringing Linda back by playing six rounds of poker with a croupier from hell. When she initially returned in torrents of color to start making pictures behind his eyes, he was right in the middle of fucking Meagan Banks. They'd opted to entice Linda out of the Badlands with sex Magick once he returned from placing the first victim at the Hollywood Bowl. Meagan was a renowned cardiovascular surgeon and a real cock-gobbler to boot, so she'd been thrilled to engage in more depraved sexual activity.

They dropped a tab of acid, then started screwing while Meagan intoned Latin blasphemies until Linda's essence channeled through their bodies. Edward had felt euphoric as his brain shifted to a blank canvas in readiness for whatever she wanted to deposit before spiritual perfection soaked inside his consciousness. Their flesh had convulsed beneath the power of the images melting his mind, more real than anything he'd faced with eyes opened. But the experience lasted only half a minute as Linda quickly returned to the underworld.

Edward reentered the house to consider his acrimonious living room. Satanic symbology covered the floor, while the walls displayed photographs of the dead. His bureau and leather couch were the only things not allied to the darkness. Stacks of occult literature formed crooked towers of esoteric information. The books were mildewed and dusty; a portrait of his father stared down from the mantle above the fireplace.

For the briefest moment, he could feel Linda's aura nearby as the pores on his skin popped out like gooseflesh. Then, she just disappeared. As if a spirit purifier had penetrated the ceiling to extract every trace of her from the room. He would eventually prevent the doorway to her torment from closing by utilizing Magick in amalgamation with blood sacrifice, crafting an invisible key capable of breaching its lock.

Edward strolled down to his bedroom and retrieved a handgun from a weapon box he kept beneath the floorboards. He didn't expect to encounter any problems while moving the corpse, but it was always best to prepare. If anyone happened to be unfortunate enough to pull him over, then he'd shoot them in the face.

He made his way to the kitchen, where he removed Jennifer's ears from a bag in the fridge. They were impeccably shaped, like a piece of exotic fruit left outside to ripen in the sun. After inhaling the aroma of raw meat, Edward returned his keepsake to the base shelf and snatched a bottle of root beer, guzzling half the drink in a single gulp. Once he completed the objective of calling in Jennifer's location, he would be free to receive additional insight.

The only way for a seeker to acquire a more profound understanding was by confronting the challenge of eternally forbidden practices every day. They must be prepared for insanity, shipwreck, and returning emptyhanded to earn a rite of passage within the demon realm. Edward had infused himself with taboo to obtain black mystical wisdom, forever craving more and prepared to do anything if it increased his knowledge of evil.

His first attempt to communicate with the dead occurred when he was thirteen, just a sad little boy intent on hearing from his deceased grandmother by burning Bible pages over her grave. It was a juvenile venture, whereby he tried to make her mad enough to jump out of the ground and manifest a way back into his life. Gram was particularly religious, and Edward had been strangely fond of her.

It didn't take long for his curiosity to evolve into a full-blown captivation that determined the direction his life would ultimately take. By the time he attended UCLA, he had spent his days seeking out people educated in mysticism and other occult practices. College turned out to be a disappointing experience that exposed most of the self-declared occultists as frauds. There'd been plenty of kids who smoked weed and messed about with Ouija boards in the hope it made them appear mysterious. But they were just middle-class douchebags, every last one of them.

A significant breakthrough occurred when he met a young professor named Earl Whiteman, who taught him the ways of satanism, voodoo, and Black Magick. Earl persuaded him to adopt wickedness and feed his passion, irrespective of any societal consequence. Edward began pandering in cruelty while he was baptized beneath a banner of malevolence, discovering the mysteries concealed within modern paganism, Western esotericism, and the concepts that permeated the counterculture of the 1960s.

Edward finished the rest of his drink and dropped the empty bottle into the trash, making his way to the front door, where he inhaled a final lungful of rust-scented air. The fragrance reminded him of the old pennies his grandmother used to store inside a jar under her bed. After making one final sweep of the living room, he stepped outside and locked the place up.

The sun had started to fade in the sky, and Edward heard a cactus wren calling to its mate as he climbed inside the van. He checked his appearance in the mirror before starting down the dusty driveway. Perhaps he'd take a quick diversion to a neglected area on the way home in the hope of luring someone unimportant back to the ranch, a vagabond or crack fiend whom he could shame beyond recognition like the other carcasses down in his shack. The sweet stinking attraction of the dead touched him in a way no living person ever would, and he needed to have a quiet moment where he treated himself to an installment of ferocity.

# TWENTY-FOUR

Addison had only just poured himself a second glass of Buckeye when the call about Jennifer Hill's body came through. The timing was inconvenient, though he quickly changed into a clean black suit and splashed cold water onto his face before driving up to Mount Lee. By the time he pulled in near the hiking track entrance on Deronda Drive, the liquor was already wearing thin.

He attempted unraveling the impetus of why the murderer was calling the bodies in while he poked the dirt on the side of the mountain. Addison considered whether the perp might be deriving inspiration from watching his handiwork on TV. There was no denying that his flagrancy had played a significant role in cultivating his notoriety. Perhaps he intended to establish some eternal disgrace by proclaiming himself the next big thing on the FBI's most-wanted list. What other reasons could he possibly have for laying her body down among the sweetgrass below the Hollywood sign?

The corpse was positioned near a sage tree a short distance from the front gates, with her arms folded across her chest. Both hands rested atop her shoulders, and she remained clothed in sports gear. Dark chunks of desiccated blood clumped Jennifer's hair as it encircled her throat like a frond of dried seaweed. Her eyes gaped up into the night as if searching for a stairway to heaven. The sliced flesh pattern where the offender had cut her ears away appeared jagged, which suggested he may have been feeling frustrated while dispensing his cruelty. A laceration on her neck penetrated down to the spine, and an inverted cross blistered at the rise of her left breast. Addison believed the perpetrator likely struggled to employ a restrained approach even though there were no signs of any sexual defilement. One thing remained apparent: the twisted shitbug had a voracious appetite for attractive blondes in their twenties, and he was moving at breakneck speed.

Addison gazed out at the city, a vast wonderland that twinkled like fireflies. The semi-gilded glow formed a hazy bubble that reached into the sky to eat away a portion of its darkness. There was a magical quality to the capital when viewed at night, a romantic enchantment that defied the harsh realities inside his head. Addison inhaled deeply, holding the air inside his lungs until he needed to draw breath. The hills were naturally aromatic, and the smell reminded him of being young and carefree, eating freshly baked pie after swimming in the lake at the back of his grandparents' farmhouse.

Jed was speaking with Coniglio beside the body. Traceable angst permeated the kid's demeanor, the same brewing frustration that he'd been carting around for the last few days. He was like a tightly compressed metal spring waiting to be released.

"What do you think he slashed her throat with?" Jed asked.

"The depth of the wound implies he used a straight razor of some kind," Coniglio replied. "There's no way a standard knife blade would penetrate so severely from a single strike. The victim died from exsanguination, which might support the theory that these murders are an occult sacrifice."

"How does her dying from a sliced throat support that theory?"

"There was no way to determine whether the perp felt connected to the blood in the first victims, due to the extreme nature of their wounds. However, he has purposely chosen to murder this girl by severing the carotid artery in her neck after hacking off her ears, and that raises the prospect his methodology involves bleeding the victims out."

Jed whistled while Addison mulled over Coniglio's awareness. Collins might be hard-pressed to reject this development as being nothing more than satanic hoo-ha.

"The corpse is in a more advanced stage of rigor mortis than either of the first two," Coniglio continued. "My estimation is that she likely expired approximately eight hours before her body was dumped here. He achieved his objective much earlier in the day, then waited until it started to get dark before driving her body up the mountain."

Forensics was combing the vegetation down the side of the slope as floodlights illuminated the crime scene. The abundant fibers, butts, and trace materials lying in the dirt were making things challenging for them tonight. It would be like gathering missing pieces from a hundred different picture puzzles and creating an image that made sense.

Jed looked over at Addison. "Now wouldn't it be a treat if they managed to find something to blow this case open," he said evenly. "The scumbag is piling up bodies faster than we can put 'em in the ground, and he ain't showing signs of slowing down. I don't think it's any stretch to declare that the investigation has officially become a freakin' nightmare."

It always amused Addison how his partner bottled the cussing whenever he found himself in the presence of a lady. The kid could be rough around the edges at times, but he was a perfect gentleman as far as females were concerned.

"What's he trying to do?" Jed continued. "Get himself a kill record?"

"I don't think so," Addison countered.

Jed looked up while shielding his eyes against the artificial light. "What do you mean you don't think so? He's completely out of control."

Addison maintained his focus on the body. "It's like I've said already. I reckon if he were concerned with matters of longevity, then he'd most likely be making more of an effort to hide the corpses, and he sure as hell wouldn't be calling them in one after the other fresh off the grill. I believe he's operating under a loose time frame of his own making. If he happens to accomplish whatever it is he's trying to do, then he'll likely become a ghost."

"A ghost, man, you really believe that?"

"Yeah, partner. I do."

Coniglio paused her work. "That's an interesting theory you've developed, Mowbray. You feel like going any deeper on it while we're all here?"

Addison composed his thoughts to streamline his response. "Well, so far he's dropped three bodies at the door in a single week, and each victim has been killed in a similar yet unique kind of way. It appears as if he's holding onto the missing body parts, and he doesn't interfere with them sexually. He's collecting pieces for a reason, and I imagine as soon as he gets all the bits he's after, then it will be game over. At least as far as advertising his crimes is concerned."

"Wow," Coniglio replied, clearly impressed.

She appreciated his brain's methodical approach as he calculated what he was going to say and how best to say it. Mowbray's allure increased with each new encounter, and his rugged masculinity appealed to the little girl inside of her. The LAPD was blessed to have him on the team, because he sure made for one heck of an adversary.

"Have you figured how to get him before he clocks off?" she asked.

"The planning part is still very much at a rudimentary stage, but I'm thinking he may end up being a single branch on a larger tree."

"Whoa, wait a second, are you suggesting he might belong to a cult?"

"I'm open to the possibility he may share an association with something bigger than himself, and I'm also considering whether we'll need to locate whatever tree it is he's attached to so that we can cut away the branch."

Jed exhaled while stretching his arms into the air.

"What?" Addison asked.

"If that Plume woman turns out to be right, then the tree could be a big part of the problem," Jed remarked as the abrasive hatred returned to his voice.

"That would make for a horrible situation."

"Damned right it would. And if it turns out to be the case, then we'll have to find ourselves a nice big chainsaw so we can cut the whole freakin' thing down."

His partner's drive had nothing to do with gaining promotion, nor did it come from a place of great empathy. He cared about people, but so did most cops in their way. It was Jed's disgust for scumbags that got him out of bed each morning, and his craving for justice could sometimes lead to trouble. The kid seemed so hell-bent on preserving his fury. Still, it was better to be burning from both ends of the candle than not to be burning at all, and Addison felt well covered with Jed at his side.

"Have you boys got any leads on this tree?"

Addison picked up on his partner's grin.

"A witch has pointed us toward a dark priest for answers." Jed explained.

Coniglio's confusion was apparent.

"A witch and a dark priest?"

"He's being somewhat facetious," Addison replied. "And he's a retired priest who's not returning any of our calls. But it's best if we fill you in with those details another time, or we're going to be stuck on this mountain all night. Surely there must be other things you'd rather be doing by tomorrow. I imagine you would have a lot on offer in your spare time."

Coniglio looked down at the corpse again to hide her smile. It sure sounded like Mowbray was fishing and maybe even complimenting her in a roundabout way.

"I think you'd be surprised," she replied eventually.

"About?"

"How many gaps there are in my social calendar."

Addison was about to say something flattering but sensed his partner's eyes all over him. One of the main drawbacks of spending most of his time in the kid's company was how he picked up on things uninvited. When the onset of awkwardness began stirring inside his gut, he turned to start making his way back up the path toward his truck.

"Where are you going?" Jed called out with a grin.

"For a smoke," Addison replied without a hint of tenderness.

Coniglio looked up at the kid with a happy smile, so Jed winked at her and touched his nose before watching his partner stomp off in the distance.

# TWENTY-FIVE

Narek sat shirtless on his third-floor balcony watching a news update on the latest Griffith Park murder victim. He sipped his strong black coffee and wondered whether the dead bitch had provided much opposition in her final moments.

Most of the saps he'd murdered had tried resisting their fate in one way or another. Some pleaded for mercy with snot and tears, while others dashed around hollering as they searched for an improvised weapon. The will to live bubbled like a dormant volcano until the Grim Reaper stared its victim in the face. It supplied Narek an additional security layer because if anyone were planning on doing him in, they'd need to contemplate how his latent fire spring might break out from within.

On this one occasion, he strangled a pimp with his bare hands after his piece misfired on the kill shot. It took Narek ten minutes to finish the sorry sack of shit while he clawed at his face with feverish desperation. The liquid growl he heard as the prick attempted to squeeze stale air up his throat was fuckin' nauseating, a sound he'd only encountered coming from a person who was in the process of having their windpipe slowly crushed. The worst of it occurred when the cocksucker's bladder gave out to saturate Narek's pants in a dark yellow stink. Notwithstanding the fact it had been hard work, it was still cool to know he could finish a man without a weapon if the situation presented.

He ended up floating out of the pimp's house on a puffy cloud of pure adrenaline. But it was undoubtedly a whole lot easier to shoot someone in the head, and when he put them down fast, they never got a chance to strike back. Even the Irish fag from Monterey Hills kicked about like a wild buck, and that was with Bedros locking him up from behind.

It had been one helluva week. Narek didn't climb out of bed on Wednesday with an expectation of whacking three people, and he wasn't a sick fuck whose cock went hard at the thought of slaying humans. Certain folk might be capable of homicide when faced with the situation of kill or be killed. He even knew a couple of guys who stabbed a woman full of holes to find out whether they could cross that line. However, it required an iron-cast determination to be an effective hitman. A ruthless indifference toward human life was essential if a person wanted to survive inside the snuff game.

Narek's primary motivation was to make sure he died with a vault full of cash. He approached his work without a hint of repentance because what he did on the streets wasn't much different from garbage disposal. As far as he was concerned, the LAPD should be kicking him a fee for doing society a favor.

He rarely got called into neighborhood disputes nowadays due to his elevated status. The lower-ranked soldiers battled on the front lines with their drive-by shootings and ongoing turf wars. The boss's consent wasn't always required to whack a notorious criminal, but his approval was essential for any target which happened to be a regular Joe. Killing a citizen brought a lot of heat, yet the LAPD might assign a couple of fair-minded detectives to investigate the execution of a known degenerate.

The city's many illegal enterprises were all expected to maintain a stringent set of procedural guidelines. Nevertheless, any boss worth pissing on would know how to give the impression they played by the rules. So long as they were perceived to be toeing the line, there was never much police opposition. Cops generally looked the other way if no innocents got caught inside the crossfire.

Every so often, Narek popped someone for personal reasons that didn't involve a bag full of money. Like the time he murdered a couple of peckerwood white boys over at UCLA after supplying them with a batch of B-grade heroin.

The cum stains were supposed to sling his smack to their classmates but decided to have a private dope party instead. When Narek eventually located them unconscious inside their dorm, he had to drop a bucket of water on their heads to hear what was already evident. He told them they had forty-eight hours to come up with his cash, and they called two days later to explain how they were still four grand short. Narek had allowed them to think they could split the difference on the next consignment, and when he strolled into their room the following day with a bag of poison junk in his hand, they couldn't get it up a vein quickly enough. He'd watched on while they foamed from the mouth and filled their pants with shit, convulsing like fuckin' retards before becoming permanently still. Best of all, it didn't even rate a mention on the news, and their deaths were confirmed as accidental drug overdoses.

Narek could only think of one instance where he'd come close to screwing things up. The night he unloaded two clips into a couple of pigs in retaliation to a tune-up he'd received a week earlier. He set the scene for a random ambush by reporting suspicious activity in an alley. When a patrol car rolled up five minutes later, he just stepped out from behind a dumpster and started blasting bullets.

He split the scene on a Ducati Panigale, riding back to Glendale without breaking a sweat. A bitch cop died, which sent the city into lockdown as the LAPD went combing the streets for a culprit. Every mobster in Cali wanted to discover who was behind the bloodshed after the law applied the blowtorch to their illicit operations.

Fortunately, Narek didn't speak a word of what he intended to do, so nobody had the chance to snitch him out. Still, it was imprudent business, and he certainly wouldn't be attempting anything similar again in a hurry.

A female news correspondent on the TV was standing beside an SUV with a satellite dish sticking up from the roof. She came across as an uppity little cunt, but she had a nice pair of perky titties, and her mouth worked like a cock vacuum. Narek turned the volume up on the television to hear what the dead girl's father was saying to the vultures gathered on his front lawn. Butchering white chicks from respectable families was a surefire way to get the attention of every lawman in the country, and it seemed only a matter of time until the crazy fuckin' pervert got apprehended.

The Armenian Mafia rarely left their corpses on the street if they could help it. A sidewalk grave was preferred when the boss wanted to deliver a message to the entire city. It was much safer to make the bodies disappear. That's why Davit dropped sixty large on the meat grinder inside his industrial warehouse.

Los Angeles was going to be blessed with lovely weather as the morning sunshine gilded the city in warm custardy light. Narek lowered his designer sunglasses over his eyes while he gazed out across to the Verdugo Mountains in the near distance. Anna was preparing him eggs like the good wife she mostly was, and Narek intended to enjoy his breakfast outdoors. Maybe later, he might give Bedros a call to see if he felt like heading over to Venice Beach. It would be kinda cool to kick back with an ice-cold Bud while they gawked at some tight young asses. An easy smirk spread across Narek's face as he looked down to the street below. Even though it had been a crazy couple of days, life really couldn't get any fuckin' better.

# TWENTY-SIX

Sean Brody pulled off Freeway 101 and continued down the road to his favorite mini-mart. All morning he'd doubted himself, questioning his ability to maintain the patient control he'd employed during this past year. Sean's desire for violence felt like it was snowballing. Everywhere he looked, more diseased minds were walking around the city—a cavalcade of scumbags begging to be put down.

He drummed his fingers against the steering wheel in time with the radio, thinking how the one advantage of living in LA was the anonymity it provided. Because aside from having to deal with his gasbag neighbor's attempted infidelity, he had no problem appearing as a washed-out face in the crowd. Almost everybody in California worked hard to emulate the glamorous movie stars they saw on their TVs, and if a person didn't look important in this town, they likely weren't. People were so caught up in the superficial bullshit of their pretend lives, posting updates on social media every time they needed to wipe their ass. No one could be bothered examining the reality of what they were presented with anymore. If the idiot box suggested black was white—the slender-minded douchebags just swallowed it whole.

Sean drove into the parking lot behind Manny's Market and killed the engine, sitting quietly for a moment while he made a mental note of what he needed to buy. The produce store was in a dying part of the city, and a beat-up red Honda was the only other vehicle in the area. Sean grabbed his wallet from the center console and put on a Dodgers cap before exiting his Chrysler to make his way inside.

The same family had operated the little market for three generations, and they knew most of their customers by name. If a product wasn't available on the shelves, all a person needed to do was ask, and Manny Junior would do his best to order it in. It wasn't too long ago when this shop was considered the heart of the community—a local clubhouse for grannies and young kids alike. Sadly, most of those customers now shopped at the Walmart that opened a few blocks up the road. The original signage still hung from the street canopy. Its bold red letters now faded to hot pink. Sean looked at the well-worn tracks on the floor when he entered the store—the trails left behind from countless feet that traversed these lanes for more than forty years.

Sean nodded at Manny Jr's son before he walked up the second aisle to get pickles for the hot dogs he intended to make for lunch. As he approached the condiment shelf, he noticed a skittish young lady standing silently by the freezer. She held a basket in two small hands and looked extremely uncertain of herself. The woman had short brown hair, olive skin, and the kind of frightened brown eyes that suggested she was accustomed to jumping at shadows. Fresh bruises formed a ring around her upper arms, and her bottom lip was split and swollen. Sean was about to inquire whether she was okay when a chubby, red-haired male moved in beside her. The guy was aged in his thirties, with large, stooped shoulders and a protruding brow. He wore faded denim jeans with a Jack Daniels T-shirt and a pair of heavy-duty work boots. A collection of silver rings covered his fat fingers. Sean observed as the girl tugged on her simple brown dress before quickly dropping her eyes to the floor.

"I can't fucking believe this," the guy accused spitefully, his fleshy cheeks shining with sweat. "This place is a waste of my time."

"Wh-why . . . what is it, Joel?"

"These burritos have got to go in the damned oven; they ain't even got the microwave ones in the freezer. I thought you said you shop here all the time, Tara. You better not be lying to me, bitch." The girl had unintentionally flinched at the sound of her name as a swell of anger began rising at the base of Sean's gut. This asshole was twice her size.

"I ain't lying to you. I promise you I ain't."

Joel stared at Tara with an unblinking scowl while he raised a hand in the air.

"If I ever find out you're playing around on me, God only knows what I'll end up doing to you. But last night will seem like a teddy bear picnic. That much I can promise."

Sean coughed as he reached for a jar of pickles, watching as the gutless snake lowered his hand and slinked off down the next aisle to get out of sight. Tara smiled meekly before following her fat cocksucker boyfriend with a subservience beaten into her over time. While Sean continued shopping, he realized something needed to be done to rectify the situation he'd just witnessed. Sean presumed the battered Honda in the parking lot belonged to the couple, and with any luck, nobody else would pull in until he'd finished knocking some sense into Joel. As soon as he collected all the ingredients required for his lunch, Sean approached the cashier, where he asked for a pack of Salems.

"How ya doin, Junior?" he greeted.

"What's up, Sean?"

"Nothing much. How's your pops getting along?"

Junior scanned the items on the counter and placed them into a bag. "He's all right, looking after Grandpa and working like always."

Sean looked over his shoulder. "Hey, man, have you seen those two in here before?"

"Yeah," Junior replied, rolling his eyes.

"What's their story?"

"I'm not sure, but the girl is always covered in bruises."

Sean paid for his things.

"Say hello to your pops for me."

"Will do, man."

Sean headed back outside to the parking lot, where he placed his shopping in the front seat and lit a cigarette, resting against the trunk of his car while he waited for the couple to finish up inside. The sun blazed orange in a cloudless blue sky, its light blending with the concrete's mica to form a constellation of tiny diamonds. A sudden wind gust swept leaves and paper across the ground, creating a clean, dust-free strip in the process. When Sean caught sight of Joel and Tara rounding the corner, he wasn't surprised to see the young lady carrying four bags of groceries a few steps behind. Sean waited until they were only ten feet away before speaking.

"Working her to the bone, I see."

Joel looked behind him in confusion. "You talkin' to me, bud?" he asked, pointing at himself.

"I sure am, and I ain't your bud."

"Huh . . . do we know each other or something?"

"Not yet."

The first sign of alarm touched Joel's face. "What the fuck do you want, man?"

Sean flicked his smoke at the dickhead. "I wanna fight ya."

Joel stopped in his tracks as if he'd met an invisible wall. "Why the hell you wanna do that for?"

"'Cause, you're a woman-bashing cunt, which is as good a reason as any."

Sean's eyes never shifted from the abusive prick, tilting his head as Joel started quivering right in front of him. His emotions gnarled together while a desire to hurt the bastard flooded his mind. An all-consuming hatred twisted fire through Sean's insides as he moved toward Joel. He felt the guy's terror leaping off him in waves—the kind of fear which could only be experienced by a weak fucking bully.

"Raise them hands of yours, Joel. Like I saw you doing to your girlfriend inside."

"No, fuck off . . . I don't even know you."

Sean smirked. "Sure, you do. I'm that promise you always knew was coming. The one you push to the back of your mind each time you set about beating up women who are half your size. Come on now, man, lift those fuckin' hands."

Joel started retreating in small, shuffling steps. "What are you talkin' 'bout? I don't beat up on no women. She fell down the back steps. Ain't that right, baby girl? Tell him, Tara, tell him how you fell."

Sean chuckled, shaking his head while moving forward. "You yellow bastards are so freaking predictable, man. Your ladies must all have two left feet the number of times they be falling down a set of stairs. Why can't you be a little more creative with your excuses? How about she fell over running away from my disgusting ass, or she tripped at the thought of having to spend another night sharing a bed with me."

Joel's eyes darted between Sean and Tara. It was pathetic. "Tell him what happened, Tara! Do it, god damn you!"

When Tara went to speak, Sean cut her off.

"Don't bother, sweetheart. This is going down no matter what you say."

Joel stopped retreating when he realized it would serve no purpose, holding his hands up in front of his face in flinching defense, a coward to his very core.

"That's better," Sean said merrily. "I'm gonna teach you an important lesson here today. Something I hope might end up changing your life for the better."

"Hey, man, I'm sorry. I won't touch her again, I promise."

"Really?" Sean asked, watching as a glimmer of hope flashed inside his eyes. It was an expression cops and battered women saw whenever an abusive male got the notion to better themselves. When they promised to speak with somebody about their problems or swore to God they'd never do it again, thinking that everybody would have to support them. The violence usually started up the following week with minor insults and threatening glances designed to make their partners feel worthless. Some of the cocksuckers probably even felt guilty afterward, but that never stopped them from reoffending.

There were many kinds of monster in the world. They didn't exist in dark wardrobes or hide under children's beds waiting for the lights to go out. Joel was a breed of beast who lashed a woman's soul, creating sounds and smells that stayed with them forever. The only monster Tara needed to fear right now was the one she woke up with each morning.

Sean landed a straight left into Joel's mouth that sent him staggering backward with a loud cry of anguish before a well-timed right hook landed on his cheek, splitting the skin below his eye, and dropping him in a filthy heap.

"Quit fuckin' whining, you yellow prick," Sean said. "Why won't you fight back, asshole?" The sight of this grown man blubbering intensified his rage. Tara was trying hard not to stare at the blood trickling down her abuser's face but got drawn back each time she went to look away. Sean grabbed a fistful of ginger hair and unleashed a flurry of punches that smashed into Joel's nose, face, and mouth.

When Sean felt a couple of teeth shatter, he straightened to survey the wretched, broken figure crumpled below him. The guy's eyes were swollen over as bloody spit drooled from his slack jaws to form gooey crimson slop on the ground. This bully appeared entirely revolting so that his exterior now reflected the man within.

Sean wiped the blood from his knuckles on the back of his jeans, then leaned down again to remove a wallet from Joel's pocket. He found a driver's license and took note of the address, crouching beside the creep's busted body where he lifted his head.

"I know where you live, prick. Are you fucking listening to me?"

Joel moaned his response.

"I'm going to be keeping my eye on your fat ass. If I see one more mark on this young woman, I'll shoot you in the head and put everyone out of their misery. You understand?"

Joel moaned again as Sean turned to face Tara.

"You're worth more than this piece of shit will have you believe. You can do so much better. If you're ever in danger or feel like you can't get away, then leave a message with the owner of this minimart. Ask for Sean, and I'll help you, okay?"

Tara nodded her head slowly with a look of genuine appreciation on her face as Sean got to his feet and dropped the wallet on the ground.

"Tell the asshole I kept this," he said, showing her the driver's license.

"Thank you," Tara mouthed.

"Don't mention it," he replied, sinking one last boot into the coward's stomach before making his way back to the car.

# TWENTY-SEVEN

Jed puffed on a cigarette while driving down the final stretch of Simi Valley road. "Third Street should be coming up on our left in a minute if my GPS decides it's going to be accurate this morning," he said indolently.

Addison looked out the window as suburban America flashed by like a movie reel stuck in fast forward. It was after four in the morning by the time he got home from Mount Lee, and he flopped into bed after finishing his whiskey. Jed had arrived at ten for the drive to Harry Bath's after they decided to try their luck at landing on his doorstep unannounced.

A dark shadow of stubble covered the bottom half of Addison's face, and he examined his careworn reflection in the side mirror. His eyes were a bloodshot haze of whiskey and weariness. The cheap black suit he'd found in the closet was crinkled and faded. He felt utterly outdated beside his partner, who appeared fresh in casual denim attire.

"Here we go, then," Jed said, pulling into the curb. "Now, let's just hope the priest is inside, or our drive out here will have been a waste of time."

Harry Bath's home gave the impression of being narrow from the front but seemed to stretch back into the property like an oversized coffin. A Californian palm tree bent toward the road from inside a ring of desert cactuses. The only other vegetation in the yard was a handful of thirsty-looking plants that appeared to have been placed arbitrarily, and the dry patchy grass looked in need of a decent soaking. Dead bugs dangled from a cloud of glistening web on the rusty mailbox near the sidewalk.

Bath's windows were coated in a thick film of red dirt while the exterior paint had started peeling away in large chunks. Simi Valley was situated in the southeastern corner of Ventura County. For the most part, the ordered little city was considered a great place to live. There were plenty of nice houses throughout the region; however, Harry Bath's property wouldn't be considered one of them.

Addison wondered what the neighbors thought of the ramshackle residence as they made their way down the priest's splintered driveway. He considered the maintained gardens across the street while climbing a small staircase onto the porch and approached the door. Addison knocked firmly, recognizing the outline of an approaching figure behind the frosted glass. The door creaked ajar to reveal an older man with cagey eyes.

"Can I help you?"

"Are you Father Harry Bath?" Addison asked.

"Yes, that's me."

"Father Bath, I'm Detective Mowbray from the LAPD homicide division," Addison began, flashing his credentials, "and this here is my partner, Detective Perkins. I apologize for imposing on you unexpected like this, but we've tried to reach you on numerous occasions over the last twenty-four hours. We were hoping to talk with you about a homicide investigation we're currently working on."

"I haven't been answering my phone of late," Bath said indifferently. "I wondered who it was calling me yesterday. Like a dog with a bone, you were."

"Yeah, well, I hope we didn't annoy you too much."

Bath remained silent, which prompted Jed to step forward. "How do you do, sir?"

"Two minutes earlier, I would have said I'm fine, but now I'm not so sure."

Harry Bath was of medium height with a thin build. His shaggy, unkempt hair appeared very brown for a man of his age. Deep wrinkles fanned across his forehead, and the gray stubble on his face was halfway to becoming a beard. Bath was dressed in cotton short pants, a grubby white vest, and tattered flip-flops.

"A homicide investigation, you say?"

"Yes, that's correct," Addison acknowledged. "But don't go alarming yourself. We haven't come here because you are suspected of any wrongdoing."

"No?" Bath retorted. "Then what brings you to my door?"

The priest's tone was similar to the one Addison reserved for God-bothering enthusiasts who occasionally passed by the house on his days off.

"We've been told you might be prepared to speak with us about a certain group of people who may be able to assist us further," he explained hopefully.

"And who has given you the impression I can do that?"

Addison reconsidered Plume's directive about anonymity as he scrambled for a response, but before he could come up with an answer, the priest asked another question.

"More importantly, what did they say about me?"

"Someone who insisted upon remaining anonymous suggested we try to speak with you. This person is under the impression that you can assist us with a particular line of inquiry we are presently exploring."

Bath's eyes narrowed into two colorless slits. "And you expect me to believe that's all this *person* said?"

Addison decided to change his approach. "Do you watch the news, Father?"

"Not if I can help it. I don't even have a television inside the house. There's nothing honorable waiting to be discovered on CBN these days."

Addison smiled politely. "I am going to entrust you with some confidential police information in the hope it may appeal to your priestly nature and persuade you to speak with us. We require this conversation to remain strictly between us."

Bath nodded his agreement.

"There is a serial killer running rampant around Los Angeles. A maniac who is responsible for the deaths of three young women, all of whom were murdered in an extremely brutal fashion. The perpetrator injects his victims with ketamine before cutting away various parts of their bodies, and he brands the shape of an inverted Christian cross onto their left breast. It also appears he may intentionally bleed them out."

Something flashed behind Harry Bath's eyes.

"We suspect he is attempting to perform an occult sacrifice, and we have also considered the likelihood he may belong to a cult. My partner and I were informed that you might know of a supposed group operating in the state several years ago. Which is the reason why we are now standing on your front porch."

Bath remained stoically silent, and right when Addison began thinking of what else he might present, the priest turned around to start moving back inside the house.

"Follow me, then. I'm prepared to give you a minute or two," he agreed.

A tingle worked its way up Addison's spine.

Jed closed the door quietly behind them as they trailed Harry Bath down a dark hallway devoid of any ornamentation. He led them into a murky living area with a limestone fire hearth and several mismatched furniture pieces.

Bath dawdled over to a grimy couch positioned against the far wall where he offered them both a seat. Addison vacillated before eventually sitting down. There was a musky odor in the air that reminded him of hunting stag inside the Piney Woods as a boy. If the space wasn't quite disgusting, it sure as hell wasn't far from being so. Coffee rings marked the oak table in front of them, while the coating of dust on the cabinets beside him was half an inch thick. All the paintings were hung crooked, and a stack of old newspapers in the corner had turned yellow with age.

A palpable sadness filled the room—a melancholy he could relate to. The brass crucifix on the mantle above the fireplace personified the loneliness and the fact there were no photos on display. Both detectives observed an uneasy silence while Bath dragged a timber chair across the floor and took a seat opposite them.

"Would either of you like tea or coffee?" he asked half-heartedly.

"No, thank you," Jed replied.

Addison raised a hand in the air. "Thanks, but I'm okay as well."

"All right, then," Bath continued. "How can I help you?"

Addison looked at Jed, who signaled for him to lead the way.

"The person who provided us with your details said there were rumors about a group who were active in the area some time back. They think these people could be involved with the murders we're investigating. Do you know who they may have been referring to?"

An intense expression crossed Bath's face. "I want to make it clear that I wouldn't usually discuss such things with anybody whom I didn't know and trust. However, the events I'll soon relay to you have weighed heavily upon my soul for many years, and perhaps a shred of positivity may yet come of this. Now I haven't got a clue what your contact has divulged about me, but I can assure you that taking a human life is not something of which I approve."

Addison leaned forward. "As I explained earlier, Father, no one has suggested you have been a participant in any crime," he assured the man wholeheartedly.

The priest appeared to appreciate the sentiment. "I'm only prepared to run through this once, so you'll need to have your notepads ready, and I'd appreciate it if you refrained from asking questions until I've finished."

Bath waited until they both agreed to his conditions before continuing.

"Back in 1994, I was running a small meeting at a house in South Pasadena, and one of the participants was a youth named Andrew King. One night, Andrew told me about a snuff club that a friend of his had become involved with. He explained how the group killed for pleasure and sacrificed people to receive an esoteric understanding of matters pertaining to their own lives.

"When I probed him further on what he said, Andrew remained unmoved and even elaborated how the affiliates murdered together at secret gatherings. He seemed to be impressed by their principles, and how he spoke could probably be defined as boasting. What you need to realize is that Andrew was an underprivileged youth with a range of mental complications. So, I naturally presumed his story was nothing more than fantasy. He often relayed outlandish tales to certain people at the meeting."

Jed leaned forward with pen in hand. "Can I ask what the purpose of this meeting was?" he inquired.

Harry Bath weighed Jed's question with a hooded gaze. "It was an intimate group for grieving people who desired to contact loved ones and angelic beings. The good kind."

The kid appeared a little disturbed by Bath's response, while Addison attempted to get his head around what he'd heard a moment earlier.

"What do you mean by the good kind?" Jed asked.

"I'm referring to celestial deities or holy angels—spirit beings from an alternate dimension who oppose demons and normally remain hidden from human sight. Before you ask anything else on the subject, let me say this: I firmly believe that both angels and demons are as authentic as you and me, perhaps even more. Yet, for whatever reason, it's usually the fallen kind who are more likely to reveal themselves to people. In any case, I don't advise attempting to initiate contact with either."

It didn't feel as if there was much scope for a response, so they stayed quiet and nodded their understanding as best they could, waiting for Bath to continue.

"When Andrew came to the meeting the following week, he was utterly paranoid, displaying symptoms of heightened anxiety. He eventually informed me how his friend was a practitioner of Brujeria, a form of Mexican witchcraft. That's how he encountered In Paucis. The Latin grabbed my attention; *in paucis*, you see, means 'the few.'"

Addison looked at his partner and was reassured to see him jotting down all the details in his notepad. "Inpawsis?"

"That's what Andrew called them."

"How do you spell it?" Jed asked.

"Capital I - n - space - capital P - a - u - c - i - s. Two words."

Recounting those past events looked as if it might have forced Bath to confront an ocean of repressed guilt as he became suddenly quiet and dropped his head. Addison believed most people detached from any horror outside their own lives to help them cope with all the suffering in the world. Because if everybody connected with a universal plane of feeling, it would crush them beneath a burden of heartbreak.

Bath slowly raised his head.

"Andrew said that his friend, another youth named Luke Green, was murdered by people associated with In Paucis, and he believed they also intended to kill him. A wealthy female doctor had promised to recruit Luke if he was willing to sacrifice an individual of her choosing."

"Are you all right, Father?" Addison inquired.

"Yes, I'm okay, thanks. These memories have been locked inside me for a long time . . . This lady told Luke he would undertake his initiation at a sacred site and that they were all going to drink the victim's blood to toast his acceptance when it was over.

"Andrew told me the inverted Christian cross was a revered symbol with In Paucis. He believed they were never genuinely interested in Luke becoming a member. It seems they fabricated his recruitment as a lure. I asked Andrew what he expected of me, but when I suggested we approach the police, he ran out the door, and I never saw him again.

"Andrew used drugs frequently, and I assumed he had psychosis. When he didn't return to my meeting over the next few weeks, I phoned the boarding house where he stayed in Pasadena, but the manager said he'd skipped town.

"A few years later, I decided to ask around as to whether anybody had seen the boys, and an associate told me she'd heard they were both dead. She claimed to have seen Luke Green's face on the back of a milk carton. After I did some additional digging, I learned that Luke had been reported missing by a parole officer from the time Andrew came to me with his story. My source also confirmed the veracity of In Paucis a few months later, although she wasn't prepared to say anything aside from the fact that they were real. The woman claimed to have a cousin on the fringes of the group."

Addison's heart skipped a beat.

"They're called In Paucis, you say?"

"*Were* called, Detective. They changed their name several years ago. To what, I have absolutely no idea. At the end of it, I don't wish to know."

"What about Andrew King? Do you know where he might have gone?"

"No one has heard from Andrew since I spoke with him last."

Addison felt momentarily speechless. He'd encountered sociopaths during his career who were capable of doing almost anything to appease their urges. Still, a cooperative of homicidal maniacs was not something he'd ever imagined possible.

"Do you recall the time these boys disappeared?" Jed asked.

"October 1994, but Andrew wasn't put on the missing person register until 1998."

"Are you getting all of this?" Addison asked his partner.

"Oh yeah," Jed replied.

"What about the boys' families?"

Bath shook his head. "Luke and Andrew were both wards of the state. Runaways who'd been in and out of foster homes and detention centers their whole lives. As I said, it was the boys' parole officers who first reported them to the police after they failed to show up for their appointments, and as far as I'm aware, their bank accounts have never been accessed. I was told the LAPD initially assumed Andrew moved out of state and that Luke had fallen victim to foul play, most likely at the hands of some vengeful delinquent from his past. But I'm sure you'll be able to verify those particulars on your databases."

"What about the woman? The one you said claims to have a

cousin who might know people on the inside. Do you know where we can find her?"

"Her name is Sarah Cross, and she once resided in Riverside County. The last I heard, she got married and moved someplace away from the city."

"Sarah with an H on end or without?"

"I have no idea."

This was a hell of a lot more than Addison had been expecting to walk away with. They had some names and a bunch of solid details to present to the lieutenant, which was a darn sight better than anything coming in on the phones.

"I don't suppose you know who the woman's cousin is?" Addison asked hopefully.

"If I did, I would have told you their name already."

"Of course. Is there anything else you can remember that might help? Did this Cross woman happen to tell you what the new name of In Paucis might be?"

"No, she most certainly did not. I've told you everything I know."

Addison turned toward his partner. "You got anything you want to ask?"

Jed looked up from his notepad and shook his head. "Nah, it sounds like Father Bath has already provided all he can."

Jed was probably right, but Addison was like a kid in a candy store. "Do you have any idea of where they may have been situated?"

Harry Bath moved to the edge of his chair. "No, I don't, and what I did uncover should clearly illustrate why I have never really spoken of this. I quit digging when it became apparent how dangerous they are."

"You sure there's nothing else you can think of?"

Bath appeared as if he might be growing impatient. "No, that's all. I hope you find whoever is responsible for killing those women," he concluded by raising himself out of the chair. "But I have someplace I need to be."

An expression of satisfaction covered Jed's face as he slipped the notepad back inside his jacket. The detectives stood to follow the priest back down the hall. Jed offered his thanks while making his way outside. Addison looked the man in his eyes.

"Thank you for seeing us, Father."

"You're welcome," Bath mumbled, gazing down at the floor.

A final question popped into Addison's head. "One last thing..."

Bath didn't react. "Do you believe they still exist today?"

"Yes, I do. You'd know better than most that inherently evil people don't often change their ways. And none of them have ever been apprehended as far as I can tell."

Addison smiled appreciatively. "Thanks again; it was very good of you to see us."

"That's quite all right. But please don't come back here. And when you see her, give my regards to Elizabeth Plume," Bath replied before closing the door in Addison's face.

# TWENTY-EIGHT

Fairmont International's luxuriant offices were situated on the top floor of a company-owned building in Beverly Hills. The high-end accountancy firm was a favorite among California's elite due to the exceptional economic thinkers they retained on staff. The Old Man was brilliant at manipulating numbers, and success had arrived soon after he established the business in 1975. He found the work to be somewhat gratifying and had always held ambitions of amassing tremendous wealth. Yet, the corporation primarily served as a smokescreen to conceal his voracious appetite for murder.

Cruelty had been part of his shadow for as long as he could remember. It all started with the small animals and birds he would trap around Presidio Heights in San Francisco as a boy. Next in line was a neighbor's dog, which he skinned alive at Glen Canyon Park, and by the time his eighteenth birthday came about, he'd already buried the disfigured corpses of two children deep inside the Armstrong Redwoods.

Most of his early victims were just kids from broken families, meaning the authorities soon lost interest in trying to locate them. Few people cared for the needy. They slipped through the cracks and had continued to provide him with fresh meat in the decades that followed. He'd never come close to being unmasked, and only in America could a mass-murdering predator become a pillar of the community.

The Old Man began thinking about Susan Rodriguez waiting inside his office while he strode through the downstairs lobby toward the elevator. She was second in the Filii Reprobi hierarchy and the foremost candidate to eventually take his chair. Her distinctive qualities had been evident from the moment his plant at

Juvenile Psychiatry arranged their introduction. Susan came from a Mexican family who assembled an empire by importing petroleum products into the USA. Her parents sent her to California to obtain a first-class education when she was ten. A teacher quickly reported Susan's sadistic leanings, and she was sent to an institution for profoundly troubled youth. The Old Man received a notification when her IQ scaled off the charts, and he took Susan under his wing a short time later. He'd been thrilled to discover her avidity for bloodshed was insatiable.

Their meeting today represented an escalating dilemma the Old Man needed to solve. Edward's recurrent theme of directing the limelight onto his pretty corpses certainly wasn't ideal. Filii Reprobi weren't accustomed to watching one of their own embark upon a killing spree punctuated by risk. His flagrant disregard of their longstanding regulations was apparent to all, and people questioned why he hadn't already reined him in.

In truth, the Old Man wanted to see whether the boy had what it took to come through this. He didn't think Edward was being motivated by the onset of delusion, not for an instant did he believe that. His old girlfriend was influencing him again; only this time, she was doing it from beyond the grave. Linda had always presented an annoying distraction; it was the very reason why the Old Man decided on Edward sacrificing her six years earlier. He knew she would have gotten in the way of his call by breaching the void inside him.

The LAPD were now tasked with hunting a wily opponent. Edward was so deliberate and orderly in everything he put his hands to, not to mention as frosty as an arctic moon. He was practically peerless among the rest of his associates—none besides Susan could match his cunning. Even then, it would likely come down to a toss of the coin. Still, the Old Man didn't want anybody to start suggesting he was ineffective in his governance, meaning he would soon be required to demonstrate his doggedness about upholding the rules. But part of him remained reluctant to bring his hammer down, and it wasn't as if he could get entangled inside any complications, for Ghost was only a phone call away.

If he permitted Edward to continue with his game, he would need to show how their virtues were being maintained. Allowing him to persist with total impunity might generate an influx of rebellious behavior, and there were already specified periods set aside where they could act without restraint.

In addition to the thirteen retreat weekends held at the Adelanto compound, they also got to spend a week at the gated estate in Mississippi during Halloween. The Old Man kept a lively collection of dirty human playthings on hand at both locations. Runaways, and street creatures he procured through various trafficking networks. A Filii Reprobi could source other prey if they wanted. However, it was supposed to be undertaken discreetly, never drawing attention to their ongoing delinquencies.

The Old Man's influence had been achieved by providing judiciously targeted individuals with inside knowledge on tainted currency. Greed usually inspired fools to tighten a noose around their neck with a sense of gratitude, and he never grew bored of seeing respectable folk sell their souls beneath the charm of a quick buck. People were easily exploited, eating from the hand of corruption for a vision painted in acid.

After exiting the elevator on the thirteenth floor, the Old Man strolled past reception, where two glamorous secretaries smiled a greeting. They both appeared enthusiastic, but he didn't bother returning their acknowledgment. The Old Man never gave much thought to adulation or softened speech, always carrying himself with an air of preeminence. Despite the fact his existence was a falsehood, he seldom deviated off course. He was the founder of Filii Reprobi, and if his manner offended, it concerned him not at all.

Saturdays were reserved for their most important clients. He surveyed the new leather couches near the interactive TV and recognized the latest number one NBA draft pick sitting alongside his manager. Olivier Woodward looked up from whatever magazine he was reading, but when the Old Man ignored him, the kid's focus returned to the article.

Fairmont International subscribed to over one hundred publications and kept an extensive library for any clients who arrived early for their appointment. They provided a stocked bar that offered everything from panda dung tea to single malt whiskey, and an assortment of pastries was available inside the kitchen. The reception area was tiled in dark granite, and the counter featured a mosaic business logo that exuded class. Sports memorabilia, contemporary artworks, and rare Hollywood artifacts provided a finishing touch. In truth, there wasn't another firm in the city that presented better.

The Old Man marched down the corridor leading to his office. When he stepped boldly through the door, he saw Susan Rodriguez sitting quietly on the other side of his desk. She didn't notice him as she studied something inside a display cabinet mounted on the wall.

Susan was dressed unassumingly in gray business slacks, a red top, and a pair of velvety heels. She appeared almost majestic with her long legs folded over to one side of her body. Her silky brown hair was pulled back into a ponytail, and there wasn't a trace of makeup on her stunning face. When the Old Man closed the door behind him, she swiveled in her chair, smiling as he gave her shoulder a light squeeze.

"Hello," she sighed.

"Hello, dear girl, how are you?" he inquired while breezing his way around the desk to his chair. Their eyes connected in a way that comes from knowing a person intimately.

"I'm okay, I guess," she replied. "A little agitated, but otherwise okay."

"I presume your concerns are all to do with Edward."

Susan appeared to appreciate his foresight even though her motives for requesting the meeting were obvious enough. It could often be challenging to read what she was feeling, but her restlessness today made her an open book.

"Can I speak freely here? Or do we need to step outside?"

The Old Man chuckled confidently.

"This room is harder to infiltrate than the Oval Office," he promised with a smirk, watching as her dark, enigmatic eyes took him in.

"I'm conscious that you have always had high expectations when it comes to Edward, which I might add is entirely justifiable. There's no denying he brings a distinct authenticity to the order. Nevertheless, these current events are unnecessary, not to mention a blatant violation of the rules.

"I was troubled from the moment the first body materialized up at the Hollywood Bowl, and the LAPD is going to be disclosing the bitch was a British medical student who arrived on a three-month visa exchange. I'm sure I don't need to point out how a butchered tourist will likely grab the FBI's attention. As expected, there are people within who have started approaching me for answers. I suppose I just wanted to hear where you currently stand on matters."

The Old Man fidgeted with paperwork on his desk, sliding it around with his manicured hands until he aligned all the edges. He was irritated by the realization he hadn't already been versed about the first woman's identity or the fact she was a tourist, and he sure as hell wasn't acquainted with being exposed on the hop.

"My contacts are keeping an eye on things and will give me a call the moment there is any reason to be concerned. I've been assured we've got nothing to worry about as of right now. The LAPD is busying itself with finding the chemicals. Besides, I was told it would all be over soon enough."

"How soon?"

"Apparently, he intends to kill six girls in total, so if we include the one from last night, then that leaves three more."

"Can we afford to be on standby? If there are any more corpses, then things might spiral completely out of control. Have you listened to the radio or watched TV over the last day? If another body is found in those damned hills, he's going to be contending with the

FBI. What if he gets caught?"

The Old Man paused to remind her of his stewardship.

"I can guarantee the LAPD won't be landing on his door anytime soon. Like I said already, I have it on dependable authority that their focus right now is finding where those chemicals have originated from, and because our own Meagan Banks supplied them, his tracks are covered. Should the circumstances change, they will notify me before any plan is enforced. If the situation requires a swift resolution, the executioner is on standby. Filii Reprobi will not be compromised."

When Susan lowered her eyes, her face reminded the Old Man of the confused child he'd first encountered at the psychiatric hospital. He waited for her to look up, recognizing how her expression portrayed a lying innocence to conceal her undeniable deadliness. It would be fascinating to know how many had perished beneath her beguilement.

"I hope you don't think I was questioning your judgment."

"Not at all, Susan," he assured her meaningfully. "I would have been completely disappointed if you hadn't come to me about this."

Susan dropped her gaze again.

"I will be sure to allay any concerns and explain how Edward is going to be chastised very shortly." It appeared Susan was anticipating Edward's punishment with bated breath.

"Did you get lunch earlier?" he asked.

"No, I haven't even eaten breakfast."

The Old Man floated out from behind his desk and placed a hand on her shoulder.

"I've found an Armenian eatery. It's nothing flash, but the food is something else."

"Where is it? Over in East Hollywood?"

"No, it's in Glendale and well worth a drive through traffic."

"Sounds swell. I can't recall ever eating Armenian food before."

"Well then, my dear girl, you are in for a special treat."

# TWENTY-NINE

Jed stopped for lunch at an old-school diner in San Fernando on the drive back from Simi Valley. They thought it might be a good idea to run through the details of Harry Bath's testimony before meeting the lieutenant. Neither of them had eaten breakfast, and the roadside café seemed a popular spot judging by the number of cars parked outside. Addison's cheeseburger came off the grill full of flavor, and the cherry pie had taken him back to Christmas dinner at his grandparents' farmhouse. He even ordered a second cup of joe to wash the food down while they squared away Jed's notes. When Addison arrived at his desk in the afternoon, he was confident their instincts had been right all along.

It took five minutes to authenticate Harry Bath's information when they ran the boys' names through their system. Andrew King and Luke Green were both reported AWOL by their parole officers in 1994. Then after a quick-fire investigation, it was presumed they had either fallen victim to a shady past or just skipped town altogether. The recorded details were somewhat nebulous—probably because the investigating officers quickly lost interest in locating them and moved on to more critical cases.

"We should probably go speak to the boss," Addison suggested offhandedly.

Jed jumped up out of his chair like a jack-in-the-box.

"Are you feeling okay, kid?"

"I don't usually look forward to a meeting with Collins, but today is strangely different. For some reason, I find myself all fuzzy about being in the man's presence."

Addison chuckled to himself while they began making their

way across the room, ignoring a couple of detectives who attempted to wave them over. When they arrived at the lieutenant's office, he knocked three times before walking through the door.

Collins made it clear he was in no mood for shooting the shit, so Addison cut to the chase by providing a rundown of their meeting at Simi Valley. He included all the relevant details, except for the piece about the two missing youths. When he finished, Addison leaned back in his chair with a powerful sense of resolution.

"This dark priest believes that your group exists then," Collins conceded wearily. "And what did he say their name was again?"

"In Paucis," Jed replied. "It's Latin and translates as *The Few*, but as Mowbray said already, Harry Bath also told us how they had changed their name at some point."

Collins massaged both his temples as color mounted on his forehead.

"And he's provided you the name of a woman whose cousin is supposed to know people on the inside?" he queried effusively.

"Indeed, he did."

Addison decided to hold back the details of the two missing youths because he wanted to drop it into Collins's lap at the ultimate moment. Too much initial information often complicated matters that should otherwise be straightforward. Part of him may have just been waiting for the man to suggest their evidence was circumspect.

Collins drummed his fingers on the desk with an ornery expression.

"How do you suggest I present this development to the captain?" he queried warily.

It was the kind of response Addison had been sweating on.

"I have some more information which you need to be made aware of. It relates to a couple of matters that Harry Bath claims occurred back in 1994."

"Well, go on, man, let's hear it."

"There was a youngster named Andrew King who attended a group Bath was running from a house in Pasadena during that same year. The priest thinks these In Paucis people murdered Andrew and another kid, Luke Green."

"Should I inquire as to what this group was for, Mowbray?"

"The group isn't important."

"Tell me about these alleged victims, then."

Addison rehashed the details.

"It sounds to me like Harry Bath has spent too much time watching fuckin' horror movies on Netflix," Collins said. "Initiation sacrifices and blood-drinking?"

"There's more, Lieutenant."

Collins exhaled impatiently, waving his hands about in the air.

"Well, get on with it. I'm listening."

Addison paused briefly, enjoying the moment.

"Andrew King believed he was in grave danger and that his friend Luke had already been murdered. Harry Bath didn't give the story too much consideration until a few years later when he did some amateur snooping. Bath discovered both Andrew and Luke are listed on the missing person register. The first thing we did after arriving here this afternoon was putting their names into our system. It turns out they haven't been sighted or heard from since the winter of 1994. The boys' parole officers initially reported them after they failed to arrive at their appointments."

Addison felt confident these new facts were enough to revolutionize the investigation, so he remained silent while the lieutenant mulled over the details. When the quiet went longer than he anticipated, he decided to give Collins a not-so-subtle nudge.

"If you were to go upstairs and relay what I've just told you to the brass, then I imagine they will probably start slapping you on the back with a happy stick. I mean, it's not like you'd be approaching them on a hunch."

"I hear you, Mowbray. But put yourself in my shoes for a second. The captain has been camped under my ass all week, hollering about finding those damned drugs. He's insisting we keep this thing on track, and he's had a hard-on for the ketamine from the very beginning. There's no denying this is the hottest lead we've acquired thus far; however, I still need to present him with facts as to why we should readjust our focus.

"The department is reeling from a year of bad press, and this story has all the ingredients of a massive shit sandwich. Have you considered what it will be like if those cocksuckers at CNN get a hold of this info? They'd be climbing over the top of themselves to start throwing out stories about blood-drinking maniacs stalking the city. It's my balls on the chopping block here, and the vultures are circling overhead."

Addison heard the brick wall quality of voice Collins got whenever things began moving in a direction he hadn't intended upon heading. The captain's fascination with finding the chemicals explained why the lieutenant had been so resistant to their proposed ideas, while the external curiosity was compounding the tension he was experiencing. One incorrect conclusion could lead to failure, and nonperformance was no light affair in the homicide division. A misguided inquiry usually resulted in devastating circumstances.

"I completely understand where you're coming from, no question. But are you implying that you don't want us to investigate Bath's info any further? As it stands, every available officer is either on those phones out there or knocking on doors, chasing up people who have given us nothing. Now, I'm sure as hell not certain this group is connected to our guy, but it's just as relevant a lead as finding those drugs. We need to get as many irons in the fire as possible. Perhaps you should just keep your cards close for now and maybe fill the brass in after we've had a chance to run with this for a few days."

The lieutenant's pained expression suggested he might be buying into the proposal, or at the very least, seriously considering their reasons. Collins looked across at Jed like he was about to ask what his opinion on matters might be before returning his attention to Addison.

"Is Bath on record with these things he's told you?"

The priest made it clear he had no intention of being spoken to again, never mind going on record. He already believed he was taking a big gamble by talking with them; besides, they'd given their word, and Addison had no intention of breaking it.

"He wasn't prepared to make an official statement. We just turned up on his doorstep unannounced, and he could have sent us on our way. From where I'm standing, Bath gains nothing by telling us what he did, and maybe there's something very substantial for him to lose. Regardless, he won't be putting his name on anything."

Collins looked at Jed again.

"Do you intend to contribute something to this discussion, Perkins? Or you happy to continue staring up at the wall with that smug look on your face?"

Jed appeared unaffected by the jibe.

"I'm all for doing some serious detective work, sir. It's why I drove down to Simi Valley with my partner on our morning off. As for my being soundless, I have complete confidence in my partner's ability to articulate what it is we would like to do."

Collins smiled.

"You know what, Mowbray?"

"What's that, boss?"

"We may just make a detective out of this guy before we're done."

Addison nodded his agreement.

"I don't know what I'd do without him."

Collins's clear brown eyes displayed an affection he usually kept hidden. "Okay, what's next?"

"The first thing we need to do is track down this Cross woman so we can try to discover who her cousin is. Then we'll keep pressing her to see if there's anything else she can reveal. In the meantime, we should probably pray that another body doesn't turn up.

Collins pursed his lips like he did whenever he was rationalizing.

"You manage to get hold of your boy yet?"

"I plan on calling his mother tonight, as a matter of fact."

Collins nodded.

"Good to hear. What we do has a significant place, but family comes first. Nothing should ever be allowed to get in the way of our kin."

The man's heartfelt avowal probably deserved a verbal response. Instead, Addison made a face. Like always, there were things he never felt comfortable discussing.

"Now that the first victim has been identified as a medical student from London, you boys probably need to be preparing for the likelihood of the Feds becoming involved."

Addison had already considered this after learning about Emma Paul earlier on.

"Any word on when her family will be arriving to formally ID the body?"

Collins leaned back in his chair.

"They're expected to be flying in sometime tomorrow afternoon. So, have either of you got anything else for me, or are we done here?" he asked disingenuously. The man was renowned for bringing his meetings to an abrupt conclusion at times.

"No, that's all of it," Addison confirmed.

"All righty, then."

Both detectives nodded respectfully before moving out into the main office. They should have been feeling pleased by the idea that they may finally be on the killer's trail, but Addison was hardly upbeat. He walked back to his desk, trying hard to ignore the apprehension in his gut about where this rabbit hole would eventually take them.

# THIRTY

The blistering heat of the past week had finally subsided, but the late afternoon sun was still toasty enough to keep Edward inside the house. He looked at the clouds through a window and saw how they were so scarlet it seemed the angels were bleeding down celestial tears. Edward had never embraced summertime—the darkness was delayed, and there were generally more people to contend with when he hunted for prey. He closed his eyes and caressed Katherine's blackened hand, imagining that Linda was seated beside him. There'd been a period when he considered preserving their parts in formaldehyde but decided to allow corruption its course. After all, a piece of fruit was at its most fertile during decay.

Meagan Banks had called him once her meeting with the Old Man concluded at the compound in Adelanto, reassuring him that everything appeared to be hunky-dory for now. The shameless slut was coming to meet with him later in the evening, and he was surprised to find himself counting down the hours until her arrival.

They were going to weave themselves into an unholy trinity as they engaged in sex rituals and blood Magick, enticing Linda to enter their bodies so they could all experience another climax together. Each new sacrifice released a fresh burst of liveliness into the realm of the dead to increase his prospect of communicating with her ghost.

The room darkened when the sun disappeared behind a mass of low-hanging clouds before a sudden gust of wind shrilled outside the door like a dying cat. Despite the steady progress he was making, a wrench of dissatisfaction stirred his spirit, poking the beast who desired to kill differently than he'd been doing of late. It required unnatural persuasion to remain confined within the guiding principles of his Aleister Crowley books.

Edward loathed operating under such restraint. There had been moments he almost surrendered to the hunger while gaping down at the ladies inside the goat's-head pentagram. He would have relished bringing a hammer down to penetrate their skulls, exploding with unchecked savagery until all that remained was red mush. Nothing compared to the thrill he received from severing tendons and pulverizing bone, which was why he'd spent half the night finding a faceless stranger. It had felt good inserting another carcass to his masterpiece beneath the shack, filling one more seat at the table of rot.

He raised a silver goblet to his lips and tasted Emma's blood, enjoying the deep coppery flavor as it soured his tongue. A tart clarity dominated the strong aftertaste of her plasma. The bitter zing wasn't apparent in the other women, and Edward wondered why. He'd been expecting his moody disposition to improve upon drinking their fluids, yet his discontented attitude and desire for violence just refused to fade away. Maybe he needed to take a drive into the city when finished fucking Meagan and entice another vagabond to a flesh-splattered conclusion. It wasn't like he'd be risking much. There were few perils to be mindful of when butchering the displaced. The good people of America only cared when the victims came from reputable suburbs and contained the potential to contribute to their society in traditional ways.

The homeless man from last night arrived at the ranch with joy in his heart after being promised a warm bed and hot meal. Edward kept half the pledge by cooking the last supper, lingering expectantly while the stinking fleabag devoured every crumb. The vagrant thanked him through rotting teeth while he gorged upon his apple pie. Then after dessert, Edward retrieved a carving knife from the kitchen drawer and ran it across the bum's face, slicing through his cheek until raw flesh flopped down onto his chin. It took a few seconds for the ridiculous smile of gratification to abandon the beggar's lips, which made things slightly uncomfortable until he stopped thinking about the food inside his belly. Upon seeing the alarm reflected inside the wanderer's eyes, Edward became unhinged, slashing ferociously until the hobo no longer resembled anything human.

Whenever torturing mediocrity, he always attempted to picture each individual in a superior form. As a newborn wrapped with white linen or a beloved sibling opening their presents under the Christmas tree. The abstract thinking prevented any triviality from infecting his mind. They were more critter than a person at the end of it, and there wasn't much glory to be gained by killing bugs. He considered himself a composer of human impermanence, and there was an orchestra of dead people ringing inside his ears.

Edward continued sitting in pensive silence while he thought about how great it would be if Linda joined them later that night. Then after a brief period, he lifted himself off the couch and walked into the kitchen, where he returned Katherine's spoiling hand to the center shelf. He needed to get moving with the business of finding another princess, and time had no intention of slowing down. Maybe a session on the DMT would relax him before tomorrow presented a new opportunity to hunt for his next lookalike.

# THIRTY-ONE

The day flashed by after the meeting with Collins concluded. Addison was now sitting inside his house, trying to come to grips with the likelihood he would be working with the FBI soon. He'd spent the past hour slumped on the couch, sipping Jack Daniel's while thinking things through, still uncertain how he felt about the situation.

When the lieutenant took the call from Special Agent Rick Sharp ten minutes before Emma Paul's identity was released, he could barely contain his smile. Sharp quickly explained how they would be coming in to meet with them the following morning before Collins's grin spread to his face. The sudden appointment interrupted Addison's plans to tidy up the house. Jed wouldn't be thrilled about coming to work on Sunday either.

Emma Paul had modified the entire playing field around the case. The FBI doesn't usually stand by waiting for an invitation to impose upon local matters when an international tourist gets killed. Addison presumed the mayor might have facilitated proceedings by implying the city's holiday appeal was being adversely impacted by the investigation. However, any such assertion was just applesauce. In all his years, Addison had never seen a case affect the number of people flooding into the region each day.

The additional resources might prove helpful in locating Sarah Cross, but the special agent in charge could also apply constraints to the LAPD's participation. From the brief discussion he'd had with Collins, it seemed likely that a joint task force was on the cusp of being formed, and their direction forward would depend on whether Rick Sharp opted to treat them as equals or errand boys with a badge.

Addison spent the afternoon running Sarah Cross's name

through a range of databases, only to be left frustrated by a lack of success with his search. It was something of a commonplace identity, which required them to work through a considerable amount of irrelevant data for a negative result. At least no more women had been abducted at this point, as far as they could tell. But that situation might change throughout the night.

He intended to have another generous glass of whiskey, then perhaps he'd swallow a couple of sleepers to cloud the pictures in his mind. It was strange how he could be a thousand miles from the event which plagued him, yet the horror was eternally present as it waited faithfully in the corridors of his next sleep. Night terrors, insights, dreams—Addison's only ever came in the shape of flashbacks and allegations. He had resigned himself to the reality there was no way to avoid the enduring sadness inside his heart. Even though his father's homicide might be considered the incident that shaped his emotions, the origin of his loneliness remained unclear. He'd spent most of his life aboard a carriage destined for solitude, and his pain tainted every relationship he'd been involved in. It wasn't as if he'd never given things a red-hot go, but no matter how many occasions he attempted to go the journey, he always disembarked at the same location.

Collins's assertion about the significance of family had got him thinking. His son was forced interstate, and his influence on the boy was now secondary at best. Addison often expressed his love for Nate through muzzled tones of constraint. He'd tried raising the kid with principles that might endure beyond life's numerous storms, never insisting on telling him how things needed to be done. He believed it was best to allow children to learn from their mistakes, while Michelle wanted to shelter their son at every juncture. It seemed she would have preferred him to remain an innocent baby forever. But Addison understood what might be waiting around the next bend. A father lying dead on the side of a road, or even a grown man without answers, sitting inside an empty house while he stared into the bottom of a whiskey glass.

Addison grabbed his phone off the couch and hit speed dial on his ex-wife's home number, listening in frustration as the call threatened to go through to her voicemail again. He was about to give up when Michelle finally answered.

"Hello," she said.

"Hey, Michelle, it's Addison. Is Nate there?"

"Yeah, hang on. I'll get him for you."

Her indifference was something he'd become familiar with long ago. It seemed an age since they'd last spoken anything warm or gracious to one another. Addison heard the boy asking who it was, followed by padded feet running on the floor.

"Hey, Pop," Nate gushed.

"Hey, kid. How are you doing, buddy?"

A three-second pause caused Addison to smile. His son was contemplative, which was something to be respected in this world.

"I'm doing great. I made the basketball team, starting point guard," he proclaimed excitedly, unable to get the words out of his mouth quickly enough.

"Really?"

"Yep, it came down to me and two other kids. The list was up on the gym wall this morning, and I got the start. The first game is in three weeks."

"Wow, I don't know what to say. You're the first Mowbray ever to achieve a starting role in a high school team. I'm damn proud of you, boy." The memory of them shooting hoops together at the house in Eagle Rock hurt. He'd experienced despondency in various forms over the years, but never more intensely than right now.

"What about when you played football for the Lone Star Rangers?"

"I only made the starting team in my senior year. Besides, the point guard is like a quarterback, and I sure as heck wasn't a quarterback."

"Mom said she saw you on the television. Will you be on again soon?"

"You know me, son. I'd rather stay incognito."

Nate laughed in a way that made the heaviness around Addison's life feel lighter. "Did you shave, Pop?"

"Well, what do you think? You tell me."

"I think probably not."

"And I think you may be right."

The boy laughed again; it was a warm, embracing sound. "How's Jed doing?"

Jed had this manner of speaking to the kid that reminded Addison of his father. Tongue in cheek, yet still serious enough to make him feel like a grown-up.

"He's great. Just surfing at Santa Monica and meeting all the pretty girls like always. I'll be sure to let him know that you asked after him. He'll be thrilled."

"Yeah, tell him I said hi. Mom told me that I might be able to come and stay with you next year on the holidays," he said, his voice scaling upward again.

"Well, that sure sounds good to me."

"Do you know how long it will take to get from Phoenix to California?"

"It all depends on how you'd be traveling, son."

"Mom said I'd have to catch a bus."

Michelle had a phobia about planes.

"If you had to ride a bus, then you'd be looking at around seven hours. Luckily, I'm happy to buy you a plane ticket to make sure you get here in express time."

Another pause went long enough to make things slightly uneasy.

"Do you think you'll move to Arizona when you retire?'

Addison heard the longing in his son's question and could almost see his dark hair and sad brown eyes; it tugged at his heartstrings. Even though he didn't like to acknowledge it, he felt guilty about how he could be so distant from the boy. The barriers were supposed to ensure Nate never had to go through what he did while growing up, but his noble intent failed to make him feel any less of an asshole.

"I sure hope so, kiddo. Now, I need you to understand that it doesn't matter where I am or what I'm doing. You will always be at the very center of my thoughts."

Addison heard Michelle calling the boy away and needed to stop himself from asking the kid to put his mother back on the phone. He'd finally managed to get through to them, and making a fuss right now wouldn't benefit anyone.

"Mom's hollering at me. I think supper's ready."

"Okay, son. You go on and enjoy your supper, and I'll give you a call again in a couple of days to see how your practice is going."

"I love you, Pop."

"I love you too, kiddo. I'll speak with you soon."

"All right."

"Okay, bye."

"Bye."

When the line went dead, he just sat there for a while, thinking of all the things he might have said to the boy, before moping out to the kitchen for a refill of Jack Daniel's. He'd started contemplating the liquor burning his throat by the time he unscrewed the lid and pulled a swig directly from the bottle. After the whiskey settled in his belly, he took a cigarette and raised his lighter to the tip while drawing the smoke deep inside his lungs.

Dinner remained an afterthought as he made his way back to the living room and slumped himself down onto the couch. Isolation could be a reasonably comfortable companion when he came to accept it, so he resigned himself to stew in seclusion until the booze kicked in to bring the curtain down on his night.

# THIRTY-TWO

Coniglio watched a dark-haired waiter float between tables in the dining zone to place her martini down in front of her. The young man smiled while he inquired whether she needed anything else before moving along to a group of twentysomethings seated nearby. A Southern jazz band was preparing to hit the stage, and she was excited to see the show. Coniglio made sure she left the office half an hour early that afternoon to get herself ready in time to arrive at the club for dinner. Her Cajun catfish had come sautéed to perfection, and the goat cheese salad blended nicely with the chargrilled flavors of the main dish.

She made a few calls earlier in the day to see if anybody felt like accompanying her to the gig, but most of her friends were married and usually required notice to hit the town. The Catalina Bar and Grill was a renowned jazz venue situated on the western end of Sunset Boulevard. Their music roster was one of the best around, and even though they imposed a two-drink limit on all non-diners, people were packing into the place like sardines.

Most of the women here tonight appeared to be under forty and were either escorted by a male companion or gathered in groups at the bar. There was a period after her marriage ended when she would have felt self-conscious about being alone at a club. As if middle-aged unattachment were a social disorder to be ashamed of. Fortunately, her attitude transformed when she made a vow to keep doing all the groovy stuff she enjoyed.

Being single no longer made her feel inadequate. Her main concern these days was deflecting the uninvited attention she usually attracted from younger guys. She enjoyed watching them walk away in surprise, unable to comprehend how a mature woman could resist an opportunity to be with a man half her age. College had affirmed how random sex was overrated. Because for her, at least, intimacy and friendship went hand in hand.

Coniglio bit unconsciously at her lower lip while thinking about how she considered inviting Mowbray along in the afternoon. It took her ten minutes to conclude she should leave him alone after being fixated on the idea of asking him out for a drink. All her courage had just dissolved each time she went to pick up the phone. Her ambiguity resulted from rejection anxiety more than anything else; she certainly didn't feel daunted in the company of men. Forensic pathology meant working with the toughest guys in town—the kind who didn't mince their words in front of a lady. If Mowbray did have a genuine interest in getting to know her better, as she suspected was the case, then it would eventually play itself out. Until such time, she was content with appreciating the obscure treasures immersed within each new day. Besides, she had a duty to focus her energy on assisting in the perpetrator's apprehension, even more so when she considered what Mowbray said about him falling off the grid.

Coniglio sipped her martini while she checked her phone, pleased to find there were no new messages from the office. Lieutenant Collins called during the afternoon with the particulars on the two missing youths, which strengthened the likelihood the perp was part of a killing league. She had tried piecing together Mowbray's hypothesis and compared it to her findings in a bid to uncover something that indicated he was wrong. But after deliberating over the crimes' voracity and patterns, the more plausible his philosophy had seemed.

The inverted Christian cross suggested the offender's connection to the occult was probably legitimate, not to mention the lack of sexually inspired violence so prevalent in most sequential crimes. Mowbray's hunch had really unsettled her. Because if he was right in his supposition about the killer belonging to something greater than himself, did it imply the group was aware of the psychopath's actions, or perhaps even approved them? She had never faced a community of evil, and it presented a scenario better left unknown.

Coniglio examined her makeup while she directed her thoughts onto something less intense. The jazz band was expected on stage shortly, and there weren't going to be any calls coming through to her phone. She was free to enjoy a few martinis tonight, and whatever tomorrow sent her way, she would deal with.

The attractive waiter was wiping down a table nearby, so Coniglio finished the drink and raised her empty glass in the air to gain his attention. She'd already spent too much time reflecting on the dead. Tonight, was all about living, and she intended to let her hair down in doing just that.

# THIRTY-THREE

An angry expression came over Collins's face as Jed apologized to everyone in the room for his late arrival. Addison observed his partner with trivial amusement, smiling at the way he pretended not to notice the heat behind the lieutenant's glare. The kid was adept at simulating unawareness when it came to the boss. Addison recognized a spark ripple across Special Agent Katy Pearce's features. It was a common occurrence whenever a lady encountered his partner for the first time. The kid often liquefied hearts with a simple hello.

Pearce looked to be Jed's age with straight honey-blond hair that hung past her shoulders. The navy-colored suit she wore failed to disguise the shapely body resting beneath. Her natural sun-kissed complexion and light green eyes complemented a self-assured style and conveyed a sense of comfort among men. Pearce may well have been the most appealing agent Addison had ever seen, but everything needed to remain above board if they were working together. Most law enforcement love affairs eventually soured, and Addison didn't want to get the FBI offside because of an aching heart.

Rick Sharp was the special agent in charge, a lanky, middle-aged African American with closely cropped, receding hair and smooth features. Sharp presented like a man familiar with determining the rules. He displayed a sophisticated composure in his approach. Dressed in a black suit with polished shoes, he made Addison feel more shabby than usual. At least Jed looked a million bucks. Collins, too, though that was commonplace for the both of them in almost every circumstance.

"Let's get down to business, then, shall we?" Sharp recommended. "I don't imagine you guys are too surprised by our presence here this morning. Your serial killer has managed to get the whole damn country into a spin. Everybody from Tennessee to New York seems to be following the investigation in some manner. The Bureau was happy to leave things in your capable hands up until now, but when CID received word of the first victim's tourist status, they decided that we needed to get involved."

Sharp paused while he fixated on the detectives. Addison assumed he was attempting to get a read on what they thought of his straight-to-the-point approach.

"Now, I know you guys have been working your butts off and are way ahead of us here," he continued. "So, I could sure use a quick rundown on where things presently stand."

Addison shifted in his chair. "You mind filling us in on your plans for the case first?" he asked, skeptical.

Sharp offered an appeasing smile. "I want to try to outline a cohesive plan on how we can best work together on this, and I don't intend to step on anyone's toes along the way. Are you guys down with that?"

Addison considered bunting back the question, but Collins was delighted by the prospect of having federal assistance, so he just pulled a face and held his tongue instead. When a scratchy silence descended into the room, the lieutenant leaned forward on his desk.

"You bet your ass we're down with that, ain't that right, Detective Mowbray?"

"Sure thing," Addison replied, unconsciously pulling at his tie. "Although I have to say, I thought you guys might have been more interested in the vigilante."

Sharp smiled perceptively. "The vigilante is targeting notorious criminals, and so long as it remains that way, then he's all yours."

"That's mighty generous of you, Agent Sharp."

Sharp opened his palms to signify a truce. "There's no need to be so formal. Call me Rick. So, who wants to kick things off?"

Collins had an unusual expression on his face which made him appear like he'd been asked a riddle he didn't know the answer to. Still, the detectives understood when to remain silent.

"We've been trying to locate where the asshole gets his chemicals from, and I've got half the division following up on anything else that comes in. My lead detectives here have recently obtained some interesting info. I'll allow them to fill you in on the details."

Addison needed to stop himself from laughing as the two agents turned their attention toward him with an unblinking stare. Talk about being thrown under the bus.

"My partner and I are in the process of tracking down a woman named Sarah Cross. We believe she knows a certain group of people who might be capable of killing in a manner which fits the crimes."

Neither agent reacted, but Sharp was eyeing him with intent.

"Can I inquire as to what kind of group they are supposed to be?" he said before looking sideways at Jed with a dubious glance. The kid remained cool and assured while leaning back silently in his chair with a pensive smile.

"A collective of some kind, and it's been alleged that their associates kill for pleasure, sacrifice people in satanic rituals, and drink human blood," Addison said.

Both agents exchanged disbelieving expressions.

"Have you guys paused to consider the kind of bullshit a story like this will cause? Don't you remember what happened during the mid-nineties?" Sharp challenged.

"We sure have, Rick," Addison responded sardonically. "The West Memphis Three were primarily responsible for lighting that bad fuse, but as far as I can tell, the entire investigation was mishandled from the very start. Unsurprisingly, the case generated a swarm of public hysteria, which led to unwarranted allegations about black rituals occurring in the suburbs. Then, after millions of tax dollars were burnt in the process, it was deemed they were all looking for something that had never existed in the first place."

Sharp's face changed slightly. "All right, tell us about this group of yours," he suggested through a forced smile.

"As you know, all three victims are similar in appearance and missing different body parts. The most recent woman had the main artery in her neck severed. The examiner believes the perp may have an affiliation with the blood."

Sharp rolled his shoulders. "But the blood loss in all three victims can just as easily be attributed to the seriousness of their injuries, can it not?" he reasoned. "The trauma was extensive."

"It isn't something we can be certain of. However, the method he used to kill Jennifer Hill supports the theory he intentionally bleeds them out. The corpses were branded with an inverted Christian cross. Are you aware of what the symbol represents?"

Sharp and Pearce nodded their heads.

"The perpetrator is using chloroform during the abductions. Then he injects the victims with hospital-grade ketamine as a precursor to their execution. There's zero evidence of any sexual assault and no frenzied attack brought on by lust. I believe he may be working his way toward a particular goal, and if he's successful, he'll likely ride off into the sunset. Or perhaps he might be attempting to control himself for reasons still unknown and is on the verge of erupting. Either way, a link to the occult seems more than probable."

Sharp appeared uncertain as he leaned forward in his chair. "I really can't see how this has anything to do with a cult, though. I'm not so sure you'd want information about the possibility of blood-drinking murderers becoming public. If it got out, you'd have every right-winger in the country calling your hotline about their neighbor next door. Don't get me wrong, I can understand why you're thinking the way you are, but we'll need more if you expect us to take your suspicions about a cult seriously."

Addison enjoyed the trace of sarcasm he heard in Sharp's voice. "I'm only just getting started."

"And I'm all ears," Sharp replied irritably.

"We recently received a call from a citizen who'd provided intel on another LAPD case several years ago. When my partner and I followed up on what she told us, we learned of a group who used to go by the name In Paucis. It's been alleged these people have been operating since the nineties, perhaps even longer."

Sharp maintained a forward lean in his chair. "In Paucis . . . is that Italian?"

"Not quite, it's Latin and translates as *The Few*, but we were advised they go by something else these days. The individual who spoke with us is well versed in these kinds of matters, and he was obstinate in his belief that the people who belong to this group still exist. He also presumed they would be highly active in occultic style murder."

Sharp kept a cynical gaze as he processed what he'd just heard. "And where are they now?" he asked. "Allegedly."

"That is what we're hoping to discover, Rick. This Cross woman we're searching for is supposed to have a relative who associated with the group several years ago."

Agent Pearce touched her partner on the forearm. "Can I ask who it was that passed on this intel to you?"

"Sure, you can," Addison quipped. "But we won't be divulging a name."

Sharp looked bemused. "And why is that, exactly?"

"Because we gave our word that they would remain anonymous. I don't know about you guys, but we in the LAPD try awfully hard to ensure our snitches continue breathing."

Sharp and Pearce communicated silently with their eyes.

"Is this informant someone you use regularly?" Pearce asked.

"Nope, it was the first and final occasion that we'll speak with them."

Sharp looked confused. "Yet you're prepared to accept their information as though it's coming from a seasoned stool pigeon. How the hell does that work?"

Jed chuckled under his breath. The kid knew what was about to come as Addison set about explaining what they uncovered in Harry Bath's grimy living room. The agents listened while he recounted the details, and by the time he finished, Sharp was fidgeting like a caged monkey while Pearce's mouth had fallen agape. Addison didn't think it was necessary to elaborate further, so he sat back and waited as they connected the dots. Neither of them appeared to be massaging their egos, and he entertained the possibility they might turn out to be okay.

"Has anybody followed up with their family or friends?" Pearce asked.

"They were wards of the state from a young age. In and out of juvie their entire lives. The details are a bit sketchy; however, it doesn't appear there is anyone to speak with."

Sharp looked over at Collins. "Can I inquire as to what your thoughts are on this?"

The lieutenant's office had suddenly become a very contemplative space.

"When Mowbray and Perkins first suggested to me that the homicides contained satanic undertones, I certainly wasn't thrilled by the notion. The last thing I wanted to do was encourage the public to start embarking on neighborhood witch hunts. Much like you, it seems. I felt the brand might be intended to create a diversion.

"The captain instructed me to focus a large portion of our resources into finding out where the asshole might be acquiring the ketamine from, and the purity of the chemical made it a valid command. But after hearing about what these two have managed to unearth, my opinion on the matter has changed. I will be assisting them however I can with the line of inquiry they're currently on."

"Who's the medical examiner?" Sharp asked, turning to Addison.

"Lilly Coniglio, who is probably best on staff," he answered, listening on uncomfortably as Jed snickered quietly beside him.

"We'll need to contact her and arrange for the victim reports to be sent over to our offices. Do you have a direct number? We can go through the regular channels if required, but I'd prefer not to waste any time where we don't need to."

"Sure thing," Addison replied, resisting an urge to shoot a frown in Jed's direction as the agents connected with their eyes again.

"Do you mind if we step outside for a moment?" Sharp asked.

Collins raised two open hands. "Not at all. Take as much time as you need."

"Much appreciated, Lieutenant. I don't imagine we'll be long."

When the two agents had left the room, Jed exhaled. "Looks like we're about to become a joint task force, Ad."

The boss's glare sent hot ice in the kid's direction.

"A task force you're damn well lucky to be a part of, Perkins. If you had come lumbering through my door ten seconds later than you did, the only thing your ass would be doing is answering those fucking phones."

Addison enjoyed watching his partner squirm. "Yeah, I'm sorry. There was a seriously bad fender-bender on the main artery, and it took me half an hour to get past the freakin' pile up," he answered genuinely.

"So, what do you think, Mowbray?" Collins inquired.

Addison knew he was referring to the FBI coming on board. "About what?"

"About them out there? What the fuck do you think I'd be referring to?"

"Well, I imagine you're in a much cheerier place right now."

Collins laughed in disbelief. "Damned right I am. But more importantly, the captain will be overjoyed. Because now we won't be the only target when the press fires off with their loaded questions."

Addison pressed back into his chair. "I guess it all depends on the way they do business and how it translates to our division. But I certainly don't want to be demoted onto the Bureau's mop-up squad."

A gentle knock ended the discussion before the agents stepped back inside the room. Sharp closed the door behind his partner as they returned to their chairs.

"Let me say, we appreciate you all sharing this hard-earned intel with us," Sharp declared. "We would like to provide our assistance in tracking down this Cross woman you've been attempting to locate, and we can also help with the search for the chemicals. There is no reason whatsoever to change anything you're presently doing. All I ask is that you share any findings with us, and we'll commit to doing the same in return."

The formation of a joint task force wasn't unexpected. Whether the investigation continued moving forward in a balanced manner was anybody's guess, but Addison sure wouldn't be holding his breath. For the sake of appearances, he nodded.

"Sure thing."

Agent Sharp seemed genuinely pleased. "Excellent. Is there anything else you think we need to know?"

Addison shook his head. "Nope, that's everything we have. Hopefully, things might change soon if we get lucky with the woman. I have a question of my own, though."

Agent Sharp extended an open palm. "Shoot."

"In the likely situation that another body turns up in those hills, are my partner and I still going to be working the scene?" he asked, staring Sharp dead in the eye.

"I guarantee you both will. We've got a much better chance of apprehending this sick asshole by working together on this. It's a definite yes as far as that goes. The only real difference is you'll be sharing your info with me, and vice versa. I think a good place for us to start is by helping you locate Sarah Cross, do you agree?"

Addison did agree; finding her was paramount. "Yeah, I certainly do."

"Great," Sharp concurred, placing his card down on top of the lieutenant's desk. "We're going to need to get a copy of everything you have."

Collins nodded. "Consider it done."

A stiff kind of unity filtered into the room as Addison considered whether the Feds' additional resources might provide the boost this investigation was crying out for. There were no assurances the group was responsible for the hills' victims but finding them was the best lead they presently had. If the cards happened to start falling their way in a couple of important areas, then some severe heat might be about to come down on the perpetrator.

# THIRTY-FOUR

Many people were wandering around inside the farmers market, making it easier for Edward to follow the young lady who grabbed his attention in the parking lot outside. He kept pace with her from twenty yards while she drifted down the aisles, pausing here and there at various food vendors along the way.

She seemed a perfect replica of Linda, and Edward considered whether his dead girlfriend had somehow found her way back into natural life. He observed her floral beach dress as it wrapped her thighs, barely containing the twisted desire that threatened to expose his genuine nature before a crowd of strangers. Her blond hair, golden complexion, and athletic body were a seamless match. Edward found himself dreaming about her bruised nakedness as his erection turned to stone. She was the precursor he'd been waiting for—the verification that his blood offerings were well received in the underworld.

When Edward went hunting for the first three women, he'd spent hours just searching for an appropriate target. But this morning, he nearly drove over the top of Linda's lookalike while turning off Third Street. She even flashed a cheery smile of appreciation after he waved her past, utterly oblivious to the fate she'd wandered into. He'd been feeling exceptionally randy of late, probably because there was nothing sexual in the way he dominated the other women. It was already a dangerous strategy to be drawing the authorities to their corpses when he finished bleeding them out, and he couldn't risk leaving any DNA inside the bodies.

The erotic burn he experienced while synchronizing their misery was eventually released in other ways. However, the pulse inside Edward's pants was unpleasantly boiling his blood. He felt like a tormented eunuch with ten young virgins sliding all over him, entirely incapable of obtaining a release. Edward would relish slurping upon her various fluids and punishing her body to the point of compliance, whittling her into an obedient little doll to entertain him on those peculiar days when he couldn't be bothered finding someone to kill.

Everything appeared to be coming along nicely. The only real impediment he needed to be mindful of was the Old Man and the conceited assholes within Filii Reprobi. Each girl had eventually found their way to him without too much bother. He spotted Emma Paul coming out of a YHA in West Hollywood before seizing her as she strolled back from a house party. Then he tailed Katherine Schneider home from a gastropub in Culver City, surprising her inside Griffith Park—of all locations—the following day. It had taken him a little longer to get his hands on Jennifer Hill after sighting her at a yoga center, and now he was within touching distance of capturing the best prize of them all.

Edward was meticulous during the abductions to ensure the victims remained in pristine condition. His strength would have been more than sufficient when it came time to snatch them, but the chloroform removed their ability to resist. He understood how everyone had a line-in-the-sand moment where fear surrendered its control and self-preservation took over. Subduing a person was quite gripping when undertaken from an unlosable position, watching them claw their way toward an illusion with a mouthful of sand. However, physical battles usually caused an injury, and he required each of the girls to be well preserved until their end.

He decided to drive out to the farmers market this morning after receiving a vivid picture of Linda during the night. They'd been walking together at this location, just as they'd done on numerous occasions in the past. Edward believed in unpacking his dreams. There was often prophetic guidance concealed among the imagery. Sleep occurred within a cryptic dimension where he frequently resolved unsettled issues. But most people just ignored their visions, and in doing so, they forfeited treasure without ever knowing it.

It was somewhat poetic to have found such a perfect replacement here. Linda had been fond of this place, singing, "Come meet me at Third and Fairfax," whenever she wanted to spend a night at home mastering a recipe. Edward recalled how he fantasized about hurting children in the restroom while Linda went searching for ingredients. It was weird how he could appreciate the attraction of the market now that she was gone. There were probably leftover fragments of his sweetheart waiting to be unearthed within the walls of these stores—familiar traces and smells. Still, sentimentality was of little concern right now because there was an accurate replica of his dead girlfriend only fifteen yards from where he was standing—an almost mirror image with a face like an angel and a body made in hell.

Edward stopped near a pie shop entrance while the doppelganger went into a store to buy fresh produce. She studied a pineapple and took a backward step to allow room for a mother with two children to pass by. After choosing a banana, his angel breezed down to the cashier, where she handed over her money with a perfect hand. Edward's arousal escalated as she rested the fruit on her thigh to apply balm onto her bow-shaped lips, waiting till she exited before positioning himself behind a group of tourists to resume his tail.

When the lookalike increased her speed, Edward slipped out from behind the travelers to keep pace. He saw that she was making an impression on several men as she moved toward the exit, and he advanced cautiously like a shifting mass of fluid while he shadowed her out the door. Edward slipped a phone from his coat pocket, pulling down the brim of his cap and scanning the area with a careful sweep of his eyes. Warm summer air hit his face, and he eased into a more casual stride.

A blaring car horn merged with the shriek of a crying baby to replace the buzz of activity from inside. Edward watched the girl approach a blue Toyota hatchback, pausing as she opened the driver's door and placed her bags on the passenger seat. The instant she entered the car, he made his move—closing space while talking loudly into his phone, timing the moment where he slammed his case against the taillight. Edward bent down to retrieve his props, and when he straightened, she was standing nearby with hands-on-hips, shaking her head like some goddess of confusion.

"Damnit, I am such a dumbass," he said sheepishly with stooped shoulders. "I was so darn busy talking on the phone and wasn't paying attention to where I was going."

A look of reprieve flashed over her face at the realization he wasn't seeking injury compensation like many low-classed scammers in the city. It was entertaining to watch.

"What happened?" she snapped.

Her moist lips caused his cock to catch fire again as he pointed his finger at the cracked paint and busted plastic, struggling for control.

"My case has collided with your vehicle, I'm afraid," he replied uncertainly, studying the slender curve of her ass when she bent over to inspect the damage to her car. He imagined biting into her flesh before she turned back to face him with a frown.

"Well, what are you going to do about it?" she asked with exasperation.

Edward crouched down to open his briefcase. He could smell a caramel fragrance coming from her legs and very nearly lost his mind.

"My name is Gary Klein; I live in Santa Monica, and seeing as this is not your fault, I'd like to pay for the repairs." His tone was legit as he removed a bogus license and extended it toward her. She studied the ID with a crinkled brow while looking at his face.

Edward raised his hands in trustworthy surrender. "Why don't you just take down my particulars, then when you get a quote for the cost to have this damage repaired, I'll send you a check. What's your name?"

He watched her expression soften.

"I'm Paige," she replied. "Paige Harding."

# THIRTY-FIVE

Addison was surprised when Coniglio called to suggest they meet up for a coffee to discuss the Bureau's participation in the case. Typically, when they were together, a crime scene was to be worked, or some cause of death needed to be determined. Her invitation was likely all business, but it still left him feeling excited.

After taking a shower, he slipped on a pair of Wrangler jeans with a red check shirt and headed out the door. The Sunday traffic leading onto Glendale Freeway was light, and he used the fifteen-minute drive getting his thoughts into uniformed alignment. He checked the time while continuing down into Echo Park, taking a left into a side street of stucco apartments and faded bungalows. Addison quickly found a parking space before checking his appearance and making his way back up to Sunset Boulevard.

Some asshole almost knocked him over as he came bustling up the sidewalk at a three-quarter pace. The young runner had a one-dimensional glare and appeared insensible of anyone who happened to be walking nearby. There was a menacing resolve to his gait. A real "stay the fuck out of my way" aura, which seemed to be the rage with many running enthusiasts these days. Headphones pumped music into his ears while his feet slapped against the ground in a monotonous rhythmical beat.

The "me first" attitude of contemporary America pissed off Addison. But he refocused on the lovely weather and how he wasn't expected at his desk until the following day. Distant buildings appeared to have been rendered impressionistic by some unknown artist in the sky. There was always a touch of randomness to grab hold of a person's attention in this city. Los Angeles was like a vast lucky dip of people, places, and things, offering everything from the good to the downright horrible.

When Addison spotted Woodcat Coffee Bar up ahead, he continued in an unhurried stroll to make his way inside. Coniglio was seated at a table halfway down the room, staring curiously at her phone. She was an advertisement for vitality in a white summer dress that accentuated her soft olive complexion. Her brown hair fell loosely past her shoulders, and there was more makeup on her face than she wore on the job.

Addison realized he was feeling unsure of himself and thought back to what Jed said while standing inside the parking station a few days earlier. There were approximately twenty people scattered throughout the room, all of them seemingly oblivious to his presence. The modern rustic interior was too trendy for his taste, although the aroma of fresh coffee beans was undoubtedly enticing.

Coniglio flashed a smile when he approached the table. Her brown eyes appeared deeply mysterious among the shifting shadows inside the room. Addison found himself briefly entranced by the liberty of her gaze, nodding while he lowered himself into a chair before a blond-haired waiter with sleeve tattoos floated up like gun smoke.

Neither of them wasted much time choosing off the menu, and they chatted in general terms until their beverages arrived. Addison was impressed when the coffee mugs were placed in front of them a few minutes later, watching Coniglio as she stirred her latte and blew softly over the cream.

"Mm . . . this is delicious," she said cheerfully. "They source the beans from an organic company in San Francisco. Their pastries are amazing as well."

Addison considered pointing out that he'd only seen her drinking tea but sipped his cappuccino instead. It wasn't like he was any kind of authority when it came to coffee; however, the flavor was much smoother than he was used to.

"I have to say, Coniglio, this here is some good mud."

She raised her eyebrows in surprise.

"You make it sound unexpected."

"I've always believed the best kind of anything usually comes out of places not so big on the interior bling. I'm more accustomed to dark corners and red-checkered table linen."

Coniglio giggled enthusiastically.

"You are Texas to the bone, aren't you? All dirt, dust, and attitude. However, I do agree with your estimation to a point. A swanky interior doesn't always equate to good produce. Nevertheless, in my vast experience of dining out, a well-presented core and quality service will often be found hand in hand."

Addison nodded.

"The Feds sure didn't drag their feet chasing you up."

"Well, if they're going to be coming on board, you'd want them to be competent. Rick Sharp seemed okay over the phone. What's your read on him?"

Addison considered the question for a good few seconds; he didn't like to estimate the character of a person he didn't know.

"He seemed all right, I guess, could have been a darn sight worse, but it's way too early to know for sure. Sharp may have played the part of the good guy to make sure we handed him over everything we've got. We'll get ourselves a better idea of what he's all about when the next body gets called in. If he holds to his word and keeps us in the loop, then their help will probably turn out to be a good thing. What about you, Coniglio? You got any secrets inside that head of yours you feel like sharing with me?"

Coniglio appeared slightly startled by his question. "About what?" she asked nervously.

"About the investigation," he chuckled. "What the heck did you think I meant?"

Coniglio felt her cheeks warming and prayed her awkwardness wasn't apparent. "I wasn't sure if you were referring to the Feds coming on board or to the case itself . . . Actually, I didn't know what you were getting at just now. But in answer to your question, I haven't found any supplementary data which might extend on what we already know. I have been thinking further on what you boys suggested at Mount Lee, though, and this thing probably is bigger than just the one person."

Addison noticed Coniglio was blushing and didn't know why.

"What did you come up with?"

"Lieutenant Collins filled me in on those two youths who went missing in 1994. He also confirmed a cult might be involved in their deaths. What are they called again?"

"In Paucis," Addison confirmed.

"Which is Latin, right?"

"Yeah. It translates as *The Few*, but apparently, they no longer go by the name."

"There's not much out there capable of spooking me these days, and I've pretty much seen it all as far as blood and guts are concerned. But a community of killers . . . the very thought creeps the hell out of me. I might end up leaving my reading lamp on when I go to bed tonight. Can you believe that?"

It was the only occasion he could remember seeing Coniglio show any sign of vulnerability, and her honesty made him feel kind of special. The transparency added yet another layer to her dynamic, jiggling at the lure he was already attracted to. Still, he could certainly understand where she was coming from. There were times when this investigation made his skin feel like it was crawling off his body. Addison usually felt vindicated if his hunches turned out to be accurate, but he may have preferred to be off the mark in this instance.

"There's nothing weird about being disturbed by all this, Coniglio, nothing whatsoever. It's a distressing thought, all right. By the way, I was going to give you a call first thing Monday morning to bring you up to speed with everything. I knew you had the day off and didn't want to intrude on your rest unless it was necessary."

Coniglio raised her hands in the air with a gentle smile.

"There's no need to explain yourself, Mowbray. I probably would have appreciated being kept in the dark until I was back in the office, truth be told."

The susceptibility he'd picked up on earlier was still present, which made her appear uncertain of herself. Not a trait he'd associated with the woman in the past. Part of him wanted to reach out and reassure her that everything was going to be okay.

"Did Collins explain how we got the name of a woman who allegedly knows someone close to the group?" Addison asked, watching as her eyes sparked into life.

"No, he didn't. Wow, have you managed to track her down?"

"Not yet, but with the Feds involved, hopefully we'll have an address soon."

Coniglio nodded earnestly. "What if those girls are just the tip of the iceberg?"

Addison thought he understood what she was getting at but pressed her anyway. "Are you referring to the likelihood there might be more than one perp involved or a whole bunch of corpses we know nothing about?"

"Both, I guess. I mean, some sociopaths manage to contain their depravity by accessing alternate platforms to get themselves off. But when a psychopath becomes active, they no longer receive much gratification by staring at an image on a screen. It's like stepping inside a cage with a starving lion and offering up a plate of vegetables. A predator will just do what comes naturally and act on the desire. If a group started killing people thirty years ago, then it goes without saying that there are victims we're not even aware of. But there's one thing which doesn't seem to fit. Why would they choose to start leaving their bodies out in the open all of a sudden?"

She was a smart lady. Addison had been mulling over precisely the same question himself, and thus far, all it did was cloud the waters. Nothing about this case was simple.

They both reached for a napkin on the table, and his fingers brushed across the back of Coniglio's hand. Then as Addison went to apologize, the look in her eyes suggested she may have appreciated the contact, so he smiled as an alternative. There was a depth to Coniglio that appealed to him more than just a physical attraction—something which had been missing in his marriage from the very start. Addison held fast to her gaze until her face started to glow in four different shades of pink. *Maybe the kid was right, after all*, he thought to himself, grinning on the inside through a belly of smooth coffee.

# THIRTY-SIX

The three Armenian gangsters made an intimidating presence as they sat at a corner table at the Abovyan strip club in North Hollywood. Narek sipped contentedly at his Ararat Brandy without a care in the world. Apart from the boss's fortified residence in Glendale, there was no safer place from which to drink the night away. Fingers of smoke twisted out from the stage to form serpent-like patterns while a world-weary dancer twirled herself around a pole. Hazy darkness saturated the lounge area in an almost swaying form as age-speckled lights provided a dim glow above the shadows.

Narek watched the stripper with a critical eye. She appeared to be well past her expiration date and needed to contemplate taking her cunt into retirement. Certain bitches must see something in their reflection that nobody else did. Or maybe they just kept looking in the wrong fuckin' mirror. Despite the wrinkled skank polluting the ambiance, he felt at home among the lingering odor of sweat, stale cigarettes, and cheap cologne. There were upmarket titty bars in town with clean air and pompous waiting staff, but they lacked atmosphere. The Abovyan was a nest of immorality where the great unwashed could come for a small taste of the players' lifestyle.

The only punters inside the joint were two middle-aged perverts who looked as if they hadn't been fucked by anything human for an awfully long time. At least they wouldn't be causing any trouble this afternoon. Davit kept ample security around to ensure the girls' safety; however, Narek and the boys would lend a hand whenever they happened to be here. Most of the regular pissants usually behaved themselves and only started bitching about the overpriced liquor after they slipped too much cash down a silken thong. Occasionally they got all hooched up to thinking their crumpled bills could acquire them a taste of the snatch on show, but a good fuckin' kicking brought them back to their senses real fast. Most problems occurred in the private rooms when the punters started demanding more than a lap dance. Stag parties often brought trouble, and weekends could get heated when 2 a.m. regulations shut down traditional nightclubs around the city.

A youthful banger named Arman tapped Narek on the arm and pointed his head at one of the fat fucks who was rubbernecking the pussy on stage. The unfortunate punter's eyeglasses magnified his peepers, and he fashioned his receding hair in a Hermes Wing comb-over. He looked the type of creep who'd get busted pulling on his pecker in a park when all the kiddies finished school. A deviant skunk from the very moment his melon popped out of his momma's clam. Davit employed middle-of-the-road dancers for the quiet shifts; germy bitches with stretched assholes who couldn't land a gig on the night roster. But it sure as hell wasn't bothering this dipshit any.

"What a stupid motherfucker," Arman declared hatefully. "He's been sitting there sipping on juice for over an hour, and I haven't seen him tip any girls, neither. We should kick his ass to the curb before he starts fiddling with his cock."

Narek took a mouthful of brandy while he considered what Arman said. The kid made a valid point, although he had no interest in taking part in a random tune-up after the events of the past few days. It was good to be sitting back, and his itch for violence had already been scratched by Jamie Callahan and the two brothers from Watts.

"Screw it, Arman, leave him be. I wouldn't be throwing any cash at that dried-out pussy if I were a customer." He slid a bag of cocaine across the table. "Just have another line and chill the fuck out. The sexy cunt will be starting soon. Then you can pick one to bounce on your cock, sit on your face, or whatever else you want them to do. Meantime, those two kiddy fiddlers will be in a dirty room somewhere fucking their hands with nothing but the memory of her C-grade tits to fall back on."

An expression of outrage flashed across the younger hood's face as he squared his shoulders like a boxer readying himself for a fight. He was an imposing kid with a muscular frame, and his beady rodent eyes never remained motionless for long. Arman looked as if he were about to contest the suggestion before slumping into his chair with a scowl. The son of a bitch was just a low-cost imitation of Narek in his Adidas tracksuit and Nike runners, another wannabe contender for the crown. Arman eyed the drugs eagerly, but his downcast expression implied he intended to brood. Bedros swooped in and tapped a generous helping of powder onto the table, a gold bracelet jangling around his wrist.

"Just one bitch, you say?" Bedros teased.

Narek understood what he was getting at. "One, two, three—who gives a fuck? The point I'm trying to make is that Rocky here doesn't need to start looking to beat up on someone every time we go out."

Bedros grinned through gapped teeth.

Arman was twenty-two and had only been initiated into the Armenian Power for three years. Like many of the younger guys, he tried to demonstrate his devotion by flexing his muscles and beating his chest like a fucking ape. It was mildly entertaining in small doses, but mostly it was a pain in the ass.

Narek was past the point of having to act ballsy. Everyone was well acquainted with his propensity for violence. He'd encountered his share of people who pretended like they were cold over the years. Brownie queens who talked a red-hot game, praying the world didn't catch onto the framework—that they were just fucking pussies. A few of them had managed to pull off the sham for a while. Then they exposed themselves by throwing out smack to a real OG and got shanked for their efforts. Narek was not one of those people, so he never had to speak a great deal about the kind of pain he was capable of inflicting.

When Bedros finished crushing the cocaine, he used a fake license to chop three lines before sucking the drugs up his nose through a straw with a thunderous snort.

"I haven't eaten anything since breakfast," he announced proudly.

Narek's mouth pricked into a smile as he shook his head.

"Yeah, well, maybe you should be doing more of this shit, brother. See if you can't crush that incessant fuckin' appetite of yours. If you continue eating everything in sight, your ticker will pack it in one day soon. Then who would I have to keep me company in the car when I have to go and kill the next cocksucker?"

Bedros stared back at him from across the table with feigned insult, disregarding Arman and his persistent sulking. Narek held firm to his gaze while he spread a fleshy hand over his heart and began breathing in short, exaggerated surges. When they burst into a fit of hysterical laughter, Arman glared at them from across the table.

"What?" he snapped.

"What do you mean, what?" Narek challenged.

"What's so funny?"

Arman had been born in Glendale Memorial Hospital, and the only thing Armenian about him was his faggy fuckin' name. He was one tough kid all right but lacked the intelligence to be successful on the street. Narek pointed toward the slobby punter they'd been scoping out moments earlier.

"That fuckin' asshole just flopped his big cock out," he confided, spacing his hands a good twelve inches apart. "It was this big, Arman. I kid you not."

The two older men sat back and observed while their comrade jumped out of his chair and set off to where the unlucky Gyot was sitting, roaring in stitches as the young hood smashed the dicklicker's face into the side of the stage and began stomping over his body. When Narek spotted the other pervert dashing toward the street, he decided enough was enough. The poor chent would likely have several broken bones and shattered teeth, which meant someone would have to drop him at the emergency room. Arman's mindlessness had provided them with a laugh, but the boss would lose his shit if the creep went belly up inside the club.

Narek slapped Bedros on the leg.

"Go stop the moron before he kills him, brother. Then tell him to pick his eyeglasses up off the floor, get the car and drop the dirty bastard to a hospital."

Bedros got to his feet, a couple of tears made a glistening trail down his cheeks.

"All balls, no brain," he replied through a grin.

Narek looked up and nodded.

"That's why so many young ones never make it to thirty," he lamented, smiling as he leaned over the table to enjoy a fat line of coke.

# THIRTY-SEVEN

The Old Man felt upbeat as he strolled along the corridor below the Adelanto compound, disregarding the terror-stricken faces that stared back at him from inside the reinforced steel cages. Annie Johnston was on his mind this evening. He'd kept her locked away for almost twenty years, and even though she no longer served many purposes, the unfortunate bitch had supplied him with something near to lasting affection. The bitter stench of her foul body drifted out to him as he neared her enclosure, and he crouched down low to call her name.

"Annie, my poor sweet Annie . . . what have you become?"

He remembered how her former brilliance had still been evident ten years ago, thinking of the long golden hair that now was a matted white mess. Annie considered him with vacant recognition. Her flesh looked as if it was melting off her bones as her cheeks sagged like jowls made of leather. Wet lesions coated her skin, and the gagging odor of human waste drenched the air around him. He recalled the pleasant taste of her youthful blood and the various ways she had attempted to please him.

Somewhere down the passage, a recently acquired runaway began pleading to be released, still unacquainted with the assurance there was no compassion waiting to be found here. The Old Man removed a jagged lump of uncooked meat from his raincoat pocket and dangled it in front of Annie's cage like a prize.

"Are you hungry?" he prodded as she spluttered cautiously toward him.

Her breath resembled a pit of roadkill as her eyes chased the beef in his hand, all misty, clouded, and yellowed by sickness. He couldn't understand how she was still alive. The Old Man had molested her body and mind repeatedly for two decades. Twisted her thoughts into a nook of nightmares, yet Annie's heart persevered, inconsiderate of all the suffering she'd endured. Protracted strands of beige drool swayed from her mouth as the entirety of her existence centered on the cut of steak in his hand. When he slipped the meat through a hole in the cage, she began ripping it apart with filthy clawed fingers like a ravenous beast—like a monster that was never human.

The Old Man decided he had seen enough of her misery, so he straightened and walked toward the whining boy nearby. The sound of his blubbering was sandpaper to the eardrums, and it only seemed appropriate to make him aware of what his future entailed. Upon seeing him approach, the weeping youth huddled up against the cage.

"Please, mister . . . there must have been a misunderstanding here. My name is Benny Jones, and I'm no one important; I'm homeless. I live on the streets of Philadelphia."

The Old Man's smile was hostile.

"The justification for why you now find yourself in this predicament might be considered somewhat arbitrary, Ben. You've been procured by Filii Reprobi and face a slow-moving, intolerable end. We'll likely start gutting you with a paring knife soon enough, but until such time, quit with the fucking begging. At least when I'm down here."

Benny's face twisted in on itself as the manifestation of dread inside his eyes charred a passage through to his core. The Old Man briefly considered butchering him right away.

"Why, mister?" Benny howled, "What have I done to you? Please let me go. I won't say a word about this if you release me. I promise you I won't."

The Old Man faked like he weighed up the boy's request.

"But how do I know I can trust you, Ben?" he teased.

"Sir, you can trust me all right. I couldn't give a hoot about whatever's going on here. I just want to get back to Philly so I can score a bump and go find a bridge to sleep under."

The Old Man's right hand closed around a hunting knife in his belt, his left on a pair of slip-joint pliers as he leaned in closer to the cage. *I'm going to enjoy this.*

"Stick your tongue out through this hole. I want to make sure you're telling the truth."

"I am telling you the truth, mister; I promise you I am."

"Then do as I have asked."

Benny gaped up at him with reluctant enthusiasm while presenting his tongue before the Old Man grabbed it with his pliers and brought down the knife in a whipping motion. Benny's screams echoed along the corridor as the Old Man inspected his flesh.

"Now, I can be certain you won't speak again. But you won't be returning to Philadelphia, I'm afraid. I'll finish this game of ours once the infection starts setting in, and someone I know is sure going to enjoy feeding on this warm offal you've provided."

The Old Man whistled "Dixieland" while walking back toward Annie's enclosure. He was satisfied that Benny's whining had been taken care of. His screams continued to bounce off the walls like a composition from the darkness—a terrible sound so delightful to hear.

# THIRTY-EIGHT

Addison thought about taking a drive to the Public Health building in Newark when Rick Sharp called with news about Sarah Cross. He would have liked to ask a few questions to verify they had the right woman but didn't want to seem arrogant, so he confirmed they'd be there shortly and told Jed to meet him downstairs with a car. It took them fifteen minutes to get to the FBI building on Wilshere Boulevard, and Sharp was waiting to greet them when they stepped out of the elevator. "Howdy, boys."

The two detectives returned his greeting.

"We sure appreciate getting the call on this," Addison said.

"Not a problem. As I said, this asshole needs to be brought down quickly, and working together seems our best shot . . . The woman is an interesting piece of work."

Sharp led them down a long, brightly lit corridor.

"How'd you manage to find her so fast?" Jed asked.

"When we put her name into Social Security and the National Drive Register, nothing came back for Riverside County. I'm guessing you boys encountered similar frustrations."

"Yeah, we did," Addison confirmed.

Sharp unlocked a closed glass door with a swipe of his keycard.

"I was attempting to formulate a plan on what we might do next when Katy walked through my door with a big happy smile. She decided to enter the name Sarah Cross as an alias in the NIBRS, and it returned as a hit. Right age, right location, right time frame. We jumped straight in the car and drove out to the address where we picked her up this morning."

"What was she arrested for?" Jed asked.

Sharp shook his head as if he were still surprised by the answer. "Animal cruelty."

"For real?" Jed said.

"I kid you not. She was apprehended in 1991 and charged with supplying dogs to an underground pit fighting ring. Her name at the time was Sarah Randall. She married Joey Parker in 1994, divorced three years later, and she just held onto his name. I was expecting we'd find her someplace on the other side of the country, but it seems she returned to Riverside County in 1999. Have you boys ever been to Cherry Valley?"

Addison's ex-wife had a niece who resided nearby.

"A small town on the edge of the city," he remembered out loud.

"Yeah, that's right," Sharp confirmed. "So, you've been out there?"

"Not for a few years."

They continued through a section of work cubicles similar to the ones used at LAPD headquarters. None of the agents engaged in open conversation or time-wasting activity as the constant tap of keyboards created a metronome-like drone. Sharp directed them past a row of modern offices and down a hall toward a conference area where a group of agents sat around a table. They didn't notice the detectives pass by, maintaining their focus on a woman who pointed calmly at charts of data on a projection screen. Sharp stopped outside a steel door at the end of the passage, where he waved them inside. Agent Pearce was standing in front of a one-way mirror, studying Sarah Parker in the next room.

"Good morning, gentlemen," she said casually.

They acknowledged her while moving in to get a look.

Sarah Parker appeared to be aged in her mid-fifties. She had stringy gray hair, a pallid complexion, and spiteful features. Her patchwork dress made her look like a witch as she stared down absently at a steel table and fidgeted with her thumbs.

"You get any gut feelings about her?" Addison asked.

It was Pearce who responded to the question.

"She's uneasy. But we haven't spoken to her yet. We just said her name popped up in a police matter, and she needed to come in and clarify a few things."

"She just agreed, no questions asked?" Jed asked.

Pearce shook her head, smiling.

"Not exactly. She certainly wanted to know what it was about. I thought she would demand legal representation, but Rick persuaded her to come along by saying we just needed to clear her name as standard procedure."

Pearce turned and gave Sharp a wink.

"He may have led her to believe it has something to do with dogfighting as well. She eventually agreed to cooperate after we promised her a ride home."

Addison admired the approach. "Anything else you were able to pick up on?" he asked.

"There's something off about her. You agree, Rick?"

Sharp tilted his head and folded his arms. "Yeah, it's kinda hard to put a finger on what Katy's referring to. I wouldn't say she presents as dangerous, but her demeanor comes across a little numb. Like maybe she'd be indifferent to nasty shit going down in the house across the street so long as it doesn't affect her personally. Put it this way, the animal cruelty charge feels like a perfect fit."

Addison nodded thoughtfully.

The red light on the camera inside the interview room was already on. All that remained was for Sharp to flick the switches to the audio recorder, and they'd be good to go.

"Who's going in to speak with her, then?" Addison asked.

Sharp extended an arm toward his partner.

"Either of you can go in with Katy. I want to let Parker know we're working together on this. It might prove helpful to mix things up in case we need to come at her hard."

Addison looked at Jed, who nodded. "All righty, then. Let's do this."

"Sure thing," Pearce replied, already heading for the corridor.

Addison followed her out to an adjacent door, where she swiped her card across the lock, waiting as the familiar clunk of double bolts disengaged before entering the room. As they made their way to the table, Sarah Parker gaped at them like they were impressions from a past that had come back to haunt her. It took Addison a matter of seconds to comprehend what the agents had been attempting to describe moments earlier. Parker's eyes displayed a kind of vacancy that suggested she was long attuned to disassociation.

"Hello, Sarah. I'm Detective Addison Mowbray from the Homicide Special Section of the LAPD, and I believe you've already acquainted yourself with Special Agent Katy Pearce. Do you have any idea why we've brought you in here today?"

When Parker narrowed her face in consideration, it gave her the appearance of a rat. Everything about her was edgy as she entwined her limbs to become a human knot.

"Dunno, maybe 'cause you've got nothing better to do with your time and want to ask me something about dogfighting, even though I haven't been anywhere near a pit for more than twenty years?" Her voice remained steady, and she seemed pleased with the response.

"Your name has come up in a current homicide investigation, Sarah. What can you tell us about a group who used to go by the name In Paucis?"

A flash of panic spread across her face, but she quickly averted her gaze down into her lap, and when she lifted her eyes, none of the anxiety remained. She stared back at them with a somber gravity one might expect to see in a penitentiary-hardened felon.

"What's the name?" she asked, feigning confusion.

"In Paucis," Addison replied. "Would you like me to spell it for you?"

Parker made a valiant attempt to look baffled but came up short.

"I've never even heard of them," she spat. "What makes you think I'd know anything about whoever they're supposed to be?"

Addison allowed a few seconds to pass while examining her eyes.

"Because we've been informed you have a cousin who's had some involvement with them in the past. We're aware that you know who these people are, Sarah. It's not going to do you much good pretending like you don't have any idea what I'm talking about."

Addison expected her to continue with the farce, but the blast of terror behind her eyes was as evident as the sun is bright. She looked like a deer caught inside the blinding glare of a hunter's headlights, preparing herself to be shot. Parker attempted to restore her composure by unfolding her arms and uncrossing her legs.

"I've got no idea what you're talking about. Not a freakin' clue. Whoever's provided that information is full of shit. You'll need to go back to the drawing board and start over again."

Addison heard Pearce scratching her thigh.

"No, I don't think so. I'm certain the information we received is good. It hasn't come from a single source. You'll have to do better than that."

There was nothing wrong with embellishing the facts when it helped put the squeeze on someone like the woman sitting across from him. Parker had given up attempting to conceal her apprehension and started chewing her nails feverishly instead.

"You can't keep holding me here," she said. "I've got no idea who those people are. So, if you intend to continue asking me questions, then I will need to see a lawyer."

Pearce touched Addison gently on the arm while she slapped a hand down on the table. Her harsh expression contravened her natural beauty.

"No fucking problem, Sarah," she declared, running a hand across the fabric of her pants again. "You can go right ahead and lawyer up if you want to. But we haven't even accused you of anything at this stage, so I don't get what your reasons are for demanding legal representation. I will say this, though: if you continue bullshitting us, then we'll be forced to find your cousin. I don't imagine it will be a difficult task—we are the FBI, after all. But when we do discover your relative's whereabouts, I'll be sure to let them know you were the one who dished out their details. I might also allow them to presume you gave us the name In Paucis as well. How's that sound?"

Pearce's smile was menacing while Parker rocked in her chair like a child. The skin around her face tightened, and her thin lips disappeared. It almost made Addison feel sorry for her. *The mere mention of their name has filled you with terror.*

"You fuckin' bitch!" Parker screamed. "Why would you do such a thing? This has got nothing at all to do with me. I'm not even one of them."

Pearce grinned like a poker player with all the right cards. "I'm doing it because I can, and you have something to do with it, Sarah. The fact their name scares you so much is indicative of your responsibility. Don't be mistaken, 'cause I'll just throw you in front of a fucking train without giving it a second's thought. Besides, I adore pit bulls. My family owned three of them when I was a little girl. They were once considered a nanny dog until assholes like you came along."

Pearce had identified the woman's fear as her main weakness and was using it against her to tighten the screws. There was an almost suffocating horror now seeping out from inside her, a complete gut-wrenching dread, the kind that made breathing difficult.

"Shit, shit, shit . . ." she cried while pulling at the hem of her dress. "Please, you've got no idea what they will do to me if you give them my name. You just can't, okay?"

Pearce looked at Addison and shrugged her shoulders. "Let's go, Detective. She's made her decision."

Parker threw her arms out. "Wait! Wait a second."

Addison didn't bother moving, watching as Pearce came to a stop and eased back into the chair. The young agent was a ruthless interrogator.

"I really can't give you my cousin's name; they'd know it was me, and it wouldn't do you any good even if I did. He's never been a part of their organization, but when word gets out about you wanting to speak with him, they'll kill us both. I don't know who it is you think you're dealing with here, but these are not insignificant fucking people. They're connected in super high places and are aware of everything going down before it can eventuate. You'll discover as much for yourselves soon enough."

Addison took note of the fact that Parker had referred to her cousin as he. It was evident she believed what she was saying, yet Pearce just shrugged, all matter-of-fact.

"We're gonna need something good from you, Sarah. I couldn't give two fucks about what happens to you or your cousin. As I said, I love pit bulls."

Addison understood why Sharp had wanted Pearce to be inside the room during the interview. The last time he participated in a joint interrogation with the FBI was in 2015. Addison walked away thinking Agent Bren Perry was the kind of person who might enjoy passing the time by counting match sticks. The guy had talked in all the moments where he should have been listening, wasting far too much time on irrelevant details. Perry probably would have said he was employing a little divergent thinking to the situation; however, a straight-down-the-line approach was where they'd needed to be. Working with Pearce was sure making up for the experience.

"There's only one person I know of who'd be prepared to speak with you about them," Parker replied eventually. "There's nothing more I can give you other than his name. If you go after my cousin, then I might as well shoot myself in the head and get it over with."

Addison and Pearce glanced at one another.

"Do you know anything about the dead girls in the hills, Sarah?" Pearce asked.

Parker appeared utterly mystified. "What? Why the hell would I know anything about them?"

"Well, you know about your cousin's group of friends."

Parker remained genuinely puzzled. "Whoa, wait a sec. Is that the reason why you're looking into these people? Because you think they might be responsible for killing those damned girls on TV?"

Addison decided to cut in. "What, you don't think they could be?"

Parker laughed through contorted lips. "You guys are heading down a dangerous path, even for law enforcement. That's your prerogative. Still, there's no way in hell the people you're asking me about are responsible for what happened to those girls. They would never dream of drawing that kind of attention to themselves. Not in a million years."

Pearce responded to her statement immediately. "This is what we're going to do, Sarah. You'll give us the name of this person who you said might be willing to talk to us, and we'll visit them. But should this turn out to be a waste of our time, then you need to prepare yourself for what we'll do next. I'm not one to make bullshit threats, and I sure as heck don't care much for people who think it's all right to look the other way."

Parker's desperation subsided. "It isn't a waste of your time. I think he scares them somehow."

"What's his name, Sarah?" Addison asked.

"Tony Anders. Reverend Tony Anders. He's a Baptist minister who runs a small church on Pico Boulevard with his wife."

Addison couldn't quite believe what he'd just heard.

"You're kidding, right?" Pearce said.

"No, I'm not fucking kidding. If you want to talk to someone who knows about the people you're referring to, then he's your man."

Addison looked at Pearce, who opened her hands with raised eyebrows.

"Why are they scared of this preacher man?" Pearce asked.

"I don't know why, precisely, but it might have something to do with a woman who got caught up in their affairs. Anders provided her sanctuary a while back, and they're both still breathing. Maybe the potential backlash of wiping out an entire church congregation saved their asses."

"What do you mean?" Addison asked.

"Exactly what I just said. Perhaps the people you're looking for didn't want to kill every member of his congregation and decided to leave him be. They even allowed him to hold onto the woman, and that isn't how they would normally do things as far as I'm aware."

Addison rubbed his eyes while he tried to make sense of things. He felt like he was trapped inside some nightmare within a dream, waiting to wake up.

"What makes you so sure he'll talk to us?" he asked dubiously. "If these people are even half as dangerous as you claim they are, then why would he speak of them?"

Parker's eyes darkened before she smiled in a soulless kind of way.

"Because that's the type of person Anders is. A real do-gooder. If you show up on his doorstep, he won't turn you away. He might not have reached out to the police, but I'm quite sure he will at least try to help you however he can. Why don't you go to West Pico Holy Baptist Church and find out for yourselves?"

Pearce pointed in the direction of the door.

"We're going to head outside to check a few of the things you've told us," she explained. "Just to make sure you're not feeding us horse shit. After that, you'll be free to go home. But you best be remembering what I said, Sarah. If this turns out to be nonsense, then we're going to find your cousin; his door will be the very next one we're knocking on."

When Pearce finished speaking, they got to their feet and headed back out of the room. Addison wasn't necessarily disappointed with the way things had turned out, although he had been hoping that Sarah Parker might provide something a little more solid. A gnawing thought remained lodged at the back of his mind. *Was it possible that some underlying evil connected this investigation to the killer?* At least they were getting closer to the people involved with In Paucis. Whether it proved to be a winning move or a step toward their demise, only time would tell.

# THIRTY-NINE

It was tranquil inside the UCLA station house where Sean Brody sat at a computer contemplating his next move. He entered Narek Avakian's name into the Laser program and studied his mugshot on the screen. There was a leaden detachment behind the hateful scowl, a homicidal indifference which suggested he might sell his children without much care.

Sean could monitor Avakian's movements from the comfort of his desk as the analytical function inside the Laser program underlined any locations where the scumbag had carried out his illegal activity. Artificial intelligence generated an accurate crime map, making it easier for Sean to cast his net. By using Laser in conjunction with the Chronic Offenders Bulletin, it left Avakian few places to hide. Yet, despite all these innovative upgrades to police surveillance, the system still favored the drug dealers, killers, and pimps who operated throughout the county. These low-life shitskids understood how to play the game.

Sean's thoughts drifted back to the night three years ago when his former partner was executed beside him. He recalled the explosive terror in Janey's eyes as she attempted to stanch the hissing of blood spraying from the wound on the side of her neck. An unbreakable sense of despair overwhelmed him in the months following her murder. A specter of hopelessness had wrapped its hands around his soul to squeeze any optimism right out of him. Janey Price was just twenty-seven years old when a single gunman ambushed them in a South-Central alley, and she perished inside their cruiser.

The LAPD wasted no time in proclaiming her a police hero. She was buried inside a star-spangled casket as the bagpipes played "Amazing Grace," and a three-volleyed gun salute cracked the skies overhead. Janey's picture went up on the Officer Down Memorial Page, and her name was inscribed on the law enforcement monument in Washington, DC.

*Big fuckin' deal, right?*

It all happened so quickly after they responded to a call about suspicious activity. The surrounding area had appeared empty when they rolled up to the scene, and neither one of them was prepared for what happened next.

Janey was speaking to the comms division when the shooter rushed into view. There was hardly time to register a reaction as the scumbag unloaded two clips through the windshield of their patrol car. Sean could only screech in protest while the faceless fuckhead fired the decisive shot into his partner from point-blank range. He remembered watching the killer scamper back down the alley, then his head started swimming, and everything went black. He awoke inside a Los Angeles hospital four weeks later.

It took seven months for his wounds to heal and another year of rehabilitation before he returned to active duty. Sean attempted to investigate the events surrounding his partner's murder whenever he managed to have a night off the booze, but all he encountered was a city overflowing with scumbags. Street justice had irrevocably modified his approach to policing, but his desire for the truth remained strong as ever.

Janey's case eventually went cold when no fresh leads came in, and the wall of silence had persisted despite a hefty reward. The mayor even offered indemnity on previous crimes to any rat who came forward with information, but it was to no avail. Sean put in for an immediate transfer from Inglewood Station House upon his release from the hospital. The last thing he needed was his coworkers to start consciously looking out for him, or worse still, catch them pausing whenever he entered a room. A few people tried to get him to reconsider, but when Sean maintained his position, they shifted him to UCLA.

Hatred became a reliable acquaintance as his culpability fueled the loathing inside him. Sean never made it to Janey's send-off, which only increased his sense of shame. At least he got to attend her memorial service at the Glendale Forest Lawn Cemetery this year. There'd been an excellent turnout to the day, as her family, friends, and colleagues assembled in remembrance of a young woman taken way too soon. Sean kept in contact with Janey's parents and called each week to check how they were holding up, always making sure there was nothing they needed.

At first, the notion of bringing vigilante justice to the streets was nothing more than a drunken fantasy to help him sleep at night. However, the origin of those thoughts emanated from his most wounded place, where a paper-thin scar covered the ache. Looking back, perhaps he was disillusioned for longer than he'd known, and his partner's murder provided the catalyst he required to act out. Vengeance overshadowed his thinking until his renegade justice concept manifested upon lifting a Ruger from a dead junkie on campus.

About a year had passed since he sent his first piece of human garbage off to an everlasting retirement. There'd been no planning or revision of the subject's patterns in advance. He merely drove around the county one night waiting for an opening. When he spotted a gangbanger stumbling along the corner of Vermont and West 75th Street, Sean just rolled up casually and shot the asshole in his face. First-degree murder had supplied him with the most awful and curative experience rolled into one. Then as soon as it was over, all he could think about was doing it again.

Sean believed he was making a statement for every victim in America. The fact it also gave the criminal underworld something new to fear was an added perk. Maybe it was sublime madness, but he thought the bangers looked more agitated whenever he passed them on the streets. That first gang-loving dickhead wasn't attributed to his hand, most likely because he didn't leave a plastic badge at the scene. But it was still odd how ballistics failed to connect the slug inside the body to those blasted into his next four.

He'd become more accomplished at choosing a target, and criminals were habitual by nature, which made tracking them a breeze. So long as he spent time in the planning, it almost guaranteed a favorable result. Remaining patient until all the pieces were aligned and never acting impulsively. One moment of sloppiness was all it would take to unravel things and hand him a life sentence in the process.

Narek Avakian's life of mayhem was rapidly nearing its end. The fucking slimeball was an Armenian Power hitman, a violent rapist, and an A-grade deviant to boot. Sean could have finished the bastard the other night when he lit his cigarette but didn't want to start rolling the dice. There were still benefits from being so close to the degenerate, like experiencing firsthand the deluded sense of invulnerability that blunted his instinct.

Sean was undecided on whether to shoot him near the apartment he owned in Glendale or out the front of his cousin's restaurant. Avakian was too busy getting high inside the Abovyan Strip Club most nights to anticipate the bloodshed coming round the bend. Oblivious to the fact there were six bullets with his name on them, and the clock was about to strike midnight.

# FORTY

Addison and Pearce sat across from Tony Anders's desk while waiting for him to finish a meeting in the hall outside. The preacher's office was furnished in a simple manner. It contained none of the glitz on show at many of the larger congregations throughout the city. An old tuxedo sofa was positioned near a coffee table on the left side of the room, and a sliding window captured the passing traffic on Pico Boulevard. A plain cross stood atop a bookcase crammed full of Bibles, and the air smelled like a blend of frangipani and cologne.

"How long have you and Rick been working together?" Addison asked casually.

Pearce uncrossed her legs and turned to face him. "This August will be two years."

"And what made you decide on spending your days chasing bad guys?"

Pearce chuckled lightheartedly. "I majored in law at Harvard and had my heart set on landing a gig at the Attorney General's Office in New York City. I don't know why I agreed to the offer for an interview at Quantico, but the Bureau wasn't even an option until I received my acceptance letter. I got assigned to the behavioral science unit, and when I met Rick, he was working as a top-level analyst at the National Center. We landed on a case together down in New Orleans in 2016. Did you hear much about the John Atticus Lorne murders?"

Addison knew the investigation well. "The tweaker creep they found in his mom's basement."

Pearce nodded. "Yeah, that's him all right. Anyway, it was the first occasion I worked with Rick, and then he became the agency's main man in California and dragged me along for the ride."

Addison understood why Sharp would want her as his offsider. "Well, the way you handled Parker inside the interview room today, I'd have to say it was a wise move on Rick's behalf. I mean, the whole pit bulls were once America's family dog approach was superb. Still, I don't imagine he needed to twist your arm."

Pearce giggled again. "Nope, no arm-twisting was necessary. I admired the man's methods and understood how coming to Los Angeles would likely turn out to be the right move for me in the long run. What about you? I can detect the twangs of Texas in your voice."

Addison moved in his chair. "You got me there. I'm Texas born and raised."

"Dallas?" she guessed.

It was Addison who snickered now. "Nope. I come from a small town filled with small-town sensibilities," he said before a double knock suspended their discussion.

Tony Anders stepped through the door and began making his way across the room, apologizing on the run for keeping them waiting. He settled behind his desk and regarded them both with a genuine curiosity, probably wondering what was coming next. The preacher had broad shoulders, ginger hair, and clear blue eyes. There was a natural warmth to the man's demeanor, unlike the religious phonies who pilfered money on the television.

Anders drummed his palms on top of his desk. "Who's who?" he said.

Addison introduced himself before waiting as Pearce did the same.

"It's not every day you find the LAPD and FBI on your doorstep," Anders proclaimed. "There have been some strange situations unfold in this room over the years, but this is a first. That said, how might I be of assistance to you this afternoon?"

Pearce motioned for Addison to lead the way.

"How do you prefer to be addressed?" Addison asked.

"People call me Tony most days," Anders joked. "Though my

wife will revert to Anthony whenever I'm in the doghouse."

There was no posturing about his manner.

"I'll get right down to it, then, Tony. We're here to find out whether you have ever come across a group who were known as In Paucis at one time or another?"

Anders appeared genuinely perplexed. "Not that I'm aware. Do you have a reason to think otherwise?"

Addison studied the preacher closely. "I take it you've heard about the three women found in the hills?"

Anders's face transformed into a portrayal of empathy. "Even if a person found themselves on the dark side of the moon, they'd still be aware of what's been going on in the hills," he lamented.

Addison acknowledged the statement with a nod. "We're trying to determine whether people from In Paucis might be connected to those murders in some way," he explained.

Anders sat back. "Can I ask who impressed the idea I can help you with this?"

"Do you know of a woman who goes by the name Sarah Parker?"

Tony Anders looked upward while apparently racking his memory. "Nope, I can't say I do," he answered.

"What about a Sarah Cross or Sarah Randall?"

"Not that I can recall."

"Well, Agent Pearce and her partner brought Ms. Parker in for questioning earlier today after we received information that she has a cousin who is possibly involved with the group. She initially rejected all our assertions on the subject, which is hardly surprising given what we know about them. But when we threatened to find her relative, she provided your name as her way out. Parker claimed you're the only person she knows of who's taken a stand against them and lived to tell the tale."

The preacher's face showed no signs of fear. "I believe I might know who this Parker woman is referring to," he said. "And I'm likely placing a lot of other people's lives in jeopardy by acknowledging the fact."

Addison fired an enthused look at Pearce. "Do you know where we can locate them?"

Anders ran a hand across the top of his head. "I think you may have misinterpreted me. I certainly don't know where you can find the group you're asking about. These people are the epitome of evil, probably unlike anything you can imagine. I don't make such a claim irreverently because I figure you've encountered more horror than any two people should throughout your careers. Nevertheless, the members of this club are rotten to their very core. They also happen to be rich and powerful; I've seen the evidence of their influence with my own eyes."

"How did you cross paths with them?" Pearce asked.

Anders smiled, as if to say, *Do you really want to know?*

"It wasn't much different to how we are meeting now," he explained. "Except, there was a man who appeared to have some type of military background sitting across from me. He placed a collection of photographs on my desk and played me a video. Then after he'd made his point, he just collected his things and walked back out the door."

Agent Pearce tapped a hand on the side of her chair. "What was in the photographs and footage?"

"The images appeared to have been taken at political fundraisers where some of our nation's most well-known names were having a great time. They were there too, I presume."

"Who's 'they'?" Addison asked.

"Them. You know, the individuals this Sarah Parker referred to. Their faces had been blurred out, but the identity of the people they were entertaining was clear."

Pearce continued her tapping. "Who did you see in the photographs?" she insisted.

Tony Anders squeezed his eyes. "I mean no disrespect, Agent Pearce; truly, I don't. But the faces I recognized in those photographs could put an end to both your careers with one call. Besides, if this meeting became known, then innocent people will die. People who have nothing to do with this."

Pearce remained unimpressed. "If this group is as dangerous as you and Ms. Parker claim, then why are you still alive today? Why would they allow you to reveal the things you have?" Her voice was broiled in skepticism.

The smile on Anders's face appeared different. "I don't have a worldly answer to your question. Simply put, they have their God, and I have mine. You should appreciate what it is you're going up against here. These people trap flies with honey, and from what I've seen, their pots are scattered everywhere."

Addison and Pearce looked at each other again. All this babble about feuding gods and faceless men in high places was starting to piss them off.

"So, let me get this right," Addison chuckled. "You won't reveal any of the names to us, even though your faith should dictate otherwise?"

Anders leaned forward in his chair and exhaled forcefully. "I don't know the identity of anyone inside their organization, and I'm just not prepared to divulge the names of the individuals who I recognized in those photographs. The consequences of doing so are too great. If it were only my life on the line here, then I'd be more helpful because this world and everything it offers is of little interest to me. I will give you the name of the group, though . . . at least it was the name when I encountered them."

Addison flicked open his notepad. "Ready when you are, Tony."

Anders released another heavy breath as he dropped his gaze. "They are called Filii Reprobi, or Children of the Fallen."

Addison checked the spelling before writing down the name and translation, thinking the likelihood they were involved was only growing stronger.

"Are you certain there's nothing else you can tell us, Tony?" Pearce asked.

Anders interlocked his fingers with a frown. "You know the identity of one of their associates, is that true?" he accused.

"Indirectly," Addison replied.

"Well, if you've set your minds on approaching them, then I'd suggest you could start there and quit expecting me to play Russian roulette with other people's lives."

Pearce had heard enough and cut in abruptly. "We will be following every piece of information that comes our way, Tony. The reason we came here today is that Sarah Parker dished your name up on a plate. I'm certain you'd expect us to keep pushing forward by whatever means if it were your daughter who happened to be one of the victims. We'll eventually put the cleaners through this Filii Reprobi cult, but before we start making moves against a person who might be directly involved with them, we need to ascertain what it is we're up against. It's called knowing your enemy; the more we know, the better our approach will be."

It was easy to detect the tone of frustration flooding Pearce's voice. She wasn't buying into the whole *my God versus their God* thing either.

Anders unlocked his fingers and leaned back in his chair. "I can hear the strain of accusation in your voice. Perhaps, you think I'm too indulgent to provide you with anything more than I have already, or maybe you presume I'm just a fool because I believe God died a criminal's death on a Roman cross. So, please allow me to repeat what I'm so desperately trying to communicate. The Filii Reprobi is unlike anything you will have encountered. I can guarantee it. And as the head pastor of this church, I am responsible for safeguarding the people's lives under my care. Remember, I only learned of their existence by chance after a woman came to me for help.

"She was involved with a Hollywood producer at the time and inadvertently stumbled upon the horror Filii Reprobi choose to indulge in. She loved this person and tried to make him see that if one can experience evil so entirely, then there must also be a paradigm of righteousness to balance the darkness. All it did was make her a target, which is why she landed at my doorstep seeking support. I have to honor her trust and protect the naivety of those who have been threatened."

"Who is the film guy?" Pearce asked.

"I have no idea," Anders replied. "At the end of it, I don't care what you think of me, Agent Pearce. I won't be speaking another word of this after you leave my office."

Addison decided to try hosing down the heat. "What do you suggest we should do, Tony?" he countered. "These young women are made victims in a way that very few ever will be. Butchered as a passing sacrifice to an evil we have not yet been able to determine. So, we could sure use your help here. Are you seriously implying that we should close up shop like they don't matter?"

Anders looked like he was running out of patience. "Not at all," he objected, clearly unimpressed by the implication.

Addison opened his hands in front of him. "Well, then, here we are."

"No, actually, it's not 'here we are.' I don't believe these people would leave behind a trail of corpses for the police to investigate. It's just not how I envisage them functioning. The media reports are claiming the victims are all missing body parts, and I fail to see how it correlates to the group of people you're currently inquiring about."

Addison could appreciate where he was coming from.

"We're not taking some wild stab in the dark on this, Tony. There are various kinds of incompetence in law enforcement, but with any luck, we're not quite that bad yet."

Anders looked mildly embarrassed.

"I wasn't implying you are acting incompetently," he said in an apologetic tone.

Addison brushed away the offense with a wave of his hand.

"The perpetrator drugs the victims with ketamine before cutting away his bits, and he might be draining their blood. We can only speculate at present, but we believe he might be using the ketamine to prolong their experience. Not to mention, there are several other elements which come across as being very ritualistic."

Anders nodded. "Sure. Look, I get it."

"He also burns the shape of an inverted Christian cross onto their left breast," Addison continued. "Are you familiar with what the symbol represents?"

Something flashed inside Anders's eyes. "An inverted Christian cross?" he repeated dolefully.

"Yes, that's correct."

Anders looked like an old porcelain doll haunted by time. "There was something else among those photos," he confided quietly. "I didn't mention it before. You need to appreciate that these people have pictures of my kids. They also showed me the home address of other families who attend the services here as well. Then there's the video taken of my parents' home in San Francisco."

Addison's gut stirred. "Go on, Tony," he encouraged.

"In one of the images, a young man was hanging over a clawfoot bath with what appeared to be a sliced throat. Now, I can't be certain as to whether the photo was even real, but I did see the bleeding shape of an inverted cross on his chest."

Addison sat back in astonishment as he contemplated whether the worst of anything imaginable might intend upon seeking him out. This case was spinning out of control like a car with an unlicensed driver behind the wheel, careening toward a collision that promised to be fatal.

# FORTY-ONE

The evening traffic along Golden State Freeway was free flowing as Edward maintained a speed just below the limit from inside the middle lane. He glanced at his reflection in the rearview mirror and noticed the dark circles beneath his eyes. The excitement of finding Linda's substitute had made sleep impossible these past couple of days, and he intended to recuperate once he'd secured his prize back at the ranch.

When Paige contacted him in the morning, her voice sounded husky, and he spent the next hour fantasizing with his cock in hand. Paige had wanted to drive out to the dummy address in Santa Monica to collect her reimbursement. Fortunately, he was well prepared for such a development, and after listening to his devious explanation, she agreed to meet at Secret Gardens.

Edward learned some interesting facts while looking into Paige's background. She was valedictorian of her graduating class in high school before undertaking an art major at Pomona College. Her best friend was a sexy brunette named Evie Popov, and her brother resided in Washington with his young family. Paige's father owned a dental clinic in Santa Ana, and her folks didn't approve of her latest beau, Gregory Pollock.

When Edward rolled up at Secret Gardens, his plan was momentarily stalled by the sight of Greg sitting beside his cargo. The young man's broad shoulders and confident manner came across like he'd be ready to rumble. It certainly wasn't ideal, but Edward had quickly regained his composure. He just smiled while drifting over to where they were seated before blasting three bullets into the big boy's chest. He'd fitted his pistol with a sound suppressor, and by the time Paige clued onto the situation, the chloroform had already begun closing down her mind. It felt good shooting the final slug through Greg's brains and settling the Harding family dispute by leaving his twitchy corpse on the sidewalk.

Edward intended to let the Old Man know that his killing spree was complete as soon as he arrived home, then he could get down to the business of exploring Paige's sweet-smelling body. Lust continued its surge inside his gut, and he almost pulled off the freeway to feed his hunger. Most Filii Reprobi displayed an insatiable appetite for sexual perversion, and Edward had participated in many of their fuck sessions over the years. But aside from the mysterious delights he enjoyed with Meagan Banks, none of it fulfilled him. He understood the concept of pushing one's carnality to the outer extreme; however, the orgies failed to invoke the same kind of energy he received when brandishing a blade.

Paige contained the potential to meld old desires with fresh possibilities. She intensified the ache in his balls by provoking the possibility of his demise, generating a beautiful discomfort that threatened his grip on reality. A decade of mystical osmosis had landed him at the gates of perdition, where a murderous inquest was headed his way. The Old Man would be expecting an adequate response to satisfy the demands coming from the obsequious assholes within Filii Reprobi.

Edward resisted the compulsion to hit the accelerator as he veered onto Antelope Valley Freeway. He'd been operating outside of time these past few weeks, looking down on things with preeminence, confident of remaining one step ahead of the game. But the girl in the back had messed with his head, and Edward wondered whether all great seekers eventually got to thinking this way. *Did Nimrod ever track a soul to the edge of civilization, only to find his quiver was empty when he prepared for the kill shot?*

If the Old Man intended to finish him off, then he'd lure Edward toward a ruse to do so, dangling a piece of bait just out of reach until he walked himself over the edge of a cliff. The best killers were skilled at presenting like prey, drawing their target into the open without creating suspicion before unmasking themselves as a predator.

A recurring riddle had been occupying Edward's sleep recently. A particularly annoying dream where he was searching for something undetermined. It mostly happened right before he awoke, and on every occasion where he thought he'd found what he was looking for, Edward came up empty-handed. After encountering each obstacle, he continued to open random parcels with renewed enthusiasm, only to discover something immaterial waiting inside.

It left him feeling deceived, like some puritanical spouse who discovered their partner in the act of fucking the babysitter. Even so, he was never affected by fear. Edward stopped being influenced by such nonsense long ago. Almost anything could be accomplished when he applied moral autonomy to a situation. The cosmos offered everyone an infinite scope of opportunity; however, most people were akin to mice on a wheel, running fast but going nowhere.

The sun continued its descent as darkness began fusing into the muted orange glow on the horizon. Edward examined his reflection in the mirror once more and saw the fierceness swirling through his eyes. They were only ten minutes away from camp cuntmore, where an empty cage awaited his doll. Then after his call to the Old Man was out of the way, he would nourish himself on Paige's flesh by unleashing the full flavor of his passion.

# PART THREE

"For the wages of sin is death"

Romans 6:23 King James Version.

# FORTY-TWO

Traces of shit lingered in the air, a relic of the two African brothers they ground into dog food a few days earlier. Narek disregarded the other men in the warehouse as he fixated on the boss. Davit was wearing a white rain slicker while he staged an impromptu inspection of his precious meat grinder. The boss was tall, sinewy, and lean with dark hooded eyes that rarely communicated what he was thinking. At fifty-three, Davit remained youthful enough to mix it with any younger men in the prime of their life, and his cruelty ensured few ever contemplated taking him on.

The boss had arranged a collection of torture implements nearby, and the floor was covered with clear sheet plastic. Tigran Grigoryan made a bleak impression as he sat bound to a chair in the middle of the room, pleading innocence through a makeshift gag. His fears were laced with electricity. The fact Narek had known Tigran for over thirty years only made the situation feel even more surreal—like an episode of the *Twilight Zone*.

They'd conquered their challenges side by side. Becoming outlaws together upon realizing the American dream was set aside for middle-class folk with pale skin. Narek recalled when they popped their cherry by sharing a younger skank at his cousin's place and blowing up mailboxes on the fourth of July. He'd lost count of the various cocksuckers they'd whacked over the years, and it was only last weekend when their wives spent the day at Disneyland with the children. None of the men in the room knew the reason why the boss had called this meeting, but from the moment Narek saw his terror-stricken friend taped to the chair, it became apparent he'd messed up in a bad way.

"What have you done, Tigran?" Bedros teased while grabbing playfully at his crotch. "I was in the middle of having my knob polished when Davit called. Now it seems I'll be cutting you into little pieces for all the fishes to feed on. But don't worry about it, chent, more work is more money, and the bitch will be waiting with open legs when I finish here."

Narek fired off a warning glare while lighting a smoke. "Shut your trap, Bedros. He ain't no spik trash you're talking to."

Bedros smirked; the cunt was enjoying himself. "Narek, my brother . . . he was somebody who had our respect; this is true. But what I see before me today is just another gyot. Isn't that right, booby?"

Tigran screamed in a garbled frenzy. It was a fuckin' complicated watch.

"How about waiting to hear from Davit before we make things more difficult for him," Narek objected. "We don't even know what it is he's supposed to have done."

Bedros made a tsking sound. "Come on, Narek, look at this chent. Have you ever seen anyone walk away from the chair he's sitting in? He was your brother for a season . . . now he is a nobody."

Narek grunted a rejoinder and blew out a smoke ring which dissipated in slow-moving wispy curls. He was feeling torn about finishing a man who was practically an extension of himself. Murdering an acquaintance could be a little tricky, but doing a genuine buddy was like being ordered to drown the family puppy as a kid. He had only killed a friend on two previous occasions and received no pleasure from the act. First-degree murder usually included desire, premeditation, and malice. Simply put, the killer wanted the person dead, planned the crime, and sought the victim out to ensure their death occurred. Each of those ingredients was missing for him here tonight.

Davit edged his way along the wall, seemingly lost in his thinking. As if he might be undecided on how things needed to play out. Then, right when Narek began considering a more pleasing outcome, the boss cut a line across the room toward Tigran's chair.

"You are a stupid fuck," he grumbled. "Deceiving your own."

The biggest threat to a criminal enterprise usually came from within; David made an example of rats to deter others from choosing a similar path. If Tigran had sold them out, then he'd be attuned to the reality that terrible consequences were fast approaching. His trial would be heard in a courtroom of impartial arbitration, where the judge didn't give two fucks about what colors a man wore or the allegiances he'd sold his soul to. Underworld enforcers maintained a ruthless set of principles, and they imposed themselves upon anyone who betrayed the code. Tigran was Narek's closest friend, but he had no problem understanding how it was better to follow an order than be on the end of one.

Davit moved in; an expression of loathing pressed to his face.

"You probably excused what you did because none of us were part of the betrayal," he suggested indignantly. "But you're mistaken, you rat fuck."

Tears streamed down Tigran's cheeks. He was a much harder man than most; however, death was no longer an abstract notion in some faraway land. The freaking walls were closing in, and he was on borrowed time, not so much living as counting down the seconds until his end. In this circumstance, there was no disgrace in weeping. Narek believed his friend's pleas would remain inside his ears for longer than he cared for.

Davit scanned each of the men in the room, straightening his shoulders while he interpreted their faces with suspicious eyes. The barn light overhead gave his slicker a metallic sheen, making him appear like some batshit crazy anti-hero from a Marvel movie.

"We all accept the responsibility that comes with being a part of the Armenian Power. This outlaw life has provided each of us with many opportunities we wouldn't ordinarily receive. I heard Levon's kid was accepted to college."

Everyone besides Narek started laughing.

"The Armenian Power has established a reputation for flying

straight," Davit continued. "But the building will crumble if we start selling people out. Keeping tight lips is one of the very first things we are taught, so this cocksucker knows what he's done."

Tigran's despair became even more profound. He'd stood opposite that chair often enough, smiling while other people's misdeeds were determined. Clemency only transpired on the big screen where mercy swooped down in the nick of time to save the day. A spirit of murder was slapping Tigran across the face with both its hands. If he were fortunate, there'd be nothing waiting on the other side except darkness. He couldn't anticipate a speedy departure either. They usually reserved an unexpected bullet for soldiers who remained faithful to the code. His oldest friend would have to seek solace in the empty void of nonexistence and pray there wouldn't be any standards to appease once he got there.

Davit stroked the side of Tigran's face, ruffling his dark curly hair with fake affection while stooping to eye level. "Our brother here has been singing like a fucking canary," he said before making his way to a corner of the room.

Narek watched the boss remove a folder from his briefcase. It contained the evidence of their comrade's misdemeanors. Bedros and Levon were reticent as they awaited further clarification, smirking shamelessly in anticipation as Tigran's wailing increased. He sought out Narek with a haunted gape, searching urgently for any sign of reprieve, for a spark of light at the end of a very dark tunnel.

Davit strolled over to the mincer, where he flicked a switch to set its grinders into motion, then he placed a sequence of photographs down on the floor before ushering them in for review. Narek crouched on his haunches to study the images which captured Tigran getting into an unmarked police car at various locations around the city.

"Fucking unbelievable," he muttered. "What do they know?"

Davit caressed the blade on his hip while he stepped his way through them.

"Nothing. I found out about this a few days ago," he said, leaning in close once more so Tigran could feel the blaze of hatred on his face. "My little mole inside GND has assured me that none of us will be subjected to any fresh investigations. This prick was only passing on street-level information. But it makes no difference to me. Squealing is squealing, and we all know it's only a matter of time until a rat starts working his way up the chain."

When Davit finished speaking, he gave Tigran's cheek one final pinch, easing the blade into his belly with a well-practiced hand as the traitor thrashed about furiously. Everybody was articulating their condemnation when Narek stepped in to have a turn at stickin' the rat. He realigned his thinking to forget the past they shared growing up together on the streets of Glendale. After all, Bedros was one hundred percent correct. Whatever this cocksucker might have once been, he sure as fuck was no longer his brother.

# FORTY-THREE

"How have you been holding up, Sally?" Tony Anders asked.

The woman's smile didn't extend further than her lips. "I've been doing . . . okay. Thanks," she replied.

Sally Ferguson was a portrait of breathtaking beauty. So much so that Agent Pearce appeared kind of ordinary sitting beside her. The former supermodel continued glancing across at the office door as if wary of an impending threat. Her eyes undermined the outward display of calm she was attempting to present.

Pearce and Sally were seated on the tuxedo couch while Addison, Jed, Rick, and Tony sat opposite them in flimsy plastic chairs.

"Are you certain that nobody knows I'm here?" Sally asked. Fear was evident in her tone as she twirled a strand of russet-colored hair around her finger.

Anders smiled. "I haven't mentioned a word about this to anyone, and these fine people have assured me our meeting will remain a guarded secret. Isn't that right, Detective Mowbray?"

"Totally," Addison said.

Sally took a swill of water and exhaled resignedly. "What would you like to know?"

"Just give us the rundown on how you came to be in contact with these people," Addison suggested. "And we'll cut in when we have any questions."

The uneasiness remained on her face as she hiked her shoulders. "Sure thing," she replied as Pearce nodded supportively.

"It's all right, just take your time," she said in a comforting voice.

Sally's smile was sudden and unsure.

"I was working as an international fashion model when I discovered my partner at the time was a member of that appalling club.

Just the memory of being involved with somebody who participated in their evil activities completely repulses me."

"By club, you mean Filii Reprobi?" Sharp asked.

Sally nodded. "Yeah, I prefer not to speak their name out loud."

"We'll keep you safe," Sharp promised meaningfully.

Tony Anders and Sally exchanged dubious glances.

"I hope so, Agent Sharp, I do," she said. "Although, I think you might be underestimating the enemy on this occasion. Anyway... my work took me worldwide, and I met Larry Springfield at a Gucci launch in Rome. We hit it off and dated for several months. Then I moved into one of Larry's houses in Beverly Hills."

"You're talking about the Hollywood producer Larry Springfield, right?" Jed asked in amazement. "The guy who made all those award-winning science fiction movies?"

Sally smiled again; still, it failed to touch her eyes. "I am. However, you need to disregard whatever you may have seen on TMZ when it comes to Larry. All that stuff is scripted, and he has a gift for presenting as lighthearted."

Agent Pearce had her cell resting on her thigh to record the interview; even so, Addison wrote Larry Springfield's name down into his notepad.

"It wasn't until two years later that everything went pear-shaped. I'd flown out to Paris to do various shoots for *Vogue* and expected to be on location for a couple of weeks. When things wrapped up ahead of schedule, I decided to come home early as a surprise. Larry hated the amount of work I'd been doing and insisted I didn't need the cash. He told me I could have whatever my heart desired; all I needed to do was ask, but the idea of becoming a Hollywood wife with a monthly allowance wasn't real enticing. My career provided independence and a function other than being Larry Springfield's arm candy. It was something of an ongoing issue.

"After landing at the airport, I took a taxi straight to Beverly Hills only to find Larry wasn't home. I went down to the study to check his schedule and noticed that his computer was open on a ledger called

Filii Reprobi. I also saw a video paused at the bottom of the screen, and curiosity got the better of me, thank God. Because as terrible as it was to discover the truth, it would have been much worse to remain in the dark. Who knows? I might still be sleeping beside a monster. Larry always kept his PC locked tighter than a bank vault. If I'd called ahead from Paris to let him know I was coming home early, then we probably wouldn't be sitting here today."

"What was in the video you found?" Addison asked.

"The footage was taken inside a Gothic-style hall. There were forty-odd people gathered in groups. Some of them were engaged in sexual activity, while the others remained nearby, drinking champagne. I couldn't hear what was said with any clarity, but about ten minutes into it, a disheveled man got dragged, screaming, across the room. He was secured to a clawfoot bathtub where they brutalized him with various knives and a cattle prod. There was a limit to how much I could stomach."

"How old was the victim?" Addison asked.

"It was hard to know for sure," Sally explained soberly. "He was filthy, like he'd been living on the streets, but if I had to guess, I'd say mid-twenties to early thirties."

"How can you be sure the footage wasn't a scene from one of Larry's upcoming movies?" Sharp said before Sally dismissed the idea by raising her eyebrows. His suggestion caused a flash of anger to cross her face, and her cheeks reddened at their center.

"I'm sure if you were to question Larry about the video, he would tell you that was what I saw. It's one of the reasons why I chose not to contact the LAPD with any of this. But when you've spent as much time in front of the camera as I have, it's not hard to tell the difference. Besides, the ledger on his computer confirmed it was real, not to mention the warnings Tony received or the fact you're sitting here in his office today."

Sharp tugged awkwardly on his tie like a schoolboy talking with the prom queen. "I don't doubt your testimony; I'm just clarifying is all. When we make our move, there can be no margin for error. Did you recognize the people in the footage?"

"Larry was filming it all. Ironic huh? But there wasn't anybody else I could identify. It was gloomy, and I was in such a state due to the stuff they were doing to that poor man. It went beyond the point of sickening— Larry could have come home at any second."

Addison decided to take things slightly off course. "Tony explained how you attempted to get Larry to see the evil of his actions, something about drawing him over to the light. Is that true?"

Sally looked at Tony with niece-like affection. "I think my dear friend was wearing his preacher's cap with you there. Tony has dedicated his life to assisting the downtrodden, and he isn't one to betray a person's trust. It's why I went to him for help when things first spiraled out of control. I started attending this church back in the nineties; it's been a refuge for me over the years. The Anders family helped me through some extremely tough periods in my younger days, and I never forgot about it. They are people who can always be relied on."

Addison looked at Tony, who appeared unaffected by the compliment.

"After I read the ledger, I packed a suitcase, jumped in my car, and booked a room at the Beverly Wilshire Hotel under my cousin's maiden name. There was never any consideration given to drawing Larry over to the light. Not after the horrors I witnessed in that footage. Hopefully, divine justice will be served one day soon, but until such time, whatever punishment they might receive would be too light, in my opinion."

Addison believed the woman was speaking truthfully.

"So, the footage was like a snuff film?" he suggested, watching as she pondered his question. "Kinda, I guess. However, I didn't see the poor man die. I reached a threshold where I couldn't watch anymore, but that's where he was headed. Still, the event came across more like a party. A celebration of pure evil is how I would phrase it."

"Did you notice an inverted cross in the footage?" Sharp asked hopefully.

Sally shook her head. "Not that I can recall. However, I was entirely shocked at the time, so there's likely going to be quite a lot I missed."

Tony Anders raised a hand in the air.

"You got something to add, Tony?" Addison invited.

"Yes, I most certainly do. If you guys approach Larry Springfield directly about what Sally has told you, it could turn out to be disastrous on several fronts. Can I inquire as to what your intentions might be once you leave this room?"

Addison looked toward Sharp. "Rick?" he asked with a furrowed brow.

"I completely understand your concerns, and I assure you everybody's wellbeing will be the very first issue taken into consideration before any decision is reached. Simply put, we won't be making a public display of kicking his door down, that's for certain."

Anders and Sally appeared somewhat appeased.

"What did you see on the ledger?" Addison resumed in single-minded fashion, prompting Sally to look uncertainly at Tony Anders, who nodded his encouragement.

"A register of names, people they held at locations referred to as either the compound or the estate. Both places appeared on multiple occasions in the archive, though I couldn't find anything further that might help determine where they are. Besides each of the names were gender, age, and acquisition price. I noticed some of them had a red line marked through the particulars. Larry had highlighted certain dates. I assumed maybe they intended to meet at those times, but I can't recall when they were. The only other thing I saw was a record of the fees Larry had outlaid to someone called the Old Man. They dated back to 1998."

Agent Pearce placed her hand on Sally's arm. "Do you recall the amounts of those payments?"

"It was a decent chunk of change, even for Larry Springfield. I'd say the values ranged anywhere from five hundred thousand to one million dollars."

A sense of astonishment flooded the room in the form of total silence. The hairs on the back of Addison's neck were standing on end while a cod knot twisted at the center of his belly. It indeed appeared as though Filii Reprobi was a serious business. No doubt palms were being greased. Addison reflected on what the Parker woman said during the FBI interview before making a note to find Larry Springfield's accountant.

"Has Larry tried contacting you lately?" Pearce asked.

Sally rubbed her upper arms and gagged in disgust. "No. When everything initially went down, he came after me like a dog with rabies, but the last time I heard from them was when they sent somebody to threaten Tony. I altered my entire lifestyle, walked away from my career, and purchased a very secure apartment in Beverly Grove. I turned my back on anyone who was attached to my former life and started again. Do you believe they're behind the attacks on those girls?"

The question caused a penny to drop inside Addison's head.

"Maybe one of them has gone rogue and is working off the chain."

Jed whistled exuberantly.

"I sure like where you're heading with this, Ad," he said. "It makes sense of certain things which have been convoluted up until now. Were those money figures you mentioned just what Larry outlaid personally?"

"As far as I could tell."

"And you said there were approximately forty people on the footage you saw?"

"Something like that, yes."

"Damn, there's a truckload of money changing hands."

Tony Anders raised an arm again.

"Go ahead, Tony," Sharp interjected.

"I wasn't embellishing the kind of influence that would be available to the individuals I recognized in those photos. They were robust American icons. If the Filii Reprobi can rely upon them for support, then you guys will be jeopardizing your careers."

"There's no need for you to worry about us," Sharp assured him. "These people could have the president's ear for all I care; it still won't affect the outcome here."

Tony Anders shook his head ruefully. "I wish I could share in your optimism, Agent Sharp," he said.

There was a dolefulness to the preacher's voice that unnerved Addison. As if Pandora's Box had been opened to reveal a bunch of dead things rotting inside. For the first time, he felt a genuine despondency about solving the case. It wasn't like he expected to walk away empty-handed, but he knew when this investigation concluded, there would likely be a colossal wreck of destruction scattered in its wake.

# FORTY-FOUR

The Old Man's grip tightened around the phone while he considered the various implications of the situation.

"And you're certain of this?" he queried.

Detective Rodgers looked cautiously over his shoulder as he paced along the pavement outside LAPD headquarters.

"They're all gathered at Tony Anders's church as we speak. Both FBI agents, the two HSS detectives, and Sally Ferguson. But I think it would be a risky move if you were to proceed with silencing the woman and the preacher."

"I don't pay for advice, Tom. I pay you for information."

Rodgers sounded like he was breathing under duress.

"When crank heads and street whores go missing, it ain't difficult for me to look the other way," he declared bitterly. "But Mowbray and Perkins are my colleagues, and nobody at that meeting can be dismissed as trash. Not to mention it was one helluva risky move I made in getting a hold of this intel for you."

The Old Man chuckled derisively. "A community-minded attitude is a bit rich coming from the likes of you, considering what's inside the folder of evidence we've compiled on your affairs. If those pictures were to find their way to the press, the only friends you'd have left would all be wearing orange jumpsuits inside a federal prison. In any case, there's no need to worry. The two detectives are not in any immediate danger at this point."

Rodgers pictured a future behind bars. "I hope your house is in order," he said eventually. "The hounds are coming."

*Don't worry*, the Old Man thought, *it most certainly is.*

"I appreciate the call, Detective," he said dispassionately.

"Like always, you will be well compensated in due course. In the meantime, if anything gets set into motion, I want to be informed immediately. Make sure you follow my instructions. Are we clear?"

The Old Man waited until Rodgers acknowledged his decree, then he ended the call and returned the phone to the cradle on his desk. He felt slightly irritated that the police had managed to make a connection with Larry Springfield. Not because such knowledge might bring Filii Reprobi trouble—it just created unwanted complications that now required his undivided attention.

Sarah Parker and Edward were primarily responsible for the current circumstances and needed to be purged of their failings as a consequence. Parker once held aspirations of joining Filii Reprobi but was declined on several accounts. Her lack of class and limited assets were just two of them. The Old Man would have already interred the hag years ago if not for her cousin's intercession. Frank Rivers promised to take on the responsibility if she ever caused a problem, and the hasty pledge was going to cost him his life. Edward's impulsivity had drawn the authorities to their gates, which meant it was time to bring the investigation to a close.

Nothing was ever too complicated for the Old Man's resolve. So he straightened his thoughts and began planning everything out in his head. He wasn't about to act impulsively. Stupid choices remained stupid choices, irrespective of the speed at which they get presented. As things stood, the LAPD had nothing besides Larry's and Sarah's names, both of whom represented the walking dead. A satisfying chill worked its way up the Old Man's spine as he envisioned his ideas unfolding. It was perfect, just like the Burberry suit he'd worn into the office this morning.

His frustrations were already subsiding as he retrieved his emergency phone from the desk drawer and hit speed dial on the one contact who could make every problem obsolete.

"Hello," Ghost answered, ready for business.

"I have a situation which requires your immediate attention," the Old Man explained calmly. "Three situations, to be exact."

"Are you coming here, or am I coming to you?"

"I'm at the office. How soon can you be here?"

"Give me fifteen."

"Have you begun surveillance on the detectives' families yet?"

"I did the recon here in LA on the rookie's girlfriend and mother. My best man is following the kid in Phoenix. All the targeted houses have already been breached."

"Great, when you get here, we'll talk more."

The Old Man ended the call and lit a Cuban cigar, satisfied with how effortlessly everything could be influenced when under his control.

He'd always been cagey about Larry Springfield. The schmuck was a shameless Jew bragger who'd been born into Hollywood royalty, and killing the asshole would be a lot of fun. But Edward was a different story. He came from a long line of generational brutality established on the sugar plantations in South Carolina.

How he'd become so enamored with the blue-collar blood of Linda Jones was anybody's guess. The Old Man despised the lower classes and homeless trash who infested many parts of the city. Their whining excuses pierced his spirit like a thousand shards of broken glass. Lacking the tenacity to improve their lives, they leeched off welfare, panhandled on the sidewalks, and fermented in their stink. If it were up to him, they would all be exterminated as turds with legs should be.

The Old Man expected Edward to forget about his working-class girlfriend and incorporate the dogma of their fraternity. But she continued to harass him, like an annoying harlot who refused to part ways. There was no place for sentiment within Filii Reprobi. If Edward had arrived at this truth, it might have prevented him from lighting a fire without thinking things through. He'd jumped the gun and was going to be reunited with Linda in a hell of his own making.

The law always attempted to work its way back from a body in the hope of unpackaging the crime. Therefore, he'd need to make sure they left nothing for them to find. The Old Man closed his eyes and chuckled soberly, thinking how Edward would be remembered as a drug-inspired lunatic. "What a shame," he whispered. "I hope she is worth it, son."

# FORTY-FIVE

Collins didn't feel comfortable with the directive Addison relayed to him, but the fact it had come from the FBI meant there was little he could do about it. Rick Sharp wanted to keep Larry Springfield's identity under wraps to make sure Filii Reprobi didn't receive a tip. It seemed like a prudent request considering Sally Ferguson's disclosure about the group, yet the lieutenant was having difficulty getting his head around things.

Addison checked the time on the wall, eager to call it a day. His shift had ended almost two hours ago, and the only thing he'd eaten was a packet of Funyuns from the vending machine in the kitchen. An image of pepperoni pizza with melted cheese tormented his mind as Collins stared across at him expectantly.

"Anders runs a small congregation, Jevonte. What reasons could he possibly have for embellishing the details?"

Collins appeared bemused.

"It's taken me all these years to discover what a great man of faith you are. The kind of detective who will take a preacher's word as being gospel."

The flippant remark contained much derision. Nevertheless, Addison did spend some time contemplating God, destiny, and the greater universe on the drive back from the church. He understood how people might get to thinking their lives were preordained for misery when childhood dreams turned to dust, and they found themselves dumped on the shores of an unwelcomed reality. Addison had pretty much abandoned his faith when his father passed and didn't anticipate it seeing a way back to him. His verdict on such matters was reasonably uncomplicated. Everybody was accountable for their own choices in life, and sometimes nasty shit happened to outstanding people. But he wasn't in a mood right now to engage in a conversation about life's platitudes with the boss.

"It's not like Anders was opposed to us moving on Larry Springfield," Addison countered. "He just wants to ensure Ms. Ferguson won't be endangered as a result."

The lieutenant appeared weary, and it was easy to understand why he might want to go in all guns blazing. It would provide something to report back to the brass at the bare minimum, and progress was a keyword right now.

"So, you're convinced Springfield is connected to the killer?"

Addison raised his eyebrows and shook his head. "Nope, but it sure seems likely."

Collins tapped a hand on his desk in frustration. "What is it with you and men of the cloth?" he said.

Addison appeared confused. "What do you mean?"

"Well, you insisted on keeping the identity of your priest a secret when the Feds came across, now you're bending over for a Baptist preacher. If I didn't know better, I might start to think the spirit of God has infected you. Did Anders mention anything about how these Filii Reprobi assholes threatened him?"

Addison realized he hadn't filled the man in on the first meeting yet. "He said a spook arrived at the church and showed him pictures of his family and various other people who attend the congregation. I guess it was more a 'we know where to find you' kind of thing. The people he recognized in the other photographs is what's got him believing we might be taking on more than we can handle. He even insinuated our careers would be jeopardized if we choose to proceed."

The expression on Collins's face was borderline admonitory. "I know how it all sounds, lieutenant, really I do. But like I said already, Anders has verified there was an inverted cross carved into the chest of a man in one of those images, a man with his throat cut no less. I mean no disrespect at all by saying this, but I can identify fear when it's seated across from me. And I'd like to think I'm capable of detecting if someone is lying. Anders didn't seem overly concerned about his well-being, but he was apprehensive when it came to others' safety. Both he and Sally were speaking honestly, of that I've got no doubt at all."

Collins started drumming on his desk again.

"You're asking a hell of a lot of me. I've already stuck my neck out for you by keeping this whole satanic cult angle from the captain. Admittedly, it turned out to be the right move. But this shit here is on a whole other level, pal."

Addison nodded before Collins continued making his point.

"These aren't trivial details you're expecting me to keep quiet here; it's game-changing intel concerning the hottest damned investigation in the country. It should be sent straight up the fucking chain, no questions asked. If this blows up in our faces, it's gonna be my black ass everyone is gunning for. No one will give a ripe royal fuck about you or Perkins, though I may find myself pushed into retirement."

Addison felt kinda lousy about the request. Still, the lieutenant was old school, and if their roles were to be somehow reversed, he would be asking the very same thing. Most case-hardened cops in the LAPD were being replaced by show ponies who spent too much time perfecting their physique in the gym. Meanwhile, an entire generation of tough guys had been put out to pasture, which made the job even more frustrating.

When Addison started in uniform, he worked on the Hollywood beat with a veteran named Eric Devereaux. One night, they were called to a suspected B&E in a seedy apartment block located down a shadowy side street at the end of the Boulevard. Upon rolling up at the scene, they spent fifteen minutes searching for signs of a forced entry, then just as they began walking back to their patrol car, a crank head came charging out of the darkness, waving a piece in the air.

Addison had fumbled with his gun clip while Deveraux

disarmed the offender and beat him into a state of unconsciousness. As the EMS vehicle drove away, his partner said how the bastard might give pause for thought the next time he considered running at police with a gun in hand. Such events barely rated a mention back in the day.

Collins lifted himself out of his chair to start pacing the office. He resembled an angry tiger in captivity, impatient for something to claw apart. His black suit was crumpled, and there were dark coffee stains on the collar of his shirt.

"I can't see how this will fall back on you," Addison said. "The FBI has the record of interview, and if anything, damaging eventuates from withholding the info, you can deny having prior knowledge of the facts. It's not as if Jed or I am going to rat you out."

Collins chuckled under his breath. "You can be a cold hard bitch at times, man."

Addison hadn't meant to imply they shift the blame onto Sharp, but the lieutenant appeared to be coming round, which was the primary concern right now. If the Feds suspected resistance on their end, then the investigation's whole tone would likely change. Trust was very much a reciprocal concept in law enforcement.

"Rick's the one who has insisted we keep Springfield's details under wraps," Addison reminded. "But I know it's a big ask all the same."

Collins lumbered back to his desk and slumped into the chair.

"How's it been working with them?" he asked through a smile.

Addison's expression reflected his surprise. "Much better than I was initially expecting, that's for sure. Not only has Rick been true to his word, but it turns out they also happen to be particularly good at what they do. We probably wouldn't have progressed so quickly without them. Pearce is one of the finest interrogators I've sat down with. The woman's ruthless."

Collins's subtle smile became a grin.

"What happens next?" he asked.

"We're going to set up detail on Larry Springfield and see where it leads us; then we'll send in the troops when the timing is right. I don't imagine it's gonna be a long wait. I'd also like to find out who the prick's accountant is. Those payments he made were substantial and would be difficult to explain away."

Collins's furrowed brow indicated he was deep in thought.

"Something on your mind, boss?" Addison asked him.

"It appears you've got this case by the tail, so I don't want this to sound like sour grapes. But have you considered what might happen if the perp isn't connected to these Filii Reprobi cocksuckers?"

It was a detective question and something which Addison had already contemplated several times in the past few hours. Everything appeared to be lining up perfectly, but the killer and the group might still be independent of one another. What Collins wanted to know was where the investigation would go if their search uncovered a broader adversary than first anticipated. Addison rubbed the tightness in the side of his neck.

"I'm feeling confident that our guy is one of them," he answered. "Maybe he's just working from a different playbook, and we'll catch ourselves two birds with the one stone."

It was the best he could come up with, and he watched as Collins placed a big paw over his mouth to stifle a yawn. "Okay, then, you got anything else for me tonight?"

"Nope, that pretty much covers it."

Collins began looking around his office as if he'd misplaced something important. "Where's Perkins?" he asked playfully.

"I told him to go home right before I came to see you."

Collins smiled again. "All righty. You and I should probably call it a day."

Addison nodded while pushing himself out of the chair before saying goodnight and walking back into the main office. He'd started preparing himself for the likelihood he was being dragged someplace he didn't want to go. What he needed was to switch everything off for a while, buy a bottle of whiskey and order a pepperoni pizza on his way home, then drink until he found sleep.

# FORTY-SIX

There was nothing suspicious on the security cameras along the front boundary of Edward's property, yet a paranoid disposition troubled his mind. More than a day had passed since he'd spoken with the Old Man and promised to stop dumping bodies in the hills.

The slippery fuck seemed pleased by the news. His manner was amiable, and nothing implied Filii Reprobi was manipulating Edward's immediate surroundings. Even so, the Old Man wasn't about to advertise a proposed strategy. Edward had seen him fillet flesh from children as his soulless eyes gazed down on them apathetically like he was dissecting a rat in biology class.

Meagan Banks—the cold-hearted bitch that she was—taught them various ways to keep a person alive. The Old Man had become proficient at removing muscle from bone as his subjects shook about in violent futility. He regulated his rage better than anybody, rarely reacting to the suffering he created, and his detachment was never more apparent than when his walls were being sprayed in crimson.

Filii Reprobi owned a cottage inside Los Padres National Forest, where they sometimes went to inflict misery in a more intimate setting. Edward and the Old Man spent a few days there during the previous summer, draining the life from two teenagers taken off Santa Barbara's streets. When they finished having their fun, the room was a shifting mass of black flies swarming over the sullied corpses on the cabin floor. Afterward, they'd both sat silently for a while, appreciating their creation as the bugs laid seeds in whatever cavities remained. That same afternoon, the two of them were seated at a diner on Paradise Road, eating pie and slurping milkshakes without a care in the world.

Edward had studied the Old Man closely in that café, watching as he engaged in small talk with an attractive waitress who looked like Jennifer Aniston. The woman inquired about their day and whether they planned on visiting the region's famous canyons and camping grounds. A few weeks later, the Old Man arranged her abduction from the parking lot behind the restaurant at the end of her shift, and she suffered a prolonged experience. Edward preserved the grill waitress's memory to recap how disingenuous appearances were for everyone involved with their organization.

The fact he had been ordered to attend the compound the following evening didn't necessarily mean he was in immediate danger. However, he needed to prepare himself for a possible ambush because if they were going to spring a surprise, it would be when he was alone in the dark at a remote location like the Mojave Desert.

Sordid impressions of Paige flooded Edward's mind as he raised himself off the couch to begin striding across the living room. One hand squeezed his throbbing cock as he opened the steel door to his storage chamber and stepped into the gloom. Paige uncurled on the ground and began pulling at the tape on her wrists while Edward scoffed at her clumsiness. He decided to do away with the enclosure, which allowed him more access to her lithe young body. It wasn't as if she could dig a way out through the floor.

Edward encouraged his arousal by swirling his fingers along the bulge in his pants until lust blistered his spirit to the point of displeasure. The vision of her dirty gleaming skin robbed his breath, and he considered whether she might become the best remedy to a glum mood he would ever find. Edward needed to lick the saltiness of her unwashed skin while bruising her body. Beat her severely, then help mend the wounds. Paige offered momentary rapture, but if he intended to keep her long term, she would have to become familiar with his sadomasochistic aspirations.

He moved across the room in shuffled steps, chuckling at the way she attempted to claw a hole in the wall as unmistakable disgust encased her. She would soon come to accept her circumstances with a different attitude once she grasped the alternative. He provided the opportunity to extend her existence as his favorite little dolly—a chance to continue breathing so long as she supplied him with the contentment he required.

Edward listened to the pattern of her breath before mounting her torso. He ripped at her lime green sundress like an excited child, sliding up her body and licking her neck like a lizard. Her sweat mixed with stale perfume to produce a salty layer of scented paste as she toiled fiercely beneath him. He wasn't deterred by her loathing, grinning while she gawped up all crazy-eyed and spicy, bucking her hips against his aching cock. Paige's resistance was about to be exposed to the hand of correction, and his discipline would be harsher than necessary.

He straddled her like a cage fighter and grabbed a fistful of honey-blond hair, inhaling the leftover floral scent of shampoo. Edward imagined sponging her in the soaps Linda once enjoyed when she eventually fell into line. Dressing her up beautifully so they could appreciate one another from across the kitchen table as he destroyed another homeless bum. For now, she remained intractable, thrusting upward in willful stupidity. Paige's shrieks were piercing as long tendrils of mucus danced around her nostrils to the melody of her breath.

Edward pinched her ass cheeks with both hands, twisting with furious delight to break the skin. He paused while she thrashed furiously before biting into her shoulder so that blood filtered over his tongue, sucking against the wound until his mouth tasted like rusted steel. When his spittle turned the color of red wine, he waited tolerantly for Paige's trembling to subside, kissed her eyes with soft lips, and got to his feet.

A little later, they would smoke some DMT together and take a spiritual journey to an alternate dimension assembled in perfect lines. When they returned, he intended to increase the breakdown velocity by separating her memory from her consciousness, rewiring her awareness into a state of total compliance.

The extent of her misery would be dependent upon how determined she was to hold onto her memories. Paige's past recollections were like rotting teeth that needed an extraction, and he was going to enjoy pulling them out slowly, roots and all.

# FORTY-SEVEN

At face value, the crime scene up at Secret Gardens presented like a botched robbery, which was why Addison wasn't notified of the event until morning. Gregory Pollock was identified as the deceased thirty-five-year-old male from a license the CSI team discovered inside Paige Harding's car. An all-points bulletin had gone out on the girl.

The detectives who drove over to Pollock's address in Huntington Beach discovered that the victim was a high-end sports executive who rented the stucco bungalow with his girlfriend. Neighbors noticed the young couple drive away in the late afternoon before verifying they were alone and appeared normal at the time.

Pollock was shot three times in his upper chest and once in the forehead. Four shell casings were recovered for ballistics, representing the first noteworthy trace evidence the killer had left behind at a scene. By the time everyone realized Paige Harding had resembled the three previous victims, they were well behind the play. Things went down beside the Self Realization Fellowship Headquarters, but all the available CCTV proved useless because the gardens created a blind spot.

Addison considered the peculiar location of the crime while he squeezed the ache at the side of his temples. He'd discarded the idea that these abductions were an act of randomness. What was the likelihood of the perpetrator driving up to Mount Washington and stumbling upon Paige Harding—a young woman who happened to tick all the right boxes?

He believed a meeting was prearranged. Perhaps the girl felt apprehensive about going there alone, so she decided to drag Pollock along for the ride. No matter how he looked at this thing, there was no way he could attribute the circumstances to their being in the wrong place at the wrong time. Which meant the perp must have been instigating an exchange before the abductions. However, on every occasion he tried to figure out what the killer's method might be, all he was getting were blanks.

Addison began mulling over Larry Springfield's possible connection to Filii Reprobi. He wondered if the renowned movie man knew the perpetrator's identity. It would have been a ridiculous notion a week ago, but the case had unearthed some strange threads of late. The brass had scheduled a press conference downstairs to provide the latest rundown on the investigation. Hopefully, the lieutenant didn't disclose the specifics of what they'd uncovered to the captain beforehand. Springfield was presently shooting a biopic in South Africa, so throwing his name up in lights wasn't the right move at this point.

Jed was about to ask Addison if he had heard back from Rick Sharp when Detective Tom Rodgers approached them.

"How are you doing, Mowbray?" Rodgers asked casually.

Addison looked over at him, irritated by the pointless question. "Up to shit, Tom. Right up to shit."

"Yeah, I can imagine. You found anything new?"

Addison studied him through a narrowed gaze. "We're still following up the same bits and pieces," he lied.

"I thought the Feds might have helped get things rolling."

"It's still early days."

Rodgers nodded. "I just wanted to let you know, Lyn has organized drinks at the Rhythm Room later tonight. She thinks it's time everyone chilled the fuck out by getting a little rat-assed."

The hip venue inside the basement of an office building on 6th and Spring had become a popular spot with many younger cops. They promoted a large group environment with jazz bands, pool tables, ping pong, and shuffleboard.

"Swell," Addison replied unenthusiastically.

"Come on, Mowbray, everybody knows you boys are living this case right now. A few drinks will recharge your batteries."

"I really can't see either of us being there," Jed said. "Paying for watered-down whiskey inside a games room will only irritate. Perhaps if we joked our way through work in the same manner as Holbrook, then ping-pong might seem appealing."

Rodgers slapped his thigh and laughed.

"Perkins, my man, are you still pissed with Lyn because of what she said the other day? You need to let that shit go."

Jed hiked his shoulders. "Whatever, man."

Rodgers offered a carefree smile. "The offer's there. We'll be meeting at six-thirty."

"Are you still working the hotline?" Addison asked.

"Nah, we started catching new cases again this morning. Your buddies at the Bureau have lightened the load around here it seems."

Addison kept his cards to himself. "Anything noteworthy?" he asked.

"What do you mean?"

"The case—is it fascinating?"

Rodgers made a face like he'd caught a whiff of something unpleasant. "Well, that depends," he said.

"On?"

"Whether you find another dead beaner from the Belvedere Familia interesting or not. Anyway, good luck finding your killer. Lyn and I are heading out to East LA to go speak with the sorry bastard's family, and we sure wouldn't want to be late now."

Both detectives observed Rodgers move back across the office in his customary macho stride before looking at one another and shaking their heads.

"What a dick," Jed said. "The fucking Rhythm Room?"

Addison grunted in agreement. The kid might still be regarded as wet behind the ears by some, but he was old school cool in all the ways that mattered.

"What are you saying, partner? Are you not in the mood for a few games of shuffleboard? I didn't think you'd pass up a chance to show Holbrook who's in charge."

Jed ignored the dig. "If our perp is responsible for shooting Pollock, it's one hell of a deviation from everything he's done thus far," he remarked.

Addison considered his partner's statement for a moment. "I think Pollock caught him on the jump, which forced the shooting, then he took the girl as he intended and split the scene."

Jed peered up from his screen with a furrowed brow. "You're set on the notion he's organizing a meet-up?"

"Pretty much. How else can you explain him pulling in across from Jennifer Hill's car right as she's headed to her yoga class? There's no way he's just driven into that parking station on the off chance of finding a girl who fits. We don't know enough of what happened with the first two, but past contact seems likely in the case of Jennifer and Paige."

Jed squeezed his chin. "You reckon he might be using a Facebook profile?"

"No, I don't think so. If he was using social media to draw them in, then how does Schneider fit? She was gay, and the Harding girl from last night had her boyfriend riding shotgun. I'm not sure how the asshole's pulling it off, but I do believe he's finding a way of getting them to agree to a meeting."

Jed stretched his neck. "Maybe he pretends to buy something from them," he said. "Or he offers them employment. We know Katherine Schneider was taking her clothes off in the name of art."

Addison shook his head. "Surely, the tech guys would have made the connection by now if that were happening. I think he probably drives to specific locations where he searches for an appropriate target. Then he does something to prompt the next meeting."

Jed chewed at the end of his pen while he considered the theory. "What if he organizes an accident or damages their car?"

"Like a fake injury?"

Jed winked perceptively. "Or a minor traffic incident."

"That's some decent theorizing, kid. We should be looking into both those scenarios. Have you got the forensic report on Jennifer Hill's vehicle?"

"Yeah, I think I've got it on my computer here somewhere."

"See if there's any mention of damage to the car."

Addison began envisioning how the kid's idea might work when his mobile started buzzing on the desk. He looked down to see Rick Sharp's name on the screen. "Howdy, Rick, I was hoping you'd get back to me."

"Hey there, Addison, we've found Sarah Parker's cousin," Sharp declared.

"Really, who is he?"

"Name's Frank Rivers. He owns a flashy legal firm over at Laguna Beach with his wife. He's wealthy and almost squeaky clean."

"Almost?"

"In 2008, a hooker named Candy Brandy filed a complaint in Vegas."

Addison nearly laughed at the name. "What was the nature of Ms. Brandy's grievance?"

"She accused him of tying her to a hotel bed against her will. Ms. Brandy claimed Rivers cut off one of her nipples and sucked the blood like a newborn on the tit. Nothing ever came of it because she recanted her statement a few hours later."

Jed was eyeing Addison from across the desk. "You heard about the incident at Secret Gardens yet?"

"We only just received the intel ten minutes ago," Sharp confirmed. "Looked like a carjacking or robbery gone wrong."

"How are you guys planning to approach this?"

"Paige Harding has thrown a bit of a curveball at our next move. We won't be driving out to Laguna Beach and knocking on his door. I want to put a detail on him, best guys available. Let's follow the asshole for a bit and see where he leads us."

It was the right play. If the FBI stormed in with the cavalry and found nothing, Rivers would likely bunker down.

"Surveillance is the way to go," Addison agreed.

"We've got his two main addresses, and I can have a team ready by the end of the day. Larry Springfield is going to be flying back later this evening as well."

Addison opened his drawer in search of Advil.

"You still there, Addison?"

"Yeah, I'm here."

"You and Jed should come over whenever you're ready."

Addison closed his eyes to block out the lights above him. "We'll head over after lunch," he replied. "We're right in the middle of something that might prove helpful."

"I hope you boys ain't holding out?" Sharp joked.

"We've started tossing a few ideas on how the perp could be following the victims, and we're also due to meet with the lieutenant. Once that's squared away, we'll be there."

"Great, I'll see you when you get here then," Sharp said, ending the call.

Jed's green eyes burned with expectation. "What did Sharp say?" he demanded.

"Just that they've located the Parker woman's cousin. There's an FBI surveillance team assembling as we speak."

"Fuck yes!" Jed said, pumping a fist into the air.

"I wouldn't start celebrating yet. We don't know if the guy is connected to the perp. He might be nothing more than a weak bastard who beats up hookers for sport."

Jed's face became inflamed. "You want me to keep looking into whether there was any damage on the Toyota from last night?" he asked, clearly enthusiastic.

Addison stood up to ease a twinge in his lower back, shifting his weight right then left from the waist down, like he used to before a game of football.

"You okay, Ad?"

He wasn't okay. Addison truly detested getting old. "I'm going to have a word with the sergeant," he replied casually. "If you happen to see Collins making his way back up here, let him know that we need to speak with him in his office right away."

# FORTY-EIGHT

Edward placed the glass pipe to Paige's lips and slapped her cheek until she inhaled the smoke, holding a hand across her mouth to ensure the hallucinogen took full effect. Hopefully, the DMT would help him to cross-pollinate her spirit with Linda's Ghost.

The harsh smoke tasted like mothballs on Paige's tongue. Then everything upended while she got sucked through a vacuum where an explosion of divine color-infused her spirit. A distant wormhole revealed a molten doorway that prevented her from escaping the void. Paige floated in a realm unobstructed by time, a sphere without any origin. When the barrier began to slowly open, she tried clawing a way back into the natural, but as the smoke saturated her lungs, she blasted beyond the gate at lightning speed. Paige experienced her birth at Saint Joseph's Hospital while her consciousness was reprogrammed inside a womb of computerized DNA. An infinite force shaped everything here, feeding her soul with mystical wisdom while Eden itself coiled around her limbs.

She saw elevations of technology in all directions, so terrifying and beautiful in their construct. The essence of perfection overwhelmed her, like a first and final breath, as she resurrected from a thousand consecutive fatalities. Interdimensional symbology glowed in platinum currents, enclosed by digital machinery that stretched on forever, forming an ultra-high-tech universe of unknowable sophistication. Angelic heralds addressed her in celestial languages as vibrations of rapture mainlined through the core of her intellect. This place felt like the nucleus of the entire cosmos, capable of exonerating every concern a person might ever know. Yet, she perceived its impermanence.

After a few seconds—*or was it ten uninterrupted lifetimes?*—Paige was transported back to the room with a fresh appreciation of her captivity. Realization dawned in an instant. Whatever she had just faced epitomized counterfeit piety where distorted holiness opposed all that she understood God to be; a treacherous expression of harmony from a world of false splendor to conceal the maggots squirming behind its façade.

When Edward began slithering about on top of her, she contracted into a ball to prevent him from groping her flesh, but it was as if she had just run a marathon and was now lying in a bathtub of wet cement. Paige's muscles were listless Jell-O, and she heaved while his crotch rubbed against her body with lustful ferocity.

Something formless had started dividing her brain into compartments of dread; its consistency was melted blackness, peeling layers from her awareness as it probed her mind.

She felt the corruption of his breath whispering in her ear.

"Welcome to your destiny, sweetheart. If you embrace your new life and look beyond the veil, I will allow you to leave this prison. We could sit down and enjoy a yummy lunch together, then afterward the three of us can fuck the day away in my bedroom."

Edward's voice came to her in shifting pictures. Everything he rambled concerned a future he wanted her to be part of. Despite all the terror coursing through her being, Paige cried out mutely to God in her heart. She used every ounce of desperation within her soul while clinging to verses she remembered from the Bible.

# FORTY-NINE

The porcelain vase exploded against the kitchen wall.

"You're a used-up ungrateful cunt," Narek screamed. "When are you going to learn that you don't make the rules around here, bitch? I make the fuckin' rules. Me, no one else."

Anna stood her ground in defiance. Her pretty cherub-like face formed a mask of disgust as she stared up at her husband's evil brown eyes. She'd endured the piece of shit and his abusive control for nine years, nine exceptionally long years. At least the kids were out with their grandparents, so she didn't need to consider them right now.

"Fuck off, Narek!" she shrieked. "You think I don't know what you get up to at that club? I'm over being your slave. Move-in with one of your whores; why don't ya?"

When the inevitable blow smashed into the side of Anna's face, she fell to the floor with a thud, unaware of the glass shards cutting her hands. Narek bellowed his unintelligible hatred while everything swayed in drunken half-circles. This situation would only end with her unconscious and bleeding, but she couldn't give a hoot right now.

Anna thought back to when she met her husband at his cousin's wedding. The deceiving asshole had acted like such a gentleman, and by the time she figured it all out, there was nothing to be done. She often contemplated leaving him, but if he even suspected she might run off with the children, he'd just rape her till she bled, then cut her throat. Being married to an Armenian Mafia hitman meant there was nowhere to run, nowhere to hide.

She raised her head brazenly, determined to speak a word

before Narek turned off her lights. Tears blurred his outline, and she couldn't string a cohesive sentence together in her mind. Anna swore at the weak bastard in Armenian as his right foot connected with the side of her head.

* * *

Narek looked down on his wife's limp body with genuine loathing. Being married to the whiny bitch felt like a curse these days. He had provided her with the best things in life, and still, she found a reason to complain. What was the big deal if he enjoyed a bit of cunt on the side? It wasn't like he didn't please her in the bedroom at least once a week. Any of the sluts at Abovyan would trade places with her in an instant. They'd love to be his wife; he could see it in their eyes whenever they sucked on his skin flute.

He stepped over Anna's repulsive shape, disregarding the crunch of glass underfoot as he made his way to the bathroom. By the time he returned home the following day, all the mess inside the kitchen would be gone. Narek slipped on a sports coat and examined his appearance in the mirror, giving his reflection a sexy grin. He looked a million bucks. Why the fuck couldn't the stupid chent just be grateful for who he was?

Maybe he needed to show her what life on the other side of the fence offered. What it felt like being married to an average Joe who gets fat on the couch watching ESPN each night. After a week of that crap, she'd be begging him to fuck her in the ass again. Narek ran a hand through his thick hair, turning sideways for a more thorough inspection. When he was satisfied with his profile, he walked back to the kitchen and collected his wallet from the benchtop, stepping over Anna one last time on his way out the door.

His cousin's BMW was parked on the street, and he needed to return it to the restaurant when he finished doing the rounds. The boys were going to collect him later in the evening, so there'd be plenty of time to enjoy Erik's mouth-watering food before they headed to the club. He'd have to buy himself breakfast, though, because Anna had been in the process of making scrambled eggs when he dropped her.

Narek had tried not to think about Tigran's final moments since leaving the warehouse or the sound his body parts made as he pulled them through Davit's mincer, but it was fucking complicated. The boss's titty bar presented a distraction, and there would be an assemblage of beautiful asses on display to help raise his mood. Wednesday nights at Abovyan were the best—it's when all the top-shelf dancers began their week. The premium snatch brought bucket loads of cash into the joint, so they were never expected to fuck someone they didn't want to. Still, none of them required much coercion when it came time to sit on his face.

Narek entered the elevator and hit the button for the lobby before leaning back against the rail while the lift descended. When the carriage doors opened, he noticed a beautiful young mother struggling with her two children and kept his arm over the sensor as she stepped inside.

"Thanks," she said, flashing him a row of perfectly white teeth.

"Don't mention it, honey," he replied, watching as the doors closed and the sexy mom disappeared. He would love to know which apartment she lived in. It was handy to keep a bit of cunt nearby for those occasions when he couldn't be assed going to the club.

As Narek made his way outdoors, he embraced the sunshine with a grin. It was a picture-perfect day for his picture-perfect life. Who'd have thought an Armenian refugee could rise to such dizzying heights? Certainly not him. A fantastic night lay ahead, and if people paid what they owed, he'd be at Yerevan by late afternoon. Narek breezed down North Central Avenue like a mythical god, firing a glance up and down the pavement as he walked toward Erik's ride.

# FIFTY

The Old Man looked around at Frank Rivers's postmodern Laguna Beach mansion. There were few places he hated more than this waterfront community of tasteless real estate and spoilt children. He always suspected Frank might eventually make a very foolish decision; however, he rendered his dues on time and contributed generously to the cause. Frank was a prominent class action attorney who'd performed miracles inside big city courtrooms, but now he faced a different kind of conviction.

"I can fix things," Frank slobbered pathetically. "Please, let me make this right."

The Old Man considered him with a numb gaze from across the dining table, thinking of terrible things he'd like to do to the idiot. Frank was of medium height with blond hair, thick lips, and suntanned skin. His unduly whitened teeth and terror-stricken eyes gave him the appearance of a rabbit waiting to be skinned.

"That ship has already sailed. The FBI will have you under surveillance before the day is out. Larry Springfield, too, once the schmuck returns tonight. This finale I'm offering is far more graceful than what Larry will be getting. So, put the gun in your mouth and squeeze the damned trigger, or my friend here will drag you away to the compound where your death will take weeks."

Frank's eyes were feral as he considered his options. Ghost smiled in a Mona Lisa sort of way, a large knife in one hand and a silenced pistol in the other.

"I'll take proper care of Sarah for you, I promise," Frank sobbed. "I'll make her regret the day she was born. Then I'll leave the country; you won't ever see me again, Clive."

The Old Man slapped him across the face.

"If you speak my name out loud again, I'll recant this offer and gut you like a fish. Your cousin will most certainly regret the day of her conception. Many times, over. I assure you of the fact. This is your final chance to eat the gun. You have ten seconds to decide."

Frank Rivers would probably be regarded as dangerous by most, but right now, he looked less deadly than a kitten taking a shit in a thunderstorm. He reached for the Glock G29 on the table with a trembling hand. His breath came in shallow gulps.

The Old Man inspected his fingernails.

"There is one bullet, and it's already chambered for your convenience," he said. "Rest assured that if you somehow live through this, we'll eventually get around to finishing the job. Should you attempt anything ridiculous, I'll bleed you out slower than you could imagine, then I'll go after your offspring to ensure no trace of you is left behind."

Frank whimpered while placing the barrel in his mouth.

The Old Man was stone-faced as he waited. "Make sure to point the gun up . . . Three seconds," he reminded.

Frank roared as he squeezed the trigger, blowing a chunk out of his skull before collapsing onto the floor with twitching limbs like a dying bug. The life disappeared from his eyes in one magical puff while the room permeated an aroma of molten steel.

The Riverses' mansion on Crescent Bay Drive featured large, sweeping lawns, uninhibited ocean views, and lots of privacy—a wonderful setting to orchestrate Frank's suicide. Serena and the kids weren't anticipated to be home until late afternoon, by which time Frank would be stone cold and stiff. Ms. Rivers was also an attorney, and perhaps a tiny part of her might feel saddened by his sudden passing, but the Old Man knew of her ongoing affair with a younger intern. The lovebirds met at a hotel several times a week, and Frank preferred cock to cunt, so the Old Man didn't envision Serena mourning him long.

Ghost crouched beside Frank's body.

"Well, that was super fucking easy," he said.

"It usually is," the Old Man replied.

Ghost operated a world-class security firm from an office Downtown. He supplied fully integrated IP network CCTV, remote access control, and intruder detection alarms to his most affluent clientele. The Old Man ordered every Filii Reprobi to use the company, which enabled him to access their properties in moments like this.

Not that he ever did much with Ghost at hand. The fine fellow worked as an assassin in the CIA's anti-terrorism unit for twenty years, where he developed a unique skill array. He'd proven dependable on every occasion the Old Man had used his services, getting the job across the line in a clean and untraceable fashion. After their meeting the night before, Ghost contacted a forensic accountant to make it appear as though Frank had been gambling away his fortune. Then he arranged for his mole inside the Treasury Department to clean house and make sure there was nothing that could be traced back to Filii Reprobi.

"I'm going to be another hour," Ghost explained. "I have to swap out the sim card in the CCTV and do a sweep through Frank's study. I want to be sure there isn't anything here that will keep the Feds interested. I've also got to give this area a proper wipe down to remove any fibers we walked inside. Should I call one of my drivers to come get you?"

The Old Man looked at the latex gloves on his hands. "That won't be necessary, but thanks all the same. I'll take your car. I often do my best thinking while I drive. You can arrange a lift back when you're done."

Ghost maintained concentration as he hiked his shoulders. "Sure thing; you're the one paying the Benjamins."

"Are you confident this plan of yours will send the FBI away?"

"So long as the two detectives play their part, then it's pretty much guaranteed. By this time tomorrow, the Feds will be holed up in a bar, getting rat-assed in celebration of a job well done. The detectives will be forced into a corner, and the loose ends will be tied off. Special Agent Sharp will have other priorities within forty-eight hours."

The Old Man's face remained expressionless. "That's very good to know," he replied dryly.

He watched the former spook going about his work. They'd arranged to have Larry Springfield intercepted at the airport when he set foot onto the tarmac. There was no need for them to rush things here either. His plant at the FBI was going to call well before their surveillance detail rolled out.

The Old Man reflected upon his meeting with Edward later tonight. The boy likely felt apprehensive about going to the Adelanto compound and would come armed. Paige Harding's photo had featured on Fox earlier that morning, and she spiritually resembled Linda Jones. It was the reason why Edward suddenly wanted to make things right. But the situation had taken an irrevocable turn, and the simplest way to restore order was by giving the authorities what they were anticipating—a drug-abusing psychopath with a monstrous appetite for murder. Edward's collection of rotting corpses beneath the shack at the back of his property would add further credence to the narrative.

News headlines kicked into overdrive after Jennifer Hill's corpse was found up at Mount Lee. *"The most terrifying killer since Bundy?"* suggested the *Times*, and CNN provided an update on the investigation at the top of each hour. Edward's shenanigans at Secret Gardens were guaranteed to intensify things, and the Old Man promised to deliver a final twist.

He intended to drop a watertight case onto the mayor's desk by tomorrow. The slippery fool was another Filii Reprobi puppet, and the Old Man possessed a large file that contained his misdemeanors. If the detectives' curiosity proved to be untreatable, then Ghost would find a way to eradicate the problem for good.

When Meagan Banks arrived at the chapel the other night, one thing became apparent. She was someone Edward thought he could trust. The Old Man demanded the lovely doctor be present for their rendezvous later this evening. He expected her to make amends for the terrible judgment she displayed by getting involved. Meagan's presence would create a false sense of security before Ghost moved in to finish him.

Edward was much stronger than an average person, although it wouldn't make a lick of difference in this instance. Ghost had mastered several fighting styles such as Brazilian-jiu-jitsu, karate, and Krav Maga, and he never conceded until his target was dead.

Ghost didn't present as much of a threat, making it easy for him to blend into a crowd. Yet despite a modest appearance, the guy was an angel of death. He'd taught the Old Man different forms of body disposal and the best ways to sanitize a room when he finished having fun. The only thing he cared about was getting paid when he completed the job.

The Old Man planned to leave Paige Harding alive; her testimony would help paint his picture. Ghost had listened carefully to the recorded audio at Edward's ranch, and he had spoken nothing problematic to the girl. At least the boy managed to get that part right. Nevertheless, in a week from now, Edward's brief reign of horror would be a fading memory while Filii Reprobi continued hiding in plain sight.

# FIFTY-ONE

They were in the process of deciding where the best position for the surveillance detail might be when a flustered agent with a bald head came bursting into the room.

"I'm sorry for interrupting, but a call has just come through about a possible suicide of an adult male at Laguna Beach. We're still awaiting clarification on the details, but the incident occurred at the Crescent Avenue address we're getting eyes on."

None of them wanted to believe what they'd just heard or consider how it might impact the investigation.

"Fuck!" Sharp yelled. "What else do you know, Mark?"

The rattled agent looked like he was sweating bullets. "All we know at this stage is that the son made a call to 9-1-1 at 4:13 p.m. When the EMT van arrived fifteen minutes later, they found a fifty-three-year-old expired at the scene. The medical examiner is there right now."

Sharp slammed his fist onto the desk. "Damnit, Frank Rivers is fifty-three!" he exploded.

"How do you want to proceed, sir?" Mark asked, uncertain.

Sharp looked at Addison; hellfire smoldered in his eyes. "Go tell everyone the whole thing's off."

"Yes, sir," Mark replied, scurrying his way back out the door.

Katy Pearce leaned forward in her chair, a dubious look on her face. "Do you guys think Sarah Parker may have given them a warning?" she suggested half-heartedly, looking first to Sharp, then to Addison, doing her best to disregard Jed.

"No, I don't think so," Addison replied. "Parker was terrified about word getting back to Filii Reprobi, and her fears were certainly no act. We should probably hotfoot it to the scene. Whoever's over there now won't even know what they're looking for."

Jed had been subdued during the afternoon as he pretended not to notice the way Pearce was sizing him up. But this turn of events switched his brain into an analytic model.

"A mega-rich lawyer happens to commit suicide on the day we're getting eyes on him," Jed asserted cynically. "Either he woke up this morning and decided he no longer wanted his perfect life, or we've got ourselves a rat who's alerted Filii Reprobi, and everything is much bigger than any of us anticipated. Just like the preacher claimed it was."

The kid's statement threatened each of them differently.

Pearce cut back in.

"Do you guys believe these assholes are killing women with increasing intent? And what, now they're turning on each other? It just doesn't make any sense."

Addison cultivated a picture that had previously been disjointed.

"Perhaps it makes perfect sense."

Sharp looked slightly irritated.

"Where are you coming from, Addison?" he challenged.

"What if one of their people has gone rogue? Maybe they let it slide until now because they presumed whoever was responsible would fall back into line. If Jed's right about us having an infiltrator in our ranks, then perhaps they decided to eradicate the threat."

Sharp remained noncommittal.

"How does Frank Rivers's potential suicide fit into that theory?" he challenged.

"We may have unintentionally contributed to his demise when we interviewed Sarah Parker. They didn't want us getting to Rivers, and now he's become collateral damage."

"What do you propose we should do?" Jed asked. "We can't sit back and wait while these scumbags play shuffleboard with people's lives. But if someone is compromised on this end, then everything we do will likely be one step behind them."

Addison furrowed his brow.

"Well, I know the leak hasn't come from the LAPD."

"What are you saying, Addison?" Sharp said.

"There are only three people in the homicide division who knew about Sarah Parker and Filii Reprobi. Two of them are sitting in this room, and the other one is the lieutenant."

Sharp and Pearce exchanged a cursory glance.

"We're not even sure Frank Rivers is affiliated with Filii Reprobi," Sharp replied uncomfortably. "How about we head over to Laguna Beach and look around his house. Let's speak with the coroner to determine whether his death was the consequence of suicide before we go making any assumptions about guilt."

Jed appeared as if he'd thought of something important.

"How about dragging Springfield's ass in tonight?" he suggested.

Sharp considered the idea before shaking his head.

"If we do that, it compromises any surveillance on him in the future. I'll send some of our guys out to the airport, though, just to be sure he makes it home in one piece."

A hesitant knock on the door brought the discussion to a pause as everyone turned to see Mark reenter the room. Rivulets of sweat trickled down from the top of the agent's head; his puffy rose-colored cheeks made him look like a goldfish.

"The deceased has been formally identified as Frank Rivers. His wife is speaking with the examiner right now," he said, almost apologetic.

Sharp appeared on the verge of self-imploding. "Who's in charge of the fucking scene?" he demanded.

"Uh . . . I'm not sure, sir," the agent stammered.

"Well, get your ass on the phone and explain to whoever's running things over there that it falls under FBI jurisdiction. Tell them to secure the place until we arrive."

Mark scurried outside like a dog with its tail between its legs.

Addison turned his attention to Sharp. "We need to get eyes on Tony Anders and Sally Ferguson, Rick."

Sharp nodded wearily. "I'll get Mark to set something up before we head out."

Addison hoped Mark was more competent at keeping people safe than he seemed.

"I've got Tony's number," he said. "I'll call him from the car to let him know he needs to be on high alert. The last thing I want is to have their deaths riding my conscience."

"What about Sarah Parker?" Pearce asked.

Sharp exhaled, frustrated, and gaped up at the ceiling. "Well, we sure as fuck can't call her, but I'll get a car up the street from her house. With any luck, she hasn't already done herself like her cousin. Not that she'd be missed, I imagine."

No one responded.

"Where are you guys parked?" Sharp asked.

"Out front," Addison replied.

"Okay, after I speak with Mark, we'll move out."

Addison watched Sharp leave the room, noting how he appeared much less confident than when they'd first met inside Collins's office a couple of days earlier.

# FIFTY-TWO

Edward closed the driver door of his Lincoln Navigator and began making his way to the chapel. He patted the shoulder holster beneath his jacket, self-assured as always, confident of remaining one move ahead of his rivals, whoever they might be.

Meagan called in the afternoon to explain how the Old Man expected her to attend their little meeting as well, most likely so he could rebuke them both together. There was nothing to suggest he was being set up, but the firearm provided additional reassurance if he'd misread the situation. Edward cast a keen eye around the perimeter of the compound, readying himself for any sudden attack.

Meagan's Mercedes was parked beside the Old Man's Cadillac, and there was nothing that might be considered out of place. The sun had faded behind a molten sky as creeping shadows swayed across the area where he now stood.

This rubbish couldn't get squared away soon enough because he sure as hell wasn't enjoying looking over his shoulder. Edward considered how Paige was getting on back at the ranch while he approached the chapel doors. They'd made some stunted progress during the day, and despite the fact she resisted his contact, he sensed her defiance waning.

Paige objected when he told her to spread her thighs, so he presented her with a set of spoiling body parts until her insolence stopped. It turned out to be a dry fuck, although that was to be expected. It would likely be some time before she desired his cock.

Edward moved through the chapel entrance with caution, listening to the murmur of conversation as it filtered down from the Old Man's chamber. When he was satisfied only two voices were coming from inside the room, he continued through the hall and knocked on the door.

"Come in," the Old Man called out cheerfully.

Edward took a deep breath in preparation for whatever chastening awaited him before entering the sanctuary. He saw Meagan Banks seated in a chair near the Old Man's desk. Her long legs, coated with tanning oil, glistened appealingly. The contemporary office was spotlessly clean with a gray polished concrete floor. An asshole Scandinavian designer crafted each piece of furniture, and everything had been positioned in a way to create a fundamental sense of internal discomfort. Tight lines and neutral hues underscored the bland ambiance. It provoked a memory of the sterile tones that received him whenever he met with his psychiatrist as a child. It was a soulless room of imagined tranquility that amplified the commotion inside his brain.

Meagan greeted him with a friendly smile, unveiling a row of shiny teeth she'd spent thousands of dollars refining. "Hello," she said, her eyes ablaze with excitement.

Edward courteously acknowledged them both before taking a seat. His heart was thumping, and he became suddenly apprehensive as the Old Man leaned forward on his desk with a smirk that revealed nothing of his intent.

"Your actions over the past couple of weeks have made a lot of people unhappy, Edward. Some of them are demanding your head, screaming for it from the rooftops. It was nice to learn you will no longer be leaving your corpses in the Hollywood Hills; however, I still need to be seen as somebody who maintains harmony. So, what do you suggest I should do to appease those among us who wish to see you punished?"

Edward had predicted this type of question on the drive over and was confident that the solution he'd come up with would prove satisfactory.

"Tell the stupid saps I will be serving an enforced suspension of six months and paying a large fine for the way I went about business. They are all so fucking attuned to their weekends here that a six-month ban will seem like a lifetime. But I won't be getting my balls zapped with a cattle prod or having my arms nailed to any walls. I believe I have a valid enough reason for doing what I did. Though in hindsight, if I could have my time over again, I would be sure to work in a manner which is more befitting of my membership."

The Old Man looked at Meagan and chuckled.

"While I agree hindsight can prove somewhat beneficial on occasion, it's always better to employ foresight, I believe. But each to their own, I suppose."

Edward felt like pulling out his gun and just shooting them both in the face. Especially Meagan Banks, the sycophantic bootlicking cunt that she was. Instead, he imagined smashing her face in with a hammer while he smiled graciously and nodded.

"Fortunately," the Old Man continued, "I have decided upon a way for us all to move forward. I'm sure you will agree that my proposal meets with all Filii Reprobi conditions."

Meagan rearranged herself in the chair, folding one sparkling leg over the other, so it pointed toward Edward. She was dressed like a slutty whore in a bottle-green skirt which barely covered her ass. Meagan had a mouth that could suck the chrome off a steel shifter; the bitch had appraised more cock than a B-grade porn star. Though she certainly knew how to stir a person into sexual enthusiasm, and Edward felt himself go hard despite the situation.

The Old Man smiled at him in a perverted way.

"Relax, Edward. You're going to like this . . . Meagan will no longer be available to assist anyone in Filii Reprobi until it has been cleared with me beforehand. She explained how she helped you in other areas, so correction is necessary to dissuade the others from being foolish. Do you agree, Meagan?"

"Yes, I most certainly do," she answered, licking her lips in an evocative manner while regarding Edward with expanded eyes. The woman was a low-down Judas betraying bitch, and he intended to make her pay for this at some point.

"Excellent," the Old Man replied. "Your predicament is more contentious, considering all the unrest you have caused."

Edward regarded him without awe, doing his utmost to remain subdued while he waited to learn what the stupid old fart had to say. Perhaps he was going to demand that he walk away from Filii Reprobi's posturing bullshit. Still, the bastard's tailor-made suit wouldn't be good for anything other than cleaning rags if he didn't tell Edward what he needed to hear.

"I appreciate your suggestion," the Old Man revealed through a smile. "It's well-considered and shows me you do indeed use foresight when it suits. But unfortunately, in this instance, it has arrived a couple of bodies too late."

Edward went to say, "I don't think so," when something tightened around his elbow, pinning his arms to the side of his body. He looked down to see a plastic cable tie and twisted in his chair to identify whoever had snuck upon him like a cat, only to find they were positioned out of sight. Panic engulfed him as he prepared to play the ace up his sleeve.

"What the hell do you think you're doing here, Clive!" he roared. "You best be thinking this through because I have an insurance policy locked away. If anything ever happens to me, the whole thing is going to come down on your fucking head. Filii Reprobi will be finished. You're an old fool to think I wouldn't prepare for a day like this."

The Old Man was genuinely enjoying himself. Whatever fondness he once had for the cretin was gone. He thought about Susan Rodriguez, confident she would never disappoint him in such a pathetic manner as he placed Edward's memory drive onto his desk.

"You must be referring to this little piece here, I presume?" he replied coldly, smiling as Edward's features became feral, unable to comprehend what was rapidly unfolding.

"I had my good friend behind you reclaim it from your safety deposit box this morning, you poor misguided idiot . . . As I said, you really can't beat foresight."

"I've got another one of those!" Edward screamed.

The Old Man tutted while slowly shaking his head as Ghost stepped into view.

"No, you don't," Ghost countered sardonically. "There are still bits of information on your computer in Palmdale, but I'll be sure to wipe them when I return your body."

A terrible realization washed over Edward's face as he transitioned from defiant to panicked in the blink of an eye, looking from the Old Man to Ghost and then back to Meagan.

"Stop!" he screeched, "I only wanted to bring her back!"

Meagan Banks glared at the pitiful sobbing mess beside her, sickened by the notion she once found him so incredibly alluring. He was no different to the loser assholes whose innards she had woven together at the Los Padres cabin all those years ago.

None of them reacted to Edward's cries. The silence articulated what everybody was thinking better than any words. The Old Man stared impassively at Edward's weeping face, listening while he bounced from one justification to the next, becoming more frantic by the second. They were impervious to his excuses, slightly fascinated perhaps, but unmoved just the same.

Edward heaved himself onto the floor in a final attempt to break free, flopping about like a fish out of water. Ghost crouched down and removed the pistol from Edward's holster. The familiar half-smile returned to his lips.

"We should get this over with before he bruises," Ghost encouraged.

The Old Man's gray eyes were hazed in thought.

"It won't matter once they find what's waiting for them at Palmdale," he assured with a chuckle.

Edward's squealing continued, high pitched and despairing.

The Old Man slid a syringe of dirty liquid heroin across his desk.

"It's time for you to serve your penance, Meagan," he said.

Ghost held Edward steady, turning his head away from the ugly sound of his screaming while Meagan prepared for action, humming a nursery rhyme like Edward enjoyed doing as she selected a vein. She could tell he was using every ounce of his strength to break the ties, but Ghost held him tighter than a vice. Meagan winked at Edward before the needle pierced his skin, watching as he opened his mouth and howled like a dog. His hands clawed hatefully at the air, and his legs kicked out wildly in front of him.

Meagan giggled as Edward's face went from bright red to a darker shade of purple. Spit foamed at the corner of his thin blue lips, and his eyes contained the accurate measure of his distress. She watched his tongue double in size while he twitched and gagged, suffocating on the poison flowing through his system, entirely powerless for the first time in his life. Edward's heels drummed and scraped against the concrete as Meagan stared into his face with contempt. A soggy breath cackled up his throat and his eyes glazed over in death. His lifeless expression gaped up at the ceiling before piss saturated his jeans to form a rusty puddle on the concrete.

The Old Man hadn't bothered moving out from behind his desk, barely watching as the heroin kicked in and strangled the life out of the prick. In truth, he would have preferred to kill the shit like the vagrants Edward kept at the back of his property. When the Old Man strolled around to where Meagan and Ghost were stooped, he gazed down on Edward's listless form like it was an object of mild interest inside a shop window. "And to think I had such high expectations for him," he said, lighting a cigar. "The main weakness in the boy's character was the way he believed himself to be indispensable. I suggest you take a close inspection of what's in front of you, Meagan. A really close inspection."

Meagan looked up at the Old Man like a child who'd received a good ass whooping from her daddy and now anticipated his restoring love.

"I understand," she replied, fluttering her lashes expectantly.

The Old Man's eyes implied Meagan was in for a busy night.

"And it would also be in your interests to forget all about my friend," he said, pointing his cigar at Ghost. "Because if you don't, you'll be begging to die like Edward."

Meagan slipped her tongue across her lips again, smiling when the Old Man's eyes swept over her curvy body and flawless legs. She parted her thighs, revealing a freshly shaved pussy as Ghost hoisted Edward's corpse over his shoulder and trudged out of the room.

# FIFTY-THREE

Addison's brain felt like someone had dipped it in a deep-fry cooker. They'd found nothing at Laguna Beach to support the theory that Filii Reprobi had murdered Frank Rivers. It seemed a clear-cut case of suicide. The examiner determined Rivers had swallowed a Glock G29 at the family dining table. There was no sign of coercion and no explanation left as to why he'd blown his brains out.

When they attempted to retrieve Frank's possessions, his wife refused to hand anything over without a warrant. Serena Rivers had clammed up after declaring that she knew nothing about Filii Reprobi, trying hard to present herself as a heartbroken wife.

Addison refilled his glass with whiskey before leaning back on the couch and closing his eyes. He thought of his recent encounter with Coniglio at the Woodcat Café, recalling the soft touch of her skin when their hands brushed. Addison appreciated how she always remained upbeat, even when a dead body lay in front of her, and the gagging trace of human shit filled the space. Mostly, he just missed the counter perspective of a woman. So, when the investigation concluded, he intended to ask her out for a meal.

He listened to the ESPN commentary panel discussing whether Tom Brady received too much latitude in games. Addison rested his glass on the table and let his mind wander, remembering how Nate recognized Brady's incomparable greatness the first time he watched him play. Addison felt a little disappointed that the boy hadn't answered his call earlier, but he was accustomed to things being this way. His loneliness had been around so long; he'd gotten used to the smell. Addison swallowed a mouthful of liquor and shut his eyes again, hoping the warm glow might draw him toward sleep. The humming vibration of his Samsung dragged him back to the present. He saw the caller ID was blocked and presumed it was someone from headquarters.

"Mowbray," he answered wearily.

"Hello, Detective Mowbray."

The hostile tone sent ice shards down the center of his back.

"Who the fuck is this?" Addison demanded.

"Who I am is not important. What I'm calling about, on the other hand—"

"How did you get this number, asshole?"

A conceited chuckle made Addison want to punch the caller in their face.

"You will be handed a gift before morning, detective. When the disease you are presently looking for is served up on a silver plate. I suggest you accept our benevolence with gratitude, then get on with the business of living your life. If you don't heed my advice, you'll have no one to blame for the resulting consequences other than yourself."

Addison's stomach lurched as his heart thumped against his rib cage.

"Filii Reprobi," he replied in a slow dragging tone.

"It's best if you forget that name."

"Is that right?" Addison countered. "I'm not the forgetful kind."

Another snicker, more irritating than the first.

"Your son, Nate, leaves for school at 8:05 every morning. The bus usually picks him up at ten past and drops him at Jefferson High about half an hour later. He has basketball practice on Tuesday and Thursday afternoons. Nate trains on the outside courts near the road because the seniors get priority as far as the auditorium is concerned. Your kid lives on Bell Avenue with your ex-wife, Michelle Cawthorne.

"Michelle has recently found herself a new friend named Peter Marshall. Peter is a math teacher at your son's school, and they are both trying to keep their romance under wraps for the time being. Nate keeps a picture of you in uniform beside a Dallas Cowboys lamp, and his room is a bit messy. A boy named Charlie Tomlinson is Nate's best pal; they ride the streets together every afternoon. As you know, children go missing every day, so be sensible, and your son will get to reach his undoubted potential. I think he has a decent chance at earning a college scholarship if he continues working on his jump shot.

"There's a package at your backdoor. Have a good look at what's inside; it should help to seal our arrangement. Your badge can't save you in this situation. You need to trust me on that. And if you tell anyone about this call, I will withdraw my offer, and your boy will get carved up like a slab of beef—you'll never see him alive again."

When the call was abruptly ended, Addison sat in shocked silence. Rage blazed his senses as he jumped to his feet and rushed to the back of the house, fumbling with the old brass handle before swinging the door open with a frantic heave. Someone had placed a manila envelope on the porch; a big smiley face in black marker mocked his despair. Addison scooped up the package, tearing the seal to discover whatever was inside. Nate and his ex-wife's color photo captured them walking down their drive toward Michelle's yellow SUV, laughing obliviously while a killer stalked them from across the street.

Addison slammed the door shut and ran to the living room to get his phone, hitting Michelle's home number and praying to every known god that she answered his call. When she responded in her usual dispassionate tone, pure relief engulfed him.

"Howdy, Michelle, how are you doing?" he asked, sensing the uneasiness in her silence. It would have been well over a year since he'd last inquired about her general disposition.

"I'm fine, Addison. Why do you ask? Is everything all right?"

Like all people, the woman had her faults, but a chump she was not.

"Yeah, things are good. I'm just trying to make small talk is all."

"Small talk," she cried. "It's a bit late for that. Nate's not here right now."

Addison's heart jumped into his mouth again. "What, where is he?" he asked much too quickly.

"He's staying over at his friend Charlie's place; they've got practice tomorrow and wanted to shoot some hoops together tonight. Are you sure everything's okay, Addison? Because you sound kinda weird."

Addison thought of the Filii Reprobi threat.

"Yeah, I'm good, it's just that it's a Wednesday night, and the boy has school tomorrow. I was hoping I'd get to speak with him. I already called earlier."

His ex-wife's extended pause suggested she wasn't convinced.

"I'll let him know you asked after him and make sure he gives you a buzz when he gets home from basketball practice tomorrow afternoon. Whatever happened to the whole let-the-boy-learn-from-his-mistakes psychology you used to preach?"

She wasn't making this easy for him.

"I guess perspectives change when your kid moves to another state. Particularly when it becomes so darn hard to reach him all of a sudden. I'll expect a call tomorrow, then."

"Sure thing. Goodnight, Addison."

"Night," he replied before staring at the phone like it was poison.

He contemplated making a call to arrange a patrol car to park outside Michelle's address but was starting to consider Filii Reprobi might be capable of almost anything. Instead, he thought about the various warnings he'd received before arriving at this juncture. The restraint of Harry Bath, and Sarah Parker's condescension, not to mention the disparaging attitude of Elizabeth Plume or the frustration spoken by Tony Anders.

Addison swallowed the remainder of his whiskey in one gulp, racking his brain for an alternative to break the shackles which Filii Reprobi had just applied to him. He'd been on the verge of sleep ten minutes earlier, but now he was amped like a crack head on a bender. As he examined the photo again, awful images of Nate electrified his thinking.

The terrible dreams he experienced at night faded quickly upon waking in the morning. But this was an entirely different proposition. His worst nightmares were being recounted with opened eyes, and there wasn't a damn thing he could do other than wait for the gift promised by those Filii Reprobi cocksuckers.

# FIFTY-FOUR

It had been a slow night at Yerevan, and the handful of customers who came for dinner proved to be a pain in the ass. The recently hired dish-pig never bothered turning up for his shift, and Erik was reading through the *Los Angeles Times* with a testy attitude.

Narek often wondered why his cousin had chosen this path. He knew most of the boys in the Armenian Power but had never wanted any part of the criminal life. Erik frequently cautioned him about playing Russian roulette with Satan, believing his life was destined to end in a blaze of violence. His cousin was still one tough son of a bitch, and much harder than many of the gangbangers within the community. He just lacked the killer instinct and cold-blooded mindset that was necessary to prosper on the streets.

Some faggot cops from the GND tried to load him up with phony charges a few years back. The fucking douchebags were expecting Erik to panic and rat out Narek's crew, but his cousin just laughed in their pig faces. He'd kept his trap sealed for over forty-eight hours while the cops stood around waiting for him to bend over. Erik's loyalty came as no surprise to Narek, though; he was a Bedrosian after all, and Bedrosians were no sellouts.

Erik looked up from the newspaper and slid a plate of dolma across the benchtop.

"Take this home for Anna and the kids," he said.

"I'm going to the Abovyan tonight, but you may as well leave it out. Bedros will eat the entire fucking plate when he gets here, then go looking for more."

Erik remained locked onto his eyes.

"What?" Narek asked, opening his hands in front of him.

"You should spend more time with your family. All you seem to do lately is sit out the back here in my little kitchen or get yourself rat-assed at Davit's strip joint."

Narek experienced a flash of rage. He hated anybody challenging him but knew better than to try standing over his relative. It had never worked when they were kids, and it sure as hell wasn't going to work inside the man's fucking restaurant.

One time, Narek got loaded at a family BBQ and said something insulting to Erik's sister. His cousin let it slide that night before asking Narek to come back to his house the following day. When he walked through the door, Erik proceeded to beat the living shit out of him. They eventually smoothed things over, and Narek remained mindful of how he spoke to bitches when his morally pretentious cousin was in the room.

"It's work, Erik; I don't choose my hours. You know that."

"Fuckin', please. I hear Bedros and those other chent dogs bragging about what happens at the club each night. Don't insult me. I'm not an idiot. What you do in your marriage is entirely your business, cousin. But Anna is a good woman, and she has given you two beautiful children. I worry for you, Narek. What would happen to your little family if somebody decided to come after you? Those boys need their father."

Narek laughed off his concerns.

"Relax, man; nothing is going to happen to me. I'm not some street-level punk who's throwing up gang signs with a can of spray paint in an attempt to get noticed. People don't wake up and decide that they will put out a contract on somebody like me. Davit is one of the most feared men in all of Los Angeles, and I'm like a son to him."

Erik discarded Narek's reassurance with a wave of his hand.

"You need to pay more attention to history. See what eventually happened to people who live the way you do. They all thought they were indestructible, and nothing could put them down, but their reputations only protected them to a point. There will always be a next-generation asshole lining up to be the kid who finished Narek

Avakian. It's just a never-ending wheel of death, like the snake eating its tail."

Narek looked down at the plate of food, unable to hold his cousin's gaze. The truth was, he did occasionally think about dying but never allowed his thoughts to linger on the notion in case doubt entered his head. Hesitation could make a person freeze at the wrong moment. Besides, Erik didn't understand life in the same way he did. There were rules in place to safeguard the more prominent players in the criminal underworld. Narek had dedicated most of his life to get to the position he was in today. He'd shed buckets of blood and was now an extremely successful gangster, not some bitch ass wannabe cunt.

"I'm going outside for a smoke," he said.

"When you come back, give me a hand to clean up so I can go home. You probably haven't even noticed, but the new dish-pig I put on failed to show his ass again tonight."

"Did the cocksucker call?"

"Nope."

Narek shook his head with a comical expression. "You want me to pay him a visit for you?" he joked.

"Fuck off, cousin."

Narek was grinning again as he walked through the dining area and made his way outside. The night air was warm, and a full moon hung above the city skyline, bathing its buildings in cold silver light.

He lit a cigarette and looked up the street until he was confident nobody was lurking behind a car. Maybe tomorrow he'd buy Anna flowers, then take her and the kids out for a movie. Erik's guidance struck a chord, and he felt a very slight pang of responsibility when he thought about his wife lying unconscious on the kitchen floor. He didn't exactly enjoy hurting her, but it felt as though he had no control over his fiery temperament. The gangster life trained him to strike hard before the other person had a chance to get ready for the blow. It was entrenched behavior, which kept him breathing all these years.

His cigarette tasted like stale dog piss, most likely because he'd smoked half the packet during the afternoon. He flicked the butt onto the road, leaving a spitball on the sidewalk for good measure. As he turned to make his way back inside the restaurant, he caught a burst of movement from around the side of the building.

Someone was coming toward him with urgency, closing the space between them in no time at all. It didn't take a genius to figure out what was unfolding—it was already too late to try sprinting for the door. The assailant sneered from beneath a black hoodie, extending a pistol in a manner that suggested he wasn't about to miss. Narek recognized the familiar flash of the gun barrel as a slug penetrated the right side of his chest, exploding through muscle and knocking him off his feet. It was like he'd been snapped in half by a linebacker who timed their impact to perfection. Narek tried reaching for the revolver he kept at the back of his pants, remembering how he'd left it in the glove compartment of his cousin's BMW. He gaped up through teary eyes, unable to comprehend what was unfolding.

The shooter stood over him victoriously. His smooth silhouette blocked the moon. Quiet laughter found a passage into Narek's mind before another two rounds ripped holes inside his guts, hammering the air right out of him. He scraped the sidewalk with his nails, seeking absolution from the unforgiving terror he faced.

Erik's earlier caution resonated in his brain like some taunting summary of his impermanence. Narek didn't feel the next slug shatter the left side of his rib cage, splintering bone while it bounced around like a pinball. Everything began to decelerate as his consciousness conveyed the grim reality that there would be no more tomorrow. The last thing he observed were two pale blue eyes glaring down at him with familiar animosity—with loathing so intense he could feel it in his spirit.

Narek heard the tinny rattle of a plastic police badge hitting the ground beside him, then his vision darkened, as the essence of goodness was absorbed by a malevolence too intense for words.

Something repulsive and decaying stood nearby, and Narek understood how it waited for him.

The demon represented the cry of every person he'd murdered and the pain behind each beating his wife endured. It had anticipated being in his presence for such a long time and was restless to become acquainted. A looping reverberation of Anna's laughter was deafening as the creature's clammy hand clutched Narek by the hair and dragged his soul off into screeching blackness.

# FIFTY-FIVE

By the time the Filii Reprobi tip-off came through to the LAPD hotline, quite a lot of activity had transpired during the night. The vigilante killer claimed another victim from the Los Angeles criminal milieu—a high-ranking Armenian Power enforcer who got shot to shit in the suburb of Glendale. The killer dropped a toy police badge beside the contorted corpse on the sidewalk, just as he'd done with the previous four.

The call came at three a.m. from an unknown male claiming to have seen a woman matching Paige Harding's description locked inside a room. The informant explained how he delivered some heroin to the property for Edward Cole earlier in the evening. LAPD quickly ascertained that Cole was a very wealthy thirty-two-year-old who inherited a fortune in 2012. Lieutenant Collins was alerted right away, and the joint task force rolled out a short time later.

Addison didn't even attempt to sleep after finding the envelope at his backdoor. He just sat inside the house waiting for the impending call, quickly realizing there was no way to alleviate his concerns. Addison had witnessed too many acts from the extreme end of the cruelty spectrum to imagine a satisfying conclusion to this present situation. Instead, he soothed his guilty conscience with an understanding that the dead were already dead. They were deceased today, and they would still be dead come tomorrow. However, his kid was alive, and if that were to change because of anything he did, then there'd be nothing left to go on for.

He watched from inside his Ford as the FBI SWAT team made final preparations to storm the property. Rick Sharp was speaking with the tactical response team leader half a mile up the road from Cole's front gates. The dull thud inside Addison's head was intense. He'd ingested some Tylenol with a mouthful of liquor ten minutes earlier, but his brain remained a hostile place. Impressions of Nate continued flooding his mind. Old memories of him sitting at the table in Eagle Rock, smiling while he ate his cereal, blissfully ignorant to the ways of the world.

The predawn night contained an edge to its darkness. There was a sense of permanence to the quiet—a haunted quality to the ether that made Addison's hackles rise. He considered turning around to start driving to Arizona until he got to his son. Just keep on going, then mail in his badge and never return.

His thoughts were invaded by two bright headlights that sliced through the retreating darkness. He watched Jed pull in beside him and lower the window. "Howdy, Ad," he said. His eyes darted nervously without ever coming to rest.

The kid looked as if he'd spent the night entertaining ghosts.

"How ya doin'?" Addison asked.

Jed kept his attention trained on the action in front of him. "Yeah, I'm okay . . . Didn't get much sleep, is all."

Addison saw his partner's face harden. "You get a nasty phone call last night?" he asked.

Jed's knuckles turned white on the steering wheel. "The motherfuckers know my mom's address," he confirmed. "They provided me with a detailed description of her bedroom, and they also left a photograph of Rosie's workplace in the mailbox. The cocksucker told me what a fine waitress she is. Much too bright to be working tables is how he put it. He said the perp would be served up on a plate tonight and that I'm never to mention Filii Reprobi again. What about you?"

Addison grimaced through a hateful gaze. "They know where Michelle and Nate live, who Nate's best friend is, and what time he goes to school. The piece of shit knew about a picture the kid has beside his Dallas Cowboys lamp. There was a photo of Nate and Michelle at my backdoor."

"Fucking incredible. What are we going to do?"

"Well, I sure ain't prepared to place my kid any danger, that's for certain. Everyone who knows anything about these assholes has warned us from the get-go. We should probably sit down with the lieutenant and reevaluate when the dust settles. Let's just wait and see what's on the other side of that gate. Then we'll go from there."

Jed didn't react, watching as Rick continued talking with animated hand movements. "You think they got a call as well?" he asked, lighting a smoke.

"Nah," Addison replied. "I've been watching him closely. He's like a kid whose Christmases have come at once. I imagine once we find whatever's been prepared on that land, the fed's will likely move along to something else quickly. Maybe Pearce and Sharp will keep chewing on the bone, but I'm guessing they probably won't."

"What about us?" Jed wondered.

Addison was about to ask whether he'd be prepared to risk his mother's life when he noticed Pearce walking toward them.

"Howdy, boys. You fellas ready to catch another sicko?"

Her unbridled enthusiasm confirmed that she'd never received the kind of phone call that had kept the two detectives awake throughout the night. So they affirmed their willingness as best they could before awaiting further clarification.

"We'll follow SWAT through those gates in five minutes, and our priority is getting the girl out alive. When you see us start to move, buckle up and fall in behind Rick and me. Best of luck, boys, and I'll see you both on the other side."

Addison watched Agent Pearce hustle her way back to a nearby SUV, envious of the fact she was operating beneath a banner of ignorance. Nothing they found was going to take away the churn inside Addison's gut. Even if things got wrapped up in a manner to satisfy the demands of Filii Reprobi, they still had Nate's whereabouts on record.

It was right then that Addison decided he would devote himself to wiping the murdering assholes off the map. He thought back to

Jed's bleak outlook regarding police justice in Angela Brown's living room.

The kid's hatred remained pressed upon his features. Filii Reprobi had threatened his mom and girlfriend. Hence, there were few misgivings about whether Addison could bank on his partner's cooperation moving forward. They needed to bide their time and stay focused, but sooner or later, the sons of bitches were going to face a form of justice they never saw coming.

# FIFTY-SIX

Officer Sean Brody examined his reflection in the bedroom mirror. The LAPD shield above his heart sparkled like precious metal beneath the ceiling lights, and the name pin on the other side of his chest was buffed to perfection. Sean stared into his blue eyes. They appeared gracious and tranquil, betraying the reality of who he'd become. He was a habitual murderer—a deadly individual by anyone's standards, but a criminal he was not.

When Sean arrived home after shooting Narek Avakian, everything felt different. As if a bubble had burst and squared the ledger from which he'd been operating. He'd begun rolling around the floor with uncontrollable laughter while he considered all he had achieved in the last thirteen months. A short time later, he was weeping from the deepest part of his soul, sobbing about everything dishonest and broken in this crooked world.

After he finished crying, the flame in his belly had lost much of its homicidal-inspired ferocity. So, he tried thinking of other ways to bring a positive change to the city without discharging a gun. It was almost like he'd been standing outside his body this past year—as if life were living him and not one part of it was his own. And now, for the first time since Janey's murder, he considered whether he might be feeling a little serenity here this morning.

Sean would be meeting a couple of LAPD buddies for a drink in Santa Monica on Saturday. Maybe he'd ask them what they thought about him transferring across to youth services. Perhaps he needed to focus his energy on preventing underprivileged kids from making bad choices; do his best to stop them from becoming the next Narek Avakian.

He was confident the LAPD would never solve the investigation into his shootings. Every day police officers were being tasked with solving the homicide of individuals who had no right to be living in the first place. Why should a cop give two fucks about people who make the world a better place when they're gone?

The prevailing immorality of modern society wasn't going to change due to him taking out some trash. But if one wicked seed could poison an entire district, then the reverse must also apply when a teenager is rehabilitated from choosing a life of crime. The deliverance concept was what got him interested in becoming a cop in the first place, before gradually losing his bearings until his partner's murder blew him entirely off course.

Sean walked across his room and opened a window, appreciating the crisp morning breeze that freshened his face with an out-of-season chilliness. Perhaps he would take a drive over to Janey's parents' place with a six-pack of Coors and hot New York-style pizza when his shift finished. Surprise them with dinner while he put some tenderness back inside his heart.

*  *  *

At first, Anna had thought the detectives were fibbing for her late husband. Like he was testing her out to see how she responded. It was the kind of twisted game the evil prick would enjoy entrapping her in, mainly if he was in the mood to smack her around. If only she could have been there to see the life get sucked out of him when he died.

She'd been praying earnestly for this moment since the birth of their first son, dreaming about it each night while he went out screwing his whores. She still needed to *grieve* for the disgusting creep at the funeral, and then they would finally be free. The bedroom safe held over three hundred thousand dollars, and the modern Glendale apartment would fetch a tidy sum. Anna could finally leave the neighborhood behind.

The Armenian Power wouldn't care much where she went now

that Narek was laid out on a slab in the morgue. They'd probably be relieved to hear she intended to move away with the boys. The only person she'd miss seeing was Narek's cousin, Erik; he had always been so kind to her. It wasn't easy to comprehend how they were related.

Anna thought about the conversation she had with Layla Grigoryan the previous evening after coming to her senses on the kitchen floor. Layla's husband, Tigran, hadn't been home since Monday night, and her friend feared the worst. She begged her to ask Narek if he knew where he was. Anna had felt sorry for her. Tigran treated his wife well, and Layla had always appreciated the perks she received from being married to a successful criminal.

All Anna ever wanted was to meet a kind-hearted, loving husband who cherished his children and respected the role of being a father. She desired a simple lifestyle away from the venality of Los Angeles. Whenever she'd tried picturing such a life with Narek around, it was like watching someone drop a snake beneath her sons' pillows.

The realization that her piece-of-shit husband was truly gone had started to settle in nicely. He was gone all right, although her recognition of the fact was abrupt and jagged like an assortment of broken glass. She could still feel him in her bruises and smell his repulsive fragrance in the ether of the apartment. Just a few more weeks, and there'd be nothing left to remind her of the monster who'd controlled her existence.

"Mom?" a sleepy voice called from across the room.

"Hey, sweetheart," she replied, walking over to scoop her youngest son up in her arms like a human bulldozer consumed by love.

The boys were still distraught by the news their father was dead, but Anna also knew how robust children could be, and she was going to ensure that in a year from now, Narek Avakian would be nothing more than a hazy memory.

# FIFTY-SEVEN

There were law enforcement vehicles parked all over the Palmdale acreage as a CBS helicopter hovered overhead to capture all the developing action. Addison was crouched beside his Ford, puffing on a cigarette while watching Katy Pearce lead Paige Harding to a waiting EMS bus. An FBI windbreaker concealed the nakedness of her bruised body, and she appeared remarkably well for someone who had undergone such a traumatic ordeal.

Addison wasn't sure of what he'd been expecting to find when the SWAT team smashed its way through the front door of the homestead, though a dead man with a needle dangling from his arm was not even on the radar.

The FBI had recovered the missing body parts and three bottles of blood from a kitchen refrigerator. Addison already understood they wouldn't connect anything to Filii Reprobi. Whoever arranged the body would have made sure they swept the place clean beforehand.

The sound of footsteps interrupted Addison's thinking, and he turned to see Jed coming toward him with a specter of loathing perched upon his shoulders. His partner was dressed like a ranger from an HBO series in a pair of skinny denim jeans and a crisp white collared shirt, once again making Addison feel antiquated in his crinkled black suit.

"Are you not coming inside?" Jed asked him.

Addison took another drag on his cigarette. "What's the point?" he replied.

The two of them eyed Edward Cole's home like it was some pedophile whom they'd been ordered to release inside a kindergarten.

"There's a shack out back," Jed disclosed evenly.

Addison continued smoking. Somewhere nearby, he heard Rick Sharp laughing with his team of agents in recognition of a successful assignment. They were whooping it up like they'd won a war, oblivious to the diversionary tricks crafted into the scene for their arrival.

"You want to take a look inside that cabin with me?" Jed asked.

Addison flicked his cigarette into the dust. "Sure, kid, why the hell not," he replied while struggling to his feet, believing it wouldn't make a lick of difference either way.

The FBI might be unaware of the structure behind the home, but Filii Reprobi would have known all about it, of that he had no doubt. Addison fell in behind Jed as they walked down the side of the house and into into a clearing that led to a dense vegetation patch. The detectives traversed a narrow path, moving with caution. They assessed the area for any danger in case Cole had primed something to take a leg. Addison saw a cabin as he rounded a slight bend. It appeared to have been constructed from recycled materials without a foundation, like a shanty dwelling from a third-world slum. Overgrown branches covered part of the entrance, and a solitary window was caked in dirt.

Addison unsnapped the clip on his gun belt as he approached the shack, pushing the door ajar with his foot. The distinct scent of rotten flesh slapped his face as specks rotated within a slender bar of sunlight, creating an impression they were standing inside a snow box of organic decay. Bile started rising at the back of his throat as the humid smell of turned earth fastened to the sickly-sweet odor of death. The stench was unmovable. It was as if they'd jumped inside an opened grave while a sheet of contamination infected their senses.

Cole had thrown down a few moldy carpets on the ground, and long clumps of plaster drooped down from the walls like hanging moss. Addison heard Jed dry retching somewhere behind him. He clicked on his flashlight and moved forward uncertainly, sweeping the dark corners of the room in search of whatever produced the stink of corruption in the air. Addison felt the killer's menace everywhere beneath the makeshift roof. His savagery and hunger pervaded the atmosphere—a sense he had dined upon his victims' suffering.

Shadows engraved his wickedness on every line and corner of this terrible place; there was no escaping his presence. An obsessive love of things was what generally turned a person evil. Severe cravings for sex, control, and luxury could cast a soul into a monster. Even so, whatever mechanism had propelled this piece of shit into action would likely have been there from his very first breath.

Addison noticed a square timber flap crafted into the floor beside a monument of jumbled trash. He waved Jed across, pointing down at the small door while covering his nose with a forearm, waiting until his partner moved in beside him. A pair of hinges were fastened to a steel brace bolted into a concrete block, and a rusty handle was attached to the middle of the timber panel.

When Addison bent down, he identified something aligned to the sinister vow he'd sensed in the predawn world outside the ranch a little earlier. Whatever he was about to view would be added to the canvass inside his head to plague his dreams and keep him awake at night.

He counted to three in his mind, then slowly raised the hatch, encountering a reek unlike anything he'd previously confronted. When Addison guided the beam of his flashlight into the darkness, he was inundated by a compilation of ten human corpses. They appeared contorted and grotesque, placed around a table amid an ocean of pulsating maggots.

Addison forced himself to scrutinize the rotting carcasses below, seeing how they were all breaking apart in chunks under the weight of their degeneration. One of the victims seemed to gape upward as streams of yellow fluid dribbled from its eye sockets.

A spray of bile burst out of him as he fell backward, the sour smell of his puke making a pleasant change. A storm stirred within Addison's mind while images sputtered behind his tightly closed eyes. He saw his father's face in the rain while lightning flashed in the sky of a moonless night before Nate ran over the ridge of a mountain, flickering with the electrical surges as he tried to outrun a flood intent on sweeping him away. Addison shook his head, taking a moment to stabilize his thoughts.

"This is worse than Dahmer," he managed as vomit exploded up his throat.

Jed remained crouched on his haunches with a hand across his face, looking pallid and wobbly. The kid was whiter than a ghost.

Addison's Samsung began vibrating in his coat pocket, and he removed it in a habitual motion without checking to see who it was. "Mowbray," he answered through gritted teeth.

"Where the fuck are you?" It was Collins, and he sounded pissed.

"We're behind the house. Walk around the back, and you'll see some juniper trees a short distance away. Then continue into the scrub until you see a cabin, but you best be covering your nose when you step inside because the stink will upset your stomach."

"Is Perkins with you?" Collins replied.

Addison considered the photo of his son, which had been distributed among the Filii Reprobi, before he said, "Yeah, he is. But the FBI isn't aware of what's waiting down here. So, come alone if you can because we need to talk to you privately about something."

"Behind the main house, you say?" Collins asked.

"Yeah, go down the right side of the property, and you'll see what I just described." Addison ended the call as another thrust of bile burnt his windpipe.

Jed had already gone outside to get air as Addison remained keeled over in disgust, unable to get going. He needed a breath but was reluctant about taking one all the same. The sound of the lieutenant's approach soon filtered inside, and Addison turned his head to see Jed pointing toward the square hole in the floor.

"Holy Mary, Mother of God," Collins said upon entering the shack, tentatively making his way over to where Addison sat hunched over in his vomit.

The lieutenant began coughing in a way to suggest he was

nearing a state of nausea, so Addison passed him the flashlight and stumbled back through the door, heaving into the dust one last time. Jed was sucking air like he'd spent the previous few minutes trapped beneath the water, which got Addison thinking how essential luxuries like oxygen get taken for granted.

He heard Collins retching within, and by the time he stumbled outside to take up an unsteady position against the wall, Addison had regained his composure.

"What the fuck is that down there?" Collins wheezed.

He was dressed in a pair of dark blue Levi's and a collared shirt like Jed, and there were several wet spots splattered over his jeans.

"We need to talk to you about a call we both received last night," Addison said.

Jed was still crouched on his haunches. "What the fuck?"

"We have to notify him of the calls. This investigation needs to appear as if it has been switched off on our end, and that won't be happening without Jevonte's assistance."

Collins waited in front of them with a mystified expression.

"What fucking phone calls?"

Addison and Jed spent the next few minutes relaying the details of what occurred during the night.

When they finished, Collins spat on the ground, outraged by what he'd just heard. A hundred different questions tormented his mind. "Unbelievable," he managed.

A protracted silence followed before Jed reengaged. "You'll keep the whole Filii Reprobi thing on the down-low, then?" he asked.

Collins looked astounded and possibly a little offended. "These fuckers took photos of your girlfriend's diner. They were inside his kid's bedroom—of course I'll be leaving them out of my reports. But what about the special agent in charge and his partner? Do you think they received a similar warning as well?"

Addison smiled wistfully.

"Nah, it sure would be a whole lot easier for us if they had, but Rick was in his element back there. My guess is they'll be drinking beers and telling jokes long into the night. Let's wait and see where they stand in a week from now. But we may need to have a chat."

Collins was looking at them in a bemused manner.

"What?" Addison asked.

"You're both planning to let this whole matter slide then? Accept the recognition soon to be headed your way and start catching new cases again as if they never existed?"

Addison never felt comfortable being dishonest at the greatest of times. He usually felt awkward even shading the truth. They had been candid with one another in arriving at this fork in the road, and he didn't see any reason to change tact now.

"I intend to nail their balls to a freaking wall," he said. "But I'll need to come across like a frightened little creep mouse to be successful. I figure it'll take some doing, particularly as I'll be working the case on my dime, but I'll get them all eventually. I promise you I will."

Collins paused as he shielded his eyes and looked up at the sky. "No, Mowbray . . . We'll get these cocksuckers by working together—you, me, and Perkins here. When they threatened you boys, they threatened me as well. I have five adult children, so I feel where you're coming from."

Addison nodded his head gratefully.

"Who wants to inform Sharp?" Jed inquired.

Collins looked at him blankly. "That would be you, Perkins," he confirmed.

"Don't know why I even bothered with the question," Jed countered as he began making his way along the narrow path to the main house.

"This is about as bad as it gets, Mowbray," Collins confided while turning around and sneaking another look inside the murky space.

"Even more so when you consider they served him up to us," Addison answered before spitting the taste of decay out of his mouth. "We need to figure out a way to smoke these scumbags out. It ain't gonna be straightforward."

Collins considered Addison's statements. "You happen to have any liquor with you this morning?"

Addison pulled a whiskey flask from his coat and handed it over.

"I must say, I'm a little bit surprised," Collins said after taking a hit.

"About?"

"I always had you pegged as a Jack Daniel's man."

Addison chuckled. "When you rely on the stuff as I do, you take it any way you can," he replied, taking a healthy pull as they waited for Jed to return with the cavalry. Addison began thinking about his desire to put a bullet in everyone associated with Filii Reprobi.

"I'm not sure I want to arrest these sons of bitches," he said flatly before pulling on the whiskey and embracing the burn.

Collins extended his arm, accepting the flask with somber appreciation. "Fair call, I reckon," he said as the two of them stared at nothing.

Addison returned the flask to his pocket and lit a cigarette, blowing three smoke rings into the morning air.

"Are you going to be making a call to Phoenix PD?" Collins asked.

Addison spat on the ground again. "I'm not prepared to take the risk, not after what I've seen here this morning. Everyone we've spoken to who's had any kind of contact with these people has clarified how connected they are. It's not as if I'd believed they were all fibbing to me; an embellishment of the facts is what I thought of their testimonies. Then these Filii Reprobi assholes called Jed and me at home—and neither of us is listed—promising they would bring the case to a shuddering halt. So, a call to Phoenix isn't going to be happening right now. Although, that situation may change, depending on what occurs next."

Collins looked at him strangely, like he'd forgotten something essential. "What about Anders and the woman?" he asked.

"They didn't mention them. But I don't want their murders on my conscience."

Addison drew deeply on his smoke. The whiskey and tar made him feel vaguely human again, sterilizing the rot he'd inhaled inside the cabin. Ever since his father's murder, he often felt invisible currents of darkness around him, roiling with determination as it attempted to extinguish his hope. Addison sensed a purified version of that same vileness clawing at his skin right now. He needed answers and didn't much care how he ended up getting them.

"You thinking we've got a rat on the team?" Collins wondered.

"I'm not sure. But an intelligent informant usually waits till rumors are bubbling to the surface before passing on information. There were only three of us who knew about Filii Reprobi, so I think if there's a rat, then it's more likely they'd be a Fed."

Addison heard approaching footsteps, rustling branches, and murmured conversation. He took one final drag on his cigarette, then stepped on the butt as Jed came into view with Sharp, Pearce, and two other FBI agents. For some reason, their faces reminded Addison of an android painting he'd seen a few years ago.

"How y'all doin'?" Addison greeted, with just enough warmth in his voice to maintain the appearance of civility as he moved toward the path.

"You not coming in?" Sharp called after him.

"No thanks, Rick. I've seen enough," he replied without concern.

The FBI could have the accolades for all he cared. His mind was already focused on the long game—finding the players behind this mask.

# FIFTY-EIGHT

The Old Man settled back on a vintage couch inside Adelanto Chapel, sipping a glass of whiskey while Meagan's slender fingers brushed against the inside of his thigh. Sarah Parker and Larry Springfield were nailed to the wall across from where he sat.

All around him, Filii Reprobi pandered in brutality, Black Magick, and sexual experimentation. He observed his protégé, Susan Rodriguez, kneeling beside a pit of glowing coals. She appeared to be lost inside some homicidal impression as she cooked an iron in the embers, smirking while she gaped up at her playthings nearby.

Sarah Parker's skin glistened with a high fever. Her breasts resembled two mounds of sagging raw flesh, and one of her ribs was partly visible through the burns on her skin. She persisted in begging for mercy, although her phrases sounded adjoined, lengthy, and stretched out like that of a stroke victim. Susan had gradually amputated two fingers from her left hand with a rusted butter knife, and the bloody stumps twitched alongside her remaining digits. The nervous system was a fantastic universe to behold at times.

Larry appeared in even worse condition than his hanging partner as his innards dangled out the lower part of his stomach. His intestines were a slick steamy pink. They looked like misshapen earthworms, so hideous and slimy yet beautiful just the same. This was art in its purest form, the kind of creativity the Old Man put his name on.

"Larry has never been more appealing," the Old Man said coldly.

"I'm only just getting started on him," Meagan replied.

The Old Man considered himself colder than Alpine snow—colder than the freeze that covered the lakes during winter. No amount of tenderness proved capable of touching the power-driven hatred within his soul. His parents had tried to breach the barricades of his heart when he was a child, caressing his face in bed each night while he imagined peeling back their skin, then feeding whatever lay beneath to a stray dog.

He was comfortable among maniacs, which was a somewhat tricky way to pass his time. Edward had believed himself to be a shrewd operator, and to an extent, he surely was. The blackmail material he managed to accumulate throughout the years affirmed the fact. But none of them could outmaneuver him on the playing board because they didn't have his connections. It was why he always slept without a hint of fear.

"I want you to keep them alive for as long as possible, Meagan."

"Of course, my darling," she whispered in his ear.

He looked around at his creation with a sense of pride. The sweet reek of opulence declared their superiority over regular folk. Filii Reprobi were exceptional and sophisticated. They disregarded every law inscribed upon the hearts of men, receiving wisdom from the Angel of Light who'd fallen from heaven like lightning. The afterlife just promised more of the same—an eternity of doing whatever they desired.

Filii Reprobi generated synchronization by providing the opportunity to experience legitimate power swirling about in the palm of a hand. But to those who get presented the chance, he expected much. Larry Springfield's torture served as a reminder to all. One careless mistake could end up costing an affiliate much more than their membership.

"What are you smiling about?" Meagan asked.

"Nothing," he answered with a grin.

"It can't be nothing. You've smiled three times this past year."

The Old Man thought about what she just said. "I never liked Larry," he said evenly. "Not one little bit."

"Why?"

"Because he is a boasting Jew brat who never had to do anything.

Life laid a golden egg in his fucking lap, and I knew he would eventually find a way to screw it up."

Meagan's eyes flamed while she stared into the Old Man's face. "Watch this, then," she teased playfully, getting to her feet and gliding across the room where she removed an ice pick from inside a metal bucket.

Larry became attuned to her presence. His mouth was slightly agape while he followed her movement with a haunted gaze. A large bag of A-positive blood had been attached to a stand nearby, sustaining his life through an intravenous line fed into his vein. Meagan purred up to him like a jaguar and grabbed hold of his head, placing the pick against his left eyeball.

"P-P-Please, Meagan . . ." he sobbed.

"Aww, what a poor little man you have become," she mocked.

Meagan's hand was sturdy from years of surgery as she applied a lazy pressure with her wrist, standing on tiptoes, her calves turned to granite. Sarah Parker began howling again due to Susan's attempt to reveal another rib, so Meagan touched her tenderly on the upper arm, encouraging her to pause for just a moment. "Check this out," she said.

Then Larry's eyeball exploded, and goo ran down his cheek while he wailed.

The Old Man was delighted. "Keep playing, girls. Keep playing," he encouraged, settling back to enjoy the show, seated on top of the world. He didn't have a care in the world right now. Even if the two LAPD detectives decided to persevere with their snooping, they could do little. In truth, he wasn't foolish enough to butcher the cop's kid, not right away at least.

If they fucked with Filii Reprobi, he'd arrange to have their asses fired. Set them up on bogus charges to make it appear as though they'd done something corrupt. It was decidedly uncomplicated, considering the various stooges who were already in his pocket. The poor saps wouldn't stand a fucking chance—nobody ever did.

It was time for him to enter the fun. He wanted to collect a little keepsake from Larry boy. A testicle maybe, or perhaps his remaining eyeball. The Old Man crept in behind Meagan and Susan, slipping his hand up their skirts to sample the wetness of their excitement. He started whistling with joy—he was whistling "Dixieland."

* * *

Jezazeal loitered in a far corner of the church, gratified by all the carnage and mayhem it witnessed. Humans were easily misguided into embracing destruction and shunning the light. It had been that way since the beginning of time. The individuals in this chapel had a few short years in which to indulge their carnal nature. Then they stood to encounter an eternity of torment beyond anything their minds might conceptualize.

Their future was endless suffering whereby their deeds would be returned ten thousand trillion times over. One millisecond at a time. The demon bellowed laughter from the bottom of its enormous belly. His glee made it down to the gate of Hades, but the black souls in the room didn't hear a sound. Deaf, dumb, and blind to their very end.

# EPILOGUE

Three Weeks Later

It was a lovely afternoon as the mild weather supplied the kind of temperature to suggest Fall was coming round the bend. Addison continued down Wilshere Boulevard toward Santa Monica, where he would meet with Jed and a couple of his buddies.

The last few weeks had gone by without incident after Edward Cole's guilt was deemed a foregone conclusion. When all the collected evidence supported the perception, he'd worked alone; the mayor let the chief know he wanted the investigation finalized. In truth, there wasn't a cop anywhere who wouldn't have filed the case away.

Most of the Palmdale corpses were street dwellers, drug addicts, and sex workers—the kind of folk who went missing without creating even the slightest stir. It was quite possibly the saddest aspect of the entire investigation for Addison. The idea that people were being killed under everybody's noses and no one recognized they were living in the first place. It got him questioning how many more there might be. How many bodies were buried across the country? Faceless casualties from the streets of America's big cities? Forgotten men, women, and children whom nobody cared for.

One of the victims they recovered from the cabin was the perpetrator's missing girlfriend, Linda Jones. Her skeletal remains had been positioned at the head of the table. A silver locket with Edward's picture inside tangled around her neck. The FBI concluded that her bones were exhumed from another site before being transferred to the location. Linda's parents revealed that their late daughter had always displayed an unhealthy fascination for the occult.

Edward Cole was initially questioned concerning Linda's disappearance but provided the police with a solid alibi. The FBI located his safe house near the city where he'd gone after Jennifer Hill's abduction to switch vehicles. It was an industrial-type unit within a secure compound situated on the edge of town. All the evidence reinforced the idea that Cole was a drug-taking lunatic who'd been captivated with Black Magick. Jed's theory about him staging a minor accident was right on the money.

Rick Sharp and his team were quickly swept away with another high-profile case: a US senator murdered during a bungled robbery attempt. Sharp implied that the FBI would maintain its interest in finding Filii Reprobi, but Addison didn't believe he had much intention of doing so. It might have been different if Paige Harding had supplied useful information that supported the existence of the group. She insisted that Cole had worked alone, and the only person he'd spoken of was Linda Jones.

The vigilante's most recent target wasn't going to be mourned by anyone other than his immediate kin. Narek Avakian was an asshole of the highest caliber who had somehow managed to avoid apprehension despite his many crimes. The LAPD was still no closer to finding whoever was responsible for the murders. Shootings were often the most complicated cases to resolve because everything was over in the blink of an eye. Detectives could quickly find themselves going round in circles, knocking on the same doors without making progress.

Addison checked his face in the mirror and was unsurprised by what he saw. He no longer felt a little crazy. Crazy didn't come close to describing the madness that now resided inside his head. These days he considered the possibility of whether he might be fully fucking insane, an authentic whack job destined for a needle in the ass and a straitjacket at the nuthouse.

Larry Springfield and Sarah Parker had both fallen off the face of the earth, and their disappearance almost motivated Rick Sharp to climb back on board. Who knew? Maybe it had. Nevertheless, if the FBI agents had reinstated their concerns with Filii Reprobi, they kept the fact to themselves. There wasn't much Addison could do if that turned out to be the case. His control was limited, even with the lieutenant on his side.

They organized round-the-clock security for Tony Anders and Sally Ferguson despite the preacher's objections but scaled it down after two weeks. Addison still contacted them each night to make sure they were doing okay.

The only lead they'd acquired thus far was the accounting company used by Larry Springfield. Fairmont International was an expensive corporation-styled practice owned by a man named Clive Fairmont. Addison soon discovered that the firm donated generously to the LAPD ball and other political charity events every year. He was presently trying to figure out a way to set up surveillance on the well-heeled Mister Fairmont to see where he might lead them.

Lilly Coniglio represented a solitary piece of happiness in his life. They'd met for coffee on four occasions now and were going on a date to a jazz club later tonight. Coniglio took things to a new level when she kissed his cheek outside the cafe earlier in the week. It was a good thing she'd been feeling shameless. Otherwise, they might still be drinking mud at the same table ten years from now.

Addison spotted a vacant parking space near the Gas Lite Bar where Jed was waiting and pulled in beside the curb with a well-practiced turn. He checked his phone for messages before climbing out of the pickup to make his way toward the taproom. The unmistakable smell of stale liquor invaded his senses as he walked through the doors. It wasn't necessarily pleasant, but it was a longtime companion, which made it comforting.

Jed talked about this joint often, so Addison wasn't the least surprised by the dark interior, reclusive booths, and old-school vibe. The kid and his buddies were seated in the corner of the room, and Addison made his way over to the table. He sat down opposite his partner, appreciating the fresh whiskey glass they had already ordered for him.

"Now that's what I call service," he remarked.

"Good thing, too, it seems," Jed replied.

Addison raised his eyebrows. "Yeah, and why's that, kid?"

"Truth be told, you look like you're hurtin' for one."

Everyone in the booth laughed in an easy, good-natured way.

"Ad, this is Clarence and Sean."

They all shook hands and settled back in their seats. Clarence was a fit African American who had a way about him that suggested he'd be a good soldier to fight alongside. Sean was more subdued but a strong character all the same. It was easy to see why the three of them had connected at Elysian Park. Even though they were different, their core values and loyal undertones appeared to be in perfect alignment.

Clarence got down to business. "Perkins has been explaining how you would like some discreet surveillance work done on a ritzy accountancy firm in Beverly Hills," he said.

Addison sipped his whiskey and studied the man closely.

"I can vouch for both these boys, Ad. No doubt about it," Jed assured him.

A palpable tension suddenly permeated the booth as a silence seemed to go on longer than expected, like a load hanging over the edge of a cliff undecided on whether it would fall.

Addison returned his glass to the table. "The surveillance needs to be performed twenty-four-seven without a soul knowing about it. My kid's life may depend on it," he said, unblinking.

Clarence's expression appeared trustworthy and committed.

"I can put in for vacation time. Not right away, it could take a while for it to be approved. How long do you think you'll need eyes on these people?" he asked.

"How much time do you have up your sleeve?"

"Nine or ten weeks, give or take."

Addison had another drop of whiskey.

"Put in for four weeks to start, and I'll pay you for your troubles."

Clarence appeared startled.

"If I agree to do this, it's because I want to help, so there's no need to pay me. The LAPD can continue doing that. I don't have immediate plans for a holiday anyway, and the GND will probably be delighted to see my desk empty for a month. Besides, Perkins is my bud—if he's in trouble somehow, then it's the least I can do."

Addison appreciated the sentiment. "What exactly has my partner told you about the situation we find ourselves in?"

Sean Brody touched Clarence on the arm.

"Perkins has only spoken to us in very loose terms. The man was mindful of not overstepping any boundaries before meeting with you first. He did enlighten us about someone threatening your families and how it might tie into the slimy shitheel you boys retrieved out at Palmdale. He also said you wanted to get a set of eyes on a certain individual and are experiencing difficulties making it happen. You can depend on us, Addison. Clarence and I are both accustomed to playing a part in the game from outside the fuckin' box."

Jed chuckled.

"And here I thought you were all ready to put your service revolver under lock and key, Brody. What happened to your vision for change?"

Sean smiled and reached for his bottle of Coors. "Yeah, well . . . the vision was good while it lasted, pal."

Jed dropped an open palm onto the table in front of Clarence. "Pay up, sucker," he said.

"You'll have to take an IOU; my wallet's all plastic right now."

Sean shook his head and swilled his beer.

"You prepared to roll with this, Ad?" Jed checked respectfully.

"Sure, kid; seems as good a plan as any."

"Well, let's fill these boys in with the specifics, then, shall we?"

As they relayed the details over the next fifteen minutes, a buzz connected the four of them. It was a part cop, part brotherhood, and part frustrated awareness. Clarence sat through their recount with his arms folded tightly across his chest, the look in his eyes betraying the calm of his exterior. Addison noticed how Sean bobbed his head sideways whenever they mentioned Filii Reprobi, like he was tossing around an idea to different parts of his brain, weighing up what he intended to do to them.

When they were done explaining the circumstances, a waitress breezed up to their table, and Sean ordered a double round of drinks.

"A man after my own heart," Addison said appreciatively.

"There are some things only liquor can soothe," Sean replied.

"True, but I need to drink cautiously this afternoon."

Sean appeared a little bemused. "Really, why might that be, Addison?" he quizzed.

"He's met the lady of his teenage dreams," Jed teased.

Heat banded in Addison's cheeks.

"Good for you, man," Clarence acknowledged.

Sean picked up a coaster and began tapping it on the table.

"These cats sound as if they might be hard to bring in for an interview," he said.

Jed shot Addison a perplexed look.

"What is the bigger picture here?" Sean continued.

Quiet returned as every sound within the bar intensified.

"Bigger picture?" Addison said.

Sean stared back at him, cold and unblinking. "Do you intend to slap handcuffs on these cocksuckers, or are they going in a ditch?"

Jed leaned back in his seat as Addison finished his glass. Sean continued tapping the coaster, only louder and faster, building to a crescendo.

"Sometimes, men are forced to do things they never imagined they could," he confided. "Other times, they choose to act in a way they never thought they'd have to. If you were to ask my opinion on the matter, I'd tell you it's probably best to make the decision. Any man compelled into action can never really be his own master. But then again, who the fuck am I? Still, there's going to be a cost either way."

The waitress reappeared and placed the drinks down onto the table before Sean requested that she put them on his tab. When she walked back to her station behind the bar, he divided the liquor between them.

A queasy twisting knotted Addison's gut. It was akin to what he'd felt all those years ago upon hearing his mother's heartfelt cries coming from the kitchen downstairs. A sense of relief raged against the furnace of consternation searing at his conscience. When he'd met Tony Anders for the first time, he saw a twinkle in the preacher's eye—a look that suggested he could see good where others found none.

Sean Brody was like the antithesis of such sentiment. His eyes were unassuming, but they reached inside to restore color to unwanted memories. Addison had an unexpected image of a face being held together by wafer-thin scar tissue, its slick purple flesh gleaming with dampness and encrusted in craters. He saw Tony Anders, too. Steadfast in faithfulness and untroubled by death, presenting his cheek to a hostile world that bade for his blood.

"Who wants to make some fucked-up things a little bit right, then?" Sean asked, raising his beer bottle in the air. He waited while they reached for their drinks, smiling without concern as their pact was sealed amid the clinking of liquor.

Addison thought about Nate having to reside in a world where Filii Reprobi wandered, and his anxiety threatened to return. He polished off his glass of whiskey and made peace with the arrangement he'd just entered, knowing the only way he'd ever feel reassured was by taking down the entire group for good.

The dimness of the room suddenly seemed hostile as shadows claimed ownership of the space, drawing power from the many secrets that had been shared within the building. Addison stood without speaking and began walking for the door.

"Where are you going, Ad?" Jed called after him.

"For a smoke," he responded with calm resolve.

He felt more robust than the man who'd entered the bar moments earlier. There was no point in repudiating the fact he wanted the bastards dead. Perhaps that vengeful part of his soul was still breathing—the part he thought had been extinguished after watching his father's killer get executed. Only now, it raged deeper, fed by a willfulness to see things through. He wouldn't receive satisfaction until all his enemies were broken, and he didn't consider what the consequences might bring. They'd threatened his boy and stood inside the room where he slept each night. The terror they sent his way would be the architect of their fall, like a returning missile destined to land in the center of its launching pad.

As Addison stepped outside, he lit a cigarette and turned his back on the afternoon sun. When his date with Coniglio ended later this evening, he was going to hit the booze. Then he'd pop a couple of pills in the hope of getting a dreamless night's rest.

# ACKNOWLEDGMENTS

I need to thank my amazing wife for listening to countless hours of this book, many times over, one chapter at a time. This book would be non-existent without your input. Thank you, my love.

Lynk Manuscript Agency, Sean Doyle and Saso Creative deserve a shout-out for all the fantastic work they did on my behalf. My editors, Michael McConnell and Jenny Scepanovic, have helped immensely on many fronts, polishing my book and making me a better writer.

Alex and Mark, you are true Blue Mountains brothers - thank you.

I appreciate all the times where Leigh Marks, Mimi, and Patrice listened to my work and provided encouragement.

And finally, to my dear mum and dad, thank you for giving me the best life any person might have. I love you both dearly.